The shrouded figure strode gracefully past him as though she hadn't heard him at all. Steel blades, as long and slender as rapiers, appeared in each of her mailed fists. Whether an act of magic or mere sleight of hand, the weapons looked real enough.

"Stand down!" Tallis said, hoping to halt the intruder as well as alert the family to the danger.

The shrouded figure did not heed him.

"Who dares?" came a furious voice in the next room.

Responding to the alarm, a well-dressed steward appeared in the doorway with a half-drawn blade of his own. The cloth-wrapped intruder thrust both rapiers into the man's torso—one in his stomach, the other near his collar—making not even a grunt in the motion. Sputtering blood, the steward toppled. The intruder stepped into the room beyond without hesitation.

Then came the screams.

EBERRON

the inquisitives

Bound by Iron
BY EDWARD BOLME

Night of the Long Shadows
BY PAUL CRILLEY

Legacy of Wolves
BY MARSHEILA ROCKWELL

The Darkwood Mask
BY JEFF LASALA

the inquisitives

The Darkwood Mask

Jeff LaSala

The Darkwood Mask
The Inquisitives · Book 4

©2008 Wizards of the Coast, Inc.

Cover art by Michael Komarck
First Printing: March 2008

9 8 7 6 5 4 3 2 1

ISBN: 978-0-7869-4970-0
620- 21775740-001-EN
U.S., CANADA,
ASIA, PACIFIC, & LATIN AMERICA
Wizards of the Coast, Inc.
P.O. Box 707
Renton, WA 98057-0707
+1-800-324-6496

EUROPEAN HEADQUARTERS
Hasbro UK Ltd
Caswell Way
Newport, Gwent NP9 0YH
GREAT BRITAIN
Save this address for your records.

Visit our web site at www.wizards.com

Dedication

To Marisa, the angel in my armor.
You gave me the will and the means to write again.

Acknowledgements

This book wouldn't be half as interesting without the etymological and artful prodding of my brother, John (who is weird). My appreciation and gratitude also go out to Josh "Irrational Number Man" Wentz and Marcy "Miredhel" Rockwell for their moral(e) support and omnipresent counsel; to fellow inquisitives Paul Crilley and Ed Bolme for cross-promotion and encouragement; to Keith Baker, for fielding so many questions; and to the New York City subway system, in whose tortuous tunnels much of this book was written.

And thank you, Mark Sehestedt and Erin Evans, for giving me this opportunity, seeing it through with me, and making it all so much fun.

Prologue

The room was small, bereft of furniture and adornment, save for a single high-backed, velvet-padded chair. The man sitting in it stared out, unseeing, through the window. His head was propped up, the lids of his eyes half open, admitting only a trace of gray light from the rising dusk.

Unaware of his surroundings, the time of day, or his own fate, the man stared forward, reliving the cycle again, the memory as present as if it were happening again right there in the small, stark room. . . .

Rejkar One stares at me as I work, his aventurine eyes uncomprehending. Over the last eight hours, I have watched their translucency increase and an almost imperceptible green light grow from within. Both are indicative of the sentience struggling to take hold within the artificial mind.

I labor to give the titan more.

I clean the shallow runes along the ocular cavities with a small brush. Between the gaps in its mask, I touch the darkwood fibers to test their resilience. These I have already dusted with trace amounts of ground Irian crystal. Routine maintenance is vital at this stage.

I feel strangely outside myself this day, somewhat detached as I explore this moment. Perhaps it is simply the importance of what I am doing and the perspective it gives me. I hear the shivering roar of the forge behind the titan, but I have learned to ignore the distraction. We all have. Today the forgemaster and his team have halted their usual work to produce a lot of thirty standard units. The demands of the world outside have increased, the need for more manpower dire.

I think of Aarren again as I work, a great man, despite his excoriation. His mastery of the intelligent mind, his respect for its fragility, overshadows my own. What his father Merrix had created—warforged titans like the one before me—Aarren perfected with the man-sized, more adaptable units, but some of us have not given up yet on improving the titans, the true "children" of the Orphanage. Marrying Merrix's work with his son's genius has been the mission of this facility for years. We have made progress, and I am proud for my part in it.

Imagine it—with sentient, rational constructs of such great strength at hand, the war could be forced to a speedy conclusion at last.

"Master, you must take some rest." At the base of the maintenance ladder beneath me, I hear the concern in my assistant's voice. Does he not understand how diligent I must be in my work today?

"One hour more," he says. "Take some rest in an hour. I will take your place then, Master." He does understand.

"That will do," I call down to him.

I return to my work, confident I will not be interrupted again.

Chapter
ONE

The Infiltrator
Sar, the 7th of Sypheros, 998 YK

Tallis surveyed the cityscape one last time.

Night was absolute in Korth, the pearly face of Zarantyr veiled by storm clouds. It was a good time for this kind of work. Tallis watched from his position along the parapets of one of the city's towers, clad in his customary black, masked and ready. The arches and linear designs that gave each building below him its own identity were lost in the darkness. Only an array of glowing needlepoints—wisplights at the intersections and residential firelight in the windows—riddled the gloom.

Along the main avenues, individual torches marched in long-established patterns—the noctivagant patrols of the White Lions. Tallis knew Korth's garrison well. They were a predictable, if tenacious lot—dangerous only in numbers or if encountered unexpectedly. The only watchmen concerning him tonight were those guarding tonight's mark.

He produced a pair of wire-framed spectacles set with dark lenses. When he settled them over the holes of his leather mask, what few colors remained of the night faded into shades of gray. The shadows nearest him vanished altogether, making every crevice and crenellation within a stone's throw sharp in arrant contrast.

For that brief moment, Tallis envied the dwarves—even goblins and orcs, for that matter—for their natural darkvision. Sharp as his eyes were, he could not see in the dark. Less fortunate criminals—like him—had to pay hard-earned gold for devices like this one.

He set his eyes upon the adjacent tower, an edifice of black stone that rose more than ten stories higher than his current vantage. Known as the Ebonspire, it catered to the noble and the privileged, housing esteemed citizens and honored guests alike. It was also considered nigh impenetrable.

Tallis intended to prove such disinformation to be simply that.

The sentries and magic wards that guarded the tower's occupants ensured that whatever he was after had better be worth the risk. To Tallis, it was well worth both the risk *and* the expense. He'd nearly exhausted his magical resources just getting this far, but at least he'd saved gold by using a simple mask. Powerful wards placed by House Medani denied all the Ebonspire's entrants the ability to disguise their true appearances with magic. It was said even changelings could not use their innate shapeshifting within.

The dwelling he was about to infiltrate housed one Arend ir'Montevik, an aristocrat from the city of Atur whose religious charities Tallis was disinclined to favor. He nearly spit at the thought. The Blood of Vol had enough followers to fill its coffers without receiving generous donations from the likes of ir'Montevik.

While the man's coin could surely pad his own depleting coffers, Tallis wasn't after his wealth. Not *this* time, anyway. He didn't know what business ir'Montevik had in Korth at present, but he would see to it the valuable scrolls in the man's possession wouldn't reach their final destination. Gold was one thing. Necromantic spells in written form were quite another.

Haedrun, the agent who'd given Tallis this job, had offered one hundred galifars for every scroll he could acquire. Such pay was paltry compared the scrolls' actual value, but Tallis respected the Red Watchers and their work. For *her*, he would do this one cheap.

And if he chanced upon anything interesting or valuable

in ir'Montevik's possessions—say, dragonshards or perhaps a choice potion or two—then it would all even out. The noble was burdened by a substantial inheritance, and when such unfortunate men failed to employ their legacies properly, it was up to men like Tallis to relieve them of it.

Tallis studied the wide tower. Every story of the Ebonspire included four flats, each overlooking Korth in one of the cardinal directions from a wide balcony. His enhanced vision could not pierce the darkness as far up as he meant to climb, but he was able to scrutinize the nearest balconies, his point of access.

There: two stories down and directly across on the tower's eastern side, Tallis spotted *another* guard. This one's ivory tabard and burnished breastplate proclaimed him one of the White Lions. A military man must reside within that flat. That balcony wasn't his target, though it was his means of accessing the Ebonspire. The guard would have to get out of his way.

A long-hafted battle-axe rested within the White Lion's reach against the tower wall, and he held a longbow in hand. His posture was rigid from the arduous instruction all White Lions received under the iron-willed General Thauram.

Thauram. It had been a while since Tallis had crossed blades with *that* particular half-elf. He still saw the scar from that encounter every time he bathed.

Tallis appraised the young soldier and saw that he was tense, expecting a problem. One of Thauram's "amnesty cases," a felon who avoided execution only by indentured military service to the city?

Tallis simmered at the irony. Here he was, one of Karrnath's true patriots, staring across to the other side of the law at this young rogue-in-knight's-armor.

"Are you prepared to bleed for your nation, little white cat?" he whispered.

Tallis looked to the street far below, waited until the patrol had passed, and knew he had only a few minutes before the next. He tapped the ring on his left hand—little more than a loop of leather marked with an arcane sigil—and felt a furtive tingle spreading throughout his arms and legs. His muscles flexed involuntarily as they adapted to the magic within.

He checked to make sure his weapon—a hooked hammer—was still strapped to its harness over his shoulder. Tallis gauged the distance, made a fist with his right hand and looked to the second ring he wore there. He pointed his fist at the Lion on the balcony, sparing a glance to the tiny dragon head that adorned the iron band.

"*Telchanak*," he said with his best Draconic accent, triggering the magic of the ring. He felt not the slightest recoil as a ghostly white force manifested from the ring and launched itself across the space between the two towers. With little more than a quiet rumbling, the force closed the distance, solidifying into the shape of a dragon's head with curling, ramlike horns. Tallis heard the guard's brief cry of surprise then the resounding crunch of his breastplate as the dragon's head slammed into him. The vaporous force faded away.

The parapets denied Tallis any chance of a running start, so he coiled his body into the structural cleft. Even the greatest athlete would have difficulty clearing the gap between the buildings, but Tallis had come well-equipped. When his feet pressed against the stone, he felt an instant surge of strength and agility in his legs, owing to the enchanted boots he wore.

He mouthed a silent, half-hearted prayer to the Sovereign Host, then jumped.

The sheer black wall of the Ebonspire thrust itself upon him. With a deftness belied by even his own body, Tallis grasped the minute imperfections in the wall with his right hand, grooves that would have been impossible to find without the augmentation afforded him by the leather ring. His left hand found the lip of the balcony one story above.

Tallis hung there for a moment against the wall until the swaying of his body slowed. From the gasping noises below him, he knew the dragon-ring's concussive power had succeeded only in knocking the wind from the White Lion. He was still a viable threat. With his free hand Tallis pulled a metal rod from his belt and dropped from the railing.

A split second later, he pressed a button on the rod and it locked in place, magically suspended in space as though held by an invisible arm of prodigious strength. Swinging from the artificial handhold, Tallis used his body's momentum to drop squarely above the stumbling guard.

"Wait! " the White Lion sputtered, struggling to rise.

"Wrong occupation, boy." Tallis grabbed the younger man's longbow. Ash, he noted with admiration—the garrison was issuing fine arms to its young recruits these days. Then he swung the hard wood against the man's face.

The crack of cartilage ended all resistance and the guard slumped to the ground. Blood leaked from his nose—likely broken. Tallis would be long gone before the man would awaken to report a disturbance.

He waited briefly at one side of the balcony in case the scuffle had been heard. Satisfied his presence was still undetected, he began to climb. The two rods he carried, as well as his boots, made scaling four more stories easier work.

All told, this certainly was easier than scaling the Starpeaks in search of an enemy redoubt. Then again, the cold Aundairian mountains hadn't been crawling with White Lions who knew his face.

When Tallis neared the appointed balcony, he locked one of the rods in place. With feet planted on infinitesimal crevices and one hand gripping the second rod, he paused to listen. Nothing but the whistle of the cold night wind. Could ir'Montevik's balcony be unguarded, after all? Most of the Ebonspire's occupants—wealthy visitors and influential citizens—had no need to guard from the outside, but a paranoid man like Arend wouldn't take chances. Tallis had expected more.

He produced a rune-carved wand of ivory from a pocket on his calf and pointed it at the balcony's edge. Muttering a series of carefully memorized syllables, his best emulation of its arcane trigger, Tallis saw a glimmer of light at the wand's end and then a second glimmer along the iron balustrade above. Even with no guards, magical wards would have been in place. If the wand had done its work, any such spells would have been stripped away. Tallis climbed higher, then pulled himself up to the balcony's rail—

—only to see an enormous figure rushing at him with a heavy blade raised.

"Blunted!" Tallis dropped to step down on the rod he'd left hanging in place, narrowly avoiding a wide sweep of his attacker's sword. He steadied himself with the balcony's lip.

"Intruder!" the guard shouted, staring down at him. The man's head was covered with a broad helmet, his voice loud and resonant. One thick-fingered hand gripped the railing, while the other held the sword, poised to kill. He wore heavy plate armor, with a steel buckler on his left forearm.

No, not armored—not in the conventional sense. The guard was a warforged, a living construct given life during the Last War and the illusion of freedom at war's end—now expected to settle down into the fragile peace. In Karrnath they'd never achieved even the "freedom" offered by the other nations. Here they were pressed into indentured service, usually in security or heavy labor.

"No, I'm not!" Tallis said. "I'm . . . family. I just . . . I knew my uncle wouldn't . . . let me in."

"You lie. You wear a mask!"

For a moment, he feared the warforged would turn away and shout for help, raising an alarm, but this was a matter of pride. If Tallis was a burglar intent on stealing from its master, then the guard would handle him alone.

Tallis could exploit that.

"You're right," he goaded. "I *am* lying. Thought you'd fall for it . . . you witless *golems* usually do."

The warforged growled at the insult and swung its blade. Tallis threw his body to one side, evading the blow, trusting his balance and enhanced mobility to save him. In the same motion, he took hold of the construct's low-swinging arm, a broad limb of fibrous hardwood and plated metal. He jumped and climbed up, easily gaining holds along the warforged's body. The construct tried to shake him loose, but Tallis scrambled over it before it could bring its weapon to bear.

Tallis was happy to see that the balcony door was closed. The curtains were drawn along the glass door, admitting no light from within. Only a sliver of the Storm Moon broke through the clouds. He could see perfectly with his darkvision lenses and hoped the warforged was disadvantaged in the gloom. Tallis loosed the hooked hammer from its strap and held it up as the construct turned to face him.

"You would serve your master better as a ladder, my friend," Tallis said, "as I'm guessing you're even easier to fight than to climb."

"I will tell him I had no choice but slay the intruder," the warforged said.

Tallis had to make this fast. He jumped forward, buoyed by magic, and made an experimental attack with the edge of his hammer. The warforged's buckler turned away the blow with ease, and Tallis winced at the sound of ringing metal. He aimed his second and third swings to hit, but the construct deflected each as easily as the first. The guard was a worthy foe, but Tallis was not one to rely on a fair fight.

"Is this all you can do?" he said. "Hide behind your shield?"

The warforged stepped forward and swept its heavy blade down. Tallis took a step back and evaded the swing then stumbled. The construct followed the feint, and Tallis rolled to the side. The warforged's defenses opened. Using the same rolling momentum, Tallis reversed his weapon and buried the pick's head deep into the fibers of the warforged's stomach.

Tallis rose, twisting the weapon to grind the wood further apart. The warforged struggled to stay on its feet. The wound would have been fatal to a living man within seconds. That the construct could stand at all was testament to its strength.

Tallis was never sure if warforged could feel pain the same

way living people did. He'd only known a few during the war, and none were particularly verbose. Reversing his weapon again, Tallis brought the hammer's head down against the construct's helmlike head. With the loud ringing that followed, he looked around to see if anyone had heard.

Still, it surprised Tallis to find a warforged employed by Arend ir'Montevik. Normally Cultists of the Blood of Vol had little use for constructs. Why bother, when their clerics could raise the dead to do their bidding? He had expected only ir'Montevik himself and maybe that musclebound goon of his to be here.

Tallis peered through the glass door and the narrow slit between the curtains to a darkened bedroom with wisplight from a common room beyond spilling in.

The door was unlocked. He slipped into the room, quietly closing the door behind him and keeping to the wall as he approached the opposite exit. He gave the room a cursory examination—it appeared empty of the scrolls he was after. He slipped his enchanted lenses in a pocket. He paused to listen to the voices in the next room.

The laughter of children startled him. It sounded like a whole family!

Tallis froze, reassessing the situation. As far as he knew, Arend didn't have children. Haedrun would have told him if the nobleman had brought family with him to Korth. So what was this?

"Papa," said the voice of a child. "It's cold here!" The boy's voice was merry, despite his words, and carried a sleight foreign accent. He heard a man chuckle. Surely not Arend! The man had no sense of humor.

Another voice joined the conversation, the assertive voice of a mother. "Rennet, take this blanket. Gamnon, you really should make a fire."

Gamnon! Tallis's stomach clenched. This was *not* Arend's family. This was a mistake. His instinct had been right—ir'Montevik wouldn't have owned a warforged. Could he possibly have chosen the wrong floor?

No. Impossible. He turned back to the balcony.

A figure appeared in the room behind him, slipping through the balcony door just as he had. Veiled head to foot in black wrappings, the intruder was lithe and tall. Tallis caught the gleam of metal gauntlets beneath the linen, but he couldn't see any eyes exposed. From its supple form, he guessed it was a woman, perhaps a professional like himself? She was weaponless.

Surprised by this development, he instinctively adopted a defensive stance with his weapon held up.

"Who are you?" he whispered.

The shrouded figure strode gracefully past him as though she hadn't heard him at all. Steel blades, as long and slender as rapiers, appeared in each of her mailed fists. Whether an act of magic or mere sleight of hand, the weapons looked real enough.

"Stand down!" Tallis said, hoping to halt the intruder as well as alert the family to the danger.

The shrouded figure did not heed him.

"Who dares?" came a furious voice in the next room.

Responding to the alarm, a well-dressed steward appeared in the doorway with a half-drawn blade of his own. The cloth-wrapped intruder thrust both rapiers into the man's torso—one in his stomach, the other near his collar—making not even a grunt in the motion. Sputtering blood, the steward toppled. The intruder stepped into the room beyond without hesitation.

Then came the screams.

*   *   *   *   *   *   *

Sergeant Bratta took the spiral stairs three at a time until he reached the final landing. He was in excellent physical shape, but the Last War hadn't trained soldiers to climb stairs as much as sprint across battlefields. Behind him two more Lions followed, laboring for breath. The silent wards had revealed the presence of intruders on the thirty-fourth floor. Not surprisingly, in the midst of the crisis, the tower's only lift had become disabled. Typical civilian device, unreliable in times of need.

He found the doors already breached, apparently forced open by the White Lions who'd been stationed outside the ambassador's door. The light in the common room came from a single everbright lantern affixed to a low table, but it had been knocked sideways and the glass was spattered with blood. A casual glance at the room revealed the fate of the soldiers. Three good men dead, as well as the civilians.

"Sovereigns!" Rage welled within him at the sight. The Lions behind him fanned out, ready to act on his command.

The only man left standing within wore a black outfit vaguely reminiscent of an army uniform, but it was slashed and torn. He was dark-haired, lathered in sweat, and holding some kind of pick. The man stood half in shadow, staring at the carnage mutely. He looked familiar, but Bratta couldn't think of how he knew this man.

"Drop the weapon!" Bratta said, aiming his crossbow.

The murderer looked up. "No, you don't under—"

"Not another word until I say so. Drop the weapon!"

The man broke into a run and dived into an adjoining room, faster than he looked. Bratta ran after him. When he stepped into the master bedroom, he saw the silhouette of the murderer retreating onto the balcony. Bratta raised his crossbow and loosed, feeling grim satisfaction when his target grunted in pain.

But the bolt didn't bring the man down. As Bratta and his men rushed to follow, he saw the murderer grasp the railing's edge and swing his body over and disappear from view.

"What in Khyber—"

On the balcony, Bratta nearly stumbled over the fallen hulk of a warforged and slipped on the blood at his feet. His subordinate dropped his axe in favor of the bow, staring over the edge in an attempt to sight down their target.

"He's a cursed wizard!" the private said. Bratta glared as the killer landed in a blur on the roof of an adjacent tower, clear across the wide gap. It seemed as if he had flown from the balcony below.

The soldier drew back his bowstring and released, but the

arrow snapped against one of the tower's parapets. Bratta loaded his crossbow as fast as he could and loosed a second bolt at the man as he disappeared into the darkness. Then he was gone.

"Sergeant," the bowman said, looking over the balcony's edge to the wisplit street below. "There's another body down there. I think it's the ambassador's."

Chapter Two

"**S**hadow, hide me," Zzar hissed in his native tongue, calling to his god among the Dark Six. He preferred to hunt in secret, waiting for his quarry to come to him.

The sun had risen only two bells ago, but already there were so many people to choose from. Zzar remembered, for just that moment, his home in the Howling Peaks and the wing of fools he'd left behind. Let them scour the mountains for the tiny scalefolk and the occasional lost explorer. Let *them* scratch at rocks when there was no sport left!

But not Zzar, no.

The humans who'd survived Zzar's attack that day had offered him a new life. "Come to our city, Sharn," they bade, speaking in perfect Terran and pointing to where the sun perished each day. "We can give you sport of a different kind. We can give you silver, esteem, and the fear you deserve."

Zzar had humored them, quit the mountains of his birth, and indulged in the sights, smells, and tastes of this city—where another wing took him in. The humans gave him silver for his hunting skills and promised him more if he was fast about it.

During the sunless hours the towers looked like a great cluster of stalagmites, pitted with glowing lights and webbed together with bridges for the flightless. It was oddly beautiful at such times. During the sun-lit hours, the city was dazzling and painful to his eyes, but he was already growing accustomed. Even so, he much preferred the hunts that took him to the highest districts, where there were more places to sit and watch and fewer prying eyes. Where it was a little more like home.

A skycoach soared close overhead, distracting Zzar from his thoughts. On impulse, he scraped one taloned hand against its hull, drawing deep grooves and dislodging a sizable chunk. As the splintered wood fluttered down into the city below, one of the vessel's occupants cursed at him. Zzar laughed in reply but held his course. Humans created such ridiculous flying vehicles to imitate his kind.

Though exciting, the encounter was all too brief, and it only banished whatever it was he'd been thinking about the moment before. No matter. It was time to focus on the hunt anyway. He'd wheeled around the crowded residential district of Ivy Towers long enough with no success. His wings unfurled to their full span, then snapped together with a surge of speed as Zzar ascended once more.

Red-glowing eyes studied the urban landscape beneath him, searching for his quarry. His employers' description returned to mind. "Her name is Soneste, Zzar. Say it with me. Soneste. A young and pretty human, hair the color of wheat, light skin. She is always armed with a thin sword and often wears a blue coat."

❊ ❊ ❊ ◉ ❊ ❊ ❊

Blackfeather Slayings Solved by Local Inquisitive

SHARN—*An inquisitive employed by Thuranne d'Velderan's Investigative Services, the Tharashk-sponsored agency located in Warden Towers, personally cracked the so-called Blackfeather case on Far, naming the man responsible for the long-unsolved serial killing of thirteen nobles in 991 YK.*

*Soneste Otänsin, a native of Starilaskur but a resident of Sharn, first
came to note for finding Shauranna Rokesko last Olarune when the royal
aide had been kidnapped by a cell of Emerald Claw agents. Now Soneste
has discovered the true identity of the killer known for fifteen years only as
the Torchfire Wraith, leading to the arrest of Aldem ir'Shorem, a former
actor and playwright once rejected by the Blackfeather Troupe.*

*"We never expected to find that devil," said Werick Faldren, captain
of the Menthis Plateau garrison of Warden Towers. "He killed thirteen
young men and women in cold blood and left the Torchfire district para-
lyzed with fear for a long time."*

*Aldem, the heir of the ir'Shorem estate, is now in the custody of the
King's Citadel and faces a dozen charges of murder.*

*"I'm very proud of Soneste," said Lady Thuranne d'Velderan, head
of Investigative Services and a dragonmarked member of House Tharashk.
"She single-handedly brought a notorious criminal to justice and closure to
the families of his victims."*

*The family of Aldem ir'Shorem, the aristocrat from Ocean View whose
guilt was brought to light by Soneste's investigation, could not be reached
for comment . . .*

The chronicle had gone to print earlier this morning, was
already available at vendors throughout the city, and would be
distributed abroad within days. Hundreds—thousands—of the
Sharn Inquisitive's readers would be seeing Soneste's name in print
for the second time. She had her own copy, of course, but she'd
already committed every word to memory, an easy feat ever since
Veshtalan taught her how with but a few moments' concentration.
Still, she couldn't wait to see her friends' reactions, couldn't wait
to hear from her mother in Starilaskur after she'd read the story.
It might just cheer her up.

The world looked different now. People walked the skybridges
as they always had. Soarsleds and skycoaches glided among the
multi-leveled districts. The Watch roved the bustling streets in
pairs. Lifts rose and fell from one level to another. Yet to her,
somehow it all seemed more invigorating. What she did seemed

to *matter,* now more than ever, and people would know it! After eight years in Sharn, she'd never felt more a part of the city. It had all started with finding the kidnapped Shauranna, but this was something more, a mystery none could solve—and she solved it, following one clue after another.

"Miss Otänsin?"

Soneste shook her reverie away. She turned her eyes from the window back to the young woman who sat across from her, who was scratching notes in a small book even as she waited for a response.

"I'm sorry," Soneste said. "Could you repeat the question?"

"How many homicide cases have you been involved in now?" The young woman wrote down her own question. She carried no bottle of ink. Soneste suspected the pen possessed an enchantment enabling it to produce its own indefinitely.

"Ten," she answered. "Three of which were solo. This one and the Rokesko case are certainly higher profile than the rest."

The young woman nodded, then turned her book face down and stared back. "Do you think the ir'Shorem family will hold a grudge against you for incriminating Aldem? Or ever seek to do you harm?"

"Uhh, I don't . . ."

The question had caught her off guard. Soneste recovered herself and looked evenly into the young woman's eyes. Soneste somehow *felt* like a veteran inquisitive talking to her.

In a job that required snooping around where she wasn't welcome, Soneste had learned how to defend herself. At her hip she carried a magewrought rapier, a few tricks in the pockets of her shiftweave coat, and she always kept her Riedran crysteel dagger hidden in one boot. The beautiful weapon had been a parting gift from Veshtalan, an apology for cutting his mentorship short a mere five months ago.

"No," Soneste said. "I don't think they're that foolish. Their favorite son is facing the gallows. The public's eye is fixed firmly upon the ir'Shorem family. They'll behave for a good long while." She let her fingers caress the steel hilt of her rapier.

"Regardless, I can take care of myself, Miss . . . I'm sorry, what was your name again?"

"Kereva. Scarla Kereva."

Of course, Soneste had memorized the chronicler's name when she'd first introduced herself—a vital skill in her trade, a task made easier since Veshtalan's tutelage—but she'd decided to remind the chronicler who *she* was by comparison. An inquisitive like Soneste shouldn't have to bother with the names of those beneath her.

Beneath? Had she just thought that?

"Of course. Scarla." It sounded like an elvish name, but the scuffs on the girl's boots and the frayed lace at her sleeve did not affiliate her with the loftier elven neighborhoods of Sharn. Scarla probably lived in an apartment somewhere in Rattlestone or Kenton—like Soneste once had. Working class.

The Rokesko case, cracked nearly eight months ago, had changed everything for her. Thuranne, her boss, had intimated that Soneste could expect cases of higher profile from now on— wealthier clients had already been asking for her—which meant she would be able to afford a higher standard of living. Perhaps prematurely, she'd already moved to a new apartment in Ivy Towers. It had a spectacular view, staring across the city chasm to look upon the towers of Middle and Upper Dura. Quite a nice step up.

Now the ir'Shorem case had brought her further accolades, as evinced by the chronicler in front of her. The second *Sharn Inquisitive* article naming her was already out, and now they wanted to print an exclusive interview with her in the next edition.

Soneste had always enjoyed her work. Yet how important, after all, was finding people who didn't want to be found, spying on unscrupulous merchants, or locating stolen jewelry for people who could hardly notice its absence? Perhaps the cases themselves would be more satisfying now. With a single apprehension, she'd brought a serial killer to justice and one of Sharn's most upstanding families under scrutiny. She had to admit, she knew she *should* be careful.

The coach continued its bobbing pace, winding around another massive tower and setting across a long bridge that led to Ivy Towers. She was halfway home from the Sivis message station.

"If I may ask, Miss Otänsin, have you ever had to kill anyone in your work?"

Soneste cocked her head. "You *are* intrusive, aren't you?"

"I won't quote you, if you'd rather. But I'm curious. Have you—"

A shadow flashed through Soneste's mind.

She turned her head sharply, just in time to see something dark and winged fly past the window. She heard the driver shout and felt the coach lurch to a stop. A heartbeat later, the entire conveyance shook as something solid and heavy landed atop it. Scarla gasped, dropping her book in favor of keeping her seat.

There was no room for Soneste to employ her rapier in the tight confines of the coach, so her long knife had to do. Soneste slipped the crysteel dagger from her boot and held it up, feeling the sleight hum of its power in her mind. Scarla's eyes widened as a reflection of the rising sun appeared to shine through the violet-tinged blade.

"Just sit still," Soneste said, then kicked the coach door open.

With her feet braced against the floor, she was half-crouched and ready to spring out. She pointed the blade forward when she saw leaden talons grip the open doorframe from above. The *Inquisitive* reporter sucked in her breath, stifling another gasp.

"Sonnnesste!"

It took her a moment to realize the assailant had spoken her name. The voice was harsh, like the scrape of metal against stone. Soneste saw the shadow of leathery wings flap as the creature lifted into the air again. The coach rattling as the weight lifted.

Soneste took the opportunity to step out the door and off to one side, keeping her back against the side of the coach. The monstrous figure dropped to the ground directly in front of her. The creature's body was as large as a tall man's, though his stooped posture brought his smoldering red eyes to her level. Gray skin the texture of roughly hewn stone, folding bat-like wings, and a pair of prodigious, curving horns made the creature's presence unsettling.

Soneste presented the dagger before her, its gleaming tip stopping only inches from the gargoyle's diabolic face.

"What do you want?" she demanded, heart racing with anticipation.

She'd only seen these things from a distance before, perched on tower eaves or winging through the night. His torso was wrapped tightly in a black leather harness, clasped at the front with a House Vadalis brooch. The gargoyle was a courier, yet Soneste saw no note or package in its claws, which flexed even now as if eager to rend flesh.

Most pedestrians gave the creature a wide berth. A few bolder ones stopped to watch.

"To Warden Towersss," the gargoyle said in a forced whisper, as if knowing the full volume of his voice was unwelcome. "You are bidden!"

"Who sent you?" Soneste asked. Gargoyle couriers were not cheap, and they were usually sent to a single destination. This one had been instructed to *find* her.

Scarla poked her head out of the coach. The coachman approached as well, his face soured by the unexpected messenger. The way he hefted the mace in his hand suggested he'd seen some action in the war and knew how to wield it.

"Vvvelderan, d'Tharassshk," the gargoyle rasped. His crowned head swiveled to face the armed coachman. A claw pointed to him in warning, and the gargoyle issued a guttural hiss that sounded like steel drawn across a whetstone. When the coachman stopped, the creature looked back to Soneste. "You will go, yess?"

"Yes, I will go," she replied. "What is your name, courier?"

"Zzar."

"Thank you, Zzar, for your obvious expedience." Soneste dropped a sovereign into one clawed hand.

The gargoyle bowed his head, his duty fulfilled, then turned and leapt from the bridge. His wings snapped loudly as they caught the air, carrying the demonic shape swiftly out of sight.

She looked to Scarla, who had stepped out of the coach and was scratching furiously in her book.

"My life isn't really *this* exciting, you know," Soneste said.

"Sure, sure." The girl laughed. "This will look great in print. Gargoyles usually just deliver packages."

Soneste nodded. "Can we finish this some other time?"

Indeed, maybe her life *would* be this exciting from now on. Despite the emergency the creature's presence implied, a smile crept onto her face.

Soneste apologized to the coachman and hailed a skycoach instead. Her mind began to wander as she fished in her pocket for more silver. Why would Thuranne send for her so urgently?

* * * * * * *

Thuranne d'Velderan's Investigative Services was always easy to find, situated at the corner of Glaive and Pike Streets. The district of Warden Towers was home to the Menthis Plateau's Watch garrison, so residents and visitors alike were forced to walk through a veritable gauntlet of lawmen to reach their destination. "Keeps most of our clients legitimate," Thuranne often said.

Soneste was greeted by her younger colleagues and tried hard to ignore the few poorly concealed scowls from the older agents. Old Roren, Thuranne's senior inquisitive, glared at her openly. As much to get away from those looks as to find out what Thuranne needed, she hurried to the door at the back of the agency's modest space.

When she stepped into Thuranne's office, she felt a wave of relief at the smile upon her employer's face. There couldn't be *that* much of an emergency. The twist of her dragonmark was visible on one side of Thuranne's neck, shades of indigo almost hidden against her brown-gray skin.

Sheaves of paper and leather-bound ledgers were stacked in great volume and perfect order, as always, upon her boss's desk. Choice clippings from the *Sharn Inquisitive* and the *Korranberg Chronicle* were tacked against one wall, while small painted portraits of Thuranne's nieces and nephews adorned the opposite wall. The older woman's workspace was, just like her, at once sedulous and intimate.

Soneste spoke first. "They called you 'Lady' in the *Inquisitive*." She removed her coat and laid it over the back of a chair. It was always a little too hot in here. The ruffled, sleeveless white shirt she wore cooled her nicely.

"It gave me a good laugh too." The half-orc's smile dissolved. She looked down at a pair of scrolls in her hand, then back to Soneste. "Only two days, girl, and already I'm dragging you back to work."

"You scared the life out of me," Soneste said, unbuckling her rapier and propping it up against the desk before dropping into the chair. "Since when do you use Vadalis gargoyles?"

Thuranne snorted, small tusks peering up from beneath her lower lip. "I figured I haven't offended my own house enough."

Soneste smiled, studying the face of her mentor and friend. The older woman looked worried. "What's happened?"

Thuranne sighed. "I need you to take a new case, Soneste, and it kills me to ask you now. If it were any other job, I'd find someone else. You've earned this time off, to say the least."

Soneste's heart sank, but only for a moment. She wanted to be taken seriously, after all. She didn't meet Thuranne's eyes yet, merely fidgeting with her latest acquisition—a serpent-shaped, gold armband with red garnet eyes.

"Why the urgency?" she asked, looking up.

"This," Thuranne said, holding up one of the scrolls, "is a message from the Justice Ministry of Korth. It was forwarded to me by speaking stone. It's about a murder that took place there last night."

Soneste's stomach clenched. Korth, capital city of Karrnath. A new case. Urgent. Here she was, sitting in Thuranne's office, probably the only one to hear about this right now. Silently, she wondered if Thuranne had considered anyone else? Maybe Roren—and why not? He was the veteran inquisitive around here.

But more than Thuranne she had chosen Soneste, she was afraid to ask how a crime in a faraway nation concerned Investigative Services, which by Thuranne's own admission was just one of many agencies in Sharn and hardly the most prestigious. Why not involve House Tharashk itself? A far more powerful entity and one capable of employing magical divination.

Thuranne unrolled the second scroll. Sunlight from the window behind her made the parchment translucent. Soneste could see the seal of the Brelish crown, its authenticity notarized by House Sivis.

"This is a letter from the King's Citadel, which came to me this morning, asking me to set someone on the Korth murder case. Now I could speculate why they sent this to *me*, but given the facts, I'd say the crown wants to avoid a messy political situation and they don't want to involve the dragonmarked houses at all if they don't have to. There are some members of the Citadel who know me, and they know that I seldom involve my own house."

"Why not send Roren?" she asked.

"You know why. He's getting on in years. I need someone younger, stronger."

"What about Abraxis Wren? He loves going abroad." Wren was a House Medani inquisitive she'd worked for when she'd first come to Sharn, a few years before joining Thuranne's agency.

The half-orc rolled her eyes. "The Citadel came to *me*, not Wren or House Medani, and they asked for you, Soneste. You've really made a name for yourself now." A ghost of a smile lit Thuranne's face. "They know you're not afraid to take on the political or the powerful."

Soneste nodded, not amused, allowing the gravity of the half-orc's words to settle in. "What do we know?" she said, resigned, but she already knew where this was going.

Things had finally begun to happen for her. Good things. Soneste had gone from the agency's most promising inquisitive to its best, seemingly overnight. She'd earned this new case, of course, but going to grim Karrnath even if she left right that moment would take up valuable time, time that meant the difference between solving the case and failing miserably. Even a one-way trip by lightning rail would take days.

"Do you know the name ir'Daresh?" Thuranne asked.

Soneste didn't, but the prefix "ir" always indicated a family of noble blood. She shook her head.

"Gamnon ir'Daresh is—was—a Brelish ambassador. He was killed on Karrnathi soil in the very shadow of Crownhome. Hence the political posture. Of course, Breland has many ambassadors and things happen from time to time. Gamnon wasn't so important that we risk the attention of King Boranel just yet. But he wasn't so minor that the murder is inconsequential. The motive is key here."

"So all we need to do is determine who the killer is and why he did it? That's it?"

"Yes. That's it," Thuranne said, a smile returning in full and bringing her orcish features to the fore. "We need to know how deep this goes. If you perceive the case to be a larger threat against Breland, then you send word back to me. The Dark Lanterns may get involved at that point, but if it's just some local lunatic, identify him and let the Karrns apprehend him. He will most likely face Karrnathi . . . *punishment*. That will be decided between the Justice Ministry of Korth and the King's Citadel."

Even as Thuranne spoke, Soneste imagined a Brelish nobleman lying dead in a cold alley with fresh blood pooling between the cobbles, a dagger twisted into his gut by a passing assassin. Almost immediately, red and black-robed clerics flocked like vultures around the body in the imagined scene.

"Wait," Soneste said. "This is Karrnath, we're speaking of. Can't their priests just . . . *talk* to the ambassador? Or what's left of him?"

Thuranne sucked her teeth. "Not with his head missing."

"I . . . see," said Soneste. "It's *that* kind of case."

"Even if it weren't, you'd be smart to avoid that sort of magic in Karrn," Thuranne said. "The Blood of Vol doesn't rule the kingdom, but they've got their followers in a good number of places. Like as not, it would be a Cult priest doing the speaking. You don't want to mix yourself up with them if you can help it."

The Blood of Vol—a cult of nefarious reputation and the former national religion of Karrnath until King Kaius severed all political ties with the Cult. The king had never been able to dissolve all connections with the Cult of Vol, but it still thrived more in Karrnath than anywhere on Eberron. The Cultists placed far too much value on blood, bloodlines, and allegedly even revered the undead.

Soneste straightening in her chair. "All right. What else do we know?"

"Very little. Only a few details were provided in the letter. The Civic Minister, Hyran ir'Tennet, will provide you the rest. He did say that there is already one suspect, spotted at the scene."

"I don't suppose that would be Gamnon's wife? A bit of revenge for some past indiscretion?" Soneste wondered if it could be that simple, a crime of passion. These were the easiest to reveal.

"No," Thuranne answered. "As the murderer also killed Gamnon's wife, their two children, four servants, and three city guards."

Two children. Soneste felt cold. This was a slaughter, no simple murder. Her imagined crime scene relocated from a slum alley to a private room in some luxurious restaurant. If a professional killer was responsible, then he may have been hired by someone else. Assassins always complicated a case. Nothing was finished until you found the patron.

"And . . . their heads too?" Soneste asked, afraid to imagine it.

"No. Only Gamnon's."

Soneste sighed with relief. "Then a cleric needn't speak to Gamnon himself. His family, the servants—any of them might be able to say what happened. We could bring a cleric of the Host and stay out of the Cult's way."

Thuranne shook her head. "It's not that simple. The ir'Daresh family were respectable followers of the Silver Flame, and Maril ir'Daresh's family has already forbidden any necromancy to be performed on her body, her children's, or the servants'—though the Host only knows how far they'll get with that claim. You might be able to work around the family, but it would take too long."

Thuranne's face softened. "Besides, put yourself in their place. Would you let Karrns raise a loved one's corpse to get answers Sharn's brightest young inquisitive could work out on her own?"

The question brought Soneste's mother to mind. She pictured her staring out their third story apartment window in Starilaskur, still waiting for her father to return home from the war. Of course, he never would.

"Point taken," Soneste said, wondering idly if the killer had targeted the ambassador's family for this very convenience. "Where did the massacre take place?" she asked. Even as she spoke, Soneste felt an unmitigated loathing for the killer. She didn't care if the children were Brelish or Karrns. No one had the right to harm a child—especially now, in a time of struggling peace. The haunted face of Shauranna Rokesko came to mind. The young aide had spent a week in her captor's deranged presence before Soneste had led agents of the Watch to their hideout in the Cogs.

"The ambassador's chambers in a tower known as the Ebonspire, a sort of hostel for prestigious visitors of the city."

"Ebonspire. Sounds like a fun place."

"Thank you, Soneste, for taking this. It might be easier than you think."

Soneste nodded. "I'd better be on my way then. Do you know when the next run leaves?"

Thuranne made a curious face. "Well, the good news is you won't have to take the lightning rail. The bad news is to you need to be there *today.*"

Chapter
THREE

Gan dreamed of the perfect woman.

She was tall and slender like he, but possessed none of the androgynous features of his race. Tresses of black shot through her snowy hair and her eyes were luminous, silver-white. On this occasion, she wore a silken gown of form-fitting red—a shift-weave garment like those he'd seen blue-blooded socialites wear in Sharn.

Gan approached his dream courtesan, poised to steal a kiss and perhaps a little more.

Of course, it wasn't exactly a dream. He'd been awake for hours now. The state into which he'd submerged himself for most of the day idealized the world and fashioned anew his imagined temptress. The Traveler knew the women of Karrnath were far too cold for him and lacked the subtlety his affections demanded. Not even the Midnight Market offered companions fitting for someone of Gan's caliber.

But now she was slipping away. To his dismay, the entire waking episode was fading, the crimson-clad form transforming into another shape altogether. She wasn't just teasing him again

27

by shapechanging. This metamorphosis was not of her—or his—volition.

Her form diffused into oblivion, slowly replaced by a voluminous shape of midnight blue. A multicolored mask of lacquered darkwood resolved in perfect, horrible clarity, framed by a deep and shadowed hood. The expression carved into the artificial face was familiar—the perpetual frown Gan feared above all others.

Powerful wizards often crafted masks and enchanted them with defensive properties to grant their wearers aid on the battlefield. Others wove divinatory powers into them to better discern an enemy's own defenses. Gan's employer had done so to hide his own loathsome face.

Gan was dimly aware that he was being held upright by strong, well-muscled arms and that he was no longer in the bedroom of his personal flat. He could just make out the shapes of workroom machinery and somewhere nearby he could hear the muffled roar of a great furnace. With each second, he became more cognizant of where he was and under whose scrutiny he was bound. The fingers that gripped his arms were rough and pitiless. Pressure had decidedly given way to pain.

"My lord?" he croaked, forgetting how dry his mouth could become.

"It was my understanding, Gan," Lord Charoth said in his dry monotone, "that dreamlily did not render its user unresponsive, drooling and oblivious to the world around him." He held up an empty glass vial in one gloved hand. Gan saw only a drop or two of the precious iridescent liquid within.

Dread wormed its way into his stomach. He couldn't bring himself to speak again.

"Indeed, I was under the impression that it induced in its user a state of euphoria which stripped him of all fear, as well as precision and strength of will."

Charoth paused, then looked up to the massive figure who held him upright from behind. "Is it your professional opinion, Master

Rhazan, that Gan is lucid and fully emerged from his episode?"

Rhazan! Gan felt the bugbear's powerful hands release him, but before he could fall, a heavy black chain dropped before his eyes. It was drawn immediately backward to close tightly around his neck, the barbed links cutting into his skin. Gan gurgled with pain and struggled for air, though he was allowed only enough to remain conscious and aware.

"It is, my lord," the thug rumbled.

Charoth turned to regard Gan again. At least he thought so. It was always difficult to tell where the Masked Wizard's gaze was directed.

"Unless, of course, the user in question is a dreamlily *addict*. As I was unaware of your dependency—or indeed of your possession of the illegal drug at all—I find myself sorely disappointed." Charoth paused again, tilting his head slightly. "Have I been remiss about your well being, Gan?"

"No, lord," the changeling managed to gasp.

How many times had he stood by as his employer spoke this calmly to men and women who'd earned his wrath? Gan had watched others beg, weep, and wet themselves under such scrutiny. He was not accustomed to bearing it himself. He steeled his nerves, determined to maintain his courage. He was, after all, too important to be dismissed from service. Charoth needed him.

"How very comforting to hear," Charoth said, straightening.

He made a small gesture with one gloved hand, and Rhazan relaxed his cruel chain. Gan was able to stand again on his own feet. He longed to massage the raw flesh of his neck, but suffered in silence to salvage his dignity.

"But there is still the uncertain matter of your whereabouts last night. I was entertaining guests, Gan, and you were not there to attend me. Could it be that you had simply forgotten? Or had I given you personal leave?"

Gan made his face impassive, relying upon the malleability of his changeling skin to hold it still. Last night's errand was one of his own freelance jobs—not something he wished to connect to his employer. In one panicked moment, he remembered that he'd fallen into the 'lily's embrace at his flat in the morning hours—what time was it now? Charoth's men must have found him there. What had they seen? What had he left out as evidence of his deed?

"Lord Charoth," came another voice, a woman's impatient hiss. "This is taking too long."

By the Traveler! Was *she* here, too? Gan hated the old crow and her condescending tongue.

"My lord," he answered, attempting a sleight bow, but his neck only rattled the chain Rhazan still held ready. "I am sorry . . . for all of this. But you *had* given me the night off, as well as today. I would never have indulged in . . . any diversions had I expected you to call on me today."

"Ahh. My own apologies, then," Charoth answered. "My memory isn't as sharp as it once was. All that remains, then, is the matter of my negligence regarding your personal vice."

The Masked Wizard gingerly pulled one glove from his hand, an act Gan had never seen before. An unpleasant aroma arose from the mottled flesh of his lord's hand. Gan could see almost every vein in the wizard's hand, resembling black worms beneath the unwholesome skin. He tried desperately not to wince at the sight or smell and knew Rhazan must be doing the same. Their lord's disfigurement was not something of which his retainers spoke. It was understood.

Charoth held up the glass vial with his hideous hand, seeming to inspect it in the firelight. There were no windows this deep within the factory, and Gan assumed they now occupied one of the storage rooms beneath factory floor. The heat alone gave testament.

"Dreamlily is a *Brelish* problem, Gan, trafficked through the black markets of Sharn. I will not waste your time or mine to ask you how or why you procured this filthy substance in our city. It has no place in my employ, and you will not use it again." Charoth tossed the vial to the floor at Gan's feet, where it shattered into several pieces.

"Of course, my lord," Gan answered, head bowed. "It will . . . not be a problem."

The old priestess laughed. She stood somewhere in the shadows beyond. Gan couldn't even glare at her.

"You mean to speak the truth, Gan, but addiction is a tenacious thing. It takes only a single *weak* link to break a strong chain. I will not have such a poison compromise your excellent skills or the integrity of my estate. Understand, you are a worthy investment, and I mean to protect that investment. Master Rhazan?"

Charoth nodded to the bugbear, and the spiked chain was drawn back again, harder now. Gan tried to scream, but the thug's fist slammed into the small of his back and robbed him of his breath. Dropping hard to his knees, his pale flesh was ground hard into the broken shards of glass. Through the haze of agony that followed, Gan was aware of his employer watching his anguish without comment. He could almost see those sickly fingers clutching the vulture-headed, blue glass cane his lord always carried.

The crushing force of Rhazan's grip returned and Charoth began to evaporate from Gan's view, as slowly as he'd first appeared.

☉ ☉ ☉ ◉ ☉ ☉ ☉

"Are you still alive?" Valna asked, drawing a scimitar of razor-edged bone. The dead woman smiled, rotted-teeth elongating into fangs, then she slashed at his throat.

Tallis woke from the nightmare with a reflexive spasm.

He opened his eyes. Distorted visions of bloodshed crowded his mind, leaking from his dreaming conscious like brackish water. He thought of the war, of the battlefields he'd surveyed and the hundreds who had fallen. Surely what happened last night could be nothing worse than that. What was the slaughter of one family compared to the thousands slain in the Last War?

"Not good," he said to the ceiling above him.

Realizing that he lay in bed, Tallis sat up. Every bruise and cut on his body chose that moment to protest the harried flight of the night before. He remembered the White Lion who had trained the crossbow at him, then looked to his leg where the bolt had pierced him. A fresh bandage was wrapped tightly around his calf, but he could barely feel it—the result of magical healing.

Tallis surveyed the room, which smelled faintly of familiar incense. The curtains of the small basement window were drawn, but he could see the glimmer of daylight beneath. His magic rods lay on a small table alongside his belt, a dagger, and his darkvision lenses—one of the frames was now empty. *Damn.* Those were on loan.

He was dressed only in his smallclothes, and the purplish flesh of the bruises along his arms and legs stood out. His torn clothing from the night before was in a bundle on the floor. His boots sat against the wall next to a fresh set of clothes, neatly folded. The crossbow bolt had made a sizable hole in the fine leather of his boots.

"Oh, *not* good," he said again, wondering how much Verdax would charge him for the repair. Flesh, it had always seemed, could be mended more easily than enchanted leather.

With a start, he realized that his hooked hammer was missing as well. He strained to remember where he'd lost it. After clearing the roof of the adjacent tower, Tallis couldn't recall what had happened next. He only remembered running.

The distant murmur of voices had Tallis moving to the door, where he cracked it open and listened. Beyond lay a dark hall with brazier light spilling down a narrow stair from the main floor. Tallis proceeded up the stairs. When he reached the first landing, he stopped to listen to the conversation in the chancel above. Sound carried well within the stone halls of the temple, especially here in the undercroft.

"—will come to an end, as all things do." The voice was strong, delivered with a conviction Tallis could associate with none other than his friend Lenrik.

"But what of his *soul?*" The other voice belonged to a woman of middling years. She sounded frightened, desperate to be convinced.

"Mova, your son was—*is*—a soul. He had a body, yes, but he has passed from it. What you saw was the vessel your son once possessed—and nothing more. That body, that shell, is a property of the crown now, and though our faith protests such indignities, in the end it does not matter. We are spiritual beings given life by the Sovereign Host—all of us—and we will transcend physical limitations at the last, as has your son."

"But . . . does Aureon *tell* you all this? Can you hear him speak these things?"

Tallis smiled sadly at the woman's words. He'd asked Lenrik the same questions long ago. What, indeed, did the Sovereign of Law and Lore relay to the elf during his daily prayers, that he could be so sure?

"Not in such words," the elf answered. "The gods find better ways to be heard. Words are the clumsy tools *we* use when we can't find that better way ourselves." The elf gave a gentle laugh. "But yes, in many ways, I do hear him. You can, too, Mova. You just have to *let* him be heard."

Not so easy, old friend, Tallis thought. What will you say if she asks you about Dolurrh? Do you give her the beliefs of the Order or your own?

Tallis crept up the last few stairs to peer around the corner into the shrine of Aureon. The sanctuary was large—the holy Octogram of the Sovereign Host carved in relief upon the marble floor and the white stone altar sculpted into the open book of Aureon's symbol—but the adjoining worship hall of the cathedral proper dwarfed the whole shrine. There were only two people sitting together in the pews.

"I will . . . try," Mova said. She looked matronly, with gray hair and tired, red-rimmed eyes.

She reached out to embrace the slim figure in the dark green cassock who sat beside her. The elf's face was youthful, but Tallis knew Lenrik was more than twice the old woman's age. Mova pulled slowly away, her hands clasping the elf's shoulders as if he were a dear son of hers. "Thank you for listening to me again."

"My pleasure," Lenrik said. "May Aureon and Boldrei preserve you, Mova." Together they rose. For one moment, Tallis thought she saw *him* watching from the stairwell.

We can't have that, he thought. Tallis turned back and returned to the room and closed the door. He walked to the wall mirror and stared back at his own disheveled image. His shoulder-length black hair showed only a pretense of order and the stubble on his chin was considerably coarser than he last remembered. What time of day *was* it?

He crossed to the corner where his and Lenrik's game of Conqueror awaited. He examined Lenrik's latest move. The elf's king was only three squares from Tallis's chancellor, who in turn shielded his own monarch from Lenrik's legionnaires. Tallis pondered his strategy for a long moment, then moved the chancellor out of the way. A bold ploy, to be sure, but Lenrik's king would not be able to advance directly.

Tallis turned his head and found himself staring into the wall tapestry, as he always did when visiting his old friend. It had been woven by Lenrik's own great-grandmother in her youth, the only relic of the elf's childhood in Aerenal. A sorceress of uncanny skill, she'd woven magic into the violet, red, and gold threads that allowed the delicate work to endure for so many centuries. As Tallis lay there, the hypnotic patterns calmed his mind, allowing his thoughts to return inevitably to Haedrun. Why would she set him up? Did she even know what she'd sent him into? Where was she now?

Haedrun was a member of the Red Watchers, an organization dedicated to purging the taint of undeath that still pervaded Karrnath. It was this focus that had attracted Tallis to the Red Watchers when he'd first learned of them. Their interests were much like his own, but when Haedrun and her superiors had offered him membership in their secret society, he had politely declined.

Haedrun had been hurt by his refusal. Though he had tried to give her reasons, he'd been unable to satisfy her need to understand. In the end, the Red Watchers were an organized network. He did not work well within such hierarchal confines. Never had.

He had to do things his own way.

Yet Tallis had maintained contact with the Red Watchers. Their shared objective kept him in touch, and he frequently exchanged information with them for mutual benefit. Haedrun was his only remaining contact among the Watchers, and after that incident with the Deneith mercenary, she'd grown cold even to him.

◎ ◎ ◎ ◎ ◎ ◎ ◎

Lenrik entered the room, unadorned as usual except for the holy symbol of Aureon that he always wore on a leather cord around his neck. He greeted Tallis with a sad smile, eyes concerned but utterly without judgment. It was a look that Tallis had needed many times, but never more than now. The memory of the previous night was still too close.

Lenrik closed the door quietly behind him. "Will you tell me about it?" he asked, sitting in a stiff-backed chair.

Tallis hesitated, then pointed to his leg. "Thanks." Lenrik waved his hand dismissively. Tallis had heard him explain it many times before. There was no longer a need to. It was Aureon's will to heal him, the priest always insisted. Tallis wasn't so sure he was doing any god's work, but they hadn't argued such theology in a very long time.

"Murder at the Ebonspire," Lenrik said. "You were involved somehow?"

"How did you know?"

"The incident is drawing quite a bit of attention. A chronicler from the *Sentinel* was nosing around among the flock this morning after worship, asking questions of everyone. There is talk of an assassination."

Tallis groaned. "When and *how* did I come in here last night? I'm a bit muddled on that part."

"You entered through the side door, making no small amount of noise when you did. Had you come one hour before that, you would have interrupted a visit from Alinda." He offered a weak smile. "I'd say we're cutting it very close this time, Tallis. You must take this one seriously."

Tallis sighed. Prelate Alinda Roerith was the head of Korth's Cathedral of the Sovereign Host. She was Lenrik's superior, a high priestess, and a politically connected heroine of the Last War. Sympathetic as the prelate would be to Tallis's opposition to the Blood of Vol and its sponsors, an encounter with her would have been very bad for both of them.

No one knew of Tallis's friendship to Lenrik, the esteemed caretaker of Aureon's shrine. Aside from his flat in the Commerce Ward, this was Tallis's only safe house in the city, and Lenrik was the only one he could trust unconditionally. Even if he evaded the Justice Ministry's scrutiny, Lenrik's religious vows would be called into question by the clergy and the prelate herself. Aureon was the god of law, and Tallis had been on the wrong side of that particular ethos for years. Mere knowledge of Tallis, much less actively sheltering him, could condemn Lenrik to excommunication or worse.

Tallis sat up. "I went there to take something—and that's all—from someone. Just another well-to-do with too much gold and an unhealthy interest in the Blood. Apparently I was set up to take the blame for the massacre of a Brelish and his family. I saw it all happen, Lenrik. There were children . . ." Tallis stopped. The memory made him nauseous. "I'm . . . I'm taking this bloody seriously, don't worry."

Lenrik folded his hands. "I heard the name ir'Daresh."

Tallis nodded, solemn. "It *was* him, Lenrik—all the more reason to think I'm being set up. He sure as Khyber *looked* different, but it was definitely him."

"Gamnon became an ambassador after the Treaty of Thronehold," the elf said. "Hence the political ramifications. Didn't you know this?"

"Sovereign Host!" Tallis cursed. He'd long since stopped apologizing to the priest for taking the gods' name in vain. "He became a politician? This is going to be complicated. What time is it now?"

"Fourth watch," Lenrik said.

"I was out that long?"

"You needed the rest." The elf looked around the room as though he would find an idea amidst the trappings of the spare bedchamber. "What will you do now? You could disappear for a while. Return to Rekkenmark, perhaps? Get away from this dark cloud."

Tallis gave the thought only a moment of consideration. "No. I can't just run from this one. I have to figure this out. The backstreets will be dark by the time I return. Besides, security's going to get tight fast. They know who I am, and some of them saw me there. Getting out won't be as easy as usual."

"You could visit *her*," Lenrik said with a grim smile. The way his friend made allowances for him warmed Tallis's heart. The Midwife, the woman in question, was as illegal as they came.

"I thought of that," he answered, "but even if I do, I can't go tonight. She's got rules about these things. And much as I love breaking rules, there are some people you just don't cross. Besides, I've never gone to her for *myself*. It would be—"

"Odd."

Tallis chuckled quietly for the first time since gaining consciousness. He fingered the frayed leather where the crossbow bolt had torn his boot. "I need to visit Verdax first, I think. I'm going to need every advantage in the coming days, so I'll be clearing a few of my things out of here. Do some trading again."

"If I can help, Tallis, I will, but I need to know what happened. Will you tell me?"

"No." Tallis stood up. "You've done enough for me. Too much. I'm not going to get you involved in this, whatever happens. The less you know the better."

Seeing the priest open his mouth to retort, Tallis held up his hand. "*No.* Not this time."

❋ ❋ ❋ ❋ ❋ ❋ ❋

Lenrik Malovyn watched his old friend go, slipping out of the west-facing sanctuary door onto the temple grounds. The grove of firs afforded Tallis enough cover to hide him, but he'd left in disguise as usual. *Sovereign Lord,* he prayed, *watch over him now. He will need your vigilance to stay safe, and if it be your will, return him to me before long. His soul needs absolution.*

The elf returned to the spare room and gazed for a moment at the Aerenal tapestry. The magecraft his ancestor had woven into the fabric formed a subtle glamer designed to relax the mind. Centuries ago, in her time, Aereni wizards who served the Undying Court often used such works of art to steady their minds before attempting complex spellwork. Shortly after crafting this family heirloom, she'd passed into the next phase of existence—mortal death.

Lenrik considered what lay beyond the ancient tapestry. Tallis wasn't the only one with secrets.

* * * * * * *

The hood was pulled over part of Tallis's face, but not so low as to suggest he had anything to hide. He assumed the gait of an older man, an easier feat now that he was limping slightly and his whole body was still sore. His left sleeve was folded up, fastened to his ragged cloak with a cheap brass pin. His arm was twisted behind him under the oversized garment, loosely bound in place and well within reach of his dagger.

Karrns were raised to respect their elders, and Tallis had no qualms about seizing any advantage he could. Add to that the uniform of a veteran and most would leave him alone. Those unfortunates who had tried to take advantage of this particular old man were inevitably dismayed to find the crippled veteran both vicious and suddenly able-bodied.

Thus disguised, Tallis exited the park and made his way across the grounds.

"Sovereigns, stay with me," he whispered, a token prayer to the Host for keeping him alive yet another day. His faith was a shallow thing compared to a soul like Lenrik's, but guilt kept him tethered to this place.

When this present crisis had passed, he intended to make another generous and anonymous donation to the coffers of the Sovereign Host. Of course, he'd need to earn some more coin to do it. The Host knew, he would be handing over nearly everything he had left to Verdax. After two years of faithful, exclusive patronage, the cranky artificer still offered him only the slimmest of discounts.

When he took to the streets, Tallis marked the White Lions wherever he saw them. He could sense the tension within their ranks, the sleight deviations in their patrols and routines. For his vocation, Tallis had made a close study of the habits and patterns of the guards of each of the cities in which he was most active—Korth, Rekkenmark, and Atur.

Every White Lion of Korth would have been briefed at the start of their shift about last night's massacre. Those who had known the three Lions slain at the Ebonspire now wore black and red brassards to commemorate their sacrifice.

But it was more than anger that disturbed the soldiers' usual conduct. Pressure had been exerted on them from on high. Tallis could hear it in their terse conversations, could see the severity of their posture.

Three men had spotted Tallis at the Ebonspire, but he wasn't sure if they could identify him. Those among the garrison who didn't know his face already would have his description by now and would be looking for him.

Playing the part of the disabled veteran, Tallis shambled his way to the Ebonspire in the city's topmost district, Highcourt Ward. The great tower was less formidable in the late afternoon light. It sure looked a lot more difficult to scale at night.

A squad of Lions stood at the base, steering pedestrians and coaches away from one side of the street. An abundance of dried blood could be seen amidst the cobbles between their formation. That must have been where Gamnon's body had hit the street. Where had they moved the Brelish's corpse? Surely not the Necropolis?

Tallis limped over to the closest Lion. "Someone die, son?" he asked gruffly.

"Business of the realm," the soldier answered. "Move along, citizen."

"Bloody shame," he said, as if his ears were failing him. He looked up to the balconies that jutted from the tower. Thirty-four stories up lay a crime scene with his name no doubt stamped firmly upon it. Might as well be notarized by a Sivis clerk. "Another noble take his own life?"

The White Lion looked more seriously at him now, but there was no recognition in his eyes. The man's voice was louder. "A foreign dignitary hammered the street, but it's not my business or yours. Move along now, old man, or you'll be arrested."

"No need to yell," Tallis said and turned away. As he made his way to Verdax's shop, his mind raced.

Chapter Four

Thuranne accompanied Soneste to the House Orien enclave. Soneste watched the bustling cityscape in silence, the skycoaches, the endless parade of pedestrians across the streets and bridges. She felt homesick already.

Soneste had donned her shiftweave clothing, currently a coat of Brelish blue. She carried only a single haversack, her weapons, and a few other items on loan from the agency. Karrnath's autumn was like midwinter in Breland, so she'd packed extra layers and a pair of thin gloves.

"Some say that a woman discovers herself when she comes to Sharn," Thuranne said when they turned a corner and saw a tower emblazoned with Orien's unicorn emblem. "But I'm of the mind that she discovers herself when she leaves it again. Sharn isn't like the rest of the world, Soneste. Stay here too long and you're not sure you're even in Breland anymore. It's a world unto itself."

"But it's Karrnath I'm going to," Soneste said with a sigh.

"Wrong," the half-orc replied. "You're going to Korth. Every city has its own personality, its own secrets and dangers. You will need to adapt, of course, but don't overlook the wonders or the history. That city is quite possibly Khorvaire's oldest. Who knows? You might miss these things when you come back to me."

"Of course," Soneste said, then fixed her boss with a stern expression. "I can't help but feel you're *trying* to get rid of me, Thura. Maybe there's a bigger case brewing that you want me nowhere near."

"Bah! Just name the bastard, then come back to me." Thuranne smirked, the very picture of a proud employer. "You'll do Breland—and more importantly, *my* agency—a great service. Now shut your mouth. We're here."

Soneste turned and looked upon the city one more time, basking in the warm sun. Not even a light rain today. Sure, this city could be hostile at times, corruption was rampant, and hypocrisy seeded every echelon of society, but Sharn was still beautiful and her years here had been among the best in her life.

They passed beneath the elaborate gate of the dragonmarked enclave.

Soneste's mind drifted as Thuranne handled the details, showing their papers to the House Orien agents and paying for the service with a letter of credit sealed with the emblem of the Citadel.

"Listen to me, Soneste," Thuranne said as the papers were processed. A uniformed man, his coat adorned with a silver brooch denoting him as a dragonmarked heir of House Orien, looked on with a polite and professional smile. "Keep yours senses sharp. You've got all the usual disadvantages of being human." The half-orc winked. "But you're still the most promising inquisitive I've got and we both know it. Just remember—"

"Watch myself," Soneste cut in. "Thuranne, I know. Mostly, I just need to worry about solving this case right. I can't take the chance of offending the wrong people."

"That's my girl," Thuranne said. "Also, be careful of Karrnathi men. They're gold for the eyes, but they're aggressive and obtuse—Khyber take them all." Thuranne gave her a quick, arm-crushing hug, then held one hand to Soneste's shoulder in the custom of orcs. "Just come back to me alive, all right?"

"I will, *Mother*," Soneste replied with a deliberate roll of her eyes.

Thuranne d'Velderan walked away, leaving only her matronly, toothy smile lingering in Soneste's mind.

❁ ❁ ❁ ❁ ❁ ❁ ❁

As she waited, Soneste busied herself with her travel pack, unwilling to let the Orien heir witness her anxiety. She swallowed then faced him again, her expression strictly professional. She'd adapted quickly enough to Sharn's exorbitant heights when she'd first come here. It was magic, too, that kept the ancient towers from crumbling to the earth. Why did *this* terrify her? Childhood stories of teleportation mishaps came to mind.

The heir led her to an intricate, marbled mosaic upon the floor depicting the House Orien unicorn.

"We will arrive in another chamber, like this one," the man explained. "You may find the sensation disorienting, Miss Otänsin, but it is painless and quite instantaneous."

She nodded, just hoping to get it over with. If her career had been climbing, then this was the precipice she would have to overcome to reach the next great mountain. I can be home again in a matter of days, she thought. Thuranne had assured her that identifying the criminal was her only duty. The Justice Ministry would be responsible for the rest.

"Are you ready?" the Orien heir asked.

"I am," she lied.

The man held her wrist firmly but gently, then she felt his palm grow hot as he tapped the power of his dragonmark, the great Mark of Passage whose curling design flowed out from his sleeve. Soneste tensed but kept her eyes open. She hadn't expected to experience such magic in her life. It was a testament to the case behind her. Or the one before her.

There came a shift of light as the subtle shadows in the chamber's stylized reliefs rearranged themselves in the blink of an eye. For a

43

moment, she felt perfectly still, then the world began to spin at an incredible speed. She took a step to right herself, but that only made the room pitch vertically.

"Assist her," the heir called out.

A young girl in the house livery appeared before Soneste and caught her from falling even as the Orien heir helped to right her again. The attendant's face was a blur, but it sharpened to perfect clarity within seconds. The world stilled, the dizzying sensation a mere memory.

"Are you well, Miss Otänsin?" the heir asked, releasing her wrist.

"I am, thank you," Soneste said, flushed. A cool gust of wind swept in from the door across the hall, reminding her that she was quite clearly *somewhere else*. When the dragonmarked heir excused himself, she looked around.

The central hall of Orien's enclave in Korth was more expansive than that of the Sharn enclave. Fewer people milled around, but many of them turned to stare at the new arrival. Anyone purchasing Orien teleportation magic was either very wealthy or sponsored by someone who was. The crowds were primarily human, though a small number of business-minded dwarves tarried here on errands of their own.

At a nearby desk, Soneste signed a transport ledger stating that she had suffered no adverse effects from the trip—absolving House Orien from all liability—then moved further into the great hall. Dim sunlight filtered down from a tremendous stained glass window that crowned the vaulted ceiling, casting the hall in a soft emerald light. Fading daylight shone through the main doors, which were propped open. The frigid air of Karrnath was already seeping into her.

She immediately noticed a distinguished, older gentleman who stood near the open door watching her closely. His gray and black uniform, along with the well-polished saber at his belt, suggested Karrnath military, but she could see no metals or emblems of rank. A civilian, then, sent to receive her.

Soneste wanted to stop and examine the veined marble of the floor and the columns rising high overhead, but she didn't want to seem a wide-eyed sightseer. She was here to represent Breland—and Brelish justice. As much as she wanted this assignment to be over, or at least explore on her own, she would adhere to duty above all. She approached the envoy. The sooner in, the sooner out.

"Excuse me—"

She reached out her hand, then stopped abruptly as a figure she had *not* noticed emerged from a shadowed alcove to intercept her. The tall newcomer wore a grotesque suit of armor, a union of hard leather plates and human bones. Dark, impassive eyes scrutinized her from within the skull-faced visor. A faint, resinous odor rose from his body.

A chill ran through her as the war-time tales of Karrnath came to mind—legions of undead soldiers marching across the fields as black-robed necromancers animated their fallen to rise again. Karrnath, as evidenced by the knight before her, was as gruesome as she'd always imagined. Whose bones made up this fiend's armor? A comrade's? An enemy soldier's?

"Apologies," the envoy said. "Miss Otänsin, I presume?" He stepped around the knight and extended his hand.

"Yes," Soneste answered him quietly, returning the knight's glare before turning her full attention to the speaker.

"Hyran ir'Tennet," the man said, introducing himself.

"Civic Minister?" Soneste asked, surprised. The head of the Korth's Justice Ministry had waited to receive her personally? This was the man who'd sent word of the murder to the King's Citadel and thereby to Thuranne. Her superior hadn't lied. This case *was* important. Soneste was grateful the handshake was brief. The minister's hands felt like ice.

"Thank you, Laedro," Hyran said to the knight. "This is the inquisitive I have been expecting."

Laedro nodded, stepping back. His warning eyes lingered on her a moment longer before turning his attention to the room at large. His presence drew stares from the scattered crowd, but

Soneste was surprised to see as much admiration as distaste from among them.

Hyran continued. "Welcome to Korth, Miss Otänsin. I apologize for the hastiness of the summons and appreciate your timely arrival. You have received our dispatch, then?"

"Yes, Minister. There are a few things I will need, and I'd like to be allowed to speak with the witnesses."

Hyran nodded, gesturing to the door. "Of course. If you will accompany me, I can escort you to the Seventh Watch Inn, where you will be staying for the duration of your visit. Or, if you prefer, I can take you directly to the Ebonspire, where you will be given immediate access to the crime scene—should you choose to have a look *before* contending with the Ministry's bureaucrats."

Soneste chuckled nervously. Hyran seemed a true Karrn—cold, more than a little aloof—but she liked his candor. "If I could visit the scene first, I would appreciate it."

"Then we will bring you there at once. Tomorrow morning you will be provided with whatever and whoever you require. The crown has instructed me—and the White Lions, our city's fine garrison—to cooperate with your efforts."

"Thank you, Minister. Are the bodies of the victims still at the scene?"

"They are, save for the ambassador's. Out of necessity his remains have been moved to the Necropolis of the Valiant, our city's morgue. You will be given access at any time."

Together they exited the enclave, the knight Laedro shadowing them like a bodyguard. They came to a wide platform where steps led to the street below. Soneste saw a lightning rail station neighboring the enclave—how *most* foreigners arrived. Then she turned her head to face the rest of the city, which rose up before her in the coming twilight.

Korth sat on a series of natural bluffs around the dark waters of King's Bay, a wide alcove in the Karrn River. Soneste imagined the city as a great cemetery on a sloping hill, cluttered with giant-sized stone slabs and mausoleums. Monuments, spires, and statues rose amid the great structures. In sheer height, the buildings of Korth could not compare to the mile-high towers of Sharn, but the dark structures and their dramatic facades brought a sense of history and solemnity to the vast gray city. The gust of icy wind that lashed at her hair and coat did little to discourage this fancy. Breland was far away indeed.

One of Khorvaire's oldest cities, Korth's foundations were laid when humans were still newcomers to the continent. Karrn the Conqueror founded the kingdom of Karrnath three thousand years ago. The city conveyed that sense of age to Soneste now, and for a moment she stood in solemn silence. At last she caught Hyran's eye, who offered a tight smile in turn. Perhaps he was accustomed to newcomers gawking at the ancient city.

At the base of the steps, a coach awaited. They climbed aboard, Laedro mounting a steed of his own. Soneste nearly balked when she saw the horse—clean white bones bereft of flesh beneath heavy barding. Empty black sockets stared out from its armored, equine skull. Composing herself, she settled herself into the coach's velveteen interior as it started into motion. The knight trotted alongside them.

The ride across the city was pleasant but somber. Soneste gazed up at the buildings as they passed. Affixed to even the humblest of doorsteps were curling, wrought iron railings, while cold fire lanterns hung from stylized hooks. The Karrns went about their business just like the citizens of any Brelish city, but she observed more military personnel among the crowds. More weapons were buckled, harnessed, or carried openly. Uniform white tabards and shining breastplates denoted the White Lions of whom Hyran had spoken. They wore open-faced, white-plumed helms and carried axes and longbows, looking more like field soldiers than city watchmen.

As they passed a lightly wooded park, Soneste craned her head only slightly—sensitive to Hyran's presence—to glimpse a multi-tiered keep floating overhead. She'd only seen paintings of it before: the Tower of the Twelve. Funded by the dragonmarked houses collectively, the Twelve was an institution for arcane advancement and the study of the mystic dragonmarks themselves. She'd never expected to see the famous tower with her own eyes.

Hyran stared out the window, his gaze lost in unreadable thought. Soneste was tempted to appraise his emotions directly, but the moment was too silent. Her powers came with a subtle display, easily unnoticed in a crowd but highly conspicuous in quiet company.

She wondered what he was thinking of her, or of Breland sending a civilian to investigate the death of one of its ambassadors. Did he welcome such help from abroad, or did he prefer delegating his own men according to strict Karrnathi protocol?

The coach wound steadily up through a maze of streets, passing from one district to another until at last they reached the highest tier of the city. A towering fortress—possibly the largest single structure she'd ever seen—rose to the south, constructed of pale stone between a pair of massive, rough-hewn spires of rock. Lantern-lit windows honeycombed the structure, while indigo flames crowned the battlements. Soneste could see the movement of scores of soldiers upon the wall and the glitter of arcane ballistae. The monolithic fortress dwarfed every other structure in the city.

"Crownhome," the Minister said, though Soneste had guessed it herself. "The home of King Kaius III."

"Beautiful," she said, marveling at the palace. A mere two years ago, a Brelish passing so casually before the home of Karrnath's king was unthinkable.

Soneste thought of Brokenblade Castle, the ancestral home of her own king in Breland's capital of Wroat. She remembered sitting on her father's shoulders as a girl, so she could look above the crowds at the massive, hexagonal keep from which King Boranel ruled the nation.

But while Brokenblade Castle was a stronghold of dark gray stone, bright banners, and courtly elegance, Crownhome looked like a fortress of bone, fully arrayed for war. The two strongholds couldn't appear more different, yet both exuded the majesty of old Galifar.

With her own nation in mind, a thought occurred to Soneste. "Is this where Prince Halix and Princess Borina now reside?"

"It is," Hyran replied with a pleasant smile. "Princess Borina is often at court. Prince Halix enrolled at Rekkenmark Academy earlier this year. He returns to Korth periodically to visit his sister, and I understand he'll be returning again soon. One of our nobles is hosting a Conqueror tournament in a couple of weeks and will be inviting competitors from across the Five Nations. I'm told the prince is an avid fan of the game."

Soneste remembered with mixed feelings when the *Korranberg Chronicle* had announced the foreign exchange that Breland had established with Karrnath, Aundair, and Thrane as a gesture of peace between the Five Nations. Kaius III's younger sister, Haydith, now lived in King Boranel's court, while his brother Gaius had been sent to Thrane. In turn, Boranel's youngest children had come to Karrnath to continue their education in Kaius's court.

The murdered Brelish ambassador came swiftly to mind. As if guessing her thoughts, Hyran continued.

"They are safe, rest assured, and well guarded. I daresay the princess is very popular among our aristocracy. She has Korth's finest attending to her at all times, as well as a fair number of misguided suitors. The prince spends most of his time among his fellow cadets at Rekkenmark. There is no safer place in Karrnath, Miss Otänsin. General Thauram, commander of the White Lions, is assembling his elite in the wake of this recent tragedy to guard them both."

Soneste looked out at the gruesome knight riding alongside the coach. She wondered how many of the "elite" were actually alive. Surely they wouldn't guard Brelish royals with Karrnathi undead.

Soon the coach pulled up before a massive tower of black stone. Hyran helped her from the coach with the grace of a well-bred noble.

"This is the Ebonspire," he said, produced a leather folder and holding it out to her. "Within this you will find a description of the scene and the death report. An agent from the Ministry of the Dead has employed preservative spells upon the suite so that you can examine the crime scene as it was found last night. Tomorrow afternoon the bodies will need to be removed, so please make whatever observations you can tonight."

"In the morning you may call on me at the Justice Ministry." Hyran pointed to the heavy doors of the tower behind her. "The concierge has been informed of your presence, and can give you directions to either the Ministry's headquarters or the Seventh Watch Inn."

"Thank you, Minister." She didn't know what else to say.

With a nod, Hyran climbed into the coach again. The conveyance rolled off down the street, and the grim knight gave her a final glare before disappearing.

Chapter
FIVE

When bells rang to mark the middle of fifth watch, Tallis left the docks and joined the dwindling crowds in the Community Ward, eyeing the people as he took up the armless veteran's pace again. The Lions had doubled their patrols, often stopping citizens to ask questions. Here and there, merchants bargained with customers, exchanging nervous rumors as well as coins. Tallis knew how to read crowds, could recognize paranoia flitting between Korth's middle and lower classes.

He couldn't blame them. There was a killer on the loose—so it was said—more deadly than most, and while most accepted the slayings that took place among the dregs of the Low District as an understandable hazard, this latest murder had reached into highest echelons of Korth society. Rumor was, the murderer was a veteran of the Last War taking revenge against all enemies of Karrnath.

Images from the slaughter assailed Tallis's mind, but he pushed them away with a soldier's resolve. When allies and enemies fell before his eyes during the War, Tallis had fought on, carrying out his missions to their end. Death on the battlefield had to be impersonal.

But this . . . this was different.

"Mourn another day," an instructor at the Academy had once said, so Tallis would not bow to grief. Yes, he'd known Gamnon as a Brelish captain during the Last War—as part of a combined attack against Cyre—but had never called the man a friend. But no matter what kind of man Gamnon had been or had become, his family—his children—could *not* have deserved their fate.

Since waking only hours ago, he'd found ways to occupy his mind. Speaking with Lenrik, even briefly, always had a calming effect upon him. Bargaining with Verdax and pawning off some of his possessions helped too. But walking the streets, lacking a plan, Tallis found his mind wandering free again. Perhaps some food would help.

He found a meat vendor racing to close up his cart before nightfall. As the streets began to empty, Tallis made his way to the Commerce Ward, chewing the strips of salted pork he'd purchased. Today it might as well have been ashes. It did nothing to console him.

A child's scream of pain shattered his attempted silence. He looked around, startled, then determined it wasn't real. The scene from last night battered at his consciousness, demanding recollection. Tallis, helpless to stop it, picked up his pace as the events of the Ebonspire began to return to him in force. Not since the Last War and the depredations of Marshal Serror had he felt such disgust.

"Not *now*," he breathed.

$\bullet \ \bullet \ \bullet \ \circledcirc \ \bullet \ \bullet \ \bullet$

According to the plaque in the lobby, the Ebonspire was forty-five stories in height. There were four separate residences on each level arrayed around a central shaft, where a lift carried guests to any level they wished to go. The lift had been disabled during the attack, forcing the responding guards to take the stairs. Soneste had asked the attendant within what powered the lift, suspecting some artifice of House Cannith. Her understanding of such mechanisms was limited to the towers of Sharn, most of which were built and accessed by Cannith ingenuity and augmented by an aerial manifest zone. As a resident of the City of Towers, it was difficult for Soneste to believe that any other dragonmarked house could be as powerful as House Cannith.

"Elemental," the bored magewright had answered her, offering nothing more.

Soneste arrived at the thirty-fourth floor, where she found five White Lions guarding the door. They stood like statues, positioned evenly to view every entrance to the level. One of the soldiers was a dark-haired woman Soneste's own age. Only her eyes turned to Soneste when she stepped off the lift. The city watch in Sharn never displayed this level of discipline, and Soneste felt certain the White Lions would not be as easily swayed with bribes or honeyed words.

Soneste produced her identification papers, but the other woman waved the document away. "Either you're the killer come again—in which case there's obviously little we could do to stop you entering—or you're the inquisitive they sent in."

"I . . . Yes."

"Three good men lost their lives defending your precious ambassador, so do me a favor, Brelander. Just name the killer so we can do *our* job."

"I aim to," Soneste answered with a nod, deciding this was not the time to correct the name for her countrymen: *Brelish*. Korth's garrison seemed as dour as its citizenry, but after dealing with silver-tongued Aundairians and self-righteous Thranes back home, Karrns were refreshingly incisive. They seemed to say precisely what they were thinking.

"If you need us," the Lion said with a dismissive gesture, "just shout."

The key the concierge had given her unlocked the door with a metallic *click* without her needing to turn it at all. It suppressed the magic wards that locked and guarded the door. The killer no doubt had the means to subvert such wards.

When Soneste pushed open the door, an unnatural cold washed over her from the dimness within. Even if every window within had been left open, it should not have been this frigid. Clearly this was the preservative magic of which Hyran spoke.

The coppery stench of blood tainted the air, muted only slightly by the cold. She'd inspected too many murder scenes to be fazed by such unpleasantness, but the lingering threat of the unknown killer kept her senses sharp, despite the presence of the guards. Killers often returned to the scene of the crime, either to remove evidence or kill again.

Soneste shut the door behind her then drew out her crysteel dagger and a silvery headband. The latter was a watch lamp, created for the Sharn Watch, but the many favors owed to Thuranne had secured several for her agency's use. Soneste slipped the mithral circlet around her head and with a thought summoned a globe of white light into the air. It floated just over her shoulder, illuminating the space around her as brightly as a torch.

The dwelling was a study in luxurious amenities. Easily five times larger than her own apartment back in Sharn, it was carpeted and filled with a variety of elegant furniture and magewrought conveniences. Beyond the foyer, she could see two bedrooms, a privy, and a dining room all connected by a lavish—though blood-spattered—common room.

Bracing herself against the severe cold, she opened the leather folder Hyran had provided. According to the death report within, a total of ten had been slain.

The first three were the White Lions of which the guard had spoken, allegedly the first to respond to the massacre only to become victims themselves. They lay upon the hardwood of the foyer in dried pools of blood. The wounds were very precise, made in the grooves and joints of the half-plate armor by a slender, piercing blade. Such injuries were undoubtedly meant to slow them down until an opening presented itself, which it had—each man had a bloody stab wound in his neck, clear through to the other side.

"Khyber," she whispered, breath clouding in the freezing air. The killer was a professional.

The death report stated that the soldiers' bodies would soon be relocated to the Necropolis of the Valiant, the city's morgue. An addendum stated that the seven remaining dead, the bodies of the Brelish ambassador and his party, were not subject to seizure by the state.

Soneste scowled. The fact that every Karrnathi citizen could be claimed by the royal corpse collectors upon death sickened her. Despite the war's end two years ago, this decree had endured, allowing the remains of Karrnath's citizens to be raised again to serve the state should the need ever arise. Was she really surprised? Karrnath was still under martial law. Here the draconian Code of Kaius prevailed over the more civilized Code of Galifar.

According to the *Korranberg Chronicle*, Karrnath's undead troops had been recalled after the signing of the Treaty of Thronehold, but it was well known that they were hidden away in tactical reserve. From the chthonic air of this grim city, she wouldn't be surprised if many of the skeletons and zombies waited somewhere beneath these very streets.

Just below the description and names of the three dead Lions was a transcript, an interview with the slain conducted by a Ministry cleric. She flipped through the report to ensure that no such spells were used upon the ambassador's wife or their attendants. Soneste, despite her annoyance, would honor the family's wishes.

The transcript was brief. Three questions had been posed to two of the dead Lions. Their cryptic replies described a "slim intruder in black garb who wielded two blades." The intruder had turned away from the civilians the moment the White Lions entered the flat. Then it killed them.

Soneste stepped past the soldiers to examine the two menservants in the common room. The upended furniture and ruffled carpet suggested a nasty fight, and both men had dropped their weapons—ceremonial sabers—where they'd fallen. There wasn't a single drop of blood on these weapons, although it was quite evident that the killer's had found their mark. A rapier's blade, Soneste decided, for she'd delivered such wounds herself, though not with such strength or precision.

She surveyed the rest of the room, rubbing her gloved hands together to stay warm. The cold fire lanterns perched upon the walls had been deliberately shattered, and only a single intact globe remained, affixed to the low table that had been kicked over. Two fingers, the pinky and ring finger from a man's right hand, lay severed on the blood-stained carpet. They belonged to neither of the servants. One man had his throat slashed open in two places. The other had probably died from blood loss, likely from the arterial wound to his thigh.

Soneste found the third servant lying near the threshold of the master bedroom, his unarmored abdomen punctured twice. An easier kill, that one. The first man to die. A black leather mask, which would cover only the forehead, eyes, and nose of the wearer, lay discarded near him. Soneste pocketed the evidence and continued her examination.

There was a confusing jumble of imprints in the plush carpet, made from the boots of the White Lions, the victims, and the Ministry's initial inspectors. And, of course, the killer. Soneste stared at the pattern, envisioning a fight that could account for it: three men moving to engage the killer as he entered the room. The killer's prints, which led in from the master bedroom—his likely means of entrance—were placed just so. They were spaced apart, as if he'd run in, but the prints went in and out again. The soldiers, those who hadn't been slain, had eventually pursued him out.

She glanced at the dead guards. From the precision of his handiwork, the killer hadn't been afraid of them. Why run at all, then? Why not slay the next three to arrive, too, and leave uncontested and on his own terms?

This was quite a puzzle.

Moving on to the other bedroom, Soneste found the door still hanging at a skewed angle. The killer had forced his way into this room. The victims within probably had sought refuge here. The locking mechanism was battered. It had taken the killer a few attempts to bash his way through the reinforced door with a heavy, blunt object. She looked around. No such object presented itself. If it was a weapon, the killer took it with him. Once the lock was broken, a vicious kick—there was a sleight print made from the boot—had forced the door.

As Soneste stepped into the room, her stomach soured.

Maril, the ambassador's wife, had fallen first, defying her attacker. Her richly embroidered skirts, a recent fashion for matrons of Wroat, were soaked through with her own blood. The nursemaid had been struck from behind, an easier kill. The two children, Renet and Vestra, had been claimed in quick succession, their bodies lying entwined. A ratty stuffed badger was still clutched in the little girl's hand.

The light from her watch lamp flared brightly, momentarily beyond Soneste's control. She steeled her mind, suppressing the anger that rushed to the fore and sought to overwhelm the light. She breathed slow and deep, just as Veshtalan had instructed. Now was not the time for emotions or the exertion of psionic energy.

Soneste turned away, needing to leave this room—at least for now. The report stated that Ambassador Gamnon had been thrown from the balcony, which was attached to the master bedroom and was likely the killer's means of entrance. She would have to examine Gamnon's body later since it had been thrown from the balcony and waited her inspection at the morgue, but she needed to see where his final struggle had taken place.

❀ ❀ ❀ ❀ ❀ ❀ ❀

The shrill cry of children heightened Tallis's awareness and set him immediately on the offensive. The shrouded intruder had come here to kill.

As he chased the lissome figure into the common room he saw chaos unfolding. Two children were pulled, shrieking, away from the furniture by a nursemaid and their mother. A second and third manservant, as well as

*the portly nobleman whose family was in peril, advanced upon the intruder
with weapons drawn. A chair was knocked over, a table kicked aside.*

"What is this?" the father demanded, and Tallis knew at a glance
that the man was certainly not Arend ir'Montevik, the one he'd come to
steal from. The last time he'd seen this man's face had been on Cyran soil
years ago. The bullish features and the soldier's body the man once possessed
had been softened by age. His eyes weren't as courageous now.

Before the Brelish could engage the intruder, Tallis was there. He swept
the pick end of his weapon at the intruder's feet in an attempt to trip her, but
the weapon passed through her legs as if she were mere illusion.

"Keeper!" Tallis cursed, aware that he was contending with powerful
magic. Those blades certainly looked real.

The four men surrounded the intruder, but she gave no sign of unease.
In a dramatic arch, the assassin swept both rapier blades at one of the
servants, slicing open his throat in two places. Blood surged from both
and the man fell. In the same backswing, she parried Gamnon's sword
stroke in a spray of fiery sparks. The noble's long sword appeared to possess
an enchantment of its own, but it did no good. All their weapons passed
harmlessly through the assassin's body yet again.

Frustrated, Tallis aimed his weapon to parry her blades, knowing
that attacks to her body would be futile. Tallis knew the presence of the
undead only too well, and he didn't think this one was one of them.

Host, he swore silently, he had not come equipped for such an opponent.
"This is not an illusion!" he said to the other men. "Use magic, if you
have it!"

The second servant fell back a few steps, just out of reach of the killing blades. He pointed his free hand at the assassin and incanted a short
phrase. Three bolts of glowing energy burst from his fingertips, slamming
into her—and vanishing again without effect.

"By the Flame!" Gamnon shouted. "Help! Someone help!"

To their credit, the Brelish noble and his remaining servant fought
well, but the assassin's blades were tireless and those few swings that
reached through her defenses could not make contact. Tallis had yet to be
attacked directly, allowing him to focus on averting strikes that would
have proven fatal to the other men.

"Who are you?" Gamnon asked, glancing to his would-be rescuer.

The assassin's blades did not allow for conversation, so Tallis ignored the question. Evidently the mask he wore made him every bit as mysterious to the Brelish. Both he and the assassin were intruders, after all, but only one was here to deal out death.

The shriek of frightened children in the room beyond came again, magnifying his fury.

The assassin stepped toward the remaining servant and swept her blades low, slicing deeply through his thigh. Blood sprayed. He dropped, screaming, to the ground. At the opportunity, Gamnon aimed an attack at her head, but she'd anticipated it. Her left rapier came up, cutting his own weapon from his hand. Two fingers dropped to the floor and he stumbled back, gasping from the pain but lacking the breath to scream.

A metallic click sounded nearby, then the front door to the apartment crashed open, and three grim-faced White Lions strode in. They were battle-hardened men—they did not blanch at the bloodshed before them.

"Stop!" one ordered as two of them advanced with axes braced. The third stood behind them, drawing back a bowstring and looking for a clear shot.

As the assassin turned to face the newcomers, some of the wrappings fell away from her head. Beneath, a steel, tightly-visored helm did little to reveal her identity. She stepped over the fallen and approached the White Lions without hesitation. Tallis let her go, taking the moment to catch his own breath. At least this would buy them some time.

"Gamnon," he said sharply. He backed toward an adjoining bedroom door, where the women and children had retreated. It cost him a few seconds, but Tallis ripped the mask away from his face and dropped it.

The Brelish looked back at him, incredulous. A semblance of recognition returned to his wild eyes. "Major Tallis?" he said. "She . . . must want me. Protect them, Major!" He pointed to the bedroom where his wife and children had retreated.

Tallis nodded as he moved, searching for some means to combat this magical threat. His wand! If it was magic that made the assassin ghostly, perhaps he could dissolve it.

He heard the clash of blades and the crunch of dented armor. An *arrow smacked against the far wall. When he heard the Lions' shouts and their bodies drop to the floor, he took comfort only in knowing that more would arrive soon. The magic wards placed upon every room's door would alert the Ebonspire's guard to the threat, and even a professional assassin couldn't survive against inevitable numbers.*

Gamnon dashed into the master bedroom where Tallis had first entered. With her opponents dispatched, the assassin turned to follow him. Tallis pounded on the other bedroom door.

"Open the door, please! You must come with me!" This was their only chance. The Ebonspire was a veritable fortress, with many places to hide and many guards to help. If he could just get them out of here, they'd be safe behind an army of White Lions and he'd be free to escape. Tallis could hear whimpering within and none came to the door. Tallis hefted his hooked hammer, ready to force the door.

Then Gamnon screamed.

Tallis sprinted across the chamber, cursing again. In all his life, he'd never felt this helpless. Within the shadowed bedroom, he saw the balcony doors had been flung open. The assassin's body was, for the first time, nearly still. Gamnon stood stiffly in front of her, her rapier-blades buried to the hilt in his body. He stared over his killer's shoulder at Tallis, disbelieving.

"Aureon, no," Tallis mouthed, moving closer. His fingers slick with sweat, he drew the dispelling wand from his belt and discharged its power. Only a tiny flicker of light pulsed from its tip and he knew the spell had failed.

The assassin pushed at her weapons forward, forcing Gamnon to stumble back onto the balcony, where he tripped on the prone warforged who lay there and fell back against the balustrade. The assassin's left blade stabbed up, skewering the Brelish's head, then swung her right blade against his exposed neck. Dead already, Gamnon made not a sound as his head came free with the assassin's second cut. Transfixed by the savage deed, Tallis wondered vaguely if the killer wasn't, in fact, even human.

"Face me!" he shouted, recovering quickly from his horror. Tallis tucked the wand away and attacked the assassin again. He knew it was in vain. Ignoring his ineffective attack, the assassin let the balustrade support Gamnon's headless corpse for a moment, then it punctured him again in the abdomen and used the weapon's leverage to shove him over the edge. Gamnon ir'Daresh's body fell into the darkness below.

"What do you want?" Tallis said.

The assassin turned at last to face him. Tallis parried every blow that the incorporeal assassin railed upon him—it was almost too easy to do. His stomach continued to knot inside him as he realized this vile creature had no intention of harming him. It had followed him into the residence, passing the wards he'd taken the care to remove—now it wanted him to bear witness. What sick game was this?

The assassin pressed past him again, striding towards the second bedroom where Gamnon's wife and children hid—and stepped through the door itself as easily as through morning mist. Tallis shouted his rage and turned his hammer upon the door itself, fighting to break through, fighting to push the nightmare from his mind.

Chapter Six

Sul, the 8th of Sypheros, 998 YK

Heedless of any who might see him, Tallis dived into the nearest alley. Halfway down the narrow lane, he doubled over, retching. The contents of his stomach emptied amidst the alley refuse, and he begged for the memories to leave his mind just as quickly, but the images of that night in the Ebonspire refused to leave him so easily. When he had nothing left to expel, he sat with his back against the wall and breathed in the sharp night air.

"Clear out, vermin," a gruff voice said, jarring him from his misery. "Take your sickness back to your own hole."

Tallis looked up as a pair of White Lions entered the alley and approached, leveling an axe head at him. His stomach was too raw to deal with this now.

"Are you listening?" the White Lion demanded.

Tallis leaned against the wall, slowly standing. He twisted his bound arm free beneath the bulk of his cloak. His hood had fallen aside, and despite his sickness it was clear he was no elderly drunk.

"Who's this?" the guard asked with mild interest.

"It's *him!*" the other shouted, his axe poised for a swing.

Rolling his eyes back in his head, Tallis let his knees buckle.

When the closest Lion moved to grab him, he pushed his shoulder hard into the man's waist and wrapped his arms around him. The soldier grunted as he fell into Tallis's grasp. His companion swiveled the weapon and struck with the flat side of the axe's head, but Tallis used the first guard's body as a shield, allowing him to take the blow.

Tallis released the groaning man and drove the heel of his palm into the other's face even as he drew the dagger sheathed at the back of his own belt. The White Lion stumbled back. Tallis stepped around the fallen man and struck at his hand with the blade.

The guard cried out and clutched at his bleeding hand as the axe clattered to the ground. Tallis started away from the alley, then stopped and glared at both men, his body burning with rage. The guards cursed and panted for breath as they struggled to gain footing again.

"You want to demonize me?" Tallis asked, unable to quell the black rage inside. "Then I'll give you a real reason."

Tallis returned and threw their weapons deeper into the alley. A single kick to each man's face brought them down again. He chose the nearest and struck him repeatedly with the pommel of his dagger, caring little for the blood that spattered his cloak.

When both men lay still, he quit the alley and stumbled into the night.

● ● ● ◉ ● ● ●

Soneste stepped out onto the balcony from the master bedroom, and immediately noted the body that lay there and the profuse amounts of blood that had spattered the scene—without a doubt, this is where Gamnon had been decapitated. The body on the stone floor was not listed in the death report, which hardly surprised her. It was a warforged.

His body of wood, steel, and stone was mostly intact. She knew little about warforged anatomy, but she guessed that the torn livewood fibers of his stomach accounted for the injury that felled him, yet the slender blades that pierced the bodies of the ir'Daresh family had certainly not dealt *this* wound. Either the killer carried an arsenal of weapons on his person or the killer had not been alone. Hyran's report said there was only one man sighted at the scene.

Soneste flipped through the papers and finally found the warforged listed under Damaged Property. Typical Karrnathi attitude. If this warforged servant had also been a friend to the deceased, it was an outright insult. Even King Boranel was said to name his warforged bodyguard a loyal and trusted friend. In fact, Boranel had prompted Parliament to issue the Warforged Decree, which had given all Brelish warforged the same rights as citizens, years before the Treaty of Thronehold granted all the living constructs emancipation.

She kneeled and examined the artificial body, noting that most of the composite plating was unmarred, save for the dried blood that spattered half of his torso and one arm. The back of his metal, helmlike head exhibited a sizeable dent, but she could find no other damage to him. Was he dead? If the damage was too severe, a warforged could not be revived, but if the injury was superficial and their life force had merely dormant, they could be repaired. This warforged might be a witness. The Justice Ministry hadn't even bothered to try.

There was no corresponding blood on the warforged's weapon. The heavy blade was still clutched in his hand, and a thick shield was welded to his other arm. If it was listed as damaged property, then it must have served Gamnon ir'Daresh. This was a Brelish warforged.

Soneste stood and walked to the balcony's edge, looking upon Korth from a new vantage. The evenly spaced cold fire lanterns and random, candlelit windows in the city below were not sufficient to illuminate the whole. The dim moon of Sypheros was veiled in the night sky, outshone by the pearly face of Zarantyr and the orange-yellow crescent of Aryth. The lackluster hues of the city seemed to extend into the heavens, as clouds half-obscured the moons. At this hour, the buildings below were just dark blocks arranged in a labyrinth of invisible streets.

More impressive were the multicolored lights of the Tower of the Twelve, which floated above a shadowed park. Even at this late hour, Soneste could see at least two airships hovering near the Tower's docking bay as powerful energies played across the base of the pyramidal keep.

An icy wind swept in from the Karrn River, stealing her wonder. Shivering, she leaned over the balcony rail, gauging the distance to the ground and imagining the killer's means of reaching the balcony. It was entirely possible that the killer had flown to this height. She glanced up again to the Tower. Any skilled wizard within that arcane institution could have provided him such means.

Under the white glow of her watch lamp, Soneste scrutinized the dwelling for another hour. In a dresser drawer she found a folder containing Gamnon's letters of credit and a pouch of galifars and dragons, along with a fair amount of jewelry. These items had been inventoried in the report by the Ministry's agents sometime prior to her arrival.

What they had not found was the small book tucked beneath the cushion of one richly upholstered chair, nor the lens of dark glass ground into the carpet on one side of the common room.

The dead were at rest now, but Soneste couldn't escape the notion that this massacre was only the beginning. What else are you planning? she asked the killer.

Soon after, she left the Ebonspire for her room at the Seventh Watch.

❂ ❂ ❂ ◉ ❂ ❂ ❂

"I don't care that Gamnon is dead," Tallis murmured, and Lenrik knew he was lying, "but . . ."

Tallis let his words trail off, his back against the wall in the spare room. After a long pause, he looked back at the elf. "Listen, Lenrik. Thanks."

The priest nodded with a sad smile. The adult Tallis had always conveyed to him a sense of courage and competency, but it was impossible for Lenrik to look upon his friend without seeing the boy he once knew. He saw him that way now, frightened beyond real comforting.

Very little could faze Tallis. Not the walking dead, not the thunderous charge of Thrane cavalry, not even death at the hands of the Seeker priests in Atur who'd put a modest bounty on his head, but guilt obviously wracked Tallis's soul more than anything else could.

"I still mean what I said," Tallis said. "I'm not bringing you into this. I'll be staying at my own flat. They're really looking for me now, but my place is still secure."

Lenrik shrugged. "I brought *myself* into this the day I asked Aureon to show me the larger course for your life."

❀ ❀ ❀ ❀ ❀ ❀ ❀

As he'd relayed the full events of the previous night to Lenrik, Tallis felt some measure of the horror melt away. With a mug of his preferred Nightwood Pale in hand and a thick woolen blanket around him, the mere company of his oldest friend made him feel grounded again. He'd been a fool to try and keep it all in. He could still picture the assassin's preternatural grace and dispassionate killing, but the helpless feeling was slowly replaced with mounting rage. Tallis would find the killer again. Haedrun was his only lead.

"The Market's not for another two nights. I can't contact Haedrun any other way. It's the only place we meet now, and that's if she hasn't hopped the rail already—"

"I need to tell you something," Lenrik said. His tone had changed. It sounded resigned. "I have met with Haedrun myself on several occasions."

Tallis looked at his friend. Lenrik seldom kept anything important from him, yet in the last few years—since the war's end—he felt that they had been growing apart. Their shared military experiences had established this friendship, but their current lifestyles couldn't be more different. Tallis had his own agenda, did what he thought was right, and subverted the law to do it. He even made a good living of it. But after his many years in the service of Karrnath, Lenrik had retired here in Korth. Now he practiced his faith in a temple, not the field of battle, serving the beleaguered people who had lost so much in the Last War.

"Will you tell me?" Tallis asked.

Lenrik nodded. "Three months ago, she started to attend my sermons. Quietly at first, always sitting in the back. Eventually she found the courage to approach me. When she finally introduced herself, I suspected she was the same Haedrun of whom you sometimes spoke."

Tallis opened his mouth, but Lenrik held up a hand. "No need to ask. She doesn't know of *our* connection."

He remembered Lenrik's words the last time they talked about their secret friendship. "No one knows," the elf had said, "except perhaps the Sovereign Host, and so far they've kept our secret."

"Haedrun suffers, as do many in this land."

As do we all, Tallis thought. For the sacrifices we are forced to make, for those who are taken from us. For those who are turned against us.

"She seeks atonement for the things she has done. I offered to counsel her. I think she was drawn to Aureon specifically because he represents stability. Order. In her grief, she could only handle one god. The Nine together can seem imposing and faceless to outsiders."

Tallis thought of the older woman, Mova, whom he knew Lenrik had met with several times before. The priest counseled many desperate people, day after day. He spent more time talking to them individually than he did preaching the tenets of the faith.

Tallis didn't expect Haedrun to be among those desperate people. He envisioned the stern woman as *he* knew her. Lovely, dark-eyed Haedrun, who had lost her children to the claws of the undead, who had gained from her pain the courage of a soldier twice her size. It seemed unthinkable that she would turn to the gods for salvation. Haedrun was the sort of woman who had saved herself. How well did Tallis really know Haedrun, after all? She was a remarkable, tragic woman, but he had difficulty counting treachery among her assets. How could she set him up for the Ebonspire crime? Or was someone else forcing her cooperation?

Lenrik continued. "She never mentioned the Red Watchers, though I could sense that she wanted to. She is trying to protect them—and me."

"A familiar pattern," Tallis said with a smile. "Would you know how to find her?"

The priest shook his head. "It is not appropriate for a priest to intrude in the personal lives of a Vassal unless invited to. I don't know where she stays in this city." His voice took on a scolding tone. "Now, if I'd *known* that the Red Watchers were giving you work again, I might have asked her anyway."

Tallis clucked his tongue. "It's enough that you let me confide in you like this."

"The assassin concerns me most," Lenrik said, rising. "I will consult the Archives of Aureon. I wonder if it was some manner of spell she was using, not a quality of the assassin herself. Spells that can make a person incorporeal are beyond the province of most magewrights and novice magicians. It sounds like you're dealing with a wizard, and a well-studied one at that."

Tallis let out a sigh. "Why not? Everything I ever knew seems to be changing."

❂ ❂ ❂ ❂ ❂ ❂ ❂

When she'd finally coaxed a fire in the hearth of her room, Soneste dropped heavily into a chair. She longed for the familiar comforts of her own apartment in Ivy Towers, but she resigned herself to the austere accommodations of the Seventh Watch. They were suitably spacious, certainly, with an adjoining closet and washroom, but the wintry chill of Karrnath in Sypheros seeped through the very walls of her second floor room.

Wrapped in a heavy wool blanket, Soneste examined the small book she'd found hidden at the ambassador's dwelling. It was Gamnon's travel itinerary, which she confirmed by comparing the handwriting against his letters of credit. The last two weeks' entries revealed that he'd been on holiday, touring the major cities of Khorvaire with his family. Setting out from Wroat by lightning rail, he'd visited Starilaskur, Passage, Fairhaven, and Thaliost before crossing Scions Sound by ship. In Rekkenmark, he'd resumed the rail line to Korth. Krona Peak, the capital of the Mror Holds, had been his planned final destination.

But fate had chosen Korth.

Gamnon had spent two days within each city. Notations listed meetings he'd arranged with various men, most of whom sounded like merchant lords. Aside from their political work, the noble ir'Daresh family had always had a hand in Breland's metal industry. So the question remained, was trade a mere side project or was the ambassador's family business in the fore? According to the information Thuranne had provided her, Gamnon and his immediate family were the last of his line. There were no surviving heirs of his estate. Who, then, would benefit from the end of the ir'Daresh family? Surely what holdings remained would be taken by the Brelish crown. The assassin would receive no vast revenue from this murder.

Unless one of the men in ir'Daresh's business itinerary knew more. Any one of them could be connected to the murder. Of special note were the two names listed for Gamnon's Korth visit: Vorik ir'Alanso and Lord Charoth Arkenen.

Chapter
SEVEN

The Justice Ministry
Mol, the 9th of Sypheros, 998 YK

After a night of restless sleep, Soneste woke early and forced herself into a meditative state. Veshtalan had taught her an exercise to focus the mind and quiet the world. To make use of the "gifts of the Great Light," as he'd called her powers, her mind needed to be rested and well-ordered. Both were hard to come by this morning, especially with the cough Karrnath's damnable climate had given her.

Opting to visit the Justice Ministry only after she got a sense of the city first, Soneste took to the streets. The killer's trail was already more than a day cold. A couple of hours assessing the people and places of Korth wouldn't make it much colder. If the killer was going to flee the city, he would already have done so. And if she had to follow him beyond the city, she would.

An icy drizzle loosed itself upon the streets only seconds after she left the inn. Donning her wide-brimmed hat, she cursed the Karrnathi weather. She didn't travel by coach. Such conveyances muted the stimuli of the city—she wanted to see Korth as its everyday citizens did. While some streets were easily navigated, the lower districts wound their streets in confusing circles. Portions of the city had been damaged by siege weaponry during the Last War, but some buildings and streets had been rebuilt, resulting in a curious mosaic of old and new.

Soneste asked for directions whenever she was unsure of her whereabouts. The somberly-clad citizens gave her Brelish colors a reproachful glare and sent her quickly on her way. By contrast, Sharn embraced such the diversity of native and foreign cultures. But if Soneste wanted to learn more, she'd have to blend in more.

❧ ❧ ❧ ❧ ❧ ❧ ❧

The Justice Ministry occupied a series of tall, if unremarkable, buildings in the shadow of King's Hill and the palace of Crownhome. What the architecture lacked in inspiration was offset by a panoply of military banners. The black, silver, and red of the Karrnathi flag were most prevalent, its wolf head embossed above the heavily-guarded gate.

Within, Hyran ir'Tennet was nowhere to be found. While King Kaius III officially ruled the capital city, the Civic Minister was given the task of handling the day-to-day details. Soneste found that a legion of clerks and barristers within the Ministry hid him well.

"In the morning you may call on me at the Justice Ministry," he'd said. So where was he? The only man with more authority in this city was the king, so she supposed it made sense that he would be difficult to track down.

All the while, her damp clothes and persistent cough magnified her impatience. Her coat of dyed sayda—commonly called Brelish blue—and her artful tongue made her feel like a barking fox among brooding wolves. The Karrns scowled whenever she made demands, but Soneste gradually made inroads. They acknowledged her at last—if only to get rid of her.

Soneste was introduced to a conspicuously stern man whom Hyran ir'Tennet had allegedly "given over" to meet with her until the Civic Minister himself was available. Whatever *that* meant.

The man was tall and quite older than she, with dark, hollow eyes. A few faint scars showed along his neck and one hand. He wore a long sword, its pommel decorated with an **R** in filigree. An army officer, retired—but Soneste knew by his own unease in this environment that he wasn't part of the Ministry. Something about him, the way his eyes studied her in turn, gnawed at her. He introduced himself as Major Jotrem Dalesek.

Soneste extended her hand. "A pleasure to meet you, Jotrem," she said. His mouth twitched in irritation at her familiar address. Good. Then their dislike was mutual.

"Likewise, Miss Otänsin," he responded, grasping her hand harder than necessary. His skin was frigid. Host, she thought, was *everyone* in this cursed country sculpted from ice? On his finger she saw a ring set with a polished black stone. Red colors swirled within. A fire opal?

"Come with me." Jotrem led her to a private office belonging to some absent clerk. After a few awkward moments, Soneste tapped her fingernails on the leather folder Hyran had given her. She leaned upon the clerk's desk as Jotrem moved to the window to stare out at the city.

"Forgive my bluntness," she said, "but is it your job to stall me? I'm getting the impression I'm not wanted here."

"Excuse me?"

"As the victims of the murder at hand were King Boranel's subjects, he is under the impression that it is most certainly *his*—hence, *my*—business."

Jotrem fixed her with a stare she couldn't quite interpret—quiet outrage?—but it gradually fell away. "I'm doubtful that your king is yet aware of this event at all. But no, Miss Otänsin, I'm not here to stall you. In fact, I will be accompanying you on your investigation."

Sovereign Host, she cursed silently. Jotrem was an inquisitive too.

Just what she needed now, a local investigator stepping on her toes. One more inquisitive was one too many for her. Always was. She didn't relish partnering with another inquisitive again, much less a Karrn.

She stared mutely at Jotrem. At least *this* one was human. In Soneste's experience, elvish blood usually carried with it an unbearable pride. Steeling her mind, she held her reaction in check and met Jotrem's eyes without scowling. "Oh? I wasn't informed of that, but I will certainly consider it."

The Karrn's lip twitched. "You don't understand, Brelander. This isn't merely—"

The door opened. Soneste felt relief at the sight of Hyran ir'Tennet. His company, while slightly strained and soft-spoken the night before, was worlds better than this astringent veteran. Jotrem nodded to the Civic Minister, though both men seemed more suited to salutes, like soldiers on active duty.

"Good morning, Miss Otänsin, said Hyran. "I hope our weather hasn't dampened your spirit yet. I see that you've met Major Dalesek.

"It hasn't yet," she replied, "and yes, I have. I thank you for the offer of his assistance, but I am better suited to this investigation alone."

Hyran regarded both inquisitives then gestured politely at Jotrem. "I assure you, Major Dalesek will be a boon to your investigation. He can serve as your guide in this unfamiliar city and *assist* you with the peculiarities of our nation. This may help you to cut through the ministerial webs of life in Korth."

Soneste noticed a near-imperceptible grimace shift Jotrem's face. Hyran had both established the partnership and relegated the older inquisitive to an inferior role within it. Clever man. She knew that she could try and dispute the Civic Minister's decree, but she would have to send a message to Thuranne and thereby the King's Citadel and then wait for a reply. A waste of time and energy. Perhaps she could handle Jotrem herself.

"I know that time is short and you have a man to identify," Hyran said.

"Or woman," Soneste said.

Hyran blinked. "Pardon?"

"The killer might be a woman," she said.

Jotrem grunted. "It *is* a man, I assure you."

Soneste shrugged, holding up the death report had given her. "Yes, my employer mentioned that there was a man identified at the scene, but I didn't see him mentioned in the report."

Hyran nodded, taking the folder from her and laying out the documents on the desk. "That is because he is merely a suspect at this time. The three Lions who came upon the scene witnessed him standing over the victims. They pursued him to the balcony, where he escaped."

Soneste imagined the event, matching the three soldiers' pursuit of the suspect with the carpet prints she'd studied last night. A perfect fit.

"One of the Lions, Sergeant Bratta, recognized the suspect—a thorn in the side of both the Justice Ministry and the garrison."

"Tallis is his name," Jotrem said with obvious venom. "A malcontent of the worst order, wanted for murder, theft, destruction of property, and treason. He's a vigilante who styles himself a Karrnath loyalist, yet he continually breaks the king's laws."

Hyran nodded. "Tallis was also a graduate of Rekkenmark Academy and member of the Order. An officer who served in Warlord Dhejdan's legion, deployed for special missions . . . *before* being tried for treason. He was accused of murdering his own squad during one such mission, including a decorated marshal in the warlord's favor. Tallis did not attend his court-martial and has eluded capture for years. Not surprisingly, his military expertise has complicated our attempts to apprehend him."

Rekkenmark Academy. Quite possibly Khorvaire's most esteemed military school. Before the Last War, nobles from every province of the kingdom would send their children to receive military instruction in Karrnath, to study the writings of Galifar's greatest military minds. During the hundred year long war, only Karrnath's sons and daughters could be enrolled at the Academy, but after the Treaty of Thronehold, the remaining Five Nations had at last begun to send their promising youths to the famous training facility again, youths such as Halix ir'Wynarn, King Boranel's youngest son.

The Order of Rekkenmark was another thing altogether. Only by graduating with honors at the academy or on the king's recommendation could one join the elite order.

Soneste glanced at the opal ring on the older inquisitive's finger. "Was he a classmate of yours, Jotrem?" she asked him. The tightening of his lips answered her before his words did.

"I *was* acquainted with him, yes," he answered, following her eyes to the ring. "Several years before he joined the Order. But Tallis is a criminal now, Miss Otänsin, a traitor to the Academy, the Order, and to Karrnath."

Hyran nodded, his voice growing cold. "Last night, two White Lions were brought in to the Jorasco house of healing. They were . . . severely beaten, to say the least. When debriefed, they claimed it was Tallis who had attacked them. If that is true, he is still in the city. The entire garrison has been given his description. Some, like Sergeant Bratta, already know his face. If you name him as the Ebonspire assassin, Miss Otänsin, I will call upon all resources and we will find him in short order."

Soneste nodded. This Tallis was dangerous, of that there was no doubt. "Minister, may I speak with the witnesses?"

Hyran nodded, slipping a new document within the folder. "Of course, and I have for you a writ which will command the cooperation of most legitimate entities in this city. Major Dalesek can take you to the sergeant and the other White Lions."

"Thank you," Soneste said. "Before you leave, I wanted to ask about the ambassador's travel itinerary." She held up the small book but said nothing of her finding it. Hyran and Jotrem exchanged surprised glances. "There are a couple of names within I'm wondering if you're familiar with."

"Of course."

"The first is Vorik ir'Alanso."

Jotrem answered this one. "Vorik's family owns a tailoring house—some say, the finest in all of Karrnath. Nearly every noble

in this town owns something from the ir'Alanso workshops." Out
of the corner of her eye, she observed Hyran absently examining the silver buttons of his sleeve. A fine uniform he wore, she
thought, no doubt custom made. Ir'Alonso's work?

Soneste considered Gamnon's family business. The two
industries, steel and fashion, seldom overlapped, unless one were
outfitting an army of armored soldiers—or, she mused, putting
clothes on warforged. "Would you know of any reason a foreign
ambassador would wish to meet with a wealthy clothier?"

"It *is* possible, Miss Otänsin," Jotrem said with a touch of sarcasm, "that the ambassador merely wished to purchase a new dress
for his wife. I understand he was traveling on holiday?"

Soneste reddened. Yes, that was likely.

"But why meet with the owner himself? Why not simply
visit the shop? His itinerary noted Vorik specifically." She let the
thought hang there, then held up the book again. "Who is Lord
Charoth Arkenen?"

Hyran looked back at her then. "Lord Charoth? Another noble,
one of the newer players in Karrnath's export industries. Owns
Arkenen Glass, along with a number of tenements and warehouses
in the city. He is a wizard, formerly of House Cannith."

Interesting. "Formerly?" she asked. "An excoriate?"

Such heirs ejected from their prestigious houses were notorious
for their bitterness. This was not surprising, as the dragonmarked
houses rivaled nations in sheer wealth and influence. Excoriation,
the legal and social severance from one's house, quite often led to a
life of crime as the unfortunate heir peddled out his house's secrets
to the highest bidder. It wouldn't be the first time she'd heard of
such a thing.

Hyran shook his head. "Not quite. Lord Charoth is a . . . *self-
imposed* exile of his house. In fact, it is well known that Baron
Zorlan d'Cannith himself once made a formal offer to Lord Charoth
to return him to a place of power within the house. The offer was
immediately rebuffed."

That was strange. When the Day of Mourning destroyed the

country of Cyre, it also claimed the lives of many House Cannith heirs, for the house's base was in the city of Eston. Among the countless souls lost that day was Starrin d'Cannith, patriarch of the house. Since his death four years ago, three Cannith heirs had vied to succeed him as patriarch of the house. Baron Zorlan, the stern head of Cannith East, lived here in Korth.

"Why would he turn down an offer from the baron?" she asked.

"None know the *true* story," Hyran said, "but everyone knows that Lord Charoth is the lone survivor of a forgehold disaster that claimed the lives of dozens of House Cannith workers. He emerged from the incident . . . disfigured."

Lord Charoth was sounding more interesting by the second. She knew interviewing a wealthy businessman on short notice was far-fetched, but she would certainly try. One thing at a time, though. "Wouldn't a man of his fame and wealth simply pay Jorasco to heal him? How bad could it be?"

"Evidently they tried. His condition was the result of some kind of creation forge explosion. There are many different stories told of what happened to him."

"Would your chronicles have anything on him?" Soneste asked.

"They may," Hyran answered. "I will grant you limited access to the Ministry archives. The *Korth Sentinel* is our local chronicle, back issues of which you can find filed there as well. After his presumed death, Lord Charoth's emergence was quite the talk in Karrnath. It even made the *Chronicle*. But this was shortly after the Thronehold Treaty. There were more momentous events going on at the time. You will also be able to peruse the few files we have on Tallis, but I admit there isn't much. The unique nature of his service in the army kept him off most records."

"Thank you, again, Civic Minister," Soneste said and meant it. "You've been very helpful. The King's Citadel will be grateful. Will I be able to find you again here?"

Hyran smiled knowingly. "Yes. Use the writ to get their

attention, but I would tread cautiously, Miss Otänsin, if you feel the need to investigate Lord Charoth. He is a powerful man."

Soneste nodded and tucked the book away. "One more thing. I examined the ambassador's warforged bodyguard. Defeated by the killer, I assume, but I think he might yet be revived. He may be another witness. Could you send an artificer to assess his condition? The sooner the better."

Jotrem shook his head. Hyran appeared to consider the request, then inclined his head, businesslike. "I will have the warforged taken to the House Cannith enclave for repair. Return here this afternoon. If it is possible to revive it, I will keep the construct here, under guard. More than a witness—it may be a suspect, no?"

Everyone is, Soneste thought, even the two of you. "Minister, may I speak plainly?"

"Of course."

"I've been given the authority to identify the ambassador's killer. If you want to find this man, Tallis, please do so. But he is not to be tried or harmed until I have decided he is guilty—or innocent—of this crime. I will not lose sight of the case at hand." Her eyes flicked to Jotrem. "Nor be distracted by a suspect some obviously wish to pin this crime on. That Tallis is guilty of other crimes, I cannot say."

Hyran nodded. "I understand your concern. We shall try none who may be connected to the ambassador's death until you give assent. But understand, Miss Otänsin, Tallis is a Karrn. He is loose in *our* streets, even now, harming our citizens. His life or death is at the behest of our jurisdiction."

She nodded, refusing to look at Jotrem's face.

❋ ❋ ❋ ❋ ❋ ❋ ❋

Sergeant Bratta's demeanor was quite a contrast to the civic minister's. While Hyran ir'Tennet suppressed his personal opinions beneath a diplomatic veneer appropriate to his station, the mouth of the sergeant before her spewed biased conjecture with every breath.

But for his stilted Karrnathi accent, she might have taken him for a member of the Sharn Watch.

"Killing women and children," the soldier said for the fifth time. "It was Tallis, I know it. Cowardly bastard. Didn't realize it until after he left, but I remembered his face."

"You've encountered him before?"

"A few months back," the Lion growled. "Sabotaged a caravan from Atur as they were coming in Northgate. Took out several of my men then too."

"Killed?"

"No," he answered.

Soneste wasn't yet convinced. She'd questioned each of the White Lions in turn, but only Sergeant Bratta had recognized the man as Tallis. The others described the man they'd seen, and it matched Bratta's account well enough, albeit with a few hyperbolized embellishments. Another White Lion at the Ebonspire, posted on a balcony several stories directly below the ambassador's suite, had been attacked by a masked man shortly before the time of the slaughter. Struck down, but not slain.

But the slaughter of the ir'Daresh family was so complete, so *deft*, that she had a hard time believing the same man was responsible. Could this Tallis have partnered with another? Magic could well be involved. How else could the killers breach the Ebonspire's defenses so easily and escape again? Perhaps Tallis had been double-crossed to take the fall?

Soneste waited for Sergeant Bratta to finish his tirade, then said, "Can you tell me how he escaped?"

"On the balcony. Jumped for the edge, so I put a bolt in his leg. If he climbed down, it would have hurt like Khyber's own breath." The man shook his head.

"But?"

"He didn't climb down. At least not much. The bastard must have been part wizard. Jumped from a balcony clear across to the next tower like a giant frog."

Such magic was not uncommon in Sharn. Some citizens,

including the Watch, even carried enchanted rings that could slow a fall should they topple from one of the lofty bridges. Soneste turned to Jotrem. "What is the tower across—?"

"A tenement complex," he cut in, "of individually owned private flats. Tallis would have accessed the Ebonspire that way. I've already searched there and interviewed witnesses. The only ones who saw an intruder were private guards, most employed by House Medani. They described a man in a black mask."

Would have been nice if you'd told me this first, she thought.

"Masked going in, but not going out?" she asked. She'd found the mask, but why would he have removed it and allow himself to be identified? That Tallis had been there, she did not doubt, but something clearly had not gone according to plan.

"I saw no mask," remarked Sergeant Bratta, irritated. "I saw his face. It was him."

To Jotrem, she asked, "Could a changeling have impersonated Tallis, knowing you'd love the excuse to go after him?"

"That was no changeling," Bratta said.

"Anywhere else, perhaps," Jotrem replied, ignoring him, "but not the Ebonspire. Kundarak magic prevents illusions or shapeshifting of any kind. It's part of the very walls, not some simple ward one can bypass with a spell."

"And the Medani guards were well enough to interview?" Soneste asked him.

There was his mouth twitch again. "They'd been knocked out."

Soneste turned to the White Lion. "Does that sound like the work of the assassin to you, Sergeant?" she asked, but the question was again for Jotrem.

"It means nothing," the older inquisitive growled. "Tallis has a long history of harming his own countrymen. Whatever shred of loyalty he maintains to Karrnath takes the form of sadism. And you Brelanders? Breland was our enemy once. I doubt he would hesitate to kill *you*, Miss Otänsin."

"Brel*ish*, Major Dalesek," she corrected, using his surname for the first and last time. "And Breland has also been Karrnath's ally. Ambassador ir'Daresh once served as a captain in a regiment alongside Karrnath. You *were* in the army, weren't you? Perhaps Tallis knew the ambassador then? Harbored a grudge for some reason, and decided to wait until *after* the war to take revenge?"

Jotrem was silent.

"Thank you for your time, Sergeant," Soneste said to the White Lion. "If I have any more questions, I will find you."

❧ ❧ ❧ ❧ ❧ ❧ ❧

Jotrem led them several levels beneath the Justice Ministry as Soneste used Hyran's writ to pass six levels of security stations. While the bureaucrats did a fine job of shuffling paperwork, Karrnath's military personnel were omnipresent. Every guard scrutinized the writ, tersely admitting them at last into the Ministry archives. Even there, two uniformed clerks lingered near to keep an eye on her. Jotrem's presence did much to allay the Karrns' hesitance to allow a Brelish civilian within their walls, but Soneste had no intention of admitting it.

"Why do you call him a traitor?" she asked Jotrem as they entered another cramped room. "If he's a traitor to Karrnath, why hasn't Tallis fled the border to seek a life somewhere else? He knows you're after him. It's only a matter of time, isn't it?"

Jotrem's hand settled upon his sword hilt as he propped his back to a wall. "Aside from his treasonous crime, Tallis has taken it upon himself to decide what is best for this nation. Apparently, harassing its aristocracy serves it well."

"Aristocracy? Is that all?"

"He has also been known to strike out against Seekers," Jotrem added.

"Seekers?"

"Followers of the Blood of Vol."

An unusual assassin, she thought. "Do you know why?"

"Why does a madman do anything?" Jotrem returned. "I couldn't tell you why."

He leaned forward and gestured to the room at large. "The annals of the Ministry say only that on some crucial mission, Tallis turned on his own men. He killed a dread marshal and destroyed the undead assigned to his unit. *That* was his first known crime, and it made him a traitor to the crown."

"So Tallis has a vendetta against the undead. Strange, for a Karrn."

"Few of my countrymen have a love for the undead, Miss Otänsin, but they are useful. Tallis has no respect for the law and the decisions of the crown. He is an embarrassment to this country, and I will see him executed for his crimes."

What is *your* problem with him, Soneste wanted to ask. Instead, she merely said, "Before his court-martial, had Tallis scorned the Blood of Vol before?"

Soneste knew something of the history of the war before her time. It had been the Cult of Vol that had brought its prowess with necromancy to Karrnath early in the war. King Kaius I had accepted their terms and raised the first undead legion against his enemies. Though his successors had tried to rid Karrnath of the Cult's grasp, they could not erase its presence from the land. Soneste had even heard that the Karrnathi city of Atur was home to a great temple of the Blood of Vol.

"It's possible," Jotrem answered. "It's an old religion in this country, and the undead soldiers it raised to support our armies were usually kept in separate military units from the living soldiers. But there were joint operations."

So Tallis was opposed to both the Blood of Vol and the undead they spawned. Was there a connection between Gamnon and the Blood of Vol? The ambassador had been one of the Purified, a follower of the Silver Flame, but the Silver Flame sought to eradicate evil, and it was commonly known the Silver Flame considered the Blood of Vol to be just that. Soneste had to find the connection. If Tallis opposed the Blood of Vol, and followers of the Silver Flame opposed the Blood of Vol, why would Tallis kill Gamnon?

Chapter
Eight

They stood outside the gates of the Justice Ministry. Jotrem seemed impervious to the cold, dressed in a single insulated layer in the same drab colors as his countrymen. Soneste fastened her coat tightly and fished for her gloves.

She decided that Lord Charoth was likelier to have knowledge of Ambassador ir'Daresh, and she wanted to speak to him without Jotrem's unwelcome glare at her back. Since he had been assigned to assist her investigation, she decided to use this to her advantage. She asked him to seek out Vorik ir'Alanso or a representative of his family to learn what appointment the ambassador had missed with the clothier.

Jotrem resisted, as Soneste knew he would, so she turned to her own method of persuasion.

"Listen, Jotrem," she said. "Together you and I will seem an interrogation party. I want to keep this Lord Charoth at ease. Perhaps he may speak more candidly to an attractive young woman, no?"

This she punctuated with a smile and a mental stab, calling upon the talents she'd honed in Veshtalan's presence not so long ago. She imagined the older inquisitive's mind as a door made of stiff clay, then she pressed against it with fingertips of her will. She couldn't peer beyond that barrier, but she could leave an impression of her choice in the clay. A seed of attraction, Veshtalan had called this particular power.

She heard the quiet whistle that heralded her power—a gentle sound with no definitive source—but amidst the bustle of the crowds Jotrem would not know its origin.

"I don't know," he muttered, then furrowed his brow in mild confusion. "I suppose . . . that makes sense."

"Visit the tailoring house," she suggested, encouraging the seed she knew was germinating within him. She indicated her blue coat and its Brelish design. "Perhaps you could find some local garments for me while you're there, to help me blend in?"

Soneste didn't mention that her coat had been partially woven with illusionary threads. Shiftweave clothing could alter its color and shape with a word from its wearer.

"Of course," he said, his expression unsure. Soneste tried not to smile, knowing that in that moment, the Karrn was finding himself inexplicably attracted to women's clothes. "We will . . . meet here at fourth watch, then."

"Watch?"

Jotrem shook his head. "We measure the day in watches. Every fourth hour is another watch. Fourth watch is noon. There are six watches in each day."

"Give me an hour more," she said.

Jotrem nodded and walked away, intent on his curious errand. Soneste allowed herself to smile at last.

Now she needed to find Charoth's estate or his place of business. It was simply a matter of asking around. She turned to leave then froze as she saw two White Lions dragging a manacled captive toward the open gates of the Ministry. He was dark haired, like most Karrns, and wore a leather jerkin. For a moment, she wondered if they'd actually found Tallis. His appearance nearly matched Sergeant Bratta's description of the Ebonspire suspect: clad in black, with an unruly, if athletic bearing. He *looked* like a soldier gone rogue.

The man struggled, uttering curses unfamiliar to Soneste. She approached cautiously as a White Lion sergeant stopped them.

"Report," he said.

One of the Lions renewed his grip on the captive's arm. "This piece of human swine accosted a merchant when the merchant refused to sell to him."

"Lower rabble," the other added with disgust and patted a small scabbard on his belt. "When we intervened, he displayed this blade and said he'd stick us if we 'laid a hand upon him.'"

The sergeant looked the disheveled man in the eyes. "Is this true? Did you resist arrest?"

"Go to Khyber, white kitty," the man cursed, spitting in the sergeant's face.

The White Lion nodded stolidly. He drew the confiscated knife from the other soldier's belt without wiping his face.

"You do not refute the crime and *are* therefore guilty," he said in a loud voice, "so let's not waste the magistrate's time, eh?"

He pulled one side of the rogue's jerkin aside and slashed the long blade across the man's stomach. Soneste's own stomach tightened as the man screamed. Citizens on the street quickened their paces, none lingering to watch. The two soldiers let the man drop.

With his wrists manacled, the captive couldn't even try to stanch the bleeding. As he writhed upon the cobbles, the soldiers watched for several long seconds. Then the sergeant stabbed the criminal again, this time at the base of the neck. His pain ended.

"Another one for the corpse collectors," the sergeant said, an order as much as a declaration.

Soneste turned away, nauseated. The watch in Sharn may have been unapologetically corrupt, but they weren't quite so free to exact judgment on a whim. Was *this* the Code of Kaius?

● ● ● ◉ ● ● ●

Soneste was directed to Charoth's estate in short order. A few crowns and sovereigns dispensed into the appropriate hands even gave her some local perspective on the so-called "Masked Wizard." He was a peasant hero in the Low District, a bogeyman among the merchants of Korth, and a mage of mysterious power. There were even rumors that the mask he wore gave him prophetic, divinatory, or vitalic powers.

Her stomach was still soured by the brutality of Karrnathi law, but now that she approached the suspect's house, she felt more composed. Whether in the halls of Morgrave University or the alleys of Sharn's Lower City—or indeed, the streets of a foreign city—this *was* what she did for a living.

Lord Charoth had elected not to return to his family estate in Highcourt Ward when he returned to Korth two years ago—only one of many times he'd spurned House Cannith. Instead, he had purchased a crumbling manor in the Community Ward and rebuilt it to his liking. The former residents had been a well-to-do family whose every scion had perished in the Last War, vacating the estate for the Masked Wizard's convenience.

The first thing Soneste noticed was the gloom around Charoth's estate. Despite the late morning hour, the sky was exceedingly dark. Cold fire lanterns lit even the major street junctions in the Low District Ward, but here they were markedly absent.

The house itself matched the city's symmetrical architecture, with smooth stone walls adorned only at its edges, sills, and eaves. The ground level was broad, but further in it rose only three stories high, dwarfed by the tower blocks on either side of the estate. None could say that the mansion lacked grandeur for its height, though. The whole structure presented a regal, throne-like appearance. The locals had taken to calling it the Murder House, and now she understood why. There was a profusion of rain spouts carved to resemble crows, and the silver-painted cornices which ran beneath every roof possessed a featherlike design.

Lovely, Soneste thought.

A razor-edged fence framed the estate like a row of stylized iron glaives, conjoined by a pair of black gates that swung gently open at Soneste's approach. Did they open for all, or was someone watching? She looked to the dark windows above, saw no one, then stopped when the short path circled around a dry fountain. A vulture-headed stone demon towered at its center, glowering at her from its frozen perch. The statue's eyes, inlaid spheres of glass, were ensorceled with a crimson light—the only exterior illumination around the manor.

As she turned to follow the path, a hideous cry arose from somewhere nearby. It was bestial but almost humanlike in pitch. Inexplicable panic seized her, and she found herself running toward the gates—which had silently closed behind her.

"Unholy Six!" she swore, turning around when she heard the sound of heavy, padded feet swiftly approaching.

It was a large animal, easily the length of a horse and covered in patchy, rust-colored fur. A mass of lesions marred its black-skinned hide. Moving low to the ground, the creature had appeared from somewhere in the yard and bounded in her direction with the litheness of a cat, accompanied by the sound of rattling metal. Soneste drew her rapier and slashed wildly, startled by the speed at which the creature closed the distance. It stopped short with a heavy *chink*, turning its feline head away from her blade.

Soneste steeled her mind and struck again, finding a moment's composure as she stabbed the animal in the exposed skin of its chest. She saw the blade disappear into the matted fur but felt no resistance. As it shifted its weight, she saw part of its body linger and fade like an afterimage. Some sort of illusionary glamer cloaked the creature, displacing its actual position. It fixed her with blank white eyes for a moment then surged forward again.

The metallic *chink* sounded again as a thick chain—affixed to a collar that appeared to float in mid-air more than a foot from its neck—stretched taught. Soneste danced away from its snapping jaws, putting several feet between them.

It could move no further. She was safe now.

"*Audsh!*" a man's voice called out from the house, "*Nerzhaat hak irezh!*" If Soneste wasn't mistaken, the words were spoken in the Goblin tongue. She tried to remember them.

The creature turned away with a mewling growl, padding back to the other side of the yard like a scolded dog. Now that she saw the heavy chain, she could see where the beast's neck appeared to be—and where it *really* was.

"Don't let the words fool you, miss." A handsome, well-groomed young man beckoned to her from the porch. "I am not his master—he won't heed my commands for long. Best if you come in now."

The brooding clouds above chose that moment to release their burden. Soneste glanced once more at the skulking animal—moving slowly away from her now, it looked more like a mangy wolf with a long rat tail—then whispered another malediction for Karrnath's weather. The rain began to fall in torrents, so she hurried up the steps beneath the prominent overhang.

The valet opened the front door. "Did you have an appointment with Lord Arkenen?" he asked with a smile of neat, pearlescent teeth.

"I did not," she answered. "I'm sorry for this unannounced visit. My name is Soneste Otänsin, agent of the King's Citadel in Breland."

The valet's eyebrows rose.

"I am here on behalf of the Justice Ministry," she explained, holding up Hyran's writ. "I know your lord may be occupied, but the matter is pressing. Please ask him if he will see me for a brief interview."

"Of course," he said. "As it happens, my lord is home. Enter, please." He stepped aside.

The valet shut the door behind Soneste, offering to take her coat. She politely declined, and the man drifted away. Soneste found a wall mirror and checked her appearance, affecting her professional veneer with ease. She removed her hat, combed her hair with her fingers, then retied the ribbon at the base of her neck. When she was finished, she examined her surroundings with a practiced eye.

The great hall beyond the foyer doubled as an art gallery, a wide corridor running left and right. According to the *Korth Sentinel,* Lord Charoth had hosted a number of exclusive showings since his reemergence. Even Baron Zorlan had been invited to the last showing two months ago.

Knowing her time was limited, Soneste set to work, feigning the idle interest of a citizen with a passing appreciation of art. In the homes of the wealthy and magical, you never knew when you were being examined in turn.

The sculptures that lined the corridor were set upon matching pedestals of gray marble. Most were works of metal or stone, some abstract and unappealing to look upon, while others were realistic, pleasing depictions. Every piece, she observed, contained some component of glass—an hourglass in the arms of a marble beggar, a monocle affixed to the gold bust of an elderly scholar, even a single fingernail in the closed fist of a soldier cast in bronze. Impulsively, Soneste produced the small magnifying lens she'd once purchased years ago in Starilaskur. "Karrnathi glass," the peddler had insisted, "none better."

Glass was one of Karrnath's chief exports, so it didn't surprise her that a former Cannith director would take part in the industry. By all reports, though, Charoth steered away from House Cannith interests. Surely Cannith East already had a hand in such revenues? But then, Cannith produced innovative devices and wondrous architecture, not everyday exports.

"This way, Miss Otänsin," the valet said when he returned, sooner than Soneste had expected.

She was led through a series of austere chambers and was left alone again in a windowless parlor rendered entirely in shades of black, gray, and white. She found the near monochrome effect unsettling, as though all life had been drained from everything in the chamber. The blue of her coat confirmed that the effect was a nonmagical one. Mere eccentricity.

She studied the room in greater detail when heavy footfalls alerted Soneste to her host's approach. The valet entered first and offered her his recurring smile. "My lord, I present to you Miss Soneste Otänsin, inquisitive of Thuranne d'Velderan's Investigative Services of Sharn, surrogate investigator of the Justice Ministry."

Soneste refrained from scowling. She hadn't mentioned her agency to the valet. Charoth's people were resourceful.

"Miss Otänsin . . ." the servant said.

The noble stepped into the room. Her expression remained assertive, but Soneste admitted to herself that the ex-Cannith lord presented an imposing figure.

"I presented to you Lord Charoth Arkenen."

Every inch of the man's body was enshrouded in a courtly robe of midnight blue. From wide sleeves she could see black silken gloves on each hand, one of which clutched a striking silver-headed cane of deep blue glass. His hooded face was concealed with a mask painted with bright, stylized colors and carved with twisting runes. She recognized it as darkwood—an uncommon, expensive wood usually imported from Aerenal. The slits of the eyes were covered with glass, the lenses too thick to reveal the eyes beneath.

Against the muted shades of the parlor, the wizard's attire stood out in livid contrast. His metal-braced boots came together as Charoth inclined his head, acknowledging his guest.

"You may speak plainly in my house, Soneste," he said with a strong, sharpened baritone. His voice sounded clear but sleightly reverberant, a result of speaking through the slender crevice in the mouth of his mask. "Am I a suspect in your case?"

Soneste looked into the impassive eyes of the wooden face, uncertain on which to focus. She recalled the sketch in the *Sentinel* that depicted Charoth's gaunt, aristocratic features and tried to visualize them now as she looked at him. The presence of the esteemed Cannith wizard was slightly unnerving, but she'd interrogated hostile criminals. Charoth was no comparison. She pushed away her unease with cool professionalism.

"Lord Arkenen—"

"Charoth will suffice," he said.

"Lord Charoth. You know of my case, then?" she returned.

The wizard shrugged. "What else would bring a Brelish inquisitive to my door? The ambassador's death was two days ago. Old news now. Many die in this city."

He gestured to a white divan, waited for her to sit, then settled himself in a high-backed chair across from her with a quiet grunt. Between them sat a low glass table, upon which sat a glass figurine of a dryad whose shape was so delicate it was almost invisible in the colorless room. She wondered if he'd designed any of these works of art himself.

"You're not a suspect at this time, my lord," she lied, defying the rumor that his mask revealed falsehoods in his presence. She would not be intimidated by this man's reputation. "Only a potential source of information. I am only here to ask you a few questions. Are you willing to aid this investigation?"

"I am always willing to help the Ministry," he said, "even when foreign dignitaries are careless and get themselves killed."

Soneste used to take notes when speaking with important suspects or witnesses. Since her brief training with Veshtalan, she'd learned to commit even spoken words to memory. It was not as easy as imprinting written words in her mind, but with focus she found it manageable.

She took a steady breath, centering her mind. "Is it your belief that Ambassador ir'Daresh brought the murder of his family upon himself?"

Charoth did not answer immediately. He took a deep, rasping breath, leading Soneste to wonder if the injuries he'd suffered had affected more than his face and skin. "It is one thing if royals from the Five Nations wish to send their whelps to foreign courts as a show of peace, but another to parade their aristocrats across national borders while the scars of war still burn."

Soneste was surprised to find his prejudice so nakedly displayed. Perhaps that was a learning point. "So you *do* approve of the exchange of royal siblings, of Prince Halix and Princess Borina staying here in Korth—which, I understand, was initiated by your king?"

Charoth nodded. "Such compromises are necessary to maintain peace. But the rulers of our lands must take care not to push the limits. The ambassador, like all of them, was taking a risk bringing his family into foreign lands. Karrnath is not Breland. Your people are well known for wagging tongues. It can bring trouble in our land. Perhaps the ambassador invited it."

Soneste shrugged, choosing to sidestep the insult to her people. "At any given time, my lord, there are hundreds—thousands—of nobles and commoners from across the Five Nations in your kingdom. What would make this particular man and his entire family victims?"

"You're the inquisitive," he answered. "You tell me. Perhaps an old rival took his holiday as an opportunity to settle a score?" He leaned forward, the grimace of his mask clearer to see, adding a touch of sarcasm to his voice. "You know how brutal those Karrns can be."

"Of course, anything's possible." Soneste needed a new direction. "May I ask, my lord, why you were scheduled to meet with Ambassador ir'Daresh if you disapproved of the presence of such nobles altogether?"

"I am a businessman, Soneste," Charoth answered. "With the war behind us, I am in the business of production and exportation. Ambassador ir'Daresh was a potential customer, nothing more. When I learned of his imminent arrival in this city, I arranged a meeting with him. A meeting of which the Sovereign Host apparently did not approve."

Caustic *and* blasphemous, Soneste mused.

"You think me callous," he continued, "but I am a realist. I have to be. I may have once belonged to a dragonmarked house, but I have lived in Karrnath all my life. It is not a forgiving land, but it is, ultimately, rewarding. You must forgive my candor."

Soneste offered a genuine smile. "You are entitled to it, my lord, especially in your own home. I am the guest here, and I do appreciate your honesty. Many men and women I have questioned in my line of work are less cooperative."

"And less interested in justice—Karrnathi *or* Brelish, as it were. I am well known in this town as an advocate of retribution, when and where it is due."

"Understood. How did you make the acquaintance of the ambassador?"

"A mutual colleague introduced us via written correspondence." He offered nothing more. Was there nothing to add, or was he hiding someone?

"Were you aware that Gamnon ir'Daresh was a Seeker?" she asked.

Another blatant lie, but if Charoth's relationship with Gamnon were strictly professional, he probably wouldn't know the man's religious affiliations. Or would he? Choosing a political follower of the Silver Flame almost ensured there would be no use of necromantic interrogation of the victim. How convenient that would be.

Soneste had found this method of interrogation effective at times, used to distract the subject into revealing more. When you couldn't find the truth, invent a new one and see if it leads you anywhere. It was how she'd found the missing Shauranna Rokesko.

"I . . . was not," Charoth answered. "That would surprise me, indeed. The Brelish aren't known for their devotion to Seeker philosophy." Of course, the method worked best when you could read the subject's face. Charoth's mask, even his leveled voice, concealed everything.

"No, indeed we're not." Soneste moved on, not wanting to be trapped by her own falsehoods. "I have only a couple more questions for you today."

The wizard gestured for her to continue.

"Do you know the name Tallis?" she asked, studying his body language in lieu of his face.

Charoth didn't shift. "If the Tallis to which you refer is the infamous dissenter, Major Tallis of Rekkenmark—yes, I know the name. He is the prime suspect in the ambassador's murder, is he not?"

Soneste leaned back, nonchalant in her manner. "Perhaps. He seems to be a local criminal, a major no longer. Did you know him personally?"

"Criminal? What Tallis *is* depends solely upon who you ask. In my opinion, he is a misguided malcontent who *wants* to be a hero but chooses the wrong friends."

"What you're saying," Soneste said, "is that you once tried to hire him, and he declined you."

Charoth laughed, a dry rasp that sounded forced. "You don't miss much, do you? King Boranel sent the right woman for this case."

Soneste shook her head and smiled. "Do not think to evade my questions with flattery, my lord. Did you seek to employ him?"

"Employ him? Yes, perhaps." Charoth gestured idly with one hand. "A man of his skill should be doing something more productive with his time than wasting it on skewed patriotism. I had hoped to hire Tallis as a guardmaster for the shipments I receive from abroad. Some of the raw materials I require for my factory are expensive and in need of greater protection. I would have beseeched the Ministry on his behalf, to grant him legitimate employment in exchange for his martial skills. It would also allow the law to keep an eye on him."

Soneste considered his words. He wasn't lying, but he wasn't telling the precise truth. Charoth was feared by many, and she could see that he exuded wealth and influence, but he fronted himself as an eccentric philanthropist as well. Could this be real? He owned many of the properties within the Low District Ward, and if rumors were true, helped to keep a lot of the city's poor employed. Arkenen Glass was doing well.

"Did he give you an answer at all?"

Charoth shrugged. "He was evasive. But then, Major Tallis spurns authority, and that would have included me."

"Do you know of any prior connections between Tallis and ir'Daresh?"

"I do not."

"One more question for you, my lord." Soneste chose her words carefully. "Tallis is a wanted man, affiliated with crimes of desertion, armed assault, murder, and treason. If his whereabouts were commonly known, he'd have been executed by now. How did you know how to find him in order to present your offer of employment?"

Charoth's response was casual. "If you mean—do I know where he hides? No, but I have knowledge of a great many things in this town. There are places you can contact a man when you do not know how to find him. And when all is said and done, everyone knows where to find me."

Soneste smiled, refraining from pursuing *that* point. She had a better sense of Lord Charoth now. She would recall this conversation, and the details of his home, with greater scrutiny when she was alone. Another gift of the "Great Light."

"Thank you for your time, my lord." Soneste paused, then stood up.

Charoth held up one gloved hand. "There is another question you wish to ask."

Soneste stared back into the lenses of the mask, genuinely surprised. Surely he isn't like me? she wondered. Even I can't read minds.

"Why darkwood, you were wondering," he said with cold satisfaction.

"No, no. I—"

"It is conducive to magical application. The eyes behind this mask are damaged. Only with magic can I look again upon the world as I remembered it."

❊ ❊ ❊ ◉ ❊ ❊ ❊

Charoth stared through the window and watched as the young inquisitive walked beyond his gate. In other circumstances, he might well have sought her employment. He liked the way she'd studied the world around her, focused on everything she saw. Unless he was mistaken, the Brelish inquisitive had been memorizing every detail.

"Gan," he said.

"My lord?" the changeling answered.

Charoth turned to regard his steward. Since yesterday's discovery, Gan's professionalism had become superb. Good. Charoth didn't expect he would need to chastise him again for possession of dreamlily, but one could never be too careful.

Given the importance of his work at present, Charoth considered allowing the changeling to use trace amounts of the drug to keep his focus. The very thought of such weakness in his employee enraged him.

Let him suffer.

"I must return to the factory. The next few days are critical to me. I am certain the Brelish will return, but not today. I want to know who else she talks to and where she goes before I see her again."

"I will see to it, my lord," Gan answered, his voice sober.

"And your men?" Charoth asked.

"They are where they need to be. They are ready."

Chapter
NINE

Tallis hobbled to the back of the line at the ticket booth in the lightning rail station. Having seen firsthand that the guards at each of the city's active gates had doubled, he was tempted to just purchase a ticket and test his disguise among the rail security. Even now, five White Lions prowled the wide concourse, watchful among the crowds. Looking for *him*.

He'd meant what he told Lenrik, though. Even if he left the city now, returning would be no easier. If the Justice Ministry was determined to find him this time, would he be any safer in Rekkenmark or Atur? What if he left Karrnath altogether?

No. He'd walk willingly into the depths of Khyber before he let the assassin drive him away from his country. He'd find that bastard and kill him—or her—himself. If he left now, he wouldn't be able to talk to Haedrun and find out what got all of this started.

Aureon, just a few more days of your favor. . . .

In front of him, an oddly-dressed shifter with a curious hairstyle and an outlandish handaxe hanging from his belt was the next up. Nice weapon, Tallis thought, then stepped back out of line.

"No good, no good," he muttered to the woman behind him, enjoying his old veteran's persona less than he use to. "My daughter won't want to see me, anyway," he explained at her questioning look.

Feigning a change of heart, he walked over to stand before the message kiosk, a wide board where travelers could post or check job listings, bounties, or brief notes for one another. This was also one of several ways to contact the Midwife, a little fact known to a select and unlawful few.

Tallis scanned the kiosk. When he felt confident no one was looking, he slipped a folded piece of paper from his own pocket and tacked it to the board. *Former Blademark seeking caravan work. Ask for Azzen at the 7th Wach.* The Midwife's street eyes would recognize the double letters in the given name and the spelling error of the cited establishment. Double *Z*s always meant Tallis.

Done with his message, he turned away—

—and found himself face to face with a grinning, disheveled dwarf in a tattered cloak. He stank of filthy clothes and too much time spent in a dockside alehouse.

"Thought that was you, Tally Boy," he spat.

Tallis knew many of the dregs of the Low District by name. Some he ignored, others he handled personally. Drazen was one he'd never really had the time or inclination to "discipline."

Beyond the dwarf, a squad of Lions was in view, actively scrutinizing the occupants of the station. Only the very brave or the very stupid argued with the city watch. None protested as the Lions pushed aside broadsheets to see whose face lay behind each.

"You need a bath, Drazen." Tallis started to move away from the kiosk, slipping his only apparent arm around the dwarf's as though requiring the assistance of a youngster to walk.

"And you need a new get-up, Tally," the dwarf laughed, speaking a little too loud for Tallis's comfort. His eyes darted to the guards, who were getting closer. "Been catching my marks at the rail station, didn't you know? Recognized you straight away."

"Now's not a good time, Draze."

"I'm thinking it's not," the dwarf agreed. "I'm also thinking even your cripple garb won't hide you from the white kitties today, eh? Unless a certain false old man pays up and a certain dwarf keeps his jawbone clamped."

Tallis wanted to stick the dwarf right then and there. "You're clanless already, Drazen," he whispered angrily. "Keep pushing it, you'll be beardless soon too."

"Last chance, Tally. Buy me a meal and a mug of Nightwood and we'll have a parley, eh? Talk about what *else* you can do for me."

Two White Lions were close, and Tallis saw them both looking in their direction with a modicum of interest. He couldn't take a chance any longer. He'd left his message for the Midwife. Now it was time to go. Drazen was an unapologetic thug and would carry through with his threat especially if food was at stake. Under any other circumstances, Tallis might have been able to turn the law against *him*.

Well—why not?

"You'll get yours soon," Tallis promised, and then he drove his elbow hard into the dwarf's stomach. As the dwarf gasped for breath, Tallis disengaged roughly and let himself fall hard to the floor.

"Guards!" he shouted, making his voice sound as gravelly as he could. "This dwarf just stole my gold!"

The White Lions turned to Drazen, whose face was twisted in rage as he labored to breathe. One of the guards pointed an axe at him as the other held his gauntleted hands out in warning. Tallis twisted around and sprang to his feet, loosing his "crippled" arm for better maneuverability.

"Hands out, dwarf!" one of the Lions commanded.

Tallis staggered away from the scene, targeting the nearest exit. As he passed a group of ticket-holders seated at a bench, he turned and pointed behind him. "Some dwarf is stabbing people!" he said with a panicked look on his face.

The travelers fumbled for their luggage and began to move quickly away in different directions. Perfect.

"No, no!" Tallis heard Drazen shouting, spittle flying from his lips. "That's Tallis there! He's playing you all for fools! Tallis! Of Rekkenmark!" The White Lions looked in his direction. One of them nocked an arrow.

Tallis broke into a run.

❧ ❧ ❧ ❧ ❧ ❧ ❧

Soneste had less than an hour until her rendezvous with Jotrem. It would be tight, but she decided she could visit the *Chronicle* archives and still make it back in time. The more information she could find on her own, the easier this would be.

The field offices of the *Korranberg Chronicle* resided within the House Sivis enclave. While not officially employed by the gnomes' Notaries Guild, the *Chronicle* used the house's scribes and magewrights to maintain their archives.

Soneste's own identification papers gained her admittance within the office, for which she was glad. She could have used Hyran's writ to shorten her wait, but she refrained. The less she waved it around, the less conspicuous her investigation would be.

When her name was called, she approached the front desk. The gnome clerk regarded her from under bushy white brows. His body was aged and lean, but his eyes were fast and sharp.

"What can I help you with, young lady?" he asked.

"I am hoping to peruse the issues that you published in the weeks following the signing of the Thronehold Treaty."

"Specific dates, young lady," the gnome demanded.

Soneste thought about it. The Treaty, which had ended the Last War, had been signed in the autumn of 996, almost two years ago. Hyran had said Charoth's return to Korth was soon after.

"May I see Aryth through Olarune of 996?"

The clerk scowled down at her from his lofty perch. That was forty-eight editions of the *Chronicle* she was asking to see. Even in broadsheet form, that would be a thick sheaf of papers to compile. Soneste knew she could produce Hyran's writ and gain access without question.

Instead, she said, "Please, sir. It would mean a great deal to me right now."

The gnome cleared his throat and shook his head. "Fine," he muttered. Soneste waited in awkward silence as the clerk wrote down her request, signed it, and finally incanted some sort of enchantment to authorize it.

He summoned another employee, a young human, who stared at Soneste with poorly-disguised interest. She was beginning to learn how to differentiate the classes of Karrnathi society. From his sensible clothing and an air of entitled self-respect, this one was clearly middle-class, but he would have been too young for mandatory enlistment in the final years of the war. He was handsome, certainly, but a bit too young for her. She was also beginning to admire the Karrns' contrast of dark eyes with fair skin. She offered him a smile, if only to expedite the process.

"Take the young lady to a reading room," the gnome ordered, handing the boy the authorization papers.

"Your weapon must remain, lady," the younger clerk said, his face turning red. He pointed to her rapier.

Accustomed to the procedure from the *Chronicle* office in Sharn, Soneste complied. She did not volunteer the crysteel dagger still hidden in her boot. After leaving the suggested donation, Soneste was led through a series of corridors lit only by dim cold fire, passing open rooms where historians and other researchers poured over giant tomes. She was brought to a small room of her own, and the boy asked her to wait as he walked awkwardly away.

An oversized open book was propped upright at the center of the room. Its pages were blank. The thick spine was bound to the tabletop by means of a rotating metal hinge, which allowed the reader to angle the contraption as desired. A cylindrical slot at the top of the thick spine was ready to receive. These viewing tomes were an invention of Sivis design, crafted by dragonmarked artificers of the house.

Soon after, another gnome clerk entered the room with a leather kit under one arm. He partially unrolled it upon the table then produced the first of the rune-scribed rods pocketed within.

The gnome held it up before her and pointed to the name and number carved in fine characters along its length. "This is Mol, the first week of Barrakas, 996," he said by way of explanation, then slid the rod into the spine of the viewing tome.

The pages of the opened book immediately flooded with large, luminous words. A moment later, the light faded but the text remained. Soneste was looking upon the edition of the *Chronicle* exactly as it had appeared in print on that day. He unrolled the leather portfolio to reveal the remaining rods. There were a lot to go through.

"Thank you," Soneste said, slipping the gnome a few sovereigns for the inconvenience, which he accepted without a word. He spoke an arcane syllable and the cold fire lamps upon the wall brightened.

When the clerk left her to her research, she immediately set to work. She was aware of the chroniclers checking in on her occasionally, despite their magical safeguards against theft, but she paid them no mind. Her eyes flashed through the large pages quickly, searching for key words that might have some association to Lord Charoth,

When she reached the month of Zarantyr, almost exactly two years past, she found what she was looking for.

Forgehold Disaster Survivor Renounces Own House
Zarantyr 11th, 996 YK

KORTH—Lord Charoth Arkenen d'Cannith, esteemed arcanist and former director of a secret forgehold, formally renounced on Zol all ties to House Cannith. The self-imposed exile stood before barristers of Korth's Justice Ministry, wearing a mask and concealing his body in dark robes. Agents of the Twelve were summoned to bear witness and scrutinize the mysterious claimant with divination magic.

Believed slain along with thirty-two other forgehold personnel in Therendor of 992, Lord Charoth reemerged last Nymm to take possession

of his family's estates. According to the director's testimony, the unethical demands placed upon him by his house superiors between 990 and 992 YK led to the forgehold's destruction.

It was not until the disaster that the existence of the forgehold, a facility sources refer to as the Orphanage, became public knowledge. Lord Charoth, the promising arcanist of the Arkenen family, was presumed dead, along with the forgehold's entire staff.

Only the director's return four years later has suggested otherwise. When asked why he delayed news of his survival, Lord Charoth explained, "I have been in dark and painful places and have tried these last few years to hide this fate. Mine have been the sins of fear and denial. Now that the war has ended, I feel Karrnath can weather such a hard truth, a truth I am ready to admit."

As a consequence of the disaster, Lord Charoth's body allegedly sustained severe damage. Jorasco healers were immediately sent to attend him when his return was announced, but the former director refused them. "It was not mere fire that has scarred me," was all he told the Korranberg Chronicle regarding his condition.

Nor is Lord Charoth willing to disclose the location of the Orphanage. "It is an evil place now," he explained. "The innovations that came from its workshops have been tainted by the unethical demands of my former superiors. I will not afflict any man or woman with the horrors of that ruin, nor subject House Cannith to further embarrassment. Despite the atrocities committed by the house, it suffered a devastating blow along with the whole of Khorvaire on the Day of Mourning. I wish the house renewed prosperity."

Added Lord Charoth, "And I wish them farewell."

Among the thirty-two presumed dead at the Orphanage was Erevyn Korell d'Cannith, chief artificer and minister of the facility. Korell was a student and friend of Aarren d'Cannith before the latter's excoriation and subsequent disappearance in 970 YK.

Agents of House Cannith could not be reached for comment.

Soneste sat back, letting the information sink in. Charoth's fate was dramatic indeed, yet how could so many people die and only one man, the forgehold's own director, conveniently survive? Others must have wondered the same, investigations undertaken. Did they yield dead ends?

This seemed all very interesting, but was this a waste of her time? Did any of this relate to her case? Aside from the ambassador's warforged sentry, what connection could there be between her case and House Cannith?

She felt a surge of disappointment. No mention of Breland or the war. Charoth was a sinister—and certainly fascinating—figure, but this wasn't giving her any indication that she was on the right path.

Soneste committed the article to memory in a manner of seconds then searched through the next few editions. Nearly one month later, a follow-up article appeared within the *Chronicle*, no doubt a result of Charoth's emergence.

House Cannith Admits Forgehold Disaster
Olarune 13th, 996 YK

KORTH—Representatives from the Cannith enclave in Korth released a statement on Zor regarding the destruction of the Orphanage facility in 992. In Zarantyr, the former director of the forgehold, Lord Charoth Arkenen, came forward with news of his survival and his subsequent rebuke of House Cannith.

The statement revealed that the Orphanage was a research facility that focused on the sentient aspects of warforged creation. While most creation forges in the late 980s produced the rank and file units that House Cannith sold to the Five Nations, the Orphanage worked to augment the warforged mind. Even warforged titans, the behemoth constructs that preceded the standard models, were continually assembled and upgraded within the Orphanage.

According to the statement, a conflagration of elemental power burned within the subterranean facility in Therendor of 992, prompting Lord Zorlan d'Cannith, regional viceroy at the time, to dispatch a rescue team to the hidden site. A thorough search of the wreckage concluded that none of the forge personnel could have survived the devastation.

"Had we known of the director's survival, the outcome of this story would be very different," Baron Zorlan d'Cannith told the Chronicle following the statement. "Lord Charoth is a man of singular grace and remarkable vision. The tragedy that befell him and its effect upon his business decisions today are a loss to us all."

When asked for comment, Lord Charoth politely complied. "The Thronehold Treaties have ordered House Cannith to destroy their creation forges, a decree I heartily commend, but had I been present during the peace talks, I would have pushed for the destruction of all existing warforged. They are obsolete in this time of peace and remain only as a reminder of the weapons of war the Five Nations have inflicted upon one another. I am ashamed for my part in their construction and will have nothing to do with them ever again. I have no desire to return to the life that I once knew."

The former director was severely scarred by the mysterious destruction of the Orphanage facility and believed dead for four years. Refusing Jorasco healers to treat him, Lord Charoth said only that the damage he suffered could not be undone.

Lady Irenta d'Jorasco, an administrator of Jorasco's hospital in Korth, explained further. "When we visited his estate, Lord Charoth claimed that his body was scarred by energies from a damaged creation forge. I cannot speak to the destructive properties of such devices. That is not our province. I can, however, confirm that Positive Energy, such as that channeled by the Mark of Healing, can be deadly if not used correctly."

House Cannith's statement did not include the whereabouts of the Orphanage forgehold. Added Baron Zorlan, "We have explained all that we can. The locations of our forgeholds remain classified. This incident changes nothing."

Soneste was unable to find anything else within 996 YK pertaining to Charoth or anything at all mentioning Gamnon ir'Daresh. She wanted to search through the 997 editions, but it would have to wait. She had to meet up with Jotrem or he'd be asking questions. Then she'd have to lie.

Soneste sighed. This was *her* investigation. Why did she have to answer to anyone?

Even so, the 997 editions couldn't be as vital. Even the highly regarded *Korranberg Chronicle* dared not scrutinize any of the dragonmarked houses too much. She committed the second article to memory and called for the gnome clerk.

Interlude

Daylight shone through the window, but the man in the velvet-padded chair remained oblivious. The door to the small room closed again, but he'd made no acknowledgement of his visitor. Instead, the memories that cycled through his mind continued.

Another voice calls out to me now.

"Master Erevyn is not to be disturbed," my assistant responds in my defense.

I set my tools down, resigned to address the matter. I turn to look at the speaker, but I know it is Leonus, my sister's eldest and a good man. I'll not berate him, of course, but he knows better than to interrupt me.

"Sverak, it's all right." I climb down the maintenance ladder as my assistant backs away with a sleight bow. His movements are respectful, as always, but unnecessary. I have come to think of him as a colleague.

My nephew approaches me, wiping soiled hands upon a rag. He looks tired, having worked at the birthing pods since morning.

"What is it?"

He glances nervously at Sverak. "Uncle . . ."

"Speak, Leonus. Please." I am mildly irritated. My work is too delicate for trivialities. What can't wait?

"Uncle, Lord Charoth is returning tomorrow. We just received word from Korth."

I feel apprehension, a small measure of fear inside me. I knew the day would come, of course. The director has been away for many months now. It has seemed the Orphanage had been neglected in favor of the Cyran forgeholds. It had only been a matter of time. He was director, not I. I suppose I expected to be more prepared. That's all.

"Thank you, Leonus. Get back to work. We all have much to do."

My nephew walks away. Sverak stands before me now. I feel the sleight touch of his hand on my arm. He has always been affectionate. Unusually so.

"Master, why do you worry?"

Chapter
Ten

As expected, Jotrem had little to offer from his side of the investigation. He'd been unable to speak with the clothier Vorik ir'Alanso directly, but he'd returned with a gray shirt and black vest for Soneste—the gloomy tones that passed for Karrnathi fashion.

There was suspicion in his eyes when he'd approached her. Of course, the subtle power she'd implanted in his mind had long since worn off. She accepted the clothing with a tense smile.

"We stay together now," Jotrem said without further comment as they walked to the Ebonspire.

"Agreed," she replied, plotting her next method of shaking him.

She recounted her interview with Charoth, omitting only her personal observations about the mysterious lord. She also described in brief what she'd found in the *Korranberg Chronicle*, not telling him that she could recite it perfectly.

"I see no obvious connection between Lord Charoth and the ambassador," Jotrem said, "and no motive on Lord Charoth's part. What has he to gain?"

Soneste had no answer for that—yet.

In the city morgue, Soneste examined the decapitated body of Gamnon ir'Daresh. His wounds were the same as those that had killed his family and servants—twin punctures of a long and strongly-thrust blade. The fact that he'd been thrown from the balcony so high up seemed to her as simple mockery, something to get people talking, but the theft of his head? There had to be more to that.

When she'd finished her exam, the undertaker touched an ice cold hand to hers. "This tragedy needn't go unavenged, Miss Otänsin," he said, his voice compassionate despite their grisly surroundings. "With your permission, we *can* speak with his retainers and ask them to describe precisely what happened to them."

Necropolis of the Valiant. The Korth morgue. This undertaker worked for the Ministry of the Dead. He, or one of his associates, could employ magic to force one the Brelish corpses to answer specific questions placed to it. Soneste considered it.

Thuranne didn't *have* to know if she consented to this. If the information the spell yielded was accurate, she could learn a lot about the massacre.

Even Jotrem looked expectantly at her.

It wouldn't be the ambassador's family she was talking to, only their mortal shells. What was the harm? She thought of the two dead White Lions, and how little their testimony had provided. Then she thought of how far she might fall if Lady ir'Daresh's family heard about the spell.

"Thank you," she said quietly, "but not at this time."

Together Soneste and Jotrem went to the Ebonspire and searched the ambassador's apartments. Workers from the Necropolis waited in the lobby, while a uniformed wizard from the Ministry of the Dead lingered nearby, awaiting Soneste's approval for removal of the bodies. The wizard had renewed the magic that had seized the ambassador's chambers with supernatural cold, but he had explained that he would allow it to fade when they were finished.

Jotrem had not been permitted to inspect the crime scene

himself until now, by dictate of the Civic Minister and his correspondence with the King's Citadel of Breland. The Karrn was a veteran of the Last War, had likely seen bloodshed Soneste couldn't imagine, but the sight of the slaughter in the ambassador's chambers subdued him.

As the older inquisitive took the opportunity to examine the scene, Soneste stood at the balcony again, this time looking out at the city in the grey cast of daylight. She looked across the gap between the Ebonspire and the adjacent tenement building—the killer's point of access. Tallis had not flown by magic, according to Sergeant Bratta's testimony. But he *had* jumped somehow.

Anyone with sufficient gold could buy potions enough to possess the abilities this killer had: great strength and speed, the ability to leap amazing distances and land safely. Soneste thought of the victims' wounds. Magic could seldom account for such skill and precision with a blade. Was Tallis that efficient?

Soneste walked back inside. Jotrem emerged from the bedroom where the ambassador's family had died, his face paler than usual.

"Please finish here," Soneste said to him quietly. "I'm going to visit the adjacent tower. I know you've been there, but I need to see it for myself."

Jotrem did not put up a fight. She told the Ministry wizard that when the older inquisitive was finished, the bodies could be moved. It was time to give them peace.

❧ ❧ ❧ ❧ ❧ ❧ ❧

Soneste stared up at ir'Daresh's suite from the adjacent roof.

In her hands she held a curious weapon. She'd found it in a shadowed corner of one of the tower's stairwells. It resembled a warhammer, if slightly smaller, with a head of heavy steel. At the other end of the haft, facing in the opposite direction of the hammer's blunted side, was a long and curving piece of metal more akin to a military pick. The silvery head gleamed as if newly shined.

The hooked hammer, it was called, a weapon of gnomish design.

Usually they were crafted for the foot soldiers of Zilargo, but this one was sized for a human. A special commission—Tallis's?

There wasn't a trace of blood on the sharp, curving tip of the pick's head—only a dried, thin substance which might have been alchemical in nature. Such a weapon could probably have damaged the warforged on the balcony.

Why did you leave this behind? she asked silently.

❀ ❀ ❀ ◉ ❀ ❀ ❀

Two levels beneath the Justice Ministry was a cell block where choice suspects were questioned before more permanent incarceration in one of Korth's prisons. Within, two White Lions escorted Soneste and Jotrem into a chamber bisected by a wall of thick, magewrought iron bars.

Within the cell, a warforged paced with anxious steps that reverberated loudly across the chamber. Upright and active now, he looked even larger and more imposing than he had before, inert on a balcony floor. Soneste cursed softly as she noted that most of the living construct's damage remained and that blood still crusted his composite plating. The Karrns had only repaired him just enough to awaken him. Despite his obvious agitation, the warforged looked worn down.

"I'm sorry you were not fully restored," Soneste said as she walked up to the bars. "My name is Soneste Otänsin. I am here on behalf of the King's Citadel to investigate the crime." She displayed her papers but the smoldering blue crystal spheres that served as the warforged's eyes paid them no mind. He advanced to the edge of the cage.

"Why am I a prisoner?" he demanded, confusion evident even through his cavernous voice. "Where is Master ir'Daresh? Vestra and Renet? They are in danger!" The warforged slammed the buckler shield of his arm against the bars in frustration.

The dissonant ringing hurt Soneste's ears. Jotrem looked bored and unsurprised.

111

Soneste frowned. Where is Master—?

"Unholy Six!" she cursed, half turning to Jotrem and the White Lions. "He hasn't even been told?"

The older inquisitive shrugged.

The warforged quieted then, clutching the bars with each hand. "Woman," he said in a hollow, pleading tone. His body was perfectly still now. "What is there to *be* told? Whose blood is this?" He gestured one three-fingered hand at the brown stains that still crusted his body.

"I . . ." Soneste looked to the leather folder in her hand, stalling. The report had listed the warforged as a piece of Brelish property, belonging to Gamnon ir'Daresh. To most Karrns, warforged were weapons of war, nothing more. It shouldn't surprise her that he'd not been informed.

She looked up into the construct's eyes. Emotion could not be read in the cold metal of its standard, Cannith-issued faceplate, but from his voice she knew there was expectation. Worry. If the warforged was somehow involved in the murder, she would expect him to be calmer or feigning resignation. If this one had been disabled *before* the slaughter took place, there *should* be only confusion.

"What is your name?"

"Aegis," he answered. "Please, tell me."

"Aegis, I am sorry that I must be the one to relay such . . . tragic news." She imagined the workroom the warforged had probably awakened in an hour or so before, a Cannith artificer poised over him, armed soldiers standing nearby just in case. "Your master has been murdered. I am here to find his killer."

Aegis said nothing at first. Had he been a man, he might have gripped the bars with white knuckles, screamed with grief and rage. Instead he turned away from her and walked back to the center of the cell with great plodding steps. He'd been the ir'Daresh bodyguard. Protecting them had been his chosen duty, his vocation, and very likely his identity. She'd seen it before— warforged as devoted to their human commanders and comrades as if they were blood. Respect born from shared experiences, not instilled in them by the forges of House Cannith.

"The children?" Aegis asked. "Lady Maril?"

Soneste shut her eyes. This was *not* part of her job. She was an inquisitive, the one called in to follow the trail of killers, find kidnapped victims, reveal clues and treachery. She was not equipped to console mourners.

Damn them. Damn Tallis or whoever did this.

"I am sorry," she said, using anger to steel herself. "Aegis, I am here to find justice for the ir'Daresh family. I am here to avenge them, and I need your help, to know what you know."

The construct turned sharply. "The half-elf intruder! He was masked."

Tallis was a half-elf? She looked at Jotrem, who nodded.

"Half-elf, was it?" Jotrem repeated, a proud set to his jaw. "The warforged confirms what Sergeant Bratta and I have already told you, Miss Otänsin. Tallis *was* there. He is either the killer or the killer's accomplice. You cannot doubt that."

Soneste ignored him, distracted by this new information. She looked to the construct, whose attention was fully upon her. "Yes, I need to know more about him and about your master. I need to know everything you can tell me."

Aegis advanced again on the bars. "I have failed in my duty!" he said. "Is this why I am caged?"

Soneste looked to the White Lions at the door. "This warforged is to be released from custody. Ask the Civic Minister, if you must, but I will see it done!" She slipped the writ from its folder and held it before them. The two guards looked to Jotrem, uncertain.

"Miss Otänsin," the older inquisitive said. "The construct remains a suspect. It is not—"

"I will take responsibility for him, and he will bear no weapons." Soneste narrowed her eyes. "Will you not 'cut these ministerial webs' and demonstrate your usefulness?"

Jotrem said nothing, but he nodded to the White Lions.

Soneste turned to face the warforged again, cognizant of the

Karrns watching her. "Aegis, we are in a foreign land, you and I. Not all facts are known to me yet, and the citizens of Karrnath do not see you as your master did, nor as I *do*. If you are released, you must go where I say and do what I ask."

"I will," Aegis answered with clear fervor.

"The warforged's loyalties are uncertain," Jotrem said coldly. "It is dangerous."

Aegis tapped his forehead, where a mystic sigil was engraved in the metal. All warforged possessed such symbols, or ghulra. Each one unique, the ghulra were a signature of their creation. "I was made to fight for Breland." The warforged's tone was solemn. "But after the war, I *chose* to serve Ambassador Gamnon ir'Daresh and his family. That is my loyalty."

Soneste nodded. "I will find your master's killer."

"Then I will serve *you* now, Mistress. I failed my master, Lady Maril, Rennet. Vestra. I will help you bring them justice in whatever way I can, but I am a warrior, not an investigator. I will guard your life and do as you request."

"You will have that chance," Soneste said, "but first I need you to tell me everything that you remember. Tell me about this masked man."

Aegis pointed one of his thick fingers through bars at the hooked hammer she'd tied to her haversack. "That is the weapon he used against me."

Soneste didn't need to look to know Jotrem was smirking.

Chapter
ELEVEN

With the pretense of needing something from her room, Soneste returned to the Seventh Watch. She asked Aegis to accompany her while Jotrem waited in the lobby, then went up to her room, Tallis's weapon in her hands.

"Please bear with me, Aegis," she said. "I am not merely biding time."

She calmed her mind, sat upon the floor, and laid her hands over the cold metal of the hooked hammer. The weapon—her one solid lead—had a story to tell, and she would do her utmost to learn it. Veshtalan had once attempted to teach her the ability to read the psychic impressions he claimed all people left on the things they touched. "If someone possessed an object long enough," the kalashtar had said, "deep imprints would form, strong enough to be analyzed by a properly focused mind. Like yours, Soneste."

"Give me something that has meaning to you—for a moment only," Veshtalan had said. As always, the kalashtar's voice was soft, patient but demanding.

Soneste had complied, slipping off the carved onyx talisman

she wore around her neck. Veshtalan had grasped the smooth, flat stone, tracing the owl-shaped object with delicate fingers then closed his eyes. A soft hum had surrounded them both and the onyx talisman appeared to glisten in his hand. After several long minutes of concentration, the handsome kalashtar had opened his eyes and smiled back at her.

"This stone was given to you by a human—your father?—when he was forty-one, a gift for his adolescent daughter, in apology for an event he'd been unable to attend."

"Boldrei's Feast," Soneste had said quietly.

The kalashtar continued. "He'd purchased it from a shifter woman somewhere on his tour of duty. She was fifty-nine, a mother devoted to her family and willing to part with the semiprecious stone to feed her children in hard times. The shifter, in turn, had found the amulet in the pocket of a dead young human, not yet nineteen winters old. That boy's father had given it to him only two days before on the day the boy had manifested the Mark of Making . . ."

Soneste had been impressed by the kalashtar's abilities, but she was skeptical by nature and knew he might have fabricated most of the information. Her father *had* given her the onyx carving when his duties in the field prevented him coming home for Boldrei's Feast that year. There was no way Veshtalan could have known that without the use of his powers, but try as she might, she'd been unable to produce the same effect with other objects—though she'd never stopped trying. Her mentor had insisted that doubt, and a lack of desire to succeed, had failed her.

As Soneste sat in perfect silence, she grasped Tallis's weapon, closed her eyes, and tried her utmost to *see* it with her mind. Several minutes of mental exertion followed, giving her a headache instead of psychic insight. She maintained her focus, willing to learn more about the man who'd carried this very metal in his grasp. She wanted, *needed,* to know more! Just when she could hold her focus no longer, she had a brief moment's image—not visual, not sensory at all, but somehow it felt more like a memory that wasn't her own. She could envision the cold metal of the hammer pass from one pair of hands to another. Small, calloused hands—a gnome's—passing the weapon over to larger, gnarled hands—a dwarf's. Then again, a new hand grasping the hammer—long-fingered, delicate but strong. A half-elf's—

Soneste stopped, her body drenched in sweat from her efforts. She washed up and returned to Jotrem again. Aegis had spoken not a word during this time.

"The Bluefist," Jotrem had answered when she'd asked him where one might purchase dwarf-made weaponry in the city. "It set up shop immediately after the dwarf-lords of Mror declared their independence. They specialize in advanced arms, but they do not supply in bulk like many of the dwarf merchants. Even the Conqueror's Host carries Bluefist blades. But hooked hammers are made by gnomes."

Soneste had shrugged. "Trust me. We need to go there."

❈ ❈ ❈ ◉ ❈ ❈ ❈

The Bluefist of Mror was little more than a block of stone with residential flats stacked above it. The only ornamentation was its entrance, a threshold stylized to resemble a miniature dwarfgate of the Mror Holds. Above it, an iron plaque displayed a blue fisted gauntlet against a gray mountain. Just beneath, a Cannith seal was carved into a wooden placard and painted black, denoting the smithy as licensed by the dragonmarked house. After Soneste had read the old *Chronicle* articles, House Cannith, an omnipresent fixture of Khorvairian society, seemed more sinister.

They took the steps to the heavy door of the armory, Jotrem leading the way. The older inquisitive carried the hooked hammer. Soneste glanced at it, imagining the invisible impressions locked away like treasures inside it. What else might she learn with that power? It was one worth mastering.

She paused to see if anyone objected to the presence of Aegis, who followed several paces behind her. The people of Korth didn't seem as hostile to him as some of the outspoken protestors in

Sharn. In Korth, they didn't seem to care about him one way or the other. The warforged was just a tool.

One dwarf stood behind the counter, while another tended the weapons arrayed on the walls. Soneste saw maces, swords, pole-arms, and more exotic arms—all gleamed as though polished and newly forged. Some of them possessed a faint shimmer, suggestive of magical properties. There was a single door behind the counter. Soneste could hear the faint ring of the forge beyond.

"Stay at the door," she whispered to Aegis, who complied.

She needed to talk to the dwarves, but there was one customer in front of her, a man wearing a bulky, hooded cloak with a missing arm. He was hardly the only maimed veteran Soneste had seen in this city—or back home. A naked broadsword lay on the counter between dwarf and customer.

Jotrem moved forward to begin interrogating the dwarf, but Soneste held him back. "We can wait," she said, irritated that the older inquisitive cared little for discretion.

"The Lions have already been through here, sir," answered the dwarf, responding to a question she hadn't heard. "Twice. Now, tell me more about your son."

"He's no Rekkenmark cadet," the man grumbled bitterly. "Not so good with an honest blade." His voice was raspy with age, yet curiously strong.

"Something simpler than this would be best." He tapped the handle of the sword dismissively with his only hand. Soneste noted the man's palm was wrapped in loose bandages. The fingers were exposed, lacking the wrinkles she'd expect to see on an older man.

The dwarf waited expectantly for his customer to go on, but the old man paused. He turned slightly, peering beyond his hood as though realizing others waited behind him. His steely eyes met hers with a casual analysis, then darted to the hooked hammer in Jotrem's hand and away again in a flash.

The old man—whom she was certain was not old at all—turned back to the dwarf without a hint of duress. Soneste exchanged glances with Jotrem. Neither of them, trained inquisitives, had missed the man's look. He nodded back and placed his hand upon the hilt of his sword.

"Tallis!" he said, an edge of triumph in his voice.

The hooded man spun in place and threw the sword he'd been discussing with the dwarf out in the air. It spun wildly at Jotrem, who took a step back and ducked as low as he was able to avoid the blade. The hooked hammer dropped to the floor as Soneste drew out her rapier.

As Jotrem fumbled to regain his footing, the hooded man threw a small bag at the other Karrn. The shapeless object struck Jotrem at the waist, its surface rupturing into a mass of brown goo.

"Good to see you again, Jotrem!" The suspect's hood had fallen away, and a shock of black hair spilled out. His face was far younger than his posture had suggested. In addition, a second arm had appeared from beneath his bulky cloak.

Everyone in the room exploded into motion.

The shopkeepers produced weapons with astonishing speed, though from their shocked, angry expressions it was unclear whom they would favor in this struggle. Jotrem was unable to draw his sword, his arm held fast beneath the swiftly hardened glob that had swallowed his hand, hilt, and belt. Tallis's eyes swept the room, searching for an escape plan. Soneste had expected him to fight—was his history not one of constant violence?—so she advanced with her sword leveled at him.

"Surrender peacefully, Tal—"

"Murderer!" another voice shouted, and Soneste felt herself being pushed aside as Aegis barreled past her. He was still unarmed, but he braced the buckler of his arm like a weapon.

"Keeper!" Tallis swore then rolled himself backwards over the dwarves' low counter. He landed lightly on his feet and stopped short before the stout shopkeeper who glared at him with a glowing mace in hand.

"Not *here*, half-elf," the dwarf warned.

"I'll settle up later!" Tallis said as he dodged past the dwarf just as Aegis reached the counter. Bolstered by his rage, the warforged crashed into the sturdy wood and reached in vain for his retreating quarry. Aegis's arm shot out, preventing his massive, metal body from pitching over the counter entirely. The warforged was nowhere near as nimble as the Karrn.

Tallis jerked open the door and ran through.

The other dwarf approached Soneste and Jotrem with a hand axe gripped tightly in one fist. "What's going on here?"

Soneste pointed to the open door and looked to the dwarf. "We're with the Justice Ministry!" she said. "Is there another way out through there?"

"Yeah," the mace-wielding dwarf spat, glaring at the door through which Tallis had retreated.

She turned to Jotrem, who struggled angrily to free himself from the alchemical glue. It was a tanglefoot bag Tallis had used against him, an invention usually used to stop an opponent from running. Tallis had come prepared to elude pursuers.

"Jotrem, make sure he doesn't double back." The older inquisitive looked incredulous at her words, but he was in no position to pursue the suspect. Besides, he'd only slow her down.

Soneste vaulted the counter herself and paused at the door Tallis had taken. "Aegis, go out the front and follow around. Take him alive!"

Without another word, Soneste dashed through the door in pursuit.

❧ ❧ ❧ ❧ ❧ ❧ ❧

Tallis plucked the dart-size crossbow bolt from his shoulder, cursing as the pain revisited. Drazen had been right. He *did* need a new disguise, something to fool anyone who knew his face. For the first time since he'd known her, Tallis couldn't wait to see the Midwife again. He'd appreciated her services before but had never needed them for *himself.* Until now.

Tallis had made his way through the back of the Bluefist,

cursing all dwarves for their cynical nature. Every weapon in the back of the armory had been under lock and key, and he didn't have time to fish around for any untended tools. He'd had to exit into the alley unarmed.

Two blocks away, the woman had nearly caught up to him. He'd led her in circles, always just out of sight. She'd expect him to disappear into the sewers or leave the district, but that wasn't his way. After doubling back once, she'd grown wise to his strategy. When they'd faced each other across one street, he hadn't expected her to take aim with a miniature crossbow.

Those little bolts hurt.

Who *was* this woman traipsing around with that old wolf, Jotrem? Not a Karrn, by the sky blue of her coat or her flaxen hair, nor any freelancing inquisitive he'd seen in Korth before. Despite the irritation she presented, he wasn't ready to confront her yet.

If I don't know you, we don't deal, he thought. It was a rule. Not negotiable.

Tallis reached a small courtyard, an intersection between the tall, utilitarian structures of the Commerce Ward. He allowed himself to pause. No sign of her yet. He might have lost her this time.

When he'd gained the last roof, she'd started to climb as well. Even the White Lions seldom gave chase when Tallis rose above street level. It was usually a tried and true way to scrap the cats.

Tucking the bolt into a pocket of his jacket for later examination, he considered the three narrow alleys before him. To the left, he saw the market throngs of the main avenue. In thick crowds he could lose her, but she'd stirred up the Lions during their chase and they would be looking for him there. In front of him, the street would lead directly to the House Medani enclave—even less desirable right now.

To his right—

A flicker of movement directly above him had Tallis diving into the right-hand alley. He looked over his shoulder and saw the young woman drop to the ground like a cat from high above, landing with only the sleight scuffle of her boots and one palm to the cobbles. In her other glove was her hand crossbow, loaded again.

"Blunted!" he said, then rose and started away down the dead-end alley.

❋ ❋ ❋ ❋ ❋ ❋ ❋

Soneste was accustomed to Sharn's spires rising high overhead and its dizzying precipices yawning before her, yet somehow Korth's towers felt more oppressive, especially in the backstreets. Their sheer walls were pressed closer together as if the city was one vast prison complex, with only a network of narrow courtyards serving as streets. Her drop from the third story had been smooth, and the hum of another of her powers faded away.

Soneste kept her eyes on her quarry, but from her peripheral vision she saw there were a couple of citizens nearby. "Call the White Lions," she bade as she gestured to one with her free hand, "There's a reward. Go now!" The other hand she raised, pointing her crossbow at Tallis.

Tallis walked backwards, facing her. She'd cornered him in an alley that extended half a block before giving way to an open sky—the edge of the Commerce Ward, which dropped in a sheer cliff forty feet above the streets of the Community Ward.

Closer to him now, Tallis appeared younger than she'd taken him for. The haughty, almond-shaped eyes of an elf were offset by a jocular mouth and longish, sable-black hair. His ears tapered only slightly. Even accounting for his elven blood, he was a good deal younger than Jotrem. They could not have been classmates. The older inquisitive might have been Tallis's superior officer.

Even as she studied him, he offered a toothy smile like a street urchin with a piece of stolen fruit. Soneste reminded herself that he'd been there at ir'Daresh's suite. He might have been party to the murder of the ambassador, his wife, and their two children. The Justice Ministry's records had listed several other killings over the course of his criminal career. Mostly other criminals, suspect politicians, and known Cultists of the Blood. What *was* he after in all this?

Tallis was clad in black like many Karrns, but his attire was tailored like a uniform, the sign of a professional man of action who wanted no restriction to his movement. He carried no obvious weapons, but two metal rods hung from his belt, as though they were death-dealing wands and he an accomplished war-mage. But by all reports, Tallis was no spellcaster. Soneste did note a single ring on his left hand—a silvery band with a stylized dragon's head on it. He didn't wear a Rekkenmark ring.

"Tallis," she began, "in the name of King Kaius III of Karrnath—"

"So what brings a fawn-eyed girl like you into Khorvaire's fairest kingdom this lovely day?" Tallis gestured at the leaden sky.

Soneste clenched her teeth for a moment. "—*and* King Boranel of Breland, surrender to the justice afforded you."

Tallis raised his eyebrows. "You came from *Breland?* Really? Say, do they still serve those Aundairian pastries on the rail dining carts? Glorious taste, but they run amuck in the Cogs, if you know what I mean."

Tallis continued his backward advance, but Soneste kept pace. She noted with satisfaction that the only door that led to the alley—the only means by which he could try another escape—was blocked up by a heavy stack of rain-soaked crates. A small, battered cart lay discarded near the alley's far end, one wheel propped against the stone wall.

"Not two days ago I walked the skybridges of Sharn," she answered with a thin smile. "Breland sends more than some noname sleuth to bring political murderers to justice."

Tallis smirked, but she could see the implications reach into his eyes. "I didn't kill that man," he said, more seriously now, "or his family."

"If you're telling the truth, Tallis, then why did you run from me?"

"I don't *know* you," he answered with a boyish grin. "A pretty girl starts to chase me with a weapon. Thrilled as I am by that, I prefer a more formal courtship."

Soneste rolled her eyes. Did he expect this to buy him time?

"You know as well as I do that they just want someone to blame," he continued. "I am apparently the only suspect? The Justice Ministry and your king are all doing an excellent job, miss."

"If you're innocent of this crime," she offered, throwing his sarcasm back at him, "perhaps you'd like to assist me in finding the real killer?"

Tallis let out a resigned sigh. "I must decline, sadly." He started to move past the propped cart, mere steps away from the bluff's edge.

Without taking her eyes away off him, Soneste drew the sleeve of her coat across the razor tip of the loaded crossbow bolt. The sealed edge of the flat pouch sewed there tore open, freeing its contents. A thin, cobalt-colored paste now slicked the steel tip.

Tallis froze two steps from the edge. "Poison?" He was incredulous, or he feigned it well.

"Blue whinnis," she said. "Just a sting, and you'll sleep for hours."

Tallis licked his lips, his hands held up. "You must *really* like me."

Less than ten feet from him, Soneste knew she couldn't miss, but his proximity to the edge made her nervous. With her free hand, she swept a stray lock of hair back from her eyes, raising her crossbow for better aim.

"Far enough!" she shouted. Hadn't this same man scaled the Ebonspire?

"Sorry," he answered with a shrug, stepping back again—

—and dropped soundlessly over the cliff's edge, falling out of sight.

Soneste cursed, lunging forward and dropping her crossbow to reach for him with two hands. As she reached the edge, she saw he hadn't fallen far at all. He clung with both hands to a pair of steel bars protruding conveniently near the cliff's edge.

No, not merely convenient. The two metal rods he'd worn at his belt hung in the empty air by some invisible magic, and as his body swung beneath them, they didn't quiver at all.

On her knees, Soneste stared down at him. *"That* was your cunning escape?"

Though exerted from the maneuver, he winked back at her. She flushed, then turned away to retrieve her hand crossbow. With speed and agility that belied his slender frame, Tallis vaulted upward and reached his feet to the edge. As he did, the floating rods released and locked again, providing him the means to leverage his body up and over the edge.

Soneste picked her crossbow up and started to turn, but Tallis was already there. A kick to her hand sent the weapon clattering against the wall. Despite the pain in her wrist, she began to draw out her rapier. Tallis grasped the blade halfway from its sheath, arresting the attempt.

"Enough!" he grunted, lifting her light frame and slamming her back hard against the wall. The force of the blow expelled the air from her lungs, and she was unable to stop him as he pressed one of the rods into her stomach.

The rod locked again firmly in place, pinning her against the stone. Dodging her kicks, he grasped one ankle and placed the other rod just beneath her foot. It held there, allowing her weight to settle on it. The pressure against her stomach subsided sleightly. Tallis drew a length of black cord from his left sleeve and coiled it fast around her wrists, binding them together.

Soneste's felt her face burn, ashamed to be so swiftly subdued. "The law will not be forgiving," she said, struggling for air. "You are admitting your guilt."

"My guilt?" Tallis shook his head, then glared up at her. His face was flushed from the struggle. "Look, Miss Not Some No-Name Sleuth from Sharn, if you'd taken the rail like most folks, you might have had the time to read up on Karrnathi justice. I was guilty the moment my name made Hyran's list as a suspect. The first poor fool you bring in will get the sword. Then everything will quiet down until the real killer kills again. Hyran means well, but politics demand retribution. *Not* justice."

Soneste stared back into his silver-gray eyes but wriggled her body slowly in an attempt to extricate herself. Tallis snapped her rapier free from its sheath then lifted the tip of the blade to her neck. "What is your name?" he asked again.

Her heart thundered inside her, but Soneste had been in situations more perilous. She glanced down the alley and saw a few curious citizens looking on from a distance.

"The White . . . Lions!" she dared to call out, her voice raw. Soneste prodded the enchanted rod at her stomach in an attempt to disengage it, a difficult feat with her hands tightly lashed.

Tallis sighed again and angled the rapier's tip just behind her neck. She winced as the tip grated against the stone. At the same time she felt the ribbon binding her hair fall away. With his hand, Tallis pulled the strip of blue linen away and held it before her eyes. "Call out again and I will stuff your mouth with your own pretty bow."

"You won't," she said.

"Fine."

Tallis turned and tossed her rapier over the bluff's edge. She heard it skitter against the cliff face before landing somewhere far below. That was expensive magewrought steel!

"Dagger take you!" she oathed.

"Your name?" Tallis asked again as he picked up her hand crossbow. The bolt had not dislodged.

Soneste shut her eyes and composed her body, inhaling slowly. If Tallis was going to kill her, he would have done so already.

In her mind, she pictured herself alone in a vast, empty chamber. Her mental counterpart sang a single, resonant note which rippled outward and formed a ghostly net in her hands. She cast it out in a circle around her, snaring errant emotions within its reach.

"If you didn't murder ir'Daresh," Soneste asked calmly, opening her eyes and staring down at Tallis, "then who is framing you? Why were you at the Ebonspire?"

With a mere thought, Soneste drew the mental net back

within her. She *saw* exasperation, doubt, and fear flow out from Tallis, invisible to those without the psychic capacity to perceive it. She heard her mental song fading away, the lingering display of her power. Tallis glanced down the alley as though he, too, had heard the unearthly sound. Her fingers found a minute button at one end of the rod.

"I don't know," he finally answered with a tired voice. With a click he withdrew the small bolt from the hand crossbow. He examined its tip, still glazed with the blue toxin. "Yet."

Soneste pressed the button and the metal rod dropped easily into her hand. She stepped to the ground to fight her way free, but Tallis immediately kicked her foot out from under her. Instead of falling, she fell into his grasp. With his arms around her body, he swept her to the ground. In the scuffle, she felt a sharp stab of pain at her wrist like the bite of an insect.

The broken cobbles of Korth's back streets were not gentle beneath her.

"I didn't kill Gamnon," Tallis said quietly, inches from her face. "Sleep soundly, Breland's lovely, nameless sleuth. And please don't follow me again."

Almost immediately, all stimuli began to recede. Sound was muted and the gray clouds grew darker still. The only things that remained focused in her field of vision were Tallis's eyes, resembling quicksilver so close to her own.

"Don't . . . do this . . ." she whispered, and started to wonder if the words were her own. Her limbs didn't respond to her at all. "Just tell me . . . what . . ."

She saw Tallis's shape moving away. A darker shape was rising over her—the discarded cart, one wheel spinning uselessly as the Karrn raised its bulk over her. All light had disappeared, and even the sudden scent of waterlogged wood was fading away from her.

Soneste felt the shame of failure as she succumbed to the poison. The last thing she could sense, in the confines of her own drowsing mind, was the raw frustration she'd seen leaking from Tallis like burning tears.

Chapter
Twelve

Soneste woke with a start sometime later. The White Lions had found her curled up beneath the cart Tallis had placed over her body. By the time she'd opened her eyes, Jotrem had come upon the scene and was standing over her with an unreadable look on his rigid face. Aegis stood behind him, flanked by a pair of White Lions who watched him closely.

Face flushed, Soneste refused assistance and climbed to her feet. Not only had Tallis tossed away her rapier, but she was enraged to learn that he'd taken her crysteel dagger. Though Jotrem waited for her in silence, she was too overcome with fury and shame to speak.

It was Aegis who eventually broke the silence.

"They detained me, Mistress," the warforged said with an emphatic gesture at the White Lions. "I could not assist you."

Soneste gave the guards a scathing look but simply didn't have the energy to berate them. The blue whinnis had been thorough. Even now she wanted to search again for Tallis, but her body had had enough. The poison's effects would melt away soon, but the day had already been a long one.

She'd been so close!

She recalled Tallis's frustration, sorrow, regret, rage. She was certain Tallis was not the killer, had not intended the death of the ir'Daresh family at all. But she was also certain that he knew more—much more—about the situation. Finding him again was imperative. It would not be easy, given that he knew she'd be looking for him now.

"It wouldn't have mattered, Aegis," she said tiredly. "He was difficult to catch, even for me."

Jotrem spoke up at last. "His flight is further evidence against him."

Soneste looked at him, incredulous. "Are you an idiot, Karrn?" Her weariness had also robbed her of inhibition. "The Ministry wants him—*you* want him dead for somehow wounding your pride and Host knows what else. Tallis *does* know something about this, yes, but he's not the assassin. What was it you told me? Oh yes." Soneste spoke with a stiff, Karrnathi accent. " 'I doubt he would hesitate to kill *you*, Miss Otänsin.' Well, I'm still alive."

Aegis slammed his fist into his arm-buckler, an obvious expression of impatience. "Mistress, this half-elf, this Tallis. I fought with him and he defeated me. If he is not responsible for the murder, he will know who is. We *must* find him."

Soneste nodded, too flustered for more words.

❋ ❋ ❋ ❋ ❋ ❋ ❋

She suspected she wouldn't find Tallis again soon—he *knew* she was looking for him now—so finding his residence was Soneste's next step. It had been only a matter of speculation and inevitable deduction. He was a customer of the Bluefist of Mror, obviously drawn to the place with its ready arsenal of unusual weapons. The dwarves of the Mror Holds were famous for their interest in commerce and the gold it could bring them. They did not question their clients as long as those clients took the effort to conceal their criminal associations.

Soneste searched the levels above the Bluefist for evidence of Tallis's presence. Jotrem followed closely, allowing her to take the lead.

To avoid upsetting any of the building's tenants, she'd ordered Aegis to remain outside with the White Lions. Apparently an *untended* warforged drew a lot of attention in this land. She'd glimpsed a few since arriving in the city, but all of them appeared to be laborers and bodyguards, usually under the watchful eyes of their employers.

Soneste moved in silence and observed every hall and stairwell, putting herself in the mind of a military man gone rogue who did not want to be found by legitimate authorities. She suspected Tallis's skill wasn't in clinging to the shadows like the thieves of Sharn. Instead, he blended in with the crowd. He was just one Karrn among thousands and did a good job seeming nothing more. Until today, he'd evaded Korth's local inquisitives and the Justice Ministry.

In her experience, men and women who did not want to be found were creative about their place of residence. Soneste knew what to look for and wasn't disappointed in either Tallis or herself.

Her mind was exhausted of its extrasensory power, so she relied on instinct alone. A few choice questions to the building's occupants and a thorough search of its halls yielded a room on the third floor that matched her criteria: remote, neighbors to blend in among, and close enough to ground level to effect a quick escape.

At the second to last door of this wing, she paused and looked closer. Jotrem looked on thoughtfully, traced a finger along the faceplate of the lock, then walked past her and stopped to look at the last door.

"It's not that one," he said.

"I think it is."

"That door is trapped. It's a decoy. Leave it."

Soneste examined the lock again, noting trace amounts of fine black powder. She dabbed at it with two fingers then rubbed them together. A revolting smell rose up from the substance. Some sort of smokestick variation? If the lock was picked and the doorknob turned, more of this alchemical powder would foul the air and probably be a warning to someone nearby. Someone . . . next door?

She looked down to where Jotrem examined the final door. He'd produced a set of lockpicks and was working at the lock.

Not bad, old man, she thought silently. How did I miss this? Soneste was still dead tired. With a sigh, she climbed to her feet and joined him. A minute later, Jotrem had picked the lock and pushed it open with one of the tension wrenches from his set.

Tallis's apartment was clean and sparsely furnished, maintained as if expecting a raid. There were no obvious weapons in sight, but she soon found a thin dagger hidden on the underside of an ordinary desk near the wall. All signs suggested that Tallis did not actually spend much time here. It was a place to sleep for him, little more, a transient space in which to wait before moving to the next.

Was this any way to live?

"Evidently, Tallis is a petty thief as well." Jotrem extracted a small velvet bag from the hollowed leg of the apartment's only chair.

He upended the bag onto Tallis's only desk and separated the objects with his wrench then left them for her to examine. Soneste felt uneasy as she looked upon them: a slender necklace on a delicate silver chain, a bejeweled bracelet, and a pair of gem-studded earrings. All women's jewelry, seeming of considerable value—and clearly none of it Tallis's.

Soneste felt the gentle pressure of the serpentine armband against her skin, hidden beneath her sleeve. She'd acquired it during the Blackfeather case, when she'd found the personal effects of the killer's victims. Their families had long since forgotten about such valuables, hadn't bothered to account for them all when Soneste went public with her findings. What they didn't miss, she'd kept as a personal reward.

Considering the appearance of Tallis's residence, Soneste assumed the Karrn didn't use such jewelry to live well. It was probably currency for his trade, a means to fund his vigilante lifestyle.

But Soneste? She'd held onto valuables that weren't hers when the opportunity arose—when she felt she deserved it. Inquisitive work had never paid well, so she'd supplemented her low income with such acquisitions. She made an active effort to get out and take part in Sharn's extravagant night life. She could walk the streets and skybridges openly, go wherever she pleased, do whatever she wanted to do. She worked for Thuranne's agency during the day, but at night she was a socialite reaching above her station. On more than one occasion, she'd even gone with friends to Silvermist, a dream parlor in Lower Dura.

Soneste tried to shake away the guilty thoughts. So what if some disreputable people also frequented the same places? Soneste certainly wasn't a criminal—not like Tallis. She was an upstanding citizen of Sharn, a tax-paying subject of King Boranel. She refused bribes, paid for her necessities by herself, and rented her own apartment. Tallis was a vagabond, a thief, and a killer in *some* capacity.

She was an agent of the law. She was far above the lowlifes with which she often had to consort.

Something caught her eye, then: a rectangle of paper tacked to the wall in one shadowed corner near the bed. Grateful for something else to distract her thoughts, Soneste left the jewelry behind. She walked over and peeled the paper loose, carrying it into the fading daylight at the window.

It was a clipping, years old, but from the cracks and rough texture of the paper she knew it was from the *Korth Sentinel*. Soneste flashed through it, gleaning the content quickly. It told of a skirmish along Scions Sound, wherein Karrnath had lost an entire infantry platoon along the rocky shore when an Aundairian company had flushed them from hiding.

"I remember that," Jotrem said, behind her. "They were outnumbered three-to-one. Twenty-six captured and systematically executed. A Karrnathi platoon discovered them and chased them off before the Aundairians could burn the bodies."

"Were you one of—?"

"No. I was still a cadet at the time, reading the chronicles along with everyone else." Prompted by the clipping, Jotrem started another round of searching. "The war was more than some distant threat here. It was a way of life, even for those who did not fight. Many Karrns keep articles such as these, remnants of the war. News of loved ones, accounts of battles. I have some of my own."

In short order, the older inquisitive uncovered a cache of rolled up papers hidden behind a panel in a wall Soneste had overlooked. I need sleep, she thought.

Jotrem began to unroll the posters upon Tallis's bed. War propaganda, she recognized instantly. Soneste had plenty of it herself in Sharn and even back home in Starilaskur. It was common enough across the Five Nations, intended to boost morale among the populace against one's declared enemies and encourage recruitment. Mostly it sowed hatred and intolerance.

She felt blood rush to her face as she looked upon some of Karrnath's war posters. One of them depicted the familiar likeness of King Boranel with scaly, bluish skin and a massive, saw-toothed glaive gripped in his hands. His mouth was stretched into a diabolic grin, framed by a slick, stringy beard. The artist had rendered the scenery underneath to make it appear as though famine and corruption flowed before Boranel. At the bottom, beneath a squad of warforged with green-glowing eyes, was a title: THE BRELISH DEVIL.

"Roll them up," Soneste said in disgust. Pride for her own king and country swelled within her.

"There *are* others here," Jotrem answered coolly as he flipped through them. "Would you care to see what Queen Barvette of Aundair looked like, or the Keeper of the Flame? Your king is not alone." He turned and held her eyes with an unapologetic stare. "I can only imagine how you Brelanders saw us Karrns."

As black crows circling carrion, she knew. As necromancers mustering the fallen to fight again. As fiends raising their own enemies from the repose of death to turn against their former comrades.

"I know," she said quietly.

Never more than now, here in this quiet apartment in the middle of Karrnath, had Soneste ever been so glad the war was over. She'd never joined up herself, but as far as she was concerned, the Last War had already claimed too much from her family. Her father, a dragoon in the Brelish army, had been killed in the Battle of Cairn Hill, and her mother, once a soldier in the captain's own unit before the two had married, had not spoken a word since.

Chapter
THIRTEEN

The derelict façade did not bear a sign, but even a casual glance at the store's front window, cracked in two places, revealed an assemblage of curiosities within. Other shops lined the slanted street in both directions, most of them closed at this early hour. Some were abandoned, housing vagrants and the less fortunate among Korth's lawless population. The icy breeze sweeping in from King's Bay didn't do much to wash away the detritus of the Low District. It gathered like eddies in every niche and alley.

Toward the end of second watch, only laborers, longshoreman, and the White Lions walked the streets. The odd warforged could be seen here and there, doing guard work or heavy-lifting. A casual glance at the unremarkable curio shop before him told him that business was slow.

That suited Tallis—and the one he sought—just fine.

He'd come here in his veteran's garb again, careful to keep his face hidden from everyone he passed. He hoped this would be the last time he needed to use this particular disguise. Tallis scrutinized the other occupants of the street, making certain everyone he saw belonged there.

With the Brelish girl on his trail, he had to be especially careful. He may have overpowered her once, but she'd tailed him like a magebred hound. Tallis was fairly certain she possessed magic of some kind. She could be working for House Tharashk or House Medani, but she'd cited King Boranel. Was she really with the Brelish government?

Satisfied that no one had followed him, he limped over to the small shop and opened the door. The hinges screeched from intentional neglect, and the small copper bell affixed to the door heralded his arrival. Rows of tall shelves made the interior even more confined. Cluttered with miscellaneous oddities, the shelves limited sight. Had this been any other place, Tallis would have been nervous about that. He liked to control his environment and command a view of all exits and hiding places. Still, he had never known a civilian locale more shielded from the law than this place. He felt genuinely safe.

Tallis moved among the shelves and soon caught the eye of the bored-looking clerk at the back. He nodded in greeting and received no response. Of course. This was how it was done.

He made his way casually to one side of the shop, idly lifting up trinkets for inspection, some of them actually legitimate objects of monetary and artistic value. There were the usual sundries: antiquated artificer tools, glass bottles of every color, porcelain dolls. He spied ivory soldiers from a Conqueror set he'd never seen before, along with Lhazaar nesting dolls, and even a mummified gnoll hand from Droaam. The shelves were well dusted, the curios arranged with a semblance of order. She actually keeps this place restocked, he mused, impressed as always.

The true worth of this shop was hardly found in its visible wares. When he neared a wall whose bric-a-brac lay behind glass doors, Tallis cleared his throat.

"Is there a key for these?" he asked aloud.

"Might be," the clerk responded in monotone. "Something interest you?"

"Yeah," Tallis said, familiar with the routine. He eyed the

collection of tiny, winged figurines, looking for the one that stood out among the rest. "This one, with a child. Some sort of sylph mother?"

"As you will," came the reply. Tallis heard the jostling of keys. "If you'll step aside, sir."

With his own apathetic grunt, Tallis stepped away to examine a shelf of rusted warforged fingers. Most were the thick, Cannith-issued digits, but he noted with interest that others were slender and articulate.

The clerk selected an unusual key from his ring then twisted it inside the tumbler. Knowing what to expect, Tallis's sharp ears caught the faint rustle of whirring gears followed by the sound of the front door locking by itself. At the same time, the glass panes of the door frosted over as if the temperature had dropped exceedingly low, obscuring its transparency.

The clerk removed the key and inserted another into the same arcane mechanism, turning again. A second click sounded from beneath an area carpet. The clerk kneeled before him and Tallis saw the faded tattoo on the back of his neck—the sigil of the Midwife's gang. Tallis wondered which one this man was. Ranec? Dorven? Not surprisingly, they seldom looked the same.

The clerk pulled open the trapdoor beneath the carpet and gestured at the narrow, spiraling stair lead into darkness. "Lastpoint," he said softly, naming the watchword for entry.

With a wink, he added, "I think."

"Funny," Tallis said.

When the trapdoor closed above him, he relied upon memory alone to find the bottom of the twisting stair. Even the elf blood in his veins couldn't penetrate the utter dark. Tallis felt another pang of loss for his darkvision lenses. Something told him the Brelish inquisitive had them now. As he walked, he removed the veteran's cloak and bundled it up under his arm.

At the end of the stair he found himself at a juncture of three dark corridors that smelled of smoke and wax. A single stub of a candle was fixed upon a wall sconce across from him, trailing a tiny wisp of smoke as it sputtered. Tallis knew the candle was enchanted to remain in its dying state indefinitely. The smoke drifted idly down the right-hand tunnel.

"Lastpoint," Tallis repeated in a quiet but clear voice. The utterance suppressed the magic, temporarily incapacitating all traps down the right-hand tunnel. Slowly he set off down the path, scanning the shadows for the tell-tale triggers.

Very few were allowed here. Even Tallis, privy to the Midwife's hideout as one of her favored clients, had to be cautious. Once, when he'd foolishly entered the perilous gauntlet after mispronouncing a previous watchword, he'd nearly lost his head to a swinging axe blade and he still bore the chemical scar at the center of his back from that damnable acid trap.

Tallis knocked on the door at the end of the last hall. A small window slid open, and two yellow eyes peered back at him.

"Unscathed this time," Tallis said, holding up one empty hand as if in evidence.

When the heavy lock shifted, the door scraped against the stone. Except for the leather jerkin he wore and the long knife held ready in one hand, the rogue standing before Tallis was the spitting image of the clerk upstairs. The yellow eyes he'd seen a moment ago had already been replaced by brown.

"Is anyone actually still fooled by that ridiculous getup?" the man asked, gesturing at the bundled cloak in Tallis's hand.

Tallis looked down at his veteran's disguise. "Some are, Ranec. I suppose it's just my amazing fortune that observant changelings like you remain an undesirable minority in this town."

The rogue's face blurred and reshaped itself, now resembling Tallis's own. He offered a wicked smile, but two of the changeling's teeth were capped with silver. "Dorven," he corrected, pointing the knife blade at his teeth. "My brother has only one."

"Can't change your teeth?" Tallis asked with disinterest. Dorven grunted and stepped aside.

The chamber beyond resembled the common room of a guild

hall, with hardwood benches and tables, a few pieces of luxury furniture, and plenty of open space. The walls were probably stone, but heavy curtains hid them from view and framed the room's perimeter. The hall conveyed a warm, comfortable atmosphere, looking as it always had. Simple. Clean.

And illegal. A pair of men argued in hushed tones over a table, a loose sheaf of forged documents spread out between them. One of the men nursed a swollen jaw. The other, a large brute with an iron prosthetic replacing most of a missing ear, wiped the errant crumbs of some vanished meal from his goatee. In the center of the room, a sly gnome cast gold coins into the air, grinning when they transformed into tiny knives as they peaked before melting back into currency.

Tallis ignored the gang and walked up to a large desk set against one wall, where the curtains parted to reveal a mural-sized map of Karrnath. Small pins riddled the surface, making the map resemble a general's battle plan. Tallis had always wondered what the pins denoted, but he knew better than to ask.

Seated at a desk beneath the map, a stern-faced young woman scratched in a thick ledger with a feathered quill. She was pretty even with the fresh, livid scar that ran along one cheek, and the monocle nestled over one eye. She scowled when she looked up at him. Tallis never remembered her name.

"What are you looking for?" she asked, clearly irritated. He noticed a small plate of cakes on the corner of the desk.

"Identification papers," he answered. "Maybe travel papers too. I will, uh . . . need this for myself this time. I could use some . . . well, professional recommendations."

"Fine," she said and started jotting down his request on fresh vellum.

"It's been a while, Tallis. I trust all is well?"

Tallis turned around at the sound of the nectarous voice. A child-sized woman sat languid upon an ottoman of dark velvet. She wore a well-tailored gown of green silk with matching jewels at her wrists and throat. The lines of her middling face were softened by emerald eyes and stylish brown hair which was arrayed with ringlets like Aundairian nobility. She looked like she'd just come from some gala of the city's elite. Even with running makeup and sleepy eyes, she carried the air of a much younger halfling.

"Not as well as it ought to be," he said, then raised an eyebrow as he looked her over. "I've never seen you look so radiant before, Midwife."

"Flattery will not lower my fee," she answered with a pout. "This appointment was made on short notice, Tallis."

Tallis held out his hands defensively. He'd meant his words.

"I'd planned to stay the morning at my engagement, but the urgency of one of my favorite clients lured me back this early. Business first. I'm certain your reasons—*and* your gold—are worth it?"

"I am sorry," he said and blew out a sigh. "The circumstances aren't optimal for me, either."

The halfling's teasing vanished. She slid from her seat and walked directly in front on him, looking up at him with professional scrutiny. Even at half his size, the Midwife's manner was imposing. Tallis always felt slightly uncomfortable in her presence. She was a mage of considerable power. Not for the first time, he wondered if she'd studied in the Tower of the Twelve. If she had any blood connections to either House Jorasco or House Ghallanda—the dragonmarked houses of healing and hospitality—she never said. Not that she, of all people, would ever reveal her true identity to anyone.

"You're alone," she stated simply, "and my friends suggest that you're not just fetching papers for another stray who needs to disappear. This is about the dead Brelish, right?"

Stray. The Midwife's term for those who were wanted by the law, bounty hunters, or the murder-minded. Tallis had come to the Midwife many times to secure new identification papers for unfortunates who needed to disappear . . . usually the innocent servants or enemies of those he'd killed or financially ruined.

The Midwife had earned her epithet for just this reason.

She ushered births into the world, not of new lives but of new identities. The halfling employed natural skill and tailored magic to create flawless identification papers that held up to intense scrutiny. Tallis knew of not a single instance in which her false papers were discovered for the counterfeits they were. He believed she could convincingly recreate identification papers for Kaius III.

The Midwife's services were not cheap. Given the amount of gold he alone had poured into her coffers, along with her numerous other anonymous clients, Tallis knew she had to be one of Korth's wealthiest citizens. He may have been a favored client of hers, but even Tallis didn't know her real name. He doubted her own gang knew her story.

"Yes," he admitted. "I'm the stray. If I just run from this, I'll always be looking behind me. Hyran, Thauram, and Host knows who else are really after me this time."

"Oh, yes. Your name has *always* been synonymous with legality in this town," she said with a smile.

"Point taken. But I've got nothing to do with the Brelish ambassador—"

"Pshhh!" The halfling waved her hand dismissively. "If you want to go carving up foreign dignitaries, by all means do so. I'm sure you'd have good reasons for something like that. You always do, Tallis. Just don't bring your mess to me, and that means not telling me about it. You came to me to give you some reprieve, and so I shall."

Tallis ground his teeth together in frustration. For some reason, he wanted her to know he was innocent of this, but the Midwife's neutrality in her clients' affairs kept her in business and away from the scrutiny of the Justice Ministry. Her very existence was a rumor, nothing more. Those foolish few who had dared to implicate her in their crimes found that her gang of loyal rogues operated well outside of these underground chambers and were capable of delivering sound retribution.

The Midwife walked a slow circle around him now, muttering to herself as she did. Tallis felt her eyes appraising him and wondered if she was using wizardry to assess him. "I've known you for a long time, half-elf. I never thought I'd have the pleasure of rebirthing *you*."

"I hope it'll be all you ever dreamed."

The halfling stopped her pacing. "The papers will be easy, of course, but you'll need more than documents to blend in this time."

Tallis spread out his hands. "What can I do?"

The Midwife called out over her shoulder. "Dorv, switch with your brother. Our client needs a new face."

The halfling turned back to Tallis. She gestured to one of her servants, who stepped forward to offer Tallis a platter of vedbread and a wheel of cheese. "Make yourself comfortable, Tallis, and let's talk about your fee."

❋ ❋ ❋ ❋ ❋ ❋ ❋

Soneste woke just after dawn, wondering if it was too much to hope that she not make any more embarrassing mistakes that day.

"Mistress," a voice boomed when she climbed from her bed, startling her.

"Host!" she swore, reaching for her boot—which she wasn't wearing. Then she shook her head. "You need to give us sleepers some time to adjust."

Soneste hadn't minded Aegis's presence in her room at the Seventh Watch. He may have been an artificial creature composed of metal, wood, and stone, but he was Brelish. She had a few war-forged acquaintances back in Sharn, and most of them were good company. She trusted this one faster than most, or it may have been pity for the loss of the family he'd lived to serve.

Warforged didn't need to sleep—nor did they drink, eat, or even breathe. Magic from the Cannith forges that birthed them also sustained them entirely. When Aegis had offered to guard her, she accepted readily. She couldn't be too careful in this city, especially since the criminal she was hunting had proved himself an efficient killer.

"I apologize," he said.

"I'm sorry. It's my fault," she said. "I'm quite used to sleeping alone. What's on your mind?"

"I've been thinking. This Tallis may have saved me."

Soneste wiped her eyes and looked at the warforged. "How so?"

"He disabled me on the balcony, but he chose not kill me. If he had not disabled me, wouldn't the assassin have killed me? I do not know. If I'd defeated Tallis, perhaps I could have stopped the assassin myself."

Soneste recalled the wounds of the victims. "I think he may have saved you."

"Or not," Aegis said, sounding harsher. "At least I would have died with honor, defending my master and his family. I should not have survived."

"We'll have answers soon, I promise you." Soneste glanced at the dent of his metal head. "I'm going to take you to a magewright shop to get some repairs today. I have an errand to run myself, but we'll need to ditch Jotrem first."

"Very good, Mistress."

"You can call me by my name, Aegis."

Recovering her rapier was Soneste's priority in the first hours of the morning. The weapon was magewrought, a perfectly balanced blade of Brelish steel she'd saved up to buy. She wasn't about to lose the sword. It was bad enough that Tallis had stolen the crysteel blade—its personal value was greater by far, a gift from Veshtalan.

Soneste searched among the fences who worked the Community Ward, threatening the hand of the Justice Ministry upon those she questioned. An enchanted rapier would have been pawned quickly into Korth's black market to avoid evidence of theft. She thought she'd found the trail, but it remained ever out of reach. Given time, she knew she could track the rapier down herself, but she felt she was wasting time not searching for Tallis.

Swallowing her pride, Soneste settled for help. She walked into the city's House Tharashk enclave, fully expecting expedience and a good deal. She cited employment in Thuranne d'Velderan's agency—drawing disapproving looks at the half-orc's family name—and found cooperation in the form of a sleight discount. Evidently, the Karrnath branch of House Tharashk didn't care much for the Velderan family or its retainers.

Nevertheless, a human heir employed the Mark of Finding to locate Soneste's missing rapier. With a pair of Tharashk mercenaries accompanying them both and Aegis clomping along behind, it didn't take her long to convince the knave who had her rapier that it was in his "best interest" to give it up for free.

The entire episode hadn't been a complete detour, for it had yielded a new lead. While searching among the rogues of Korth's underground she learned the existence of the Midnight Market, a secretive bazaar that set up only night each week. On Zol.

Tonight.

● ● ● ◉ ● ● ●

"Drink this." Ranec unstoppered a small vial of black liquid and held it out to Tallis. While he'd worked on Tallis, applying skills both alchemical and mundane, the changeling had worn his own face. Tallis had never quite grown accustomed to the pallid skin and vague features of changelings, so he tried not to stare.

When he swallowed the thick solution, Tallis felt an uncomfortable strain on his muscles throughout his body then a fierce itch along his scalp. He winced. "Can I scratch?"

"Best to wait," Ranec said, and sure enough, within a few seconds he felt normal again—although his hair had flowed down over his eyes.

"Come, see. I think you will agree that the change is sufficient."

The changeling led Tallis from the stool to a full-length mirror where he stared in wonderment upon his own reflection. His hair, once almost shoulder length, had grown longer—was *still* growing as he watched—until it fell to his shoulder blades, curling slightly as it did.

"Aundairian ladies love this philter the best," the changeling said with a smile. Ranec's face reshaped to resemble a human's now that his work was complete. He bound Tallis's hair into a tail with a thin leather cord.

Although his face was still his own, Tallis's features had been altered in subtle ways. His brows were slightly arched, his silver-gray eyes had shifted to green, and even his ears appeared to have a sharper point. His face was perfectly clean shaven.

"Now, these affectations will disappear over the course of a few days," the changeling explained, "so do whatever it is you need to do, sooner than later."

Next Ranec gestured to a bench, where a fine coat of forest green with silver buttons was folded neatly with a shiny brooch resting atop it. When Tallis tried the coat on, both men looked into the mirror at his image. The changeling smiled again, and Tallis noted the single silver-capped tooth. He felt like he was trying on fine suits at ir'Alanso's Clothier. It made him vaguely uncomfortable.

Finally, Ranec produced a matching tri-cornered hat and placed it on Tallis's head. "These garments and the signet brooch are accounted for in the Midwife's fee."

"Thanks, Ranec. You're really good at this."

The changeling gave a half bow.

Soon after, the Midwife emerged from another room, now dressed in the work clothes Tallis was accustomed to seeing. Her attire included a many-pocketed apron and a pair of thick lenses which she'd tucked up into her hair.

The Midwife held out a slim metallic case. She flipped it open to display new identification papers within. "Ranec, add a portrait to this," she said, handing the case over to him.

She turned to Tallis as the changeling produced a set of colored inks. "You are now Findel d'Lyrandar, an upstanding member of the Windwrights Guild. It's just one of the names

I put into circulation some time ago, so there will already be a record of you active in this city."

Tallis nodded. "Where am I supposed to be from?"

The Midwife gave him a funny look. "I know you can't convincingly pull off an accent, so you're still from Karrnath. However, you spent some time in Cyre during the months of tenuous peace between the two nations. You lost your immediate family on the Day of Mourning—convenient, eh?—and are now based out of Rekkenmark. You come to Korth all the time, for pleasure as much as business. Maybe you have a lover who works somewhere in the Temple Ward?"

Was that a veiled reference to Lenrik? No, she couldn't know about him. Even if she did, she wouldn't care. Information to the Midwife was armor and weaponry, to be used only when necessary. She'd get along well in Zilargo, Tallis had always thought.

"Lyrandar. Windwrights Guild. Pious sweetheart. Yes, sounds like me." Tallis smiled. "Do I possess a dragonmark?" He pulled up one sleeve, on the chance that Ranec had somehow applied a false tattoo without his knowledge.

"No. Believe me, you don't want *that* much attention. Your father did, however, and you've just hoped to live up to the prestige he once commanded within the house. Don't try to fool anyone for too long, Findel, especially real members of House Lyrandar. The papers will show your reader precisely what they expect to see and nothing more. Don't linger. Just show it and move on."

"Marvelous work, as always."

"I know," she answered, accepting the compliment, "but I don't want to see you here again. King's fire is on you, and the authorities are stirring all over the city. Clear things up or don't come back. Fair enough?"

The Midwife's motherly tones carried a true sense of menace. Tallis looked to Ranec, who minutes ago had gently applied a shaving razor to his throat. Now the changeling fingered a fine-bladed stiletto.

"Fair enough."

❀ ❀ ❀ ◉ ❀ ❀ ❀

Soneste searched the archives of the *Korth Sentinel* for two hours before finding the same article that Tallis had tacked to his wall. With Jotrem working nearby, she quickly skimmed the article and buried it again among the stacks of broadsheets. She wasn't about to discuss the particulars of her research with him.

The full article described an event which place in 974 YK. Twenty-six sons and daughters of Karrnath were put to the sword by the Aundairians who'd captured them. Before they could burn the bodies—an Aundairian policy when battling Karrns—the enemies were routed by a platoon of undead infantry led by a bone knight. The recovered bodies were, of course, claimed by the royal corpse collectors and became property of the state.

Why was this article of such interest to Tallis? Or was it some arbitrary clipping, meant to mislead anyone who found his residence?

Soneste spent the next hour cross-referencing the skirmish against a roster of the dead maintained by the Ministry. Hyran had granted her limited access to Karrnath's archived casualty reports. The battle was a minor one and hadn't even been named, but the date allowed her to find the names of the fallen.

Then she found something, the fifth name on the list from that unnamed battle in 974 YK.

Recruit number 966-5-1372. Captain Tallis.

Chapter
FOURTEEN

The Midnight Market
Zol, the 10th of Sypheros, 998 YK

At sunset, Tallis had taken to the streets again, confident he could move around freely in his new disguise. He'd followed every possible lead in search of Haedrun, yet every dead end pointed back to the one place he might be able to find her—the Midnight Market.

Having confirmed the Market's location for this week, Tallis set out to find himself something to eat. He turned onto one of the major roads and was startled by a lone figure trudging towards him, moving slowly away from the docks beneath a suspicious burden.

It was an older man, the lower half of his trousers soaked through as though he'd opted to take a midnight swim in the river but had changed his mind at the last moment. He carried a large, leather-wrapped bundle over one shoulder and steadied his pace with a metal-shod staff. Two feet, one missing a shoe, stuck out of the bundle at one end.

Under the circumstances, Tallis knew he ought to just keep moving, but something about the man gave him pause. Perhaps it was the holy symbol of Dol Dorn the stranger wore around his neck or the glimmer of moisture in his eyes. Despite his solemn burden, the man was no corpse collector. He looked more like some errant pilgrim.

"Need some help, friend?" Tallis asked, surprised that he really meant it.

The man looked him up and down then smiled sadly. "I fear not," he answered, continuing on with weary steps. "He's already dead. I thank you, though."

"Of course," Tallis said in parting, doubting the man even heard him.

He watched the stranger walk away. Maybe it was the man's dignified bearing or the holy symbol he wore, but he'd brought Lenrik to mind—a resilient, battle-hardened man who hadn't let the war steal his compassion from him. It weighed heavily on Tallis that he'd relied so much upon his old friend in this crisis. He'd been forced to stay the night in Lenrik's undercroft yet again.

The Brelish inquisitive had found his flat. The ever-predictable Jotrem had staked it out all night from across the street, counting on Tallis to return like some idiot cutpurse. At least the Brelish girl knew better. She'd pulled whatever clues there were and left it behind. Still, it wasn't safe for him to return there again. The Justice Ministry would have it on file. Damn it, it had been one of his favorite haunts.

But edible birds didn't live long—he had to let it go.

Still, how long would he need to keep relying on Lenrik? Tallis supposed that'd depend on what he learned from Haedrun tonight. The thought helped him refocus. There was work do to.

❋ ❋ ❋ ❋ ❋ ❋ ❋

It was midnight. Tallis left Aureon's shrine and made his way, tier by tier, down the city. Whenever he passed a patrol of Lions, he strode by with the pretense of an important house errand. The signet brooch upon his lapel proclaimed his affiliation with the Windwrights Guild, and that was enough to satisfy most without comment. Under other circumstances, Tallis might have enjoyed playing up the role of a scion of the House Lyrandar, but this wasn't a time for role-playing. This was survival.

In the plaza at the center of the Community Ward, Tallis passed beneath the giant-sized statue of Karrn the Conqueror. He glanced up at the grim, marble countenance of Karrnath's namesake and greatest hero. The famous warlord had fought for and established human civilization upon Khorvaire millennia ago. In his wake, Karrnath and eventually Galifar itself had been founded.

A small entourage of well-dressed revelers emerged from the street on the opposite side of the plaza. Despite their languid stroll, a handful of guards kept pace on either side.

Tallis felt a stab of fear as he realized the latter were members of the Conqueror's Host—the king's own royal guard, among the finest soldiers in the land! They weren't wearing their customary silver and black surcoats, no doubt pretending to be hired bodyguards so as not to draw attention, but Tallis recognized the signature greatswords strapped to their backs, weapons specially commissioned at the Bluefist of Mror. Not many would.

To his dismay, the young revelers moved to intercept him. The nobles walked close together, most hanging upon each other, a couple bottles of Nightwood passing back and forth among them.

"Where at this late hour do *you* go, friend?" one of the men asked, slurring the words. The girl on his arm giggled.

Tallis doffed his hat and offered a smile, aware that the flanking soldiers were eyeing him. Under the wisplights, his brooch gleamed silver and bright. "To Rivergate, my young friend. I must charter more vessels to ensure a steady stream of exotic wines into the keeping of gentlemen such as yourself."

There were awkward laughs and a "Well, carry on!" or two in response, but Tallis caught the eye of a young woman in their midst who was obviously *not* amused by her companions' antics. Something in her pretty face—an expression, perhaps—reminded him of the Brelish inquisitive. This girl was at least a few years younger than she, but the secluded look in her eyes seemed familiar somehow.

Tallis gave a half-bow to the entourage and continued his

course. When he had left them behind and entered another darkened avenue, Tallis stopped and looked back. Wait, he thought, the Conqueror's Host! Had that young woman been—?

"Keep moving," issued a strident voice from the shadows.

A figure in black and white resolved itself from the darkness. Tallis could not repress his scowl in the face of the tall figure in bonecraft armor who held a broadsword freely in hand. Very bad memories rose to the fore, but Tallis pushed them away.

"Of course," Tallis answered. "I only—"

"Look to your own business," the knight said. Tallis felt the presence of a second knight walking on the other side of the street, eyeing him dangerously.

"As you say, sir," he replied without enthusiasm. A delayed parlance would lead only to violence. Now was not the time to act on principle alone.

Tallis soon entered the Low District, letting the cool air calm his nerves. He was heedless of the quiet, vacated streets, reflecting as he was upon the brief encounter.

Unless he was mistaken, that had been Princess Borina herself—youngest daughter of Breland's own king—in the company of Korth's gallivanting aristocrats. Gamnon's death certainly *had* increased security within the city's garrison. It only made sense that the royal court would be taking new steps to ensure the safety of *all* its foreign guests.

And rightly so. King Kaius III was one of the chief supporters of lasting peace. Lacking children of his own, he'd sent his sister to Breland and his brother to Thrane as part of the diplomatic exchange.

And now? Bone knights escorting Brelish royalty. Tallis choked at the irony.

● ● ● ◉ ● ● ●

Without further incident, he reached the district's western edge at the base of the cliff wall that sequestered it below the manors of the High District. There he spied his destination, a narrow street junction with a lone wisplight swaying from its post under the cold autumn breeze.

For just a moment, the pure white light flickered as if the lantern's magic were failing—then it shone anew. Two minutes later it pulsed again, confirming the location of the Market for those who knew how to look for it. Utter darkness lay beyond the lantern's reach.

The Midnight Market appeared every Zol at the appointed hour, each time in a new location within the Low District. None could say in advance where it would set up again, but the shadow players who planned its movements had ways of spreading word of the next location to the right people.

The Justice Ministry knew about the Market, of course, but on those rare occasions when it gathered the resources to find it, the fences and their clientele always vanished into the Low District's innumerable dark holes. Finding the Market's planners was impossible. The few rogues the White Lions had caught were incapable of revealing the next location. In a city where even petty infractions were punishable by death, the criminal element had to compensate.

Tallis turned the corner, passing easily through the curtain of magical darkness that concealed tonight's chosen street from ignorant passers-by. He was once told that the effect was supplied each week by an anonymous heir of House Thuranni who possessed the Mark of Shadow.

Behind the magic veil, artificial twilight reigned. A host of candles and floating magelights displayed a city block full of dubious, whispering hawkers, street fences, and purveyors of every vice and contraband available in Karrnath.

Tallis fell easily into the crowd and began his hunt for Haedrun.

Soneste's eyes returned again and again to the alley across from her where a hovering ball of light flickered with tiny threads of electricity. She kept her back to a building with shattered windows and questionable occupancy, wondering if the buoyant light was a spell effect or some sort of urban fey. It was distracting.

She had confirmed the Midnight Market's existence with one of the Justice Ministry's less savory prisoners. For his cooperation she was able to convince his keepers to lessen the man's sentence—to a faster and more painless death than General Thauram, commander of the White Lions, had planned for him.

It was then a matter of finding one of the criminal's old acquaintances and following him to the Market as the hours grew late. The attraction she'd planted in the thief's mind to find spiderdust hastened her quest. Soneste had a good eye for addicts.

It had been a gamble. The Midnight Market didn't cater to the lowliest of Korth's criminal elements, but her mark evidently knew where a dangerous substance like spiderdust would be available. Soneste silently thanked Olladra for the goddess's favor so far. She'd had enough setbacks and humiliation already in this uncouth land.

She'd spent the rest of her day scouring the city, plying her skills among the seedier echelons of Korth society. Tallis's name was known by many, but none she had questioned knew definitively where he could be found. He had a reputation as a burglar and saboteur of discriminating taste and expensive rates. Most of the time, he could be contacted at the Midnight Market. Soneste wondered if this was how Lord Charoth had once found him.

Soneste studied the crowds from beneath a low-hanging hood. With a spoken word, she'd altered her shiftweave clothing into one of its four other nested outfits. She'd used this kit before in the lower districts of Sharn, emulating the attitude of a shadow-dwelling mercenary. Having studied and apprehended city scum so many times, she knew how to adopt their manner and body language. Whenever a passerby looked at her for more than a couple of seconds, she returned the glare with hostility.

Aegis sat upon the ground beside her with a sheet of canvas thrown over him. If he walked free, there would be no concealing his construct nature—the Host knew, in this land he would inevitably attract attention.

Given the nature of the Market, she was comforted knowing the warforged was near. The magewright had managed to make some repairs. He wasn't fully restored, but he looked a lot less like someone's damaged property.

"How much longer must I wait, Mistress?" Aegis said, his whisper alarmingly loud.

"Not long," she whispered back.

Indeed, Soneste did not have to wait long. After scrutinizing every face in the crowd for the last half hour, she finally spied a man of Tallis's bearing, though his attire gave her pause. He wore a fine coat of deep green with silver buttons and brooch, a tricorn, and an elegant rapier at his belt.

"This might be him," she said quietly to Aegis. "Stay here unless I call you." She heard an unhappy grunt in response.

The man approached along the street, eyeing the crowds as carefully as she. Soneste tossed one of the daggers she'd purchased earlier onto the cobbles in front of him. The action garnered a few twitchy glances, but the man in the green coat merely stooped to retrieve it. She immediately stepped away from the wall to approach him, her hood and scarf concealing most of her face. In her left hand she held two more daggers by their blades, as though she'd been juggling the three of them.

"Sorry," she called out, forcing an impassive tone and an Aundairian accent.

Giving her only a cursory glance, the man handed the dagger back to her, hilt first. She saw a stylized dragon's head on the ring of his right hand.

"Not a good place for throwing blades around, lady, as I'm sure you know." He moved on without another word.

It *was* Tallis, and how different he looked. His face was clean-shaven now. The coat and hat were obviously recent purchases, and the longer hair might have been the work of illusionary magic.

Feigning interest in browsing the Market, she fell into step far enough behind him to remain unnoticed. Tallis moved slowly himself, making an effort to talk to various parties. He looked like a Lyrandar dandy in his kit, but Soneste suspected it served his need to look less like his infamous self.

As she scanned the vendors arrayed on either side of the narrow street, Soneste was again amazed at the audacity of the Midnight Market. Scores of men and women of disparate races carried out illegal transactions of every kind. A fur-cloaked Lhazaarite captain argued with a Karrn huckster, a manacled young man kneeling beside them. A wiry shifter was purchasing glowing bottles from a haughty, loud-mouthed artificer. Soneste even saw a group of surprisingly well-dressed goblins exchanging coffers with a man who might have been a priest of the Dark Six.

Tallis soon stopped to inquire among a cluster of men who looked better suited to the cells of Thronehold Prison than freedom on the streets. Soneste paused at a vendor's table so as not to draw suspicion, feigning interest in the wares before her.

"What is your need, lady?" a sibilant voice asked. Soneste looked up to see a woman swathed from head to toe in saffron garments. Her eyes, the only part of her body unconcealed, were vivid yellow with black, slitted pupils.

Soneste's stomach lurched. The woman was yuan-ti, serpent-blooded folk from Xen'drik and the far south. The true severity of the Midnight Market finally took hold within her. She felt a strong desire to quit this place and call the White Lions down upon the whole affair.

No. The Market would endure despite her. The Justice Ministry could not effectively locate it or stamp it out. She felt blasphemous thinking it, but Soneste wondered if perhaps Korth *needed* the Market.

Certainly the Sharn Watch, itself rife with corruption, could never expose every vice in the City of Towers. Crime was everywhere back home. Soneste been in this city for two days, and already she'd seen a world of difference. Korth was a place of extremes. The streets were safer, yes, but martial law engendered in the Karrnathi populace a dichotomy of moral choices. The Midnight Market and all its lawless indulgences had undoubtedly spawned under the unforgiving Code of Kaius.

Soneste examined the small vials the yuan-ti had revealed under a velvet cloth. Poisons, all of them.

"Blue whinnis," she said.

Without hesitation, the snake woman selected one small jar and held it up to Soneste. The paste within was darker than she was used to seeing, but it was at least two applications of the incapacitating poison. "Platinum, twenty-six pieces," the yuan-ti said, her accent sharp.

Sovereign bitch, she thought. Twenty-six dragons! She could get it for eighteen back home.

"Twenty," Soneste said in turn. "Your formula is unfamiliar to me."

"Stronger," the snake woman hissed. "My people make it better. Twenty-five."

Soneste prepared to bargain further, but she saw Tallis was moving on. "Twenty-five," she agreed, hoping she wouldn't regret the purchase. She made the exchange quickly then hastened after her mark.

For the next fifteen minutes, she shadowed Tallis as he moved among the crowd, dispensing coins—and unless she was mistaken, threats—among the knaves of the Market. When he thought no one was looking, he produced a vial of liquid from his coat and drank its contents quickly. A potion? She half expected him to fade into invisibility, but there was no apparent effect. Protection of some kind, perhaps? He moved as if he were expecting trouble.

Soneste's instincts brought her closer to him as he approached a group of Lhazaarite sailors in fur-trimmed cloaks. Just beyond them, she spied the north end of the curtain of shadow that blanketed the Market. From the inside, one could see out into a visible if muted world. Not for the first time, she wondered if the curtain also blocked sound.

Soneste moved close enough to overhear their conversation.

"Tallis?" The largest of the Lhazaarites leaned in closer to get a better look at the Karrn.

"Javey. Yeah, it's me. I've cleaned up and become another arrow in the bunch, see?" Tallis stroked his smooth chin and grinned.

"Walk out of here, Tallis. I'm serious. Haedrun doesn't want to see you." He hefted a massive cudgel in two hands.

Haedrun. The name was unknown to Soneste. Someone complicit in the ir'Daresh murder, or someone Tallis knew who could help him escape the city? Perhaps another Lhazaarite who could give him passage by ship?

"Sorry, I've got to talk to her."

Ahh, a woman.

"She didn't tell you why, did she?" Tallis continued. "Help me out, Jave. This is important."

"No! Walk away." Javey glanced around as his three comrades began to fan out around Tallis.

One of their number was a well-muscled woman with a heavy cutlass in hand. All of them wore thick leather armor and fur-lined capes and the other two carried well-worn short swords. From what Soneste had heard back home, Lhazaarites did not go down easily.

Tallis tapped the silver brooch on his coat. "I'm part of the Windwrights Guild now. Better sailors—even the lowliest of Lyrandar cabin boys—than the *greatest* of Lhazaar princes. Did you know?"

Javey, a bigger man than Tallis by far, swung his cudgel at the Karrn's midsection. Tallis sucked in his stomach, barely avoiding the rib-crushing swing.

"Come now! Sleights we can forgive, Jave!" Tallis shook his head. He gripped the hilt of his rapier with one hand, but did not draw it. "Debts we can forget, but take another swing at me, and we'll never share another drink again."

The big man actually seemed to take the words to heart, pausing as he hefted his cudgel back against his shoulder. "No," he said at last, maintaining his stance. "Walk Tallis!"

"Fine."

Tallis started to turn away then spun back sharply. He pulled at the grip of his sheathed rapier and the whole shaft pivoted at his hip. The tip of the sheath, evidently weighted for just this purpose, slammed hard into the big man's groin. Javey sucked in air as he stumbled, groaning, to his knees.

The other three raised their weapons and spit Lhazaarite curses. Soneste tensed and gripped the hilt of her rapier, uncertain whether to let this play out or reveal herself by helping the Karrn follow this lead.

Tallis drew out his weapon at last. In place of a blade, a slender glass vial half the length of the sheath was attached to the hilt. Some sort of cloudy gray liquid swirled within.

Full of tricks, isn't he? Soneste mused. Tanglefoot bags, false weapons. What next?

Growling, the Lhazaarite woman closed in first. A seasoned warrior, she made a few wild swings merely to test Tallis's skill. The other two sailors maneuvered slowly at his back. Soneste almost called out in warning, but held her tongue and watched.

"I don't think that trick will work the same on you," Tallis said to the woman, looking down at Javey who still lay on the ground, coughing. "Or . . . *would* it?"

"You had your chance," the woman snarled, diving forward with a well-aimed strike.

Tallis had taken his measure of her as well. He jumped back a pace—putting himself dangerously close to the other two—and held out his strange hilt-vial to intercept her blade as though parrying with a blade of his own. The glass reservoir, predictably, shattered—

A cloud of thick, nubilous mist exploded from the impact.

The air was muddied with the gray fumes, obscuring all sight.

Soneste couldn't make out Tallis or his three opponents, but she heard the slap of metal against leather, and the solid rap of a fist against flesh. Several times.

"Blunted!" was all she heard from Tallis.

Soneste looked around to see if any of the Market's other attendees planned to intervene. The scuffle had attracted some spectators, but even those looked on with only passing interest. She tried to make herself appear as one of them, relaxing her hands and pretending to inventory her pockets.

The alchemical cloud dispersed quickly. Tallis stood panting, only a single cut along one arm showing that he'd been attacked in turn. A blade had sheared through the fine green coat, but the wound bled only lightly. Even Tallis's tricorn hat was unmoved. The Lhazaarites lay upon the ground, ushered swiftly into unconsciousness. He knew where to hit and how to hit hard. Soneste felt a pang of empathy for the sailors. She noted the blackened eyes, the bloody noses, and the red welts on the Lhazaarites. Tallis had obviously exhibited restraint with Soneste when he'd defeated her. He was capable of considerable violence.

Tallis didn't tarry. He sat down casually beside Javey, who looked at his fallen comrades in despair. Tallis picked up the big man's cudgel and turned it over in his hands.

"One more time, Javey. This is bigger than you and me, not worth losing *all* you have. Haedrun."

The Lhazaarite's sickly face looked up at Tallis. "I can't . . ."

Tallis looked around to gauge the onlookers. His eyes passed right over Soneste, but he made no indication that he recognized her. Then he looked back at Javey and jabbed the butt of the cudgel into the man's mouth, splitting his lip.

"Haedrun?" he asked calmly. "Or did you not wish to keep your teeth?"

"Kol. . .Korran!" the man cried, spitting blood. "Stop, Tallis . . . I'll tell you."

"That's quite enough! Leave the man alone."

Soneste and Tallis both turned their heads at the bold voice of the newcomer. He wore a chain hauberk and held a long sword readily in one hand. Though the man carried himself like a professional soldier, she could see no insignia upon his uniform. His hawkish features were indistinct in the gloom of the Market, but he looked a little older than Tallis.

The expression of hostility on his face drew Soneste's hand back to the hilt of her rapier. By the Sovereigns, how many enemies did Tallis have?

"I know why you're here," the man said, "but this is your mess. Leave Haedrun out of it."

Tallis stood and faced the soldier. "It surprises me to see you here, Bentius, but it sounds like you know where she is."

"Leave Haedrun alone. Your only chance to survive this is to run, before I hand you over to General Thauram myself."

Tallis's expression darkened with suspicion. "I can't leave her out of this. She's the reason I'm *in* this at all."

Bentius closed the distance between them, pointing his sword at Tallis. As he moved, Soneste observed a severe limp in one leg. Soneste had seen something like that before. A once-broken kneecap, healed by magic but probably not soon enough to fully restore it.

Tallis dropped the cudgel and held his hands out in a show of truce. Soneste had seen him in action enough now to sense the tension building within him, especially when he appeared unarmed.

"You brought this on yourself, half-elf." Bentius gestured with his blade to the Lhazaarites on the ground. "You make too many enemies. Did you really think this pathetic Lyrandar get-up would hide you here?"

Soneste noticed a number of dark figures emerging from the crowd of spectators who'd already begun to watch the unfolding scene. They were armored with studded and banded leather and each wore a mask bound tightly to his face with thick straps. Soneste felt a chill across her spine as she realized they weren't merely masks but the metal faceplates of common warforged. The effect was intimidating, made even more unsettling with living eyes staring through the open sockets. Every one of them was armed.

A circle was tightening around Tallis. Soneste herself was shouldered aside by a half-orc brute with a warhammer. She counted seven thugs in all.

"I'm not here to hide, Bentius. I'm here to talk." Tallis winked. "Say, how's that knee doing?"

Tallis noticed the armored thugs gathering around him, but he seemed undaunted. Soneste had the sense that Tallis had fought and triumphed against numbers before, but it was obvious this was about to get ugly. Her mind raced. Surely he couldn't survive this one? She considered running to fetch Aegis, but she didn't know if she'd make it back in time.

"Since when did you run with the Steel Face?" Tallis asked with casual interest.

Bentius glanced over to a man standing near Soneste and nodded. She saw one of the thugs point a large crossbow at Tallis and take aim. She sucked her teeth.

"Host," she swore quietly to herself then slowly drew out her own rapier.

"You don't want this outcome, trust me," Tallis said with a sigh, then sprang into action. With his gloved hand, he swatted Bentius's sword tip away and lunged for the man himself.

The crossbowman took the cue and loosed his bolt. His aim was true.

Chapter
FIFTEEN

Tallis had expected to meet Bentius tonight—had *counted* on it—and he expected the rogue mercenary to know better than to confront him alone. The Host knew, Tallis had nosed around long enough among the mercenary's acquaintances to flush him out. After their last meeting—in which the hot-tempered Blademark had wrongly accused Tallis of courting Haedrun—Bentius would be aching for vengeance. Still, hiring the Steel Face was a little unexpected.

The click of a triggered crossbow was unmistakable. As he lunged for Bentius, Tallis felt an unpleasant pressure in his stomach as the thick bolt slammed into him—then broke apart without causing injury.

He'd come prepared. What was a few hundred galifars, after all, on the good chance that someone would try to feather you? Tallis would gladly pay Verdax a few hundred more the next time too. Unfortunately, the potion's effects would do nothing against the hand-held weapons now arrayed against him.

With the mercenary's blade turned aside, Tallis found a grip on Bentius's collar. He pulled one of his rods free and slammed it across the man's face twice, hearing the tell-tale crunch of a breaking nose. So much for all that armor. As Bentius clutched at his own face, Tallis shoved him roughly at the nearest assailant. The Steel Face thug stepped back, allowing Bentius to drop awkwardly to the ground, and swung his mace.

Tallis knew he could escape them all easily, but that would get him nowhere. He'd wanted to find Bentius and he'd done so. Now he needed to survive the Blademark's new friends long enough to make use of the man. He drew from his belt the strange dagger he'd taken from the Brelish girl. A quick look around revealed troublesome odds.

When the next thug closed, he ducked just beneath a killing sword stroke, countering with a vicious stab into the man's armpit. The thug dropped his sword and clutched at the streaming arterial wound. Tallis kicked him aside and looked for the next.

Two men were upon him immediately, and the tip of one's long sword caught him on the left forearm. It hurt like the fires of Khyber but it wasn't serious—for now. Tallis grasped the blade itself with his gloved hands, ignoring the pain as it sliced through the fine leather, even as the thug braced his grip to prevent it from being pulled away. Instead, Tallis pushed inward and redirected his strength *up* to slam the pommel against the man's eye. The blow loosened the thug's grip, at which point Tallis wrenched it free and hit him again in the same place. The thug dropped, squaring Tallis off with the second man. Tallis gripped the hilt in one hand, dagger in the other, and took a deep breath.

He hated swords. From the day his father had tried to teach him how to use one to the day Tallis had been tested with the Rekkenmark Sword Drill, he'd hated them. Swords were just big, heavy knives and a great deal more predictable than most other weapons.

The Steel Face thug was a head taller than Tallis and held his blade ready. He would expect Tallis to start swinging, expect to parry and return, so Tallis threw his sword with all his strength at the man's head. It spun through the short distance, moving erratically through the air. The thug swung wildly to knock it out of its path, which he did effectively.

Tallis lunged for his throat. The man tried to bring his weapon back, but he wasn't fast enough. The tip of the violet-tinged blade sheared easily through stiff leather and skin, coming to a stop only when it hit the collar bone. With a scream, the thug retreated, trailing blood behind.

This hadn't bought Tallis a lot of time, but he used it to reassess the battlefield. To his surprise, only one opponent was ready to face him, a dwarf whose unruly beard spilled out beneath the jawless faceplate. In his hands he spun twin axes with considerable skill. Over the dwarf's shoulder, Tallis saw the remaining Steel Face thugs facing a new combatant.

An ally?

She wore a dark, hooded cloak and scarf, shifting her feet to stay in constant motion. For one fearful moment, Tallis thought it was the Ebonspire assassin, concealed by cloth and nimble of motion, but there was something different about this woman's movements. A flash of fair hair confirmed it was someone else.

She knew how to lead her opponents, to allow them an offensive strategy to tire them out. With a rapier in hand, the woman searched patiently for a vulnerable place to strike. Tallis saw one of the thugs already lying on the ground near her feet, clutching a wound in his leg. Whoever she was, Tallis felt a surge of gratitude for her assistance.

He also hoped he didn't have to fight her, too, when this was over.

Tallis brought his attention back to the dwarf, just in time to dodge a pair of axe blades. They chopped the air beside him, allowing him to step just inside the dwarf's reach. The dagger scored the studded leather he wore, but Tallis wasn't close enough to dig deeper. As the thug drew back for another series of swings, Tallis ducked down, feigning a bad step. He locked one of his rods in place at his knee level. He moved back, feigning exhaustion as he eyed the dwarf.

"Khyber!" he gasped. "That beard could use a good wash. Smells like rat piss."

With a growl, the dwarf surged forward, raising both axes. He hit the magic rod where it hung—suspended in the air—and he buckled over it, arms flailed ineffectually as he struggled for balance. Tallis grabbed one arm to still it. A single dagger slash across the fingers of that hand had the thug yelping in pain and dropping both weapons. He followed up with a pommel blow to the head. It took three to drop the stubborn dwarf. Tallis retrieved his rod and looked to the mysterious woman.

Three Steel Face men surrounded her now. She dodged the first few attacks with considerable agility, but she was clearly outnumbered by seasoned fighters. A half-orc with a mace slammed her in the shoulder. She groaned and dropped the sword in her hand from the incapacitating shock that must be coursing through her arm.

The woman managed to evade the clumsy swings of the other two. Tallis realized with a start that she was the woman who'd been juggling daggers near the market's entrance.

The woman paused for a moment and simply *stared* at the hulking half-orc as if in challenge. Even Tallis wouldn't have wasted such precious moments for that! What could it gain her against such a foe? To his surprise, the half-orc used his mace predictably, the swing taking exactly the same angle as his last strike. The agile woman easily stepped away from it.

Tallis moved to join her but felt a painful jerk at the back of his neck.

"Keeper!" he swore, turning to see an eighth thug not ten feet away with an empty crossbow pointed at him.

Half hidden by the metal faceplate, the thug's mouth twisted in dismay. Irritated by the attempt to kill him *yet again*, Tallis threw the only legitimate weapon he had. The violet-tinged blade caught the thug in the neck.

Tallis didn't waste time to see the man's fate. He turned to assist his ally, only to see her backhanded to the ground by the half-orc. The thug's other hand was now empty and bled from the wrist. The hulking half-orc looked like the kind of man who was just as dangerous without a weapon. He lunged angrily at the prone woman.

Before his massive hands found purchase, the half-orc grunted in shock. Blood and bits of ruined flesh burst from his armored chest. His mouth fought to scream even as he died, dropping without a sound. Behind him stood a tall, heavily plated warrior with a faceplate of his own and eyes that shined with a soft blue light. In two gauntleted hands—to Tallis's utter horror *and* delight—was his own hooked hammer! The pick's end dripped with gore.

This was no member of the Steel Face gang. It was a true warforged, and its glowing, crystalline eyes were very much alive. The construct threw aside the canvas tarp that had wrapped it like a cloak and turned immediately to the next thug, whose hesitation at the sight of the warforged cost him dearly. The thick buckler attached to the construct's left arm rammed into the man's face, wrecking his nose and knocking him out cold in a single strike.

Buckler? By Khyber—

The warforged at the Ebonspire, Gamnon's bodyguard. Tallis had disabled the construct on the balcony, using the very weapon now gripped in its hands.

If the same warforged was *here*, that meant—

"Tallis!" The woman rolled to her feet.

"Host . . ." Tallis swore quietly. The Brelish inquisitive. In the tumble, her hood and scarf had fallen free releasing the wild spill of blonde locks unraveling from a braid. Her eyes had been rimmed with black makeup in Karrnathi fashion.

Still wary of the dangerous warforged, Tallis glanced back to Bentius, who was climbing to his feet, one hand at his face. He couldn't let the mercenary leave the Market. He had to deal with him here and now, but now he had to deal with the Brelish too. His control of the situation had slipped away.

"Tallis, please," the inquisitive said. "Just wait. Let's talk." She held her hand out even as the warforged began to pursue the remaining Steel Face thug. "Aegis, let him go. We're done." The warforged halted then jogged back with loud, clomping steps.

Most of the spectators had retreated a safe distance. Few even looked their way now. Tallis nearly thanked the Dark Six that none would summon the authorities *here*, but he still felt he owed that to the Sovereign Host.

The warforged fixed its glowing eyes upon him, reminding Tallis of an angry gorgon stamping at the ground—symbol of the very house which created it.

"You are not absolved, intruder," the warforged said to him.

"Aegis, calm down." The woman approached Tallis, hands still empty. "My name is Soneste, and I'm here for the same reason you are. To find the *real* killer."

Tallis backed away, unsure whether to run again or take his chances with Bentius in front of her. "Oh, *now* you give me your name? I asked you several times yesterday, but forgive me if I'm not yet convinced of your motives, miss."

"Who's your friend?" Soneste asked, pointing to Bentius, who was now aware of Tallis and began to limp away. She gazed at the mercenary, her attention focused, and for a moment Tallis thought he felt a hum in the air. He watched as the man seemed to freeze in place. He hadn't seen the Brelish cast any spell. Was it magic or something else?

"Bentius d'Deneith," Tallis answered. "An *unmarked* man out of favor with his own house. A man about to die."

"You can't just—"

Tallis turned back to her. "With all due respect, *Soneste*, this is my world, not yours." He gestured to the Market street behind her. "If you want answers, let it be."

Soneste stared back with open disgust. She'd retrieved her rapier but moved no closer. The warforged, Aegis, stood beside her. Its posture suggested it wouldn't be handing him his weapon back anytime soon.

He'd deal with that later, then.

Tallis pulled the violet-tinged dagger from the thug he'd dropped with it, wiping the blood on the dead man's leather. He casually walked over to Bentius and kicked him to the ground.

Tallis eyed the blade. "It looks like crystal, but I'm guessing it's quite a bit stronger, right?"

Bentius had shaken free from whatever paralytic spell had seized him. He glared at Tallis defiantly, but he was too sore to fight back. "We had a disagreement last time, Bentius, and it didn't turn out well for you." He looked at the man's knee, the one he'd once broken. It wasn't the same, but at least the man could walk again. "I let you live and this is how you repay me?" Tallis reversed his grip on the dagger, blade pointing down. "'Once he is shown to be intractable, a wise ruler allows his enemies no means of retreat or surrender.'" He peeled back part of the chain of his hauberk, exposing the man's good leg. " 'Only utter destruction prevents a foe from rising again.' "

In one quick motion, Tallis scraped the blade across the man's calf, cutting through clothing and drawing a line of blood—but to everyone else around it might have looked as though he's stabbed clean through the man's leg. The expected scream drew the attention of still more onlookers. Soneste advanced on him, her face incredulous.

"There is no call for this!" she said as she began to fish through her pockets for something. Tallis glanced at her briefly, offering no reply. He pulled the blade up again. Bentius spewed out a stream of curses and struggled to stanch the blood.

"I wanted to find Haedrun," Tallis said to Bentius, letting the blood from the dagger drip onto the mercenary's face. "Too late now, Benty. At least you won't have to hurt any more, right" The man struggled in vain to get free.

Tallis raised the blade again, point down, eyeing the man's ear. He tightened his grip.

"Enough, Tallis! Here I am."

With relief, he looked up to see Haedrun emerging from the shadows.

Chapter
Sixteen

Enemies and Friends
Zol, the 10th of Sypheros, 998 YK

The woman was tall, her frame athletic and strong. She was a Karrn for sure, her dark features resolute and proud. Lines of worry creased her face, though she could hardly be five years older than Soneste. Haedrun had a warrior's bearing, but in place of chain or mail, she wore a suit of supple, gray leather. In one white-knuckled fist she held a long sword whose blade caught the faint cold firelight and magnified it preternaturally.

"You're a bastard, Tallis," she said, pointing to Bentius. "Fix him. Now."

From the tone in her voice, Soneste assumed the Deneith mercenary was someone close to her. A brother, perhaps? No, her voice wasn't that panicked. A lover? An old friend?

Tallis looked down for a moment at Bentius. The mercenary struggled with his injured knee, too agonized to speak. "Can we talk now?" he asked the woman.

"I'm here now." Haedrun stared daggers at Soneste. "Is this waif a friend of yours?"

Tallis met Soneste's eyes. If he says I'm working for the Justice Ministry, she thought, this will end here. Haedrun was probably an outlaw like him and wanted nothing to do with Korth's authorities. Soneste returned his gaze, hoping her expression was unreadable. He won't tell the truth, she felt sure.

"Can I trust you?" he asked.

"If *you're* not even certain—" Haedrun began.

"I want what you want. Justice, not scapegoating. I'm your chance to prove yourself innocent." Soneste pointed a thumb at Aegis. "He's with me."

Tallis looked them both over carefully. "Fine." He nodded to the Karrn woman. "She's a friend."

"Wonderful," Haedrun said. "Maybe we can invite General Thauram too?"

Soneste allowed herself a sense of relief. In truth, Tallis had likely agreed so he could keep an eye on *her*. He couldn't know what else she knew. Unless he wanted another fight, he had little choice in the matter.

Tallis pulled a small potion vial from his coat. He looked around to see if anyone else was watching or listening. "Your answer?" Tallis asked Haedrun.

The woman pointed at Bentius. "Give it to him. Then we'll talk, but not here."

Tallis dropped the vial within the mercenary's reach. "There you are, Benty. Lead on," he said to Haedrun.

"You first," the woman said, pointing her blade at Soneste and then waving it northward. Beyond the curtain of shadow, she could see Korth's waterfront. "You're staying in front of me, you and your walking shield."

Soneste complied, pulling Aegis with her. "Thank you for disobeying me," she whispered to the warforged. "You saved my life, I think."

"It is what I said I'd do, Mistress," Aegis said. "Sometimes I succeed."

"I'll never forgive you for hurting them like that," Soneste heard Haedrun say to Tallis.

The Karrn grunted. "Now let's see if I can forgive you."

❦ ❦ ❦ ❦ ❦ ❦ ❦

When they passed through the curtain of shadow, the natural lights of Korth's early hours returned. The Storm Moon hung full overhead, casting its flickering image into the dark waters of King's Bay.

Tallis watched the inquisitive, Soneste, as she walked in front of him. She moved with the easy gait of a natural thief. What was her part in all this? He was glad to have found Haedrun again—at last, he was getting somewhere—but he couldn't stop wondering about Soneste. Had she followed him to the Market, shadowed him all day? Did she know of the Midwife?

Answers for later.

"Brelander," he said, deliberately adding a derisive tone to the imprecise term. When she looked back at him over her shoulder, he looked pointedly at the warforged and the hooked hammer he carried. "I would very much like my property back."

"And I would very much like *mine* returned," she answered.

"Naturally. A trade, then?"

The inquisitive looked to the warforged. ""Give it to him, Aegis."

"Mistress, are you sure?"

"Yes. Can you wield this?" She held her rapier out to the warforged, which gleamed in the moonlight. Was that the same weapon he'd tossed over the bluff's edge just yesterday? He'd thought for sure it would have been nabbed quickly. Every Karrn knew a good blade when he saw it.

The bulky construct eyed the slender, fine-pointed blade. "I'd . . . rather not."

Despite himself, Tallis nearly laughed. They made their exchange.

Soneste retained both her sword and the curious, violet-tinged dagger. The warforged seemed content without a weapon. Tallis knew the thick buckler attached to its forearm was weapon enough.

The hooked hammer came into his hands with pleasing

familiarity, like an old friend. It seemed so long ago that he'd lost it, but it'd only been three days. He pulled a handkerchief from his coat and did his best to wipe the pick's head clean of blood. Fortunately, mithral was easier to clean than most metals.

His arm still hurt from his injury—it needed to be dressed soon. He shook the thought away and looked to Haedrun. The Red Watcher was eyeing Soneste as if she expected an explanation, but Haedrun herself had much to explain.

Haedrun led them in a wide, staggered line out to the waterfront, steering clear of the White Lion patrol routes. She kept furtive watch behind them, ensuring that none followed without her observance. Only the odd sailor or vagrant marked their passing, but she seemed unconcerned with these.

They came to an empty and precarious pier whose repair had clearly not been a high priority after the war. Where the dock touched the wharf, a dilapidated warehouse with shattered windows stood, silent as a corpse. When Haedrun led them through a broken door, Tallis noticed that part of the building was still in use. Against the south wall, lumber was stacked nearly to the rafters. The walls shielded them from the wind but did nothing to neutralize the cold air.

Shadows stirred at the base of the woodpile.

Tallis pushed Soneste aside and swept the curved hook of his weapon low to the ground. A man, armored much like Haedrun, tumbled to the ground. He cursed and looked up at Tallis, rubbing at his shins. "I wasn't going to attack." The rogue climbed to his feet and slipped the dagger in his hand away.

"Any more shadows?" Tallis asked Haedren.

"Just the one," she answered, then flicked her eyes at Soneste. "You're bringing someone I don't know. It's only fair. He's one of us and a friend I can trust."

"What we have to talk about doesn't concern him." He looked to the stranger. "Get out, or I'll make certain you don't hear."

Haedrun sighed, then looked to the man. "Just guard the door. We'll be fine."

As the other Red Watcher disappeared outside the door, Haedrun led Tallis to the open space at the center of the warehouse. Soneste watched them carefully, eyeing every shadow and following behind. The warforged joined her but kept its smoldering blue eyes upon the door.

"You know what happened, Haedrun. You gave me that job, so talk."

"I know," she started, not looking him in the eye.

"You gave me the information. I accepted, went precisely where you told me, and it was a setup! Ir'Montevik isn't even in town."

She looked him in the eyes. "The source *was* good. Something . . . must have changed."

"Who was your source? Another Watcher?"

"No," she said. "My superiors didn't even know about this job."

Tallis felt some measure of relief. He didn't want to hear that the Red Watchers had been compromised. The organization was young and entirely too small. He wouldn't join them, but he wanted them to do well.

She went on. "This wouldn't have been sanctioned by the Watchers, not without more information, especially with ir'Montevik staying at the Ebonspire. That's why I turned to you, Tallis."

"What was it?" he asked.

"I received a tip that ir'Montevik was coming to Korth to visit the Temple of the Blessed Lineage to make a delivery of scrolls —something new, spells that could disguise the undead . . . make them look, feel, even *smell* like living, so they'd be able to walk the streets openly, gather in untold numbers wherever the Seekers wanted them."

"Sounds like something the Ministry of the Dead would know about," Tallis said.

"No," Haedrun replied. "This is something else. These spells could affect great numbers and last a very long time."

"Who was your informant?"

"It's not that simple."

"Damn it, Haedrun! I watched two children run through by the killer!"

The woman's eyes widened. "Sovereign Host," she breathed. "I'd heard the Brelish had his family there, but I . . . didn't know."

"Two children, Haedrun. Just like *yours*. They didn't deserve to die. The job *you* gave me led the killer right to them."

Haedrun's eyes misted, and she blinked, trying to counter grief with rage. The Red Watcher looked away, fighting with herself. Guilt tore into Tallis like a torrent of knives, but he couldn't let those responsible for all of this get away with it. What—and *who*—was she hiding?

"Their names were Rennet and Vestra."

They both looked to Aegis, who had spoken the words, its crystal eyes burning like blue fire. Of course, the warforged had been guarding Gamnon's family before Tallis had disabled it. Tallis had probably spared the construct from dying itself at the hands of the assassin. Aegis seemed a formidable warrior, but it couldn't have stopped the killer any more than Tallis.

Beside the warforged, Soneste did not take her eyes from Haedrun. Tallis realized that the Brelish had probably been the one called in to examine the bodies of the victims. She'd seen the aftermath, all the blood. . . .

"Who gave you all this information?" she asked. "That's who sent the assassin."

Haedrun held her blade up and turned furious eyes on Soneste. "Don't you dare accuse me!"

"Just tell me," Tallis said quietly.

Haedrun shook her head in disbelief, as if trying to deny the events that had unfolded. Aegis turned sharply to face the door, but Tallis continued to watch Haedrun carefully. She was his—and probably Soneste's—only lead.

Haedrun wiped her eyes angrily then sighed. "There was an elf I'd been following in Atur. He was Red Watcher material, but I had to be sure about him before I said anything else. One night, he approached me first. He'd known I was following him. He claimed to be a member of Aerenal's Deathguard. That's when he told me about ir'Montevik and the scrolls . . . he must have been working for the Seekers—"

"Mistress!" Aegis interrupted. "The guard is gone."

Haedrun and Tallis looked to the broken door, where the other Red Watcher had exited to stand guard.

Soneste had drawn her rapier and looked up. "Above us!" she shouted.

Interlude

At night, the window of the man's room was shuttered tight. There were no lights within, but what did it matter as he sat alone in the dark with only his living memories as company?

Lord Charoth enters my workroom. His manner is imposing, as always, and his expression evinces the temper for which he is well known. He is not happy with me. "Where is this new 'servant' of yours, Erevyn?"

"My lord, it is good to see you again. Welcome back."

My assistant appears in the doorway and pauses, uncertain whether he is permitted to enter at this time. Charoth looks over to him in obvious astonishment.

I realize, perhaps for the first time, that my assistant is not easily defined. I did not construct him for war—only to assist me with the delicate work of our unusual creation schemas. His mind is keen, his manipulation of the relics demonstrative of his skill. Sverak has been an asset to me and to the facility.

As the director looks upon him now, I realize for the first time how frail he must appear.

Sverak would resemble a common warforged if he had been built with the usual composite plating that protects the more integral framework, but I did not intend him to see combat at all. I expected he would not have the need to physically defend himself. His darkwood body is banded at the joints with metal strips. Silver and steel components do comprise his torso, needed to bind the living fibers and the creation patterns together. Even Sverak's head and face are narrow, no wider than a human skull. The simple, hinged jaw common to most warforged forms an apathetic rictus.

Despite my assistant's singularity, the Orphanage is still an engine of war. As I look upon the livid face of my superior, I realize that my accomplishment with Sverak may be construed as impudence.

My assistant looks to me for guidance.

"What . . . have you done, Erevyn?"

"My lord, Sverak has been invaluable to my work—to our work." I turn to my assistant. "Sverak, this is Lord Charoth Arkenen d'Cannith."

The warforged is barely three months old, but he already knows who Charoth is—the man everyone in the facility knows and respects. And in truth, fears. Many have been demoted or released from service under his unforgiving management.

Lord Charoth looks back to me, and I wonder if I, too, will soon be released.

He strikes the ground with his staff. "Warforged are not mere novelties, Erevyn, to be adopted as pets or homunculi for the serving."

"I know that, my lord." He must give me time to explain how much Sverak has accomplished for me—for us all—in three short months.

"No, you do not," he says with terrible calm. "You, to whom the workers of this facility look for guidance and leadership—a minister of the house, an example of what they aspire to be!—do not understand at all."

Lord Charoth steps close to me, his tall frame more imposing in close proximity. The smile of approval that all who answer to him crave, it is gone for me. Instead, this frown of disappointment weighs upon me.

"House Cannith produces many great things, and the warforged are our crowning achievement, yet we do not simply create walking constructs to fight a tragic war in the stead of living men. We have spent thousands upon thousands of man hours designing the training programs needed to give these living weapons the proper psychological instruction to do what they must. These programs teach strategy, the concepts of life and death, the tenets of war, but most of all they teach obedience. Obedience to their makers and to those who purchase them."

I swallow and struggle to find my voice. "Lord, I assure you, Sverak is obedient, and he is more intelligent by far, more capable than—"

"There is a reason we make no exceptions to these rules, Erevyn. Do you recall the early experiments of sensory deprivation? Select units were buried alive. For weeks. Months."

"Yes, lord. I know." Denied anything to occupy their minds or explain their perceptions, they went insane. "But this place—here, at my side, there is no such risk."

Sverak steps into the room now. He is always concerned for me. It must unsettle my sensitive assistant.

"Esteemed director," Sverak says to him. "Please do not concern yourself with such trivialities. I am lucid."

Charoth whirls on Sverak, aiming a wand at him as he does. "Do not presume you can address me!"

Sverak stares back at him without a word.

Charoth faces me again. His hand touches my shoulder, briefly, and his grip is strong. Agitated. "Keep it here with you. I must think on this. We will revisit this soon, Erevyn, I promise you. Perhaps the creation energies you have wasted can be salvaged still."

Chapter
SEVENTEEN

Crossing Blades
Zol, the 10th of Sypheros, 998 YK

An inexplicable chill sank through Soneste as she felt more than saw shifting in the darkness of the rafters above. A shadow had separated from the rest, moving with preternatural grace. Soft as a whisper, it sprang from beam to beam, almost directly overhead.

"Above us!"

Like a creature borne on the wind, the nebulous shape floated down from the shadows, led by a long blade. Tallis turned sharply, bringing the curved head of his weapon to deflect a strike aimed directly at Haedrun. The blade was turned aside, but the figure—little more than an indistinct, humanoid shadow—had anticipated Tallis's deflection. It kicked sideways, the force of the blow pushing him back. He stumbled, trying to keep his feet.

The fluidity of the assailant's form unnerved her. Soneste hesitated, then steeled her will and raised her weapon against it. At the same moment, Haedrun surged forward with her own sword.

A second blade appeared in the assailant's other hand, and it parried both attacks with ease. Aegis ran to join the fray, leading with his shield. Nearly surrounded, the figure vaulted backward, the rapier-blades vanishing in the same motion.

Soneste's mind raced. Was *this* was the Ebonspire assassin? Tallis had recovered himself and braced his hooked hammer again, his face twisted in loathing.

"What is this thing?" Haedrun shouted.

"Use magic!" Tallis said. Soneste saw him pull a black wand from a pocket of his coat. "The bloody thing can't be harmed with weapons."

Soneste focused on the shape of their enemy, who paused at a distance and appeared to study the four of them with unseen eyes. She had only one power that had ever proven effective in a fight, a mental trick that could force an opponent to repeat its previous action. She recalled the assailant's last maneuver—a brief retreat—and willed it to effect the same action again immediately.

After a moment's concentration, Soneste exerted her will, but she felt the invisible power disperse around the assassin's mind as if unable to find purchase. In the same instant, the creature sprang into motion, advancing again without fear. The twin blades seemed to *unfold* from nowhere with blinding speed, appearing in its grasp again.

Aegis was there to intercept, striking out with one empty hand to accept the assassin's attack. One blade skittered off the composite plating, while the other stabbed clear through the wood components of his arm. Entangled, the assassin was unable to move clear of Aegis's true attack. The buckler on his left arm crashed into its body, slamming it to the ground. Soneste heard the bang of metal against metal—was the assassin armored beneath its raiment of shadow? regardless, they *could* hit it.

Tallis and Haedrun were ready, standing beside one another as in a military formation. Soneste could see that they'd fought side by side before.

The assassin gained its feet in one fluid motion, dodged another heavy swing from the warforged, then stabbed both rapier-blades through the center of Aegis's artificial body. A dark, alchemical fluid leaked from the exit wound at his back. The warforged dropped loudly to the floor and lay inert. Soneste cursed.

Tallis pointed his wand at the assassin and a narrow beam of fire stabbed through the air. When it struck the assassin, the fire flickered harmlessly away.

"Khyber," Tallis cursed, abandoning the wand. He stepped in front of Haedrun, ready to engage it.

The assassin closed the distance. Tallis swung—

—and the creature danced around him with liquid grace, focusing its attack fully upon Haedrun.

The Red Watcher was ready for it, watching the flashing blades with a veteran's eye. She countered one rapier then sent the second blade out wide. Still the assassin was too fast. It spun its body in a complete circuit, stabbing with both blades at frightening speed. She cleared the first . . .

Her defenses opened.

The assassin's second blade pierced the stiff, boiled leather of Haedrun's armor and slid deep into her body, stopping only when the creature's shadowy hand struck the leather. The woman hissed from the pain, lacking the breath or focus to do anything else.

"Sovereigns," Tallis gasped, taking that moment to bring the hammered end of his weapon into the assassin's back at full force.

The loud slam of metal shook the thing's body. It did not react to the blow, evincing no pain at all. It merely pulled its blade from Haedrun's chest. A steady river of blood followed the length of metal out.

Soneste reached out and caught the woman in her arms. If she could have one moment of peace, perhaps she could stem the flow of blood and save Haedrun! She carried bandages, even a minor healing draught.

Dol Arrah, she prayed, let her live!

Tallis struck again, reversing the weapon and bringing the sharp pick's head against the assassin's back. She saw the figure jerk as the pick caught somewhere on its body. Although she was unable to gauge its wounds—uncertain if the creature could even suffer injury—Soneste knew it was still a very real threat. Tallis had settled into a soldier's calm, focused now that he discovered he could actually strike the enemy.

But the assassin had eluded him again. Its hand flashed out, the rapier blade stabbing forward yet again. Soneste cried out as she felt the air displaced by the blade and the spatter of warm liquid upon her face. Haedrun's body twitched in her arms.

The assassin's blade had punched clear through the woman's neck.

"Oh, gods," Soneste mouthed.

With Haedrun eliminated, the assassin changed its strategy. It pivoted and began to engage the Karrn. She could have sworn it was a feverish smile she saw upon Tallis's face. Rage and frustration poured into his body, and she understood why he'd become the infamous man that he was. He knew how to read his opponent, even one as fast and deadly as this, and retaliate with a strategy of his own.

Soneste laid Haedrun upon the ground and backed away, trying to decided her next course of action. Tallis traded blow for blow with the assassin, accepting minor wounds from its rapier blades as he crashed his weapon again and again into the creature. The unmistakable clang of denting metal was proof of armor beneath its veil of shadow.

Feeling frustrated and impotent, Soneste drew forth her crysteel dagger. In her grasp, the exotic weapon seemed to resonate with kinetic power. Against this unnatural enemy, she would take whatever advantage she could get. It seemed impervious to both her mental powers and the wand Tallis had employed.

Though she could see no wounds in its shadowed form, Soneste believed the assassin was losing. With a half prayer to the Sovereign Host, she circled around the creature, ready for an opportunity to end it. For one fleeting moment, she met Tallis's eyes. He nodded.

The assassin surged forward with both bloody weapons again, piercing Tallis in the leg. Soneste took that moment to strike. The crysteel disappeared into the shadow of its back and she felt it meet the resistance of a thin layer of metal then sink through. The assassin spun, sweeping its left blade low to trip her up.

But Tallis was ready. He arrested the swing, stepping hard upon the tip of the rapier with one boot, then he brought the pick's head down in a two-handed grip. With a jarring shriek, something gave way. Soneste thought she felt a fine spray of cold liquid in the air, but it dissipated quickly.

She saw part of the assassin's shadowed body break lose and heard it clatter to the floor. She expected to see blood, but there was none. The assassin's left blade had vanished altogether.

The creature may have survived injuries that would have slain a mortal man, but it could only take so much punishment. Released from its brief restraint, the creature strode away. But Tallis had already sidestepped, anticipating a retreat. It halted, as if to consider its predicament. At the same time, its veil of shadow began to dissolve. She saw the glint of metal underneath.

To her surprise, the creature turned wordlessly back to face *her.* One rapier remained in its grip; the other gone with its missing hand. The assassin, its shadow unraveling more with each second, thrust its lone weapon toward her with supernatural celerity.

Soneste turned the blade aside, but it came in again.

Then a third time. She didn't know how many times it struck, but she couldn't parry fast enough against its speed. She heard Tallis call out, then a terrible fire erupted deep within her. She looked down in muted denial at the rapier blade that had somehow made its way into her body.

Her killer had become an armored knight of lissome form, a helmed dreamshape with a black-slitted visor. She wondered distantly if she had invented it in a state of delirium.

The world raced around her at a frightening pace, with clashing blades and whirling steel, but Soneste felt her part in it slowing down. Tallis shouted again, his voice sounding hushed, faraway. He implored her quietly and urgently to stay with him. The ground collected her, the shadows in the rafters above cajoled her.

And ushered her into a vast, empty sleep.

◦ ◦ ◦ ◉ ◦ ◦ ◦

"Host, no!"

Tallis watched for only a second in shock as the Brelish slid from the assassin's blade and dropped to the floor. The assassin made no second attack against her to finish her off as it had Haedrun. It turned and struck back at Tallis again, but its blows were feeble. Deliberately ineffective.

The last vestiges of its shadowed form dissolved, leaving him facing the same killer he'd met at the Ebonspire. He knew it couldn't be a man or woman at all—there was a spirit or demon housed in that slender, steel-armored frame.

The assassin sprinted away from him. It was wounded now, the metal of its body caved in and pierced in ways that would have killed a living soul. Tallis started to pursue, knowing he could keep pace with it with his enchanted boots.

A glance back at Soneste told him she was alive still. Her cloak lay open, her shirt stained in blood, but she was still alive. If he left her now, she would die. Haedrun lay, staring into the shadows above with wide, unseeing eyes. She was gone already.

"Khyber!" he cursed, looking to the retreating assassin once more. The creature had leapt to one of the broken windows, aiming to flee to the docks. If he faced it again another day, he knew with grim certainty that it would be strong again.

"Another day, then," he promised, seething with rage he could not express.

Tallis stowed his weapon and ran to Soneste. Stanching her wound the best he could, he searched hastily through her pockets for anything that might help but found only a single unidentifiable vial. If it wasn't a healing draught, it could kill her instead. One of her pouches yielded the missing lens of his darkvision spectacles, which he pocketed quickly.

As he sheathed her rapier, he turned to look upon the aftermath of the fight. Haedrun, lying undignified in a pool of blood. The warforged, Aegis, immobile upon the ground. Cold night wind whistled through the jagged windows of the warehouse. Lying on the ground beside Haedrun was what appeared to be a hollow metal gauntlet—the assassin's hand. He scooped it up and tucked it into a coat of his pocket, then he kneeled briefly beside the Red Watcher, touched a finger to her forehead, and quickly buckled her sword at his belt.

I will return for you, he promised.

Lifting Soneste into his arms, Tallis exited the building, staring up at the city. The bluffs rose like steps to the topmost tier, where the Cathedral of the Sovereign Host—and help—awaited. A maze of streets, White Lions patrols, and a race against the woman's own heartbeat lay before him.

As he began his trek, Tallis thought of the pilgrim he'd encountered earlier, walking with his burden away from the docks of the city. The man's friend had already been dead. One more corpse in the darkness of a Karrnathi autumn.

Aureon, he implored the night sky, keep this one alive. Please.

❁ ❁ ❁ ❁ ❁ ❁ ❁

"Find Haedrun Kessler," its master had said. The words still echoed through every fragment of its being, giving it purpose when there had been none moments before the order was given. "Follow Soneste Otänsin until she finds the man Tallis, who will in turn lead you to Haedrun." Those last seventeen words had been unnecessary. It could have improvised the means of finding its quarry, but its master's ignorance had narrowed down its options and led it to be damaged in an unnecessary fight.

"Silence Haedrun when you have found her and be sure she is dead before you return," the voice had continued, giving the first objective a terminus. "Her usefulness has ended."

It didn't need or care for explanations. Motive was inconsequential, a useless quality of the listless denizens of the material world. It lived only for movement and function.

"Kill *only* this woman. Abort only if your own destruction is imminent, then return and report."

Behind its master, the other construct had looked on without comment.

Chapter
Eighteen

Soneste opened her eyes, remembering the visceral pain of sharp metal sliding into her belly. She pushed the blanket down and delicately probed her body. Bandages had been tightly wrapped around her stomach and waist. Only a dull ache remained, but her mind recalled the agony with perfect clarity. She had trained her mind to store both images and words in her inquisitive work, but as a consequence even her unpleasant memories were often retained.

She was safe now, she felt that much. Where was she—a Jorasco house? Recovering from such a wound would have taken weeks naturally, so she knew magic been used to heal her. Her sharp eyes caught the shape of the Octogram carved in relief above the room's only door, symbol of the Sovereign Host.

She sat up and looked around. The room was spacious and comfortable, with an outline of morning light framing heavy curtains high on the wall above her. The wall opposite her housed a tapestry, finely woven with threads of violet, red, and gold. In a corner between the two was a small table only large enough to accommodate the game board sitting there. Carved figures of rosewood and ebony, resembling kings and soldiers,

were arrayed within alternating squares of light and dark—
Conqueror, one of Karrnath's favorite pastimes.

There was a mirror affixed to the final wall with a dim cold
fire lantern ensconced beside it. Below that, her shiftweave clothing and gear had been neatly folded on a small table, along with
her boots and satchel.

Her weapons were nowhere to be seen.

Soneste stood, ready to assess her whereabouts. As she moved,
an echo of the pain returned. She sucked in a breath and steadied
herself with one hand against the bedpost.

The door opened and a brown-haired elf wearing green
vestments stepped into the room. He bore no obvious weapons
but carried a cloth-wrapped bundle in his hands and a broadsheet rolled up beneath one arm. It didn't look like the *Korth
Sentinel*.

"I wouldn't walk just yet," he said. "Please, take your time.
Recover your balance first. That's key."

Soneste was grateful to note that whoever had tended to
her—*this elf?*—had left her undergarments in place. She'd spent
more than one night in a Jorasco hospital before, and it had looked
nothing like this. Their rooms were small, stark, and efficient; this
one was amateur yet homey. The halflings of Jorasco were more
professional, perhaps—and ultimately more effective—but they
would have cared less about a dying woman's modesty. A faint
aroma lingered in the air, but it smelled more like incense than a
healing poultice.

"I'm well enough," she answered, sitting back down on the
bed. If she couldn't look around just yet, she would glean from this
elf whatever she needed to know.

"The wound is cured, but some pain will linger. The blade
scraped against one of your ribs. If you can wait a while longer, I
will use a spell to take the edge off."

"Do I have a choice in the matter?" she asked. "Or am I
prisoner here?"

"You can choose to wait patiently," he answered, lips curling into the hint of a smile. "Or you can choose to wait impatiently. I'd recommend the former."

"You're a priest," Soneste said, then gestured to the room itself. "I'm somewhere beneath the cathedral, right?"

"I am a servant of Aureon, yes. My name is Lenrik Malovyn. It is a pleasure to meet you, Soneste Otänsin." He did not confirm her location, but that was evident enough.

Soneste noticed a bronzewood amulet carved in the shape of an open book around his neck. Most priests of the Sovereign Host were not devoted to a single member of the Host, but she knew there were exceptions. Aureon was the Sovereign of Law and Lore, the god of knowledge and the patron of those who upheld order.

"And you are a friend to Tallis," she said with a smirk, looking at the bed beneath her with a new light.

This is where the Karrn had hidden away the night before. Once she'd discovered his apartment, the basement of Aureon's shrine must have become his only sanctuary. Lenrik Malovyn was, no doubt, one of the reasons the Justice Ministry had never caught this particular vigilante. The Civic Minister wouldn't have looked to Korth's own clergy.

She recalled the man she'd seen executed by the White Lion sergeant. Martial law was omnipresent in this city, in this whole nation. For consorting with a man wanted for murder and treason, what would Lenrik's fate be if Soneste exposed him?

While investigating various locations within the city the day before, Soneste had stopped here in the Cathedral of the Sovereign Host. She'd spoken briefly to the Vassals—priests and laymen alike—and had heard from all of them in glowing terms about the heroine and high priestess who served as prelate to the cathedral.

"Tell me, do your superiors know that you, a priest of the god of law, harbor a man wanted for breaking *many* laws?"

"As it stands, Prelate Roerith does not." Lenrik's almond-shaped eyes looked much older than his youthful appearance. Like most humans, Soneste could not accurately guess an elf's age. His face showed only the slieghtest touch of time.

He sighed deeply. "Will you not cooperate, Miss Otänsin? Tallis wanted only to save your life. There are less savory places he could have brought you. As it is, he brought you to me. Did he err in this?"

Soneste flushed, but her shame only stoked her. "He *should* have brought me to the Jorasco enclave. I'm here in your city by request of the Justice Ministry and the King's Citadel of Breland. Your government would have paid for my care."

"All of the dragonmarked enclaves are under watch by the White Lions, and we were under the impression that you'd keep hunting him as soon as you were well enough to do so. The Justice Ministry would like to see him clapped in chains and brought to judgment—which is to say execution—and you have been trying to hasten that fate, haven't you? I'm rather fond of Tallis, so I can't say I disagree with his decision."

"How do you know him?" Soneste asked. "Are you party to all his crimes?"

"You speak vaguely of past crimes," the elf said, "but you know he's innocent of the crime that brought *you* here, don't you? It was a risk for him to bring you to me for healing, for my own reputation and his safety, a risk we were both willing to take."

That's putting it mildly, she thought. In her time sifting through the records at the Justice Ministry, she'd seen the unforgiving Code of Kaius cited frequently. Both Tallis and Lenrik would be swiftly tried and summarily executed.

"Alternatively, Miss Otänsin, he could have left you to die."

Wait a moment, she thought. She'd only given Tallis her first name. "How is it you know my surname?" she asked.

The elf smiled, the expression seeming genuine. "Well, you *have* given a number of people in this city your full name recently. The Civic Minister's writ leaves quite an impression in its wake, yet that is not how I know your name, Miss Otänsin."

Lenrik held up the broadsheet he'd carried in with him. "I

was particularly interested in the story of the missing royal aide, Shauranna Rokesko, who was kidnapped by the Order of the Emerald Claw and very nearly sacrificed." He unrolled the packet and displayed its heading: *The Sharn Inquisitive.*

Soneste fell silent. She didn't know what to say.

"Your investigations have made it into the public eye more than once," Lenrik said. "Old loremongers like me tend to take interest in foreign affairs, especially fascinating stories like this one. So yes, I've read the name 'Soneste' before hearing it again last night when my friend Tallis carried an injured Brelish woman bearing the same name through the church doors."

Soneste couldn't meet his eyes.

Lenrik tapped the broadsheet again. "Shauranna Rokesko, from what I've heard within the faith, was a very special soul. Her presence in that meeting at Sovereign Towers was very important—more than you know—and you made that happen. You have a growing reputation for helping a great many people by saving a few."

"Where is Tallis now?" she asked quietly.

"He'll return soon. He went to pay his final respects to an old friend."

Haedrun. The thought sent a wave of guilt crashing against her. She could still remember the warm blood of Tallis's friend on her face, spilled so mercilessly. Even Aegis had fallen to the assassin. Was he dead or merely incapacitated again? He hadn't been in top shape in the first place.

"Haedrun was a Red Watcher," he said sadly, "One of a number of men and women dedicated to the riddance of undeath from our nation. In the last days of the war, she lost her husband and two small children to the corrupting touch of ghosts. They were vengeful spirits raised by Karrn mages, but the necromancers themselves lost control of them. Commanding the dead is not a perfect art nor a righteous means to an end. The Red Watchers are a society devoted to purging this taint of undeath. With entities like the Ministry of the Dead still in power, you can imagine how this forces them to operate in the shadows."

"So does Tallis," she said, "but he isn't a Watcher himself?"

"No. He has his own reasons, both for hating the undead and for not joining the Red Watchers." Lenrik seemed to search the air for the correct words. "Most of the Watchers are not outlaws. Tallis has never wanted his problems to be anyone else's. This is why I do not bring my colleagues into affairs like this. Their ignorance protects them."

And you? Soneste wondered. How does a priest of the god of law justify lawlessness of any kind?

Lenrik pulled up a chair, sat, and looked directly at Soneste. "I know, this is coming from a priest. I won't preach to *you*, Miss Otänsin. You aren't a member of my congregation. I don't even know if you consider yourself a Vassal, but you must understand that while necromancy has made Karrnath infamous to the rest of Khorvaire, it has also corrupted us from within. Priests of the Blood teach that the source of all life lies within people, within blood itself, and not with gods at all. It's an attractive notion, certainly—that we need look only *within*, not without, to find all the answers we crave— but the Cultists of Vol go too far. They do not let the fallen lie in peace, instead raising them as champions to their cause. Undead creatures desire only to destroy, to kill, to *take* life. The king was right to sever all ties to the Cult when it grew too powerful, but it has never lost its grip on the nation."

A long silence followed the priest's sobering words. In three short days, Soneste had learned so much more about Karrnath than she'd ever expected. Since she was a girl, she'd thought of the land ruled by King Kaius and his successors as a place where the dead walked again. It was easy to forget that not all of its people approved of such atrocities.

"What does undeath have to do with any of this?" she asked. "The evidence I've found doesn't suggest the use of necromancy in the least."

"That is true," he admitted. "We don't yet know why Haedrun and the Red Watchers were involved in the murder. I only wanted you to understand what the loss of Haedrun means to Tallis, myself, and our nation."

Soneste looked around the room. She needed to keep the elf talking.

"You say Prelate Roerith is ignorant of Tallis's personal war against the Blood of Vol because he doesn't want to share his problems, but he obviously does bring his problems to *you*."

Lenrik chuckled sadly. "I don't know that he has a choice in that. I have known Tallis for too many years."

"Will you tell me how you do know him?" she asked, feeling like the *Sharn Inquisitive* reporter who'd interviewed her only a few days ago. "Off the record," she added with a half smile.

"Before his commanders recognized his talents and he was sent to Rekkenmark, Tallis served in a regiment ordered to secure the southern border against the advances of Cyre. I was the chaplain assigned to that regiment out of Vurgenslye, though the colonel saw me as little more than one of his field healers. Tallis and I became fast friends in hard times."

Soneste listened to his words but simultaneously planned her escape. The high window above would open onto temple grounds, but it was probably too narrow for her to climb through. The door seemed her only option, though she shouldn't rule out the possibility there were other, hidden exits. Lenrik was a priest, but he was also a war veteran. She didn't know if she could knock him down if it came to that.

"That's all, then?" Soneste asked, prompting him to continue. "Comrades-in-arms?"

The elf shook his head. "Actually, I did meet him before that. You see quite a long time ago, my father had a falling out—you might call it—with the rest of my line. We left Aerenal when I was still a child and settled in Karrnath, and I became a Vassal of the Sovereign Host. Eventually I joined the clergy. The Undying Court of Aerenal is my heritage, but not my faith."

"And Tallis?" Soneste asked.

"Well, I attended the Gods' Grace Academy in Tanar Rath

and was in seminary still, visiting temples and shrines throughout the nation, when I first met the man you've been hunting on the Justice Ministry's behalf. Tallis was a boy at the time, not yet old enough for military service."

She was finding this elf's company very agreeable despite her intention to escape. She was sympathetic to what he was saying, and she believed that Tallis was largely innocent of the ambassador's murder, but she would not abide imprisonment at their hands. That was not their decision to make.

Soneste considered her extrasensory talents, trying to decide which one would best allow her to manipulate Lenrik.

❂ ❂ ❂ ◉ ❂ ❂ ❂

It was later in the morning when Tallis returned to the undercroft of Aureon's shrine. He hadn't stopped moving since Haedrun's death, hadn't lingered on the horror or succumbed to sleep.

The truth was that Haedrun had lived her life much as he had, knowing every day that her work invited death. Both he and the Red Watcher had expected to die at the hands of their enemies, not peacefully in their sleep someday. They'd even laughed and shared a drink or two over the notion.

Weariness pressed against his mind, but Tallis pushed back. Again. He paused at the bottom of the stairs when he heard the unmistakable sound of feminine laughter behind the door. It felt good to hear even a moment's levity. He ached to be a part of it, but he knew, right now, that he couldn't be.

Tallis opened the door to see Soneste talking with Lenrik in quiet tones. The woman sat upon the bed, dressed now, looking healthy and composed. Lenrik sat in the chair across from her, a cloth-wrapped bundle in his lap. Both turned to him when he entered.

"Is she safe?" Lenrik asked.

"The collectors won't have her," he confirmed, hating himself for ending their conversation with such grim words. There was still much to do. His mind was all business. To Soneste, he said,

"When I returned, your warforged was gone. It may have walked away itself, I don't know."

"I understand. Listen . . . Tallis?" Soneste stood, and he could see the bandages wrapped around her lower abdomen. Only a small amount of blood had seeped through. Her color was strong. "Thank you," Soneste said, awkwardly. "For . . ."

"Lenrik is the one to thank," he answered. "I'm no healer."

"You know what I—"

"Now, now," Lenrik said. He stood. "Enough pleasantries and uncomfortable sentiments. Let's talk about the business . . ."

The elf held up the bundle and pulled the cloth aside.

". . . at *hand*." There lay the silvery, hollow gauntlet that had been cut from the assassin's arm. Soneste's eyes fixed on it with sudden interest.

"How does your god put up with you?" Tallis asked with a stifled laugh and a roll of his eyes. Despite the badness of the joke, it felt good.

"Aureon is the most patient of the Host, didn't you know?"

Intricate spiraling designs were carved in filigree upon the gauntlet, and both the palm and lames along each finger comprised numerous fine hinges. This was more sophisticated than any piece of armor he'd seen before. At the center of the palm a slot opened up that ran to the cuff, where Tallis had severed it from the rest of the arm. In the low light he thought he detected a gold sheen to the metal.

"Is this steel?" he asked.

"I'm not sure," Lenrik answered. "It's remarkably flexible."

Soneste ran a finger along the slotted palm. "This is where the blades deployed, but where did they go? The creature had them out in no time, and they'd disappear as quickly."

Lenrik pointed to the cuff, which had been scored by Tallis's weapon when the cut was made. "Is it possible that the gauntlet just slipped free, leaving the wearer's hand exposed? This glove is entirely hollow."

"No," Tallis and Soneste answered at the same time. Both had seen the assassin in its deadly work. Tallis continued. "There was no living person beneath this armor. When I cut this gauntlet loose, there was no hand beneath, and no blade fell free."

They stood in silence for a moment. Lenrik sighed and sat down again, staring at the mysterious hand. "I've searched through the Archives of Aureon but found very little with which to identify this. I have heard of animated suits of armor, but most of those are attributed to undead spirits. They're usually only guards, whose orders are reactive in nature."

"The Blood of Vol," Tallis affirmed. "Some new model fresh from the pits of the Crimson Monastery."

"But why use such a spirit against a Brelish dignitary?" Soneste asked. "Does it serve Cultists of Vol to stir up political conflicts? To threaten the peace?"

"Depends on who you ask," Tallis said. "I'd think it would. The Blood of Vol grew powerful early in the Last War because of what it offered King Kaius. If there was war again, there'd be renewed need for their assistance."

Lenrik shook his head. "Many in the Ministry of the Dead are practicing Seekers, but not all. There are plenty of men who can raise the dead without relying on the Blood of Vol."

Soneste looked to Tallis. "Why try to pin all this on you?"

"They've been looking for a way to remove me for years," he answered simply, "but could this really all be just to get *me*? Try and get the law to take me down since they can't?"

Soneste tapped the metal hand again. "What if this is some kind of warforged? Why assume this is the work of the Blood of Vol?"

Tallis manipulated the fingers of the gauntlet, trying to imagine it upon a warforged scout. "I've never seen any warforged with five fingers before. Not even those who can sling spells look quite like this. You think House Cannith has something to do with this?"

"It might." Soneste seemed distracted by the possibility. Then she met his eyes. "What were you doing at the Ebonspire? Who is this ir'Montevik that your friend spoke of?"

Tallis sighed. "I was going after *him* that night. He's a man with more gold than he deserves. He'd be all too happy to see the Blood of Vol take power again. You heard what Haedrun said. We were *both* expecting ir'Montevik at the Ebonspire, but it was Gamnon there instead. The whole thing was a set-up. I'd known Gamnon years ago. He was jut a captain then, when our regiments were working together."

Soneste shook her head. "I've read through every record the Justice Ministry has on you, Tallis. I didn't see anything in there about Gamnon ir'Daresh or any allied regiments."

"There's a lot that happened in the war that's not on record," Tallis answered. He instantly regretted his tone. He was tired.

"Before the attack," Soneste said to Lenrik, "Haedrun said the one who gave her the tip—which we *know* now was a set up—was an elf with knowledge of powerful scrolls in ir'Montevik's possessions, spells that could disguise the undead in great numbers 'so they'd be able to walk the streets openly, gather in untold numbers wherever the Seekers wanted them.' She said the elf was a member of the Deathguard in Aerenal? Do you know what that is?"

Lenrik frowned. "The Deathguard? It's a religious order opposed to the Blood of Vol. Understand, the Aereni make a vast distinction between true undead—like those employed by the Ministry of the Dead or the Seekers—and the deathless of the Undying Court." The elf looked thoughtful. "Yes, a member of the Deathguard approaching her with news such necromancy would certainly catch her attention."

"Irresistible bait to the Red Watchers," Soneste said.

"So it was all just a ruse," Tallis said. "Ir'Montevik wasn't in Korth, and there never were any such scrolls. I'm concerned more with who this elf was." He turned to Lenrik. "I'm going to take the gauntlet to Verdax. He might be able to learn more from it."

The elf nodded in agreement. "I really ought to carry out the rest of my day as usual." He looked to Soneste. "If Miss Otänsin's absence is eventually noted, I don't want to look suspicious. Mova requested another session with me later today, so that will occupy me for some time."

"Lovely," Soneste said with obvious irritation.

"Yes, you're staying here," Tallis said.

"Tower spit!"

"Listen, just get some rest first and we'll talk about this some more when I come back. I can't have you——" Tallis paused when he heard a soft trill in the air. Where was that sound coming from? It seemed to ring from every direction. Lenrik looked around, too, as even the elf's sensitive ears seemed unable to place the source. "What is . . . ?"

The inquisitive stared back at him with a strange intensity in her hazel eyes. Even though he knew he ought to leave her behind right now, Tallis felt an inexplicable need to stay with her.

He felt Lenrik's eyes upon his, but he didn't want to look away from Soneste. He felt a curious itch inside his mind. What *was* this?

"You want to bring me along," Soneste said.

She was right. He did. It made perfect sense. "I don't really know," he answered. The world seemed a mite dizzy.

"Listen to me, both of you." Soneste walked over to where her boots lay and began to put them on. His eyes followed her every movement. She laced her boots as she spoke, her words nonchalant.

"Lenrik, I spent the last hour sitting here talking with you. I've enjoyed your company and I appreciate both your hospitality and your healing. I am truly indebted, but I've traveled very far from my home to carry out an investigation in the name of the King's Citadel. To that end, I've also spent this time with you analyzing various means of escaping this room and have determined two viable options—only one of which involves the obvious door."

Tallis looked around. What was the other?

"And Tallis?" Without looking at him, she continued to speak, lacing up her other boot. She pushed a lock of her blonde hair away from her eyes. "You're watching me now without full possession of your own will. Disheveled as I am, you would follow me straight to Dolurrh itself. And it wouldn't be *your* choice at all. It would be mine.

"A moment ago I planted a temporary seed of attraction in your mind. Call it a spell if you want, but it isn't. It's a something a kalashtar in Sharn taught me to master. Even now, you are finding my words more compelling, my rationale more sound, than you ought to. I did this because two days have passed since my arrival in Korth, and I've yet to identify the man or woman behind the ambassador's assassination. I can't afford to waste any more time and neither, I suspect, can you.

"I'm being honest with you so you will trust me. I submit to you a treaty of mutual benefit. Should I meet up with Jotrem, or anyone else affiliated with the White Lions or the Justice Ministry, I will not give you up. Indeed, I will not have *found* you at all. In turn, you will help me solve this case. It is what you've been trying to do alone, right? Clear your name of this murder?"

"And exact vengeance," Tallis said gruffly, his own words sounding foolish to him after what she'd just said. A kalashtar? He'd heard of psionic powers, but he'd never experienced any. Either way, damned effective.

"Correct," Soneste said, standing up now. A smile played upon her lips. "As I said to you the other day, in the name of King Kaius III of Karrnath *and* King Boranel of Breland, we will see justice done. We work together on this, and we start by pooling our knowledge. I need to know what you know, and I'll tell you what I've learned."

Soneste held out her right hand. "Do we have an agreement?" she asked with a wink.

She was a cunning creature. Tallis had *never* been comfortable in a partnership. He even kept Lenrik at arm's length when it came to his work against the Blood or other dubious parties, but given the circumstances—and the lingering affects of the attraction—he decided he could make a temporary arrangement like the one she was suggesting.

Tallis grasped her hand firmly. "We do."

Chapter
Nineteen

Soneste related to Tallis the events of the last two days, omitting nothing and carefully reading his face as he listened. He looked dead tired, but his attention was rapt. The attraction she'd planted in his mind wore off sometime during their discussion, but his eyes never wavered from her.

Tallis was guarded in his side of the story. He recounted events beginning with his infiltration of the Ebonspire, saying nothing about the nature of his work or whereabouts prior to the incident. Most of her clues lined up, but the identity of the assassin remained beyond their reach.

It was late morning when they set out from the cathedral, Tallis in his Lyrandar disguise and Soneste in her blue coat. Soneste looked carefully around, afraid Jotrem might track her down. She wanted to search for Aegis, but she knew they had to follow the only lead they had first. Tallis had insisted they take the metal hand straight to an acquaintance of his named Verdax.

"There must be dozens of artificers in this city who can tell us about this thing," she said as the massive Cannith estate came into view.

Even as she eyed the gorgon seal above its gates, she thought again of Lord Charoth and his estrangement from the house. He was mysterious enough to have hidden motives, but he seemed to want nothing to do with warforged or constructs. As she looked at the gauntlet in her hand, she felt certain the assassin was a construct.

Tallis's description of Charoth wasn't much different than anyone else's. The Karrn had been invited to Charoth's glass factory last year, had been made an offer of service, and he'd declined. Lord Charoth was evidently many things: taskmaster, businessman, aristocrat, a man both loved and feared—and a wizard

The *Korranberg Chronicle* had painted an intriguing, colorful picture of the man. If he'd been truly offended by Tallis's refusal to work for him, it seemed to Soneste that Charoth wouldn't need to go to such lengths to take revenge. Perhaps if she asked some members of the house about Charoth, she could learn more.

"Let's try House Cannith," Soneste said, pointing up at the enclave. "They're obviously the most likely to know about what kind of creature can live in animate armor."

"No," Tallis answered. "The dragonmarked enclaves are quickly notified when criminals of a certain caliber are at large. I'm one of those. Besides, Verdax is one artificer I know I can trust."

So this Verdax was probably an outlaw too. Lovely.

They walked the streets in silence, winding slowly down the district tiers of the city. Feeling slightly on edge, Soneste imagined the eyes of every White Lion upon her. She knew the soldiers had been shown portraits of Tallis and were told to keep their search for him as discreet as possible, but whenever she glanced up at him, she was impressed with his new disguise.

In his green coat and hat, few gave him a second glance. He conveyed nobility without the flagrant extravagances she saw among Sharn's elite. They even passed unscathed through two White Lion checkpoints. The city's security tightened with each passing day, especially in the upper districts and the palace of Crownhome. Tallis's papers, identifying him as Findel d'Lyrandar, held up each time. Whoever had forged his papers and his new appearance had done an amazing job.

Even so, they couldn't have hidden the grief that tightened his quicksilver eyes or the rage that pursed his previously wicked grin into a fierce scowl. She reached out and squeezed his hand, surprised to feel how warm it was. He was the only Karrn without ice water coursing through his veins.

"I'm sorry about your friend," Soneste said quietly.

Tallis didn't answer right away. They walked two blocks before he acknowledged her intrusion at all. "I know."

Soneste was surprised when Tallis led them down to the waterfront. A profusion of masts and half-collapsed sails filled the docks. Workers of every race and social class walked this way and that, carrying rigging, ordering inferiors around, and arguing. She searched the mass of people, hoping on a whim to spot Aegis, but the only warforged she saw were hauling cargo to and from river vessels. The din of the crowds and the cadence of dockworkers' song swallowed all other noise. The latter sounded more like battle hymns than river shanties.

"Your artificer is down *here?*" Soneste shouted to be heard. She noted a crowd of roustabouts loitering outside a nearby alehouse.

"Pray join us, Bluebird!" one of the men called to her. One of his mates held up a bottle and made a lewd gesture with it.

Angry words came unbidden to her lips, and her face flushed. "Keeper's swine—"

"Come on, Bluebird," Tallis said with a half smile, taking her hand in his again. "We're almost there."

The Karrn steered her out onto the furthest pier at the east end, passing into the shadow of the bluffs that rose high along the city's edge. The pier itself cried out for repair and some of the pilings looked ready to break free from it altogether. A cluster of damaged ships crowded the dock. Soneste knew very little about seamanship but was fairly certain none of these ships would sail again. Some of them didn't even have masts and were too ramshackle to be elemental-powered vessels.

"Watch your step," Tallis said, pointing out broken planks in their path. He stepped up to what Soneste first assumed was an oddly-shaped dockhouse. It resembled a miniature barge with a rusted iron protrusion serving as the pilot house. She could barely make out the name written on the hull, *Kapoacinth,* amidst thick layers of mildew.

"This was a salvage tug during the war," Tallis explained when he saw her scrutiny.

"Was," she concurred.

Atop a short ramp, they stepped aboard and Tallis rapped the head of his hammer against the vertical hatch which passed for the door. Soneste winced at the jarring sound. She eyed the hand-sized porthole on the door when she caught a flicker within the thick glass. As they waited, Tallis unbuttoned his coat. Buffeted as they were by the bitter riverside winds, Soneste thought him mad.

When there was no response, Tallis hammered again.

A massive reptilian eye filled the porthole, flicking left and right. Its vertical pupil dilated against the daylight behind them. A hellish red glow limned the great eye.

Soneste she reached for her dagger. "What in Khyber . . . ?"

Tallis chuckled, removing his jacket and tucking it under an arm.

An illusion, perhaps. Many arcanists employed fearsome, if harmless defenses such as this in their shops and homes. Soneste found it difficult to believe this floating piece of junk housed a legitimate workshop.

"Who is you?" a harsh voice issued from the door, the sound amplified through invisible pipes.

"You *know* who, Verdax," Tallis answered. "Let me in. I'll make it worth your while."

"Bringing ssstranger?" the voice accused, the eye fixing on Soneste. She looked around to see if anyone else noticed the shrill voice. None did.

"Yes. Just open up."

"No!"

"Very well." Tallis withdrew the metal case that housed his identification papers, propped it open, and cleared his throat.

"Verdaxensoranec!" he said in a loud voice. A few heads near the crumbling dock turned their way at the sound. The angry red eye widened and swiveled around. "You are hereby ordered, in accordance with the Justice Ministry of Korth *and* the Code of Kaius, to submit to an authorized search of the *Kapoacinth* as requested by the Windwrights Guild of House Lyran—"

There came a furious hiss, followed by the metallic *pop* of the ship's door as it unsealed and swung ajar. Tallis clapped the metal case together. "Better let me go first. He hates people he doesn't know." Soneste made a face. "What? You wanted to come, didn't you? By the way, you might want to take that coat off."

On the other side of the door she saw a protruding eyehole at waist level, inlaid with a thick lens that disappeared into the metal. Tallis led her by hand through a cramped and dark walkway that smelled like lamp oil and snake skin. A ramp brought them into the belly of the small ship, where a sudden, stifling heat enclosed them. She removed her coat quickly and folded it over one arm.

The air remained uncomfortably warm and was as black as night until Tallis triggered something upon one wall. Yellow-globed lanterns flared to life with cold fire, illuminating the space. Distaste and wonder both warred for her favor as she looked upon the room.

Soneste had seen arcane workspaces before, had visited magewright shops in Sharn and even glimpsed research chambers in Cannith Enclave. The interior of this boat looked like it comprised the leftover parts from *those* places. Every horizontal surface was littered with a perplexing array of tools and inorganic parts. Hooks and chains jutted from the ceiling and walls, holding whatever failed to fit anywhere else. Tucked in an alcove beside her was a sheaf of legal documents. Against the far side of the shop, a large storage bin was propped half open by something covered in a filthy tarp. She felt an aqueous murmur somewhere beneath her feet, as though the boat itself was powered by churning water.

Soneste's gaze settled at last upon a small, reptilian figure that stood fuming up at her like a tiny bull. For a moment she thought the creature was stuffed, until its glowing red eyes narrowed. No taller than a halfling, most of its scaly, gray-brown skin was covered by a suit that combined a workman's smock with studded leather armor. A pair of oversized goggles perched atop his head, contesting with the two black horns that sprouted there—a kobold.

Most of his kind lived in tribes and laired in caves, setting traps for the unwary and venturing out only to raid. Soneste had never heard of a kobold artificer.

Tallis pointed at her. "Verdax, this Soneste. She's clean." He indicated the kobold in turn. "Soneste, this is Verdax."

"Master Verdax," she said with a half-bow, holding back a smile.

"Shhrk! Where she is from?" the artificer demanded with a hiss.

Tallis opened his mouth to reply, but Soneste cut him off. "Listen," she said, producing her identification papers and holding them out for the kobold's inspection. "I work for Thuranne d'Velderan's Investigative Services, a freelancing inquisitive agency with ties to House Tharashk. I am here on behalf of the King's Citadel of Breland and the Justice Ministry."

Verdax's eyes bulged. The lips of his canine snout peeled back to reveal a collection of tiny sharp teeth. One clawed hand reached for a wand sticking out of his largest pocket.

"I am not here for *you*, Verdax." She pointed at the papers tacked to the wall. "I have no interest in seizing the *Kapoacinth*, for which I'm assuming you possess legal ownership, nor of investigating your business here. We're only interested your help."

The kobold turned his baleful gaze upon Tallis. He had yet to address her directly. "She is law! Cannot be trust!" he screeched.

"Look, she's with me. *Me. I'm* the one wanted by the law, right?" Tallis added, "And Verdax . . . she's from Sharn."

The kobold's glare faltered, quickly supplanted by a sinister, dragonlike smile. He looked back at Soneste. "Tell with me about City of Towers, warmblood."

"Another time," Tallis said. "There's something I really need you to look at right now."

Soneste placed the cloth bundle on the central worktable. Verdax lingered a moment as if lost in a dream, his toothy grin only slowly fading. He mounted a metal step ladder that had been fused to one side of the table and peeled back the cloth. Soneste imagined him constructing various other devices right there, standing on the tabletop like an artificer's homunculus, yet the more she looked around at the wands, potions, and sundry magic items, the more seriously she took the peculiar kobold.

Verdax prodded the empty gauntlet with interest, turning it over and hefting it in nimble claws. At last he looked up at Tallis. "Settle first! Then we gold-talk."

"Fine." Tallis nodded at Soneste. "This will only take a few minutes."

The Karrn and kobold moved to the other side of the shop. Tallis produced the fire wand he'd used just last night, handing it to Verdax. "This was discharged only once in my possession," he began. "I promise you. You can check it yourself."

Soneste watched as Tallis pulled a surprising number of items from his coat and pockets, including a handful of small potion vials. She spied the two metal rods he carried at his belt, but he didn't remove them. From the bargaining session that followed—hushed tones punctuated by the kobold's shrill exclamations—Soneste deduced that Tallis borrowed most of the tools for his peculiar trade but that he did, in fact, own a few of them himself. The gravity-defying rods and the gnomish hooked hammer were probably his. The rest, it seemed, he rented in exchange for gold or temporal magic findings.

Soneste busied herself with her own inventory but quietly studied the space around her. She knew only a little about magic but knew enough to know that Verdax owned a veritable arsenal of arcane equipment and weaponry. Between the basement of Aureon's shrine and this unassuming little watercraft, Soneste knew she'd found Tallis's primary haunts. She already knew a lot about this man. Once this investigation was over, what would happen next? He seemed too careful to just let her go, truce or no truce.

Her eyes kept returning to the storage bin across the way and its tarp-covered protrusion. Was that a *limb*?

"Good," Tallis said when their business had concluded. "Now take a look at that thing!"

◎ ◎ ◎ ◎ ◎ ◎ ◎

Verdaxensoranec didn't appreciate threats. His time was valuable, his skills underappreciated, his hard work underpaid and forced into unlawful measures. But this female warmblood had been gentle enough with her implied threat. She was diplomatic, for a human, yet had she come in the company of anyone other than Tallis, Verdax wouldn't have risked treating with her at all.

The offer of payment allayed his concerns, but talk of Sharn spurred his efforts. The sooner he identified the metal hand, the sooner Tallis and the female would leave and come back again. Hence, the sooner he would learn more of the City of Towers. He'd certainly had enough of the City of Danger. Karrnath was a cold, unpleasant land, and it had made his scales ache for years. The warm caves of his homeland in the Ironroot Mountains were more comfortable, but he'd quit them in favor of more enlightened company.

Alas, Sharn! The famous City of Towers offered an acceptable climate *and* endless arcane resources. Someday he would get the *Kapoacinth* there! The warmblood claimed to be an agent of the king of Breland. That might prove useful toward that end.

Thus inspired, Verdax set upon the strange metal hand. He settled the goggles over his eyes, and the fine filigree of the gauntlet sharpened to perfect clarity. This was a curious metal, to be certain. For a device such as this he knew he would need to call upon the skills bestowed upon him by the mighty dragon Eberron. He prefaced his scrutiny with the purifying words of a Draconic incantation, summoning the first infusion he would require.

Verdax fell into his work. Time faded away, along with the feckless prattle of the warmbloods nearby.

When he'd learned all that he could, he dropped his goggles on the tabletop and stretched. His stomach snarled at him, reminding him how long he'd been ignoring it. Tallis and his female sat wearily nearby, but their eyes came alert when they saw he was finished. A sheen of mammalian sweat slicked their too-smooth skin—especially the Karrn. Oh yes, as if it had been so hard sitting there doing nothing!

"What's the answer?" Tallis asked, uncharacteristically impatient. The half-breed elf was normally a respectable customer.

"Steel is not steel," Verdax answered. When Tallis prompted more of an explanation—what was so hard to understand?—he continued. "Shrrk! Steel is mixed, not steel only. Different alloy. Unsure of ore. Not from real mountain."

"Yes, and . . . ?"

"Not mithral. Not adamant."

"Adamantine, right," Tallis corrected, rudely.

"Yes. Hand is pulled from construct. Living metal."

"Verdax," the female interjected. He *thought* he'd been talking to Tallis. But no matter, this female would assist his career with her knowledge of Sharn and its societies. "This hand came from a creature composed entirely of armor. Could this armor have been animated with necromantic magic? With undead spirits?"

"Shhrk! No. Hand is pulled from *construct* body." Hadn't he just said this? This was very simple to understand. Verdax began to question this kingly agent's intelligence. "Construct not real *alive*. Construct not dead or undead."

"Of course," she answered. "Could this hand have come from some sort of unusual warforged?"

Verdax laughed, and the female made a surprised face. It was funny. "No. Not is . . . ordinary." He waved a claw at the junk bin on the other side of the room, the thought having reminding him that he really ought to inspect his latest yield.

In all his years on the salvage crew, Verdax had never once seen a warforged with five digits upon its hand, nor seen a material simultaneously hard and flexible like this. The swirling arcana etched into the grooves of the gauntlet was not suggestive of Cannith work. They were runes of a different sort, nothing like the schemas he'd once pried off the shell of a warforged titan.

"Not Cannith, not artificer make. Is wizard work."

The female's eyebrows rose, as if this was some astounding revelation. It really wasn't, though. Verdax had learned that much from the hand at first glance.

"Is there anything else you can tell us about it?" Tallis asked.

"Construct powerful. Elemental, but not. Force in construct outside my work. I cannot say. Not know. Wizard work." Verdax hated the common tongue of Khorvaire's most populous races. Draconic was so much more articulate and easier to pronounce. He'd only learned this cast-off language of the Five Nations to advance his career.

"So that's really all? You can't determine what this thing came from?"

"Give you discount on hand identify," Verdax answered, feeling generous and patient. The half-breed was a good customer and the secrets of Sharn awaited.

"Can you at least tell me where I *can* find out more?" There was that impertinence again.

"Yes," Verdax responded. There really was only one place in Karrnath he knew of where one might find out more. He pointed one clawed finger up. "Tower of Twelve."

Tallis and his female exchanged worried glances. Mystery and power surrounded the dragonmarked institution that floated above the City of Danger. It didn't frighten Verdax, of course. He'd love to visit the halls of the Twelve and study relics as ancient as the Dhakaani Empire, but he'd long since given up the notion of visiting. He certainly doubted Tallis, of all the warmbloods in this city, would be welcome there.

"Good luck!" he offered them both and set to rewrapping the metal hand.

"Do you think it's possible?" Tallis asked the female.

"It is," she replied, sounding distracted, "but I'd probably need to provide a good reason. I'm not sure Hyran's writ is enough. The Twelve does not answer to the Justice Ministry or to any government, for that matter. This may require me to tell them about the assassin and the hand."

Tallis sighed. "More will die if we don't track this thing down."

"Keep death away here," Verdax warned, not liking the turn of their conversation.

The female turned her attention full upon him. There was a sneaky look in her eyes, like she was investigating him. "Verdax, you pointed to that bin a moment ago. Can I ask what you keep in there?"

Worthless but potentially useful junk, he thought. At least until last night, when one of his dockside associates had made him an offer. The wharf-dweller had found something that he knew a salvager like Verdax might be interested in. It had cost the kobold fifty gold coins, and he had yet to determine if the trade had really been worth it.

"Junk," he answered.

"Specifically," she pressed. "What is under that tarp?"

Verdax hissed. "Breland warforged. Damaged life core, but fixable. Found last night. Will make new helper, not having to feed."

Tallis raised his hornless brows, and the female smiled big, showing her garish, flat white teeth. Her voice rose in a funny pitch as she spoke. "Master Verdax, you are a most resourceful kobold. I have one final request of you."

Chapter
Twenty

Soneste set out from Verdax's shop with Aegis beside her. The warforged's composite plating was repaired, the deep cuts made by the assassin's blade smooth again. The artificer's infusions had restored Aegis to his full physical capacity. Verdax charged her several times an acceptable amount, but now wasn't the time to argue cost, especially since the funds weren't her own. She knew what they were up against now, and the assassin evidently knew how to find them. She needed Aegis at his best. It would take a lot more than a few rapier stabs to bring him down again.

Despite his mended condition, the warforged's spirits were low.

"I have failed again," he said.

Soneste rapped on the pauldron that served as the warforged's shoulder. "I paid for your repair with the Citadel's gold. You're called to serve a duty, Aegis. To Breland. You haven't failed your king yet."

"I have been disabled twice."

"Well, me too. First by Tallis and then . . ." Soneste instinctively touched her stomach. She could still feel the tight bandages beneath her shirt and remembered all too well the blade sliding into her body. "Last night . . . I nearly died. It was Tallis and his friend who saved me."

"You *found* Tallis, Mistress," Aegis said. "Why are we leaving him again?"

"We're not. We're working together now. In saving me and burying his friend, Tallis has had no rest. He needs it now. And there are some places I must go that I cannot take him. We're meeting him in the park at four bells."

"I do not trust the half-elf."

"Aegis," she said, "he's not our killer and you know that now. We've faced off against the real one. Now we have to trust Tallis, and we *cannot* give him up to the Justice Ministry or to Jotrem. Promise me you will say nothing about last night."

When he did not answer, she stopped him. "Aegis. Promise me in the name of King Boranel—the very liege of your former master, Gamnon ir'Daresh. Promise me, for Rennet and Vestra."

"And Lady Maril." The warforged looked down at her, the fibrous wood that served as his muscles flexing as he stood tall. "I promise."

Soneste smiled. "Thank you."

* * * * * * *

Soneste secured permission with the Justice Ministry for passage and admission to the Tower of the Twelve, but Hyran's writ could not guarantee her a meeting with one of its wizards. She had to wait two bells until the proper document was notarized, transportation with House Vadalis was arranged, and approval from the Twelve was given. Soneste left the Ministry's headquarters, intent on a new destination to pass the time.

"I take it you've been busy, Miss Otänsin?" a voice called out to her.

Jotrem stood waiting for her just outside the gate. He excused himself from a conversation he'd been having with one of the White Lions standing sentry. The older inquisitive's calculating eyes looked

Aegis up and down, no doubt observing the warforged's immaculate condition. She had no intention of justifying anything.

"Something like that," she answered, not slowing to talk.

"Where have you been?" Jotrem asked.

Soneste chuckled darkly. "I'm sorry, Jotrem. The Civic Minister said you would 'serve as my guide in this unfamiliar city.' I am not required to confide in you or share with you the results of my own independent investigation. If you'd like to register a complaint with the Ministry bureaucrats, feel free. I have work to do."

Jotrem fell into step beside her, his familiar scowl returned. "I did not see you leave the Seventh Watch this morning," he said.

"I guess my day started earlier than you expected."

"Where are you going?" he demanded.

"You wish to help, then?"

"Of course, Miss Otänsin."

"Well, thanks. I wish to find Lord Charoth again. I've thought of another question for him. Now that I've already visited him once, I don't think it matters if you're with me."

Soneste saw Jotrem rub his hands together for warmth as they walked. He caught her glance, and he lets his hands fall again. "I've done work of my own," he said. "Lord Charoth, unlike many of the nobles of this city, spends most of his time at work. That is where we will find him now, at his factory. That you found him at home the other day was mere chance."

"Lead on, then," she said, glad she didn't need to return to Charoth's brooding estate.

"What do you intend to ask him?" Jotrem asked.

"You'll see." Soneste didn't have to look at him to sense the man's frustration. She had another trick to use against Charoth now. It was a gamble, but one worth taking.

For a man unaffiliated with one of the dragonmarked enclaves, Lord Charoth's place of business was impressive. Arkenen Glass comprised several facilities, but most prominent was the glass factory near the bluff's edge of the Commerce Ward. Beyond producing mundane glass products, Arkenen Glass supplied the Tower of the Twelve exclusively with reinforced glass for its windows and laboratories alike.

The building was long, five stories high with a clawlike chimney rising from the center of its crenellated walls. From within this architectural grasp dark vapors churned into the sky.

Jotrem's presence proved more than useful. Among other Karrns, he was persuasive and commanding. Without needing to display Hyran's writ, he gained entrance to the factory and convinced one of the senior workers to lead them directly to Lord Charoth. Soneste had to admit, Jotrem certainly had knowledge of his city, and she found herself wondering if she ought to have included him more in her investigation. But how would he have handled the Midnight Market? And she really didn't want Jotrem to meet up with Tallis again. That couldn't go well for either man.

No. She'd been right to go her own way.

The only caveat had been denying Aegis entrance. The man at the factory doors had made an incredulous expression when he first laid eyes upon the warforged. He was emphatic about the construct remaining *outside* the building. Aegis complied after Soneste instructed him on what to say if anyone troubled him.

"Everyone who knows of Lord Charoth also knows he has no love of warforged," Jotrem said quietly to her as the worker led them through a series of chambers.

Soneste recalled Charoth's quote in the *Korranberg Chronicle*: "*Had I been present during the peace talks, I would have pushed for the destruction of all existing warforged. They are obsolete in this time of peace and remain only as a reminder of the weapons of war the Five Nations have inflicted upon one another . . .*"

They entered a room larger than any Soneste had ever seen. Engines of glass production filled the factory floor, manned by scores of workers. At the far end of the hall, two enormous, brick-walled cylinders rose halfway to the ceiling, capped with spinning blades that funneled thick, acrid fumes into the vents above. Attached to the base between the two monstrous machines a metal furnace roared with fire. The air was filled with the drone of churning machinery. Metal walkways stretched across the room on several levels.

A team of men in protective gear were busy repairing the brick wall of one of the vats. Behind them, facing the nearest vat, a glass-walled room had been built into the wall overlooking the factory floor. An open-air metal bank of stairs led up to its door fifteen feet above the ground level. The room's size and prominence told Soneste this was Charoth's own office.

Looking for his robed and masked appearance through its transparent wall, Soneste was surprised to hear the wizard's sonorous voice much closer at hand.

"Just one moment," their escort bade them, approaching a knot of workers who had gathered around the former Cannith lord.

It was strange to see Charoth outside the sterile silence of his manor. Although he looked exactly the same, stately in his dark robes, metal-shod boots, and painted mask, here in his factory and among his employees he seemed more animated. His presence commanded respect.

Soneste pictured Charoth in the subterranean levels of the Orphanage, with magewrights and artificers operating under his orders as did the glassworkers she saw before her. Having never been to a Cannith forgehold, her imagination supplied the details: Spike-armored warforged stood as sentries as more of the living constructs emerging from a yawning creation forge. Charoth, unmarred and unmasked, stood in observance—a stern director with eyes like a hawk, searching for flaws among the facility's creations.

"Ahh, Miss Otänsin!"

The vision faded away. The nearby workers quieted and turned to look at Soneste, an audience of dozens. This was *his* world, she reminded herself cautiously. "Good morning, Lord Charoth."

"It is a pleasure to see you again," the wizard said, his mask turning sleightly as he looked at Jotrem, "and a surprise. But I fear your presence suggests that there is yet a killer to be found."

Soneste flushed. "Yes, there is."

Jotrem spoke, breaking the tension. "It is an honor to see the inside of your factory, my lord. I have always admired it from the outside."

"Thank you . . . ?"

"Major Jotrem Dalesek, my lord," the older inquisitive said, casting his head down with respect.

"Would you mind if we spoke with you?" Soneste asked. "We ask for only a moment."

Charoth tapped the base of his cane firmly upon the ground. "Of course," he answered then waved his gloved hand to the workers around him. "Give me some privacy."

"Lord Charoth," she began when the men shuffled away. "I have seen a good deal more of your city now. I merely wish to ask you some follow-up questions, now that I have . . . context."

Charoth nodded. Soneste found herself staring at the narrow lenses that filled the eyeholes of his mask. She wondered what color his eyes were. "Have you found your prime suspect yet?"

"Briefly," she answered, remembering her first meeting with Tallis in the alley—not far from here, in fact. "But I'm wondering why he hasn't yet left the city. You would think a guilty man would run. I know from experience now that he is resourceful."

"He is at that," Charoth responded, his voice unreadable. "I would not easily be able to locate him for you, if that is what you intended to ask. I suppose I *could* attempt to have him contacted."

A man like Charoth had the influence and—no doubt—a sizable network of informants. In her experience, even the most upstanding nobles had eyes in the underworld.

"There is no need, but thank you." Soneste slung her haversack from her shoulder, unfastened it, then fingered the cloth-wrapped bundle of the assassin's hand. "I wanted to ask you about a piece of evidence I acquired."

"Of cour—" he began. Charoth turned, lifting his glass-eyed gaze beyond her. "Excuse me," he said with unexpected venom in his voice.

A team of men approached led by a well-dressed, middle-aged dwarf with a long silver beard partially braided and bound with small crystal beads. Between the exotic stones and his stiff, even stride, Soneste pegged him as Mrorian noble. He walked with a sleight limp but eschewed any means of support. Dwarves from other parts of Khorvaire didn't carry themselves with quite the level of smug pride as those from the Holds. His team of laborers included well-muscled dwarves and a pair of particularly enormous men.

"Why were my workers given such resistance at the door, Lord Charoth?" the dwarf demanded. His accent confirmed Soneste's suspicions. "My papers are good!"

"Master Doragun!" Charoth bellowed, startling Soneste and arresting the attention of everyone else in the vicinity. "You misled me!"

The Mrorian stopped, his ruddy cheeks darkening. "I have done no such thing!" he answered with mounting anger.

Charoth struck the floor with the base of his glass cane. Electricity gathered at the stroke, then faded away. "Your men are no doubt respectable, honest workers, Doragun, but you said nothing of *those!*"

The wizard pointed with one gloved hand and all eyes turned to the pair of men at the back of Doragun's team. Clad in over-sized workman's clothes, the "men" were, in fact, metal-plated juggernauts who made even the enormous Aegis appear slim. They stared back with flickering crystalline eyes, awaiting their employer's defense.

Soneste tensed when an eight-foot-tall figure bristling with coarse brown fur padded onto the scene. A bugbear! Taller *and* cleaner than most, the tall goblin's body was clad in a leather jerkin. A long black chain wrapped several times around his muscled frame like a piece of armor. One end hung over his shoulder, weighted with a thick metal spike. The creature's lips twisted with obvious bloodlust, prominent incisors slick with saliva. He moved to stand beside Charoth, evidently quite willing to attack at his lord's command.

"Be still, Master Rhazan," Charoth said, but his masked visage had not moved.

Jotrem saw the bugbear as well, scowling as he placed one hand to the hilt of his sword. For one brief moment, the bugbear flicked its beady red eyes at the older inquisitive.

"Who I retain is not *your* concern," Doragun returned. "You summoned me to perform a service, wizard, not to evaluate my staff."

Charoth's rage felt like a gathering storm. Jotrem shifted uncomfortably, while the factory workers looked away to avoid their lord's wrathful attention. The men nearest the bugbear drifted away.

"Warforged are unwelcome in my presence," Charoth said, "and they are forbidden in my factory. You will remove them from the premises immediately and expel them from your team while you operate under my contract!"

The bugbear snarled loudly. Charoth held up a hand to silence him.

Doragun gritted his teeth, flustered. The contractor stared defiantly up at the former Cannith lord, nervously smoothing out his silver beard. His bearing was haughty, but beneath the baleful gaze of the wizard's mask, his pride was tested.

"My lord," the dwarf said at last, "Ang and Tar are my best men. Their work is solid but delicate. They would be a boon to your—"

"No!" Charoth screamed. "They are *not* men!"

Soneste knew an opportunity was upon her. She abandoned her original plan, then shut her eyes and gathered her focus with a moment's concentration. She formed the astral net with her mind then opened her eyes as she cast it into the empty space between Charoth and the Mrorian. Amidst the tension in the crowd, the spectral note of her mental voice went unnoticed.

"Lord Charoth," the dwarf continued to protest, his face bright red.

Soneste willed the net to return. Emotional residue from all around snared within its invisible strands, slipping easily back into her analytical mind as it did.

The fury of an injured pride bled from the dwarf's psyche. From the bugbear, Rhazan, Soneste could feel only bestial aggression mingled with a desire to please his master. He was obviously ordered to keep a distance when his master was conducting business.

Her net nearly slid without yield across Charoth's mind. She felt from him a resistance she'd never experienced before, yet the emotions surging from the wizard were too strong to be missed.

There was anger, outrage at Doragun's continued protests. But something overshadowed it all. What was it?

Soneste's telepathic net snared other errant emotions from the workers nearby—apprehension in some, interest and even amusement from others not the subject of the wizard's ire.

Sharp anxiety flowed from Jotrem beside her. It seemed absurd, especially for a hardheaded veteran like him. Was the Karrn afraid Charoth would level his anger against them? With the arrival of the Mrorian and his warforged, their interview was all but forgotten.

She maintained her concentration seconds longer, determined to learn more.

"This is not a matter of efficiency, Master Doragun," Charoth was saying, his voice cooler now but carrying with it unmistakable menace. "This is principle. The work each warforged does for you denies a handful of honest, hard-working men who need the silver to feed their families. Karrns and Mrorians, it matters not. These walking weapons are not even worth the detritus from which they were produced!"

Doragun's warforged workers took a couple steps forward, as if unable to bear the insult any further. Then Soneste felt it, flowing from Charoth like gushing oil.

Irrational, unmitigated fear.

"Take them *away!*" the wizard roared, magic carrying his baritone across the whole factory. Rhazan stepped in front of Charoth, clasping the spiked chain over his shoulder. The dwarf contractor stepped back, grumbling to himself in indecision.

Soneste relinquished her empathic power then took Jotrem by the elbow. "Let's go," she whispered. The older inquisitive complied all too quickly, and they walked unnoticed away from the scene even as the glassworkers around them began to disperse.

Jotrem led them to the factory doors as Soneste's mind churned. What had happened to this man in that secret Cannith forgehold those six years ago?

Interlude

Someone had been talking to him, but the man in the velvet-padded chair did not hear the voice or the words. His mind was in another time and place, following the same path of memories as if a new outcome could be reached.

I have renewed my case to Lord Charoth once again, but he cannot be swayed.

His months abroad have changed him. Outwardly, he is the same man. Severe, demanding, reliable. But there is a hardness in his demeanor, tempered perhaps by firsthand exposure to the war that rages outside the Orphanage. House Cannith labors, in other forgeholds across Khorvaire, to make weapons, armor, and devices to bolster each nation.

Most would say this is to make the house rich. Others, like myself—and perhaps Lord Charoth at one time—like to believe that the devices of war that we create will ultimately replace the combatants entirely, will rid the need for shedding the blood of living men and women.

Both the director and I were raised in Karrnath. Our father land, Charoth informs me, is not faring well. Two legions were recently crushed by the dwarves of the Mror Holds in an unwise attempt to seize some clan holdings. The Regent Moranna was forced to abdicate her position, and Kaius III, recently come of age, has taken the throne. Karrnath is weak, its enemies many.

A sense of heaviness falls on me as our discussion concludes. In the silence, I know I have two options: submit to Lord Charoth's order or resign my position under his command. Either way, Sverak will be destroyed. What does it really matter? I must ask myself. He is a tool like all warforged.

Distant shouts draw our attention to the door. Lord Charoth, strong in body as well as mind, draws out his favorite wand. He opens the door and runs out like a watch sergeant investigating a crime. All that transpires in the Orphanage is the Director's responsibility.

I follow behind warily.

When we step out onto the lower balcony, the sight before me stops me cold.

Chapter
TWENTY-ONE

Ancient Arcana
Wir, the 11th of Sypheros, 998 YK

"No more secrets, Miss Otänsin," Jotrem said as they waited outside the extravagant stables. "Tell me about this gauntlet you found."

She turned and faced the older inquisitive. "Look, I'm taking you with me. I'm even leaving Aegis behind. I'm not going to explain this twice. Wait and see."

Most visitors to the Tower of the Twelve were members of a dragonmarked house and therefore had their own in-house means of accessing the floating keep. Few residents of Korth had reason or need to ascend to the Tower, but House Vadalis—bearers of the Mark of Handling—maintained a small but profitable compound at the edge of Wollvern Park where infrequent petitioners could borrow their exotic beasts. Hyran's writ and a handful of complimentary galifars had secured Soneste and Jotrem with two pegasi and two skilled riders.

The flying steeds were a mated pair, beautiful and intelligent animals that cheered Soneste the moment she looked at them. One was black, the other white and gray, with magnificent feathered wings that beat the air seconds after they mounted up.

The Tower of the Twelve was a pyramidal fortress of smoke-gray stone floating high above the tree-lined colonnade of the park. Magic coruscated silently along the underside of its massive base. Elemental airships landed or disembarked along the docking platforms that jutted from several of the thirteen tiers. It seemed a place far removed from the natural order of the world, and why shouldn't it? The Tower housed the collective efforts of centuries of arcane study.

As they rose into the air she looked down at the Tower's great shadow which shrouded the park. She gripped the Vadalis rider more tightly around the waist, and despite the cold, she enjoyed the purifying sensation of the wind through her hair. The last day had seen an excess of blood and some dizzying revelations—plausible criminals, a paradoxical priest, and a tinkering lizard. What did the next day hide?

Soneste's black-coated pegasus landed on the Tower's lowest dock as gently as a stag upon the forest floor.

"Thank you," she said to the rider, dismounted, and waited for Jotrem to climb down from the gray-feathered mare.

Four guards met them with ready weapons and polite words. Resplendent in lavender tabards and shining chain shirts, the guards wore the chimera insignia of House Deneith and rune-carved helms. Soneste guessed them to be duskblades of the Defenders Guild, warriors who wedded martial skill with arcane magic.

She displayed her papers and the Civic Minister's writ even as one of the men probed them with a spell of divination. Soneste hoped her association with House Tharashk would help.

"You will be granted admission," one of the duskblades said after reading the documents in their entirety, "but only a minister of the Twelve can expedite your request. You will have to wait."

"Thank you. That will be fine." Soneste had expected this. "Please just remind your superiors of the time sensitivity of the matter."

A pair of tall and aureate metal doors swung open at the guards' command. Soneste hesitated, excited. Some of Khorvaire's most impressive magical advances had been conceived within this institution: the speaking stones of House Sivis, the lightning rail of House Orien, and even the warforged were allegedly first devised in the Cannith workshops. Soneste smiled, imagining the look on Thuranne's face when she told her about her visit to the famous Tower. Few people without strong dragonmarked affiliation were allowed inside.

A cool wash of power flowed across her body as she stepped over the threshold. She guessed it to be a thorough analysis of all magical and psychic trappings on her person. She could sense even the Riedran crysteel of her dagger register under its scrutiny, no doubt observed by an unseen wizard. Could it read her mental talents?

After Jotrem had stepped through the threshold, two robed arcanist approached from within. "Excuse me, sir," one of the young men said, "We need to speak with you alone."

Soneste turned. "What's wrong?"

Jotrem's face flushed, but he didn't look surprised. "It's all right. This will only take a moment. I will join you within." The older inquisitive steered the arcanist out of earshot, perhaps too hastily.

The other arcanist beckoned for Soneste to follow.

⬡ ⬡ ⬡ ⬡ ⬡ ⬡ ⬡

The prodigious hall served as both waiting room and museum gallery. It was furnished with elegant chairs and tables neatly arrayed with game pieces, while bookshelves and statue-adorned alcoves formed the wide perimeter. Large stone models of the Twelve Moons floated smoothly overhead along unseen currents. A handful of other visitors idled across the chamber.

Soneste studied a series of plaques upon one wall. One vaunted prestigious students, while another, smaller plaque displayed the names of blacklisted students—even the Twelve had its outcasts, she mused. She scrutinized the latter, comparing the list against her considerable roster of memorized names should any prove of use for the future.

She turned at the sound of approaching steps. Jotrem offered his customary frown, but there was something else in his eyes, a cunning she hadn't noticed before.

"What was that about?" she asked. "What are you carrying that they found of interest?"

Jotrem lifted up his right hand, displaying the opal ring of the Order of Rekkenmark. "It was this," he said without even looking back at her. "When I retired from active service, I paid for an enchantment to be placed upon it. The effect shields my body from certain spells often used against inquisitives in Karrnath, but the magic is technically . . . necromantic in nature. I suppose that makes it suspect, so I was questioned about it."

"Ah." Soneste settled herself in one of the richly upholstered chairs, staring into the orrery above. Necromancy? Magic involving the dead questioned in Karrnath, of all places? She didn't buy it. Jotrem was lying to her.

As they waited, Soneste kept an eye on the older inquisitive. What did he have to hide? Her thoughts turned to Tallis. She had allied herself with a wanted criminal, risking far more than her investigation in doing so, and he was trusting her to keep her word.

Before Soneste had left Verdax's shop, she'd demanded that he get some sleep. With Olladra's favor, what she learned here would point her to the assassin's lair. Tallis needed to be rested for whatever came next. She didn't know yet if the next phase of the plan would involve the Justice Ministry or not. Either way, they had agreed to rendezvous in Wollvern Park.

"Miss Soneste Otänsin?"

A woman's voice rolled across the hall, buoyed by some minor enchantment, stirring her from her thoughts. Jotrem had remained standing and approached the speaker without hesitation.

Soneste leapt to her feet and joined him at an open doorway at the far side of the hall where a woman only slightly older than she waited. She wore a red and gold academician's tunic and a pair of spectacles that enlarged her inquiring eyes. The crooked shape of the Mark of Finding extended from the woman's hairline and framed one eye.

"Miss Otänsin? I am Lady Erice d'Tharashk, savant wizard in service of the Committee of the Twelve. I have been asked to assist you in identification of a piece of evidence?"

Soneste introduced herself and Jotrem. Erice led them on a winding path through a network of corridors lit by the most elaborate cold fire lanterns Soneste had ever seen. A gray cat emerged from the shadows of a doorway and slinked purposefully behind them. A familiar, Soneste mused.

As they walked, Lady Erice spoke. "I admit, I was surprised your request had come to *my* house. Most identifications are brought straight to the Canniths for obvious reasons."

Soneste had deliberately avoided inquiring with House Cannith. There was too much uncertainty surrounding the House of Making as far as she was concerned. She wanted a fresh perspective.

"My agency in Sharn has ties to House Tharashk," Soneste replied with an innocent smile. Erice's accent suggested she had not been raised in Karrnath. Soneste would use that. "My employer, Thuranne, is of the Velderan family of Tharashk. I thought some familiarity was in order."

Soneste inclined her head at Jotrem, who walked behind. "You see, Karrnathi hospitality has me homesick."

The women giggled. Jotrem offered an uncharacteristic half smile. Did a sense of humor lurk somewhere within that cold stone body?

The savant soon led them into a small laboratory several levels up where Tharashk maintained its research facilities and classrooms. When Erice had shut the door behind them, she gestured to an empty table. "You are carrying out an investigation, aren't you, Miss Otänsin? Does this relate to the Brelish ambassador?"

Soneste pulled the cloth-wrapped bundle from her haversack. "I'm sorry," she answered genuinely, thinking of Jotrem whose eyes were ever upon her. "I'm afraid I can't speak freely about the nature of the case. In fact, your objective examination of this evidence would be especially useful."

"I understand."

Soneste placed the assassin's metal hand upon the tabletop. Erice and Jotrem both moved in with interest. "I *will* tell you that this hand was taken by force from an armored assailant. I need to know everything possible about it, particularly the nature of the armor it came from, and if magic is involved, I need to know what kind." She pointed to the scored cuff where Tallis had cut the hand free. "This hand was part of the rest of the armor, not merely a detachable gauntlet."

"I will see what I can learn," Erice said, intrigued by the hand.

What she had deduced so far Soneste could only guess. A scholar of the arcane probably knew of countless possible origins for a creature composed of solid armor, but likely only a spell would begin to unlock the true secrets.

Soneste idled in the laboratory, taking care not to offend the savant by tampering with the tools of her trade. When she could do so unnoticed, Soneste studied Jotrem. His posture and sleight body movements were as stiff as usual, but there was something subtle about him that puzzled her. Occasionally, he blinked unusually long periods of time. That seemed . . . familiar.

Meanwhile, the gray-furred tomcat studied *her*. Soneste knew that familiars were intelligent, not merely dumb animals, so she smiled and waved once. Occasionally she watched Erice work. The savant's examination of the hand was quite unlike Verdax's. Where the artificer had woven temporal patterns upon the metal itself, Erice seemed to focus more upon her own spell than its object. She chanted softly and conjured divinatory magic around the hand, which formed a misty wreath. Erice studied the complex array of auras that took shape within.

At last, her work finished. The savant sat down, removed her spectacles, and rubbed her eyes from the strain. Soneste gained her feet and approached the table. Jotrem snapped to attention and merely looked on.

"Did you learn anything?" Soneste asked, feeling dumb asking the obvious.

"It is a wonder," the woman said somewhat distantly. "I should have guessed it. The design was so unusual."

"Lady Erice?"

The woman looked up. "I'm sorry. Yes. I can tell you a great deal more now."

Jotrem sidled forward.

Erice indicated the metal hand. "This belongs to a spirit called a nimblewright. Its entire body is mechanical in nature, a hollow shell of armor. It is, for all intents and purposes, a construct."

Soneste blinked. Except for having a name for it, this didn't tell her anything new. "I see. A construct, like something House Cannith would produce? Like warforged?"

"Not quite." Erice pointed to a diagram on one wall, which depicted the core design of a standard-sized warforged: a fibrous wooden musculature, steel, adamantine, or mithral composite plating which encased the frame like armor, and various elements of stone. "A nimblewright is in many ways far more complex and in others not *as* complex as a warforged. They weren't *produced* like warforged were, churned out of creation forges in mass production. Instead, a single mage of great power might create *one*—much like a servitor golem. In fact, like golems, nimblewrights weren't exactly cost-effective—certainly not in a time of war—which is why the Canniths invented the 'forged.

"Both a nimblewright and a warforged possess the ability to adapt to their surroundings, to improvise and strategize. Even a warforged titan has some level of adaptability, if not true sentience. Golems are expensive and deadly but ultimately unable to think for themselves. Nimblewrights are more like 'forged in this regard."

Soneste compared the savant's words against all she'd witnessed. "So what, aside from cost, truly separates nimblewrights from warforged?"

"Nimblewrights, unlike 'forged, are not free-willed. They are more proficient instruments of martial combat, but they obey their creators only—or one who is designated as their master. Centuries ago, wizards of the Twelve created nimblewrights as personal bodyguards and sentries. Some still guard the inner vaults. I've even heard that some were used as spies at the beginning of the war."

"Or assassins," Soneste said, unable to keep the bitterness from her voice.

"Yes, possibly." Erice's voice softened. "But not many of these exist anymore. I've never even heard of one being created in my lifetime."

Soneste looked at the laboratory around her. The creature had most likely been fashioned *here*, within the walls of the Tower of the Twelve, probably by some powerful wizard hiding behind layers of magical and political protection. The nimblewright's master could be here.

But if nimblewrights were used as guardians of the Tower, what was one doing loose in the city below? *Someone* had commanded the nimblewright to kill the ambassador and his family. And Haedrun.

Yet not Tallis or me, she thought. According to the Karrn, the nimblewright had fled after wounding *her*. What were its orders, if not to kill everyone investigating the massacre?

Jotrem interrupted. "Are you telling me there is one of these deadly constructs in Korth, acting solely at one man's behest? *That* is the assassin?"

"Yes," Soneste answered reluctantly. Then another thought occurred to her. "Lady Erice, you said the nimblewright was a construct 'for all intents and purposes.' But not in truth?"

"Well, it is. Normal constructs are simply valuable materials animated by elemental spirits—in the case of golems, earth elementals bound into an artificial body and commanded into mindless obedience. The nimblewright, however, is animated by an elemental spirit of water. This makes them fast, agile.

"What makes the nimblewright most effective is its

shapechanging ability. It can wear the illusion of any other person, so it can walk among regular people. Like changelings, but more powerful. Not many constructs can do *that*."

Soneste remembered the fluidity of the assassin's movement and the shadowy illusion it wore in the warehouse. This, no doubt, explained how it had followed them undetected. The nimblewright might have *been* one of the drunks or the sailors they'd walked past or had simply tailed them like a shadow. According to Tallis's account, in the Ebonspire it had worn its true form—steel armor on every inch of its body. Even the nimblewright couldn't defy the Ebonspire's illusion-stripping defenses.

"Is there anything else you can tell me about them?" Soneste asked. "Any vulnerabilities or immunities?"

"I . . ." Erice began to look flustered. "I suppose they would share many characteristics with golems, an immunity to magic used against them, but maybe not all. I . . . I don't know much, Miss Otänsin. I am a scholar, not a war wizard, and this is hardly House Tharashk's purview. I could try and find out more for you, but I would need to consult with Cannith wizards."

"I understand, but there isn't time. Can you do me just one more favor? I need to know who specifically created *this* nimblewright. Can you find out, just from this hand?"

Erice nodded. "I can try, but I don't know *when* I could find—"

"Please, Lady Erice. Time isn't on our side," Soneste said. "The nimblewright whose hand we're looking at killed the Brelish ambassador Gamnon ir'Daresh three days ago. It also killed his family and their servants. Since that day, it has been trying to kill those who can implicate its master. You're my last lead, Lady."

❖ ❖ ❖ ❖ ❖ ❖ ❖

The gray cat was watching them both as they waited for Lady Erice to return. Soneste tried to ignore it, but she suspected it would relay what it witnessed to its mistress. In the back of her mind, she was afraid that Lady Erice would tell someone else about Soneste's discovery, that news of her meddling would reach the wizard who commanded the nimblewright. If the killer behind it all knew she had a lead, wouldn't he have her followed?

Soneste did her best to keep from fidgeting.

"When *did* you encounter this . . . nimblewright?" Jotrem demanded at last. He licked his lips, which she noticed had become increasingly dry. Was he nervous here?

"Last night. I found Tallis again, and I followed him discreetly. He must have marked me, because he got away. Then I was attacked by the real killer—the nimblewright."

"I don't appreciate your lies," Jotrem said. "I am very interested to see if you will tell them to the Civic Minister as well. Do you not want your agency—or the King's Citadel—to remain on amiable terms with Karrnath's government?"

"You saw the killing wounds, Jotrem," she said, ignoring his threats. "You know the nimblewright's is the hand that dealt them."

She touched the groove in the palm of the steel hand. "The construct's weapons came from here. Long narrow blades, like a rapier." She rattled her own weapon. "Even Tallis isn't strong enough to do what we've seen."

"Very well," Jotrem said. "But how do we know Tallis isn't the creature's master? We know he was there."

"He's no wizard, and you know it."

"Yes, but Lady Erice told us that *another* could be designated as master."

The door opened and the savant entered the room with a thick sheaf of scrolls in her hands. There was a smile upon her bespectacled face. "I found something."

"Boldrei bless you, Lady!" Soneste blurted. "I will see that a sizable donation is made to Tharashk's interests here."

The savant waved the words away and began to unroll the papers upon the table. She leafed through them, discarding some in a separate pile and taking greater interest in others. From her vantage, Soneste could see that each of the documents contained the lofty diction of contracts, as well as lines of arcane writing she would never be able to decipher. At the bottom she saw notarizing Sivis marks.

Erice compared the designs inscribed upon the hollow underside of the steel hand with the arcane sigils inscribed upon the contracts. Sheet after sheet passed through her hands as Soneste waited, anxious. The savant seemed to be enjoying her search. Perhaps at heart, everyone in the House of Finding was an inquisitive. Soneste allowed herself a smile as she watched the woman.

Just when Soneste could wait no longer, the bookish woman squealed triumphantly and pulled a scroll from the sheaf. "Aha! This nimblewright, model seventy-two, crafted in the month of Eyre in 783 YK, was commissioned by Sehrok d'Phiarlan, a minister of the Committee of the Twelve. It was then gifted to the Malovyn family of dignitaries in Aerenal, who were granted ownership."

Malovyn.

Soneste's smile melted away. Lenrik Malovyn.

Chapter
TWENTY-TWO

"Malovyn," Jotrem said as they climbed atop the pegasi once more. "You know this name. Who is it?"

Soneste ignored him, holding tightly to the Vadalis rider as they galloped from the loading dock. The black-winged stallion spread its wings and caught the cold air currents.

She felt sick. Fixing her eyes upon the conifers of the park below, Soneste lifted one hand up, watching her fingers tremble ever so sleightly. Could she have missed the clues?

Soneste swore she could feel a malevolent tension in the air. The clouds were swollen now, promising rain, and the wind was noticeably colder. Was this her imagination, some souring side effect of her extrasensory powers? In truth, she hadn't used them as much in the last month as she had in the last few days.

When they touched down, she tipped the riders and walked from the Vadalis compound. Jotrem caught up to her. "I will find out for myself, if I must. Malovyn: it's someone you've met here in this city, isn't it? I'm certain I'll find the name in the Ministry records."

She turned to meet Jotrem's eyes, but she felt like she was

staring straight through him. A nauseating sensation roiled within her mind, like some sort of psychic runoff. Or was it just what betrayal felt like?

"I need to verify this for myself first. Promise me that you will *not* share what you heard with anyone else. Yet." She carried a copy of the arcane contract in her bag—her final request of Lady Erice—knowing she would need to show it to Tallis. Assuming he wasn't complicit as well.

Aureon forbid, she prayed. She can't have misjudged everyone.

"Then place some trust in *me*," Jotrem said. "Tell me. Maybe I can help."

Soneste continued to stall, too distracted by this development to effectively steer Jotrem away from this line of inquiry.

"Go," she bade the older inquisitive as they approached the gates of the park. "Find the name if you must. I have one more lead to follow before I confide in you. If you will be patient with me, Jotrem, I will share with you what I know."

At any other time, she might have appreciated the simple beauty of the tree-lined path that wound beyond the gates or the wash of autumnal color in the thinning branches and leaf-strewn grounds. Even the trees of Karrnath looked regimented, spaced out evenly like a row of pillars.

"Say what you will, Brelish," Jotrem said, keeping pace with her. "We are beyond trust. I can either be a hindrance to you or a boon. I helped you visit Lord Charoth on short notice. I can help again."

Brelish? she thought. Jotrem had called her *Brelander* before. Was he trying to win her favor at last?

Soneste was still half a bell early for her rendezvous with Tallis. If she put her mind to it, she could get rid of Jotrem in that time. "We'll see," was all she said.

She casually made her way to the location Tallis had described: the statue of a robed Karrn, a royal wizard and chief advisor to Kaius II. A cluster of thorny bushes framed the pedestal. At the base huddled a vagrant in a filthy cloak. The man rubbed his hands together to keep warm.

Lovely. She'd need to clear *him* away too.

Soneste glanced around to see if any White Lions were near. In the distance she could see a patrol of four, but nothing else seemed amiss in the park. How did the White Lions treat the homeless here? she wondered.

She approached the vagrant, fishing for a couple of crowns, just enough for him to purchase a bowl of stew. "Sir, do you need a hot meal?"

Just then, Soneste recognized the oversized cloak the man wore. Didn't Jotrem? They'd both seen it before.

"Don't waste your coins," Jotrem said as he stopped beside her and glared down at the vagrant. "Cheap ale is the only thing you'd be buying this man."

The homeless man leaned up as Soneste held her copper coins out. "That's hardly fair," he said with a strong voice. His right hand flashed past her outstretched hand and gripped the hilt of Jotrem's sword. He jerked it free even as he rose in one smooth motion.

"Tallis!" the older inquisitive gasped.

"Good to see you again, Jotrem!" the Karrn said with his crooked smile, smacking the man hard in the chest with the pommel of his own long sword. "Twice in as many days!"

Jotrem groaned and staggered away, but Tallis kept on him, pulling a thick leather sap from the bulk of his ragged cloak. He dropped the sword, gripped the weighted weapon, and slammed it against the side of Jotrem's head.

Soneste's reflexes were numbed by anxiety. She moved to stop him, but she gave up after his second blow. The third dropped the inquisitive heavily to the ground. Soneste stood as still as the statue above them as she watched Tallis make sure the attack had gone unnoticed. He stripped Jotrem of all weapons, pausing only a fraction of a moment when he spied the black opal ring on the older man's finger. She marked his troubled expression before it melted away into his usual self-assuredness.

When he finished, Tallis removed the oversized cloak—wearing his green Lyrandar coat beneath—and wrapped the inquisitive in it. "Time to retire this thing anyway." Tallis pushed the unconscious inquisitive into the bushes and out of sight, tossing his weapons into another bush.

Soneste pitied the older man such indignities, but she hadn't liked Jotrem since the moment she met him. The *next* time she met him, things were sure to be ugly.

Tallis stepped back out, brushing off his coat. "Sorry about that," he said with an awkward smile. "I like to be early for meetings, though I admit I imagined our secret tryst would be more romantic than this. And I *didn't* think you'd bring your boyfriend." Tallis winked, but Soneste didn't appreciate the joke.

Soneste wanted to yell at him, but the news she bore hung over her like the storm clouds above the city. "How am I supposed to explain this later? You're driving a wedge between me and the Ministry. This will only hurt us both." Her words lacked conviction. Her relationship with Jotrem was hardly a concern right now.

"What's wrong?" Tallis glanced up at the Tower of the Twelve, frowning. "You learned something, didn't you? Something bad."

Behind him, Soneste saw Aegis approaching them on the path. A small crowd of children trailed him, some of them pelting him with small stones and litter from the streets.

Tallis rolled his eyes. "It's a good thing we're not worried about drawing attention to ourselves."

A larger stone rebounded off Aegis's steel-armored back. The loud noise made Tallis wince—and drew the attention of several passersby, who eyed the construct suspiciously.

"Cannith trash!" the oldest boy jeered, as if daring the tall warforged to attack him.

Aegis stopped and turned to face the children. "You are very astute, young master Karrn," the warforged said to the boy. "I am, indeed, cobbled together from the dust and dross of a Cannith forgehold. It is a wonder I can move at all."

Soneste wanted to smile, but Lady Erice's words had frozen

in her mind. She called out to Aegis. The children began to slip away, one by one, as the warforged approached the safety of two adults.

Soneste slipped her haversack free. "Tallis, let's take a walk."

She explained what Lady Erice had told her about nimblewrights and the nature of their possession. Aegis walked behind them, listening without comment. As they neared the far side of Wollvern Park, she handed Tallis her copy of the arcane contract. When he finished reading it, the Karrn stopped. His expression was dark, more confused than worried.

"What is this supposed to prove?" he said, turning to look at her as they walked. He looked calm, but his tone was hostile.

Soneste sighed. "Nimblewrights obey only the orders of their master. This particular one—our assassin—was given to the Malovyn family. Lenrik's family. Only a Malovyn can command it."

For the first time since she'd met him, Tallis was speechless. Anger and denial warred in his quicksilver eyes.

"Tallis," she said with a whisper, not wanting to be overheard. "Don't dismiss this out of hand. Your emotions will mislead you."

"No, this just isn't right. Lenrik isn't . . . I *know* him—better than anyone else on Eberron." He looked back at her. "Better than I know *you*."

Soneste wished for something else, some hidden clue to disprove her own fears and substantiate her doubts. She'd only met Lenrik this very morning. She felt like she'd gauged the elf's character fairly well. She'd enjoyed his company and had understood why Tallis had confided in him.

The Aerenal tapestry came unbidden to mind. What if her earlier supposition about that had been right? Tallis had known the elf most of his life, but the deepest deceptions were personal.

"Does he have any other family in Khorvaire?" she asked.

"No. He's the only one. His father is dead. The rest . . . are still in Aerenal or someplace. No contact." He shook the paper in his hand, looking as though he would tear it up. "Even if this thing is accurate, the thing's master *could* be someone else. In Aerenal. Some relative."

"Commanding the creature here in Korth? That's a very big coincidence."

Tallis shook his head. "If this was true, why didn't Lenrik try and stop us from identifying the nimblewright's hand if it could implicate him? If he *was* involved somehow, why would he allow us to find out more? We'd find out the truth eventually. He'd have held onto it to be safe, promising to find out more in the Archives of Aureon. It's all a lie."

"I don't know. I know it doesn't make perfect sense, which is why we need to approach this carefully."

"*You* don't need to approach this at all. I'll talk to him." Tallis glared at her then began to outpace her.

Soneste hurried to keep up, the heavy footfalls from behind reminding her that Aegis was still with them. "Listen, you can't just confront him about it." Tallis kept moving, as obstinate as Jotrem had ever been. "Damn it," she said. "You're such a Karrn!"

When they exited the park, a squad of White Lions tore past them on the street, responding to some emergency. A sergeant barked orders to his men, and Soneste heard only the words "lightning rail." She watched them as they disappeared around a street corner, desiring to know what errand demanded their presence so urgently. She *could* follow them or find out at the Justice Ministry, but she couldn't let Tallis go to the cathedral alone. Things had become entirely too dangerous.

"Slow down," she demanded. "You're going to attract attention. I'm coming with you. Just slow down!"

Tallis said nothing, brooding as he walked.

"Tallis," she said quietly. "Before you go barging into the cathedral, we need to learn more—"

The Karrn stopped sharply, snatched one of her hands, and pulled her close to him. As her body pressed against his, he looked into her eyes—then bent her arm behind her back. He applied pressure just so, sending a wave of agony through her arm. She gasped from the pain.

Still Tallis held her gaze. He'd chosen his moment well. They stood out of sight of most foot traffic, and those who passed by could easily take their posture as a lover's embrace.

Soneste heard Aegis stepping close behind her. "Unhand her or die," he said, his tone deadly.

"Another step," Tallis warned the warforged without shifting his gaze, "and this arm will break."

"Aegis . . . just wait," Soneste managed through her pain. She tried to think. The slieghtest movement of her arm in any direction sent a surge of fire through her nerves. She considered a psychic attack, but she wasn't sure she could muster the concentration for it.

"Remember our truce!" she said to Tallis. "For your king and mine."

He leaned in close, his lips close to her ear. "Kaius and Boranel don't know about any of this." Tallis's voice was pure scorn. "They wouldn't care if they *did*."

"I'm here to help," she said softly. "I don't want to believe Lenrik is involved in this any more than you do."

"You're here for your case." There was a long pause. Soneste could feel the tension in his body, the anger in his grip. "Leave me—leave *us*—alone, Brelish." He released her arm then shoved her away. Hard.

She would have fallen to the cobbles gracelessly, but Aegis's strong hands caught her and held her upright. She composed herself, mind astir with both rage and sorrow. She looked back to see Tallis already some distance away, his pace quickening into a run. Soneste turned to the warforged.

"I *have* to follow him."

"But Mistress, he will—"

"He won't." She pointed in the direction the White Lions had run down the street. "I need *you* to find out what's going on. Follow the White Lions from a distance if you can. They're headed to the lightning rail station, I think. If anyone questions you, just give my name and the Civic Minister's, Hyran ir'Tennet. Then wait outside the cathedral. That's where I'll be."

"Yes, Mistress."

Chapter
TWENTY-THREE

Speculations of Death
Wir, the 11th of Sypheros, 998 YK

The Cathedral of the Sovereign Host loomed high above the treetops of the temple grounds, its towering belfry spearing the gray sky and rivaling even the spires of Crownhome. Tallis had seen it a thousand times, but it brought him no comfort now. Men had constructed an edifice in worship of the gods, but where were the gods now? Where was the justice so vaunted by Aureon's teachings?

In his new guise, Tallis decided it would be best to enter the cathedral through the front door, to visit Aureon's shrine and speak to the priest like anyone else would.

Tallis couldn't quiet his mind. Images, conversations, and shared moments streamed through his head in a hundred disjointed pieces. Lenrik, the humble elf priest who'd given Tallis's family an extra loaf of bread when food was scarce back home in Teryk. Lenrik, who'd risked his life time and again in skirmishes upon the Karrnath-Cyre border just to heal the sons and daughters of Karrnath . . . and occasionally the orphans of Cyre. Lenrik, who'd brought Tallis himself back from death innumerable times.

That he could be party to the murder of innocents was unthinkable. Lenrik had known Gamnon as well as Tallis, and *he* was less likely to bear a grudge against the arrogant Brelish captain.

How could he be tied to this construct, this . . . nimblewright? To the Ebonspire murder? Lenrik hadn't known Tallis would even be anywhere near the Ebonspire that night, not until Tallis himself had told him about it the next day.

But he *had* known Haedrun, hadn't he? She'd mentioned being approached by an elf before the assassin attacked them at the docks. Was that Lenrik, after all?

"Fury's madness," he swore, anguished at the thought. Perhaps it had all been some horrible coincidence.

What was Soneste playing at? Anger surged through him when he thought of the Brelish inquisitive's argument, for seeding this doubt within him at all. He didn't know her, and *she* couldn't possibly know him or Lenrik. So she'd found "evidence" in the Tower of the Twelve? Perhaps the Twelve, with its great influence, had instigated the whole event, fabricating evidence to redirect blame.

But why Lenrik?

Adopting the confident bearing of a Lyrandar guildsman— feeling none of it himself—Tallis strode up the steps of the cathedral and passed through the main doors. He nodded to the Vassals who greeted him, but he couldn't offer a smile in turn.

He marched down the central aisle of the worship hall, heedless of the great pillars he passed and the Sovereign scripture carved upon them. Above him, a magical panorama of the night sky and its unclouded moons drew the eyes of visitors and priests alike. Tallis had stared into its mystic depths many times before, somehow finding a modicum of comfort in its terrible beauty. The dark firmament made Eberron and all its wars seem so small.

Not today.

A spiraling stair on one side of Aureon's sanctuary led him down to the undercroft. Therein lay the caretaker's personal chambers, where none but Lenrik or Prelate Alinda were officially permitted.

At the bottom of the steps, he passed adjoining rooms—study

chambers, a vestry, and the eminent Archives of Aureon. It had been a place more comfortable for Tallis than any other in Korth.

"Lenrik?" Tallis called out, hearing only his own echo return. From its hiding place in the vestry, he retrieved his hooked hammer. It felt wrong—blasphemous—to wield a weapon in this place. At last he entered the spare room that Lenrik had converted to a healing chamber, where Tallis and Soneste had both woken with mended wounds in the last few days.

Once inside, Tallis set about examining every corner, every detail, as if it were the scene of a crime. He looked at their game of Conqueror in the corner. Tallis's chancellor had been deposed by Lenrik's general in an unexpected maneuver and now lay discarded off the board. The elf's king was poised for a final strike against his own. Tallis felt a chill.

"Tallis," a voice said softly, and he whirled with his hammer ready to throw. Soneste stood there, her hands held out to show she meant peace.

"I told you—" he began.

Soneste pointed to the wall. "Look. The tapestry."

He followed her gaze, expectant. When he didn't move, she walked across to stand in front of the Aerenal tapestry. She slipped her fingers behind one edge, peeling the layered fabric away from the wall to see behind it.

Tallis stared at the violet, red, and gold threads and the beauteous spiraling patterns they formed. For a moment, Tallis succumbed to the glamer, but his trance ended abruptly when the tapestry shifted.

"Help me with this," Soneste said, trying to push her way behind the heavy fabric.

He pulled the bottom of the tapestry up and away, giving her room. She prodded delicately at the smooth worked stone—looking for something? Some hidden niche in the wall? Tallis stared in shocked silence as one of Soneste's fingers disappeared into the masonry. She reached tentatively further, until half her forearm had disappeared.

"Illusion," she murmured, more absorbed by her work than the discovery itself. "It's not warded or trapped. It's just . . . a disguised door."

"How did you know this was here?" he asked. Tallis had learned over the course of his career how to identify and even disable many magical traps and hidden doors. Most of the time, one didn't need magical expertise so much as an aptitude for disrupting someone else's, yet in all this time, he'd never found *this*.

"I didn't." Soneste sounded honest. "When I was here with Lenrik this morning, I just imagined it was possible there was a door behind this."

The art of possibilities. Soneste seemed to excel at that.

"Slowly, now," she said. She pulled a silver metal circlet from her haversack and slipped it around her head. Immediately, a white ball of light formed in the air above her shoulder. She stepped through the hidden door and vanishing from sight. For some reason he didn't understand, Tallis did not want to enter. He didn't want to know what Lenrik had hidden away.

But circumstances demanded it. He followed, finding that he had to push aside a heavy curtain that lay across the unseen threshold. As he did, Tallis breathed in a spicy, souring aroma which seemed to cling to the fabric but had not drifted into the bedroom behind him.

※ ※ ※ ※ ※ ※ ※

The chamber in which they found themselves was small, unremarkable in itself with a low, vaulted ceiling like many in the undercroft. It would take time to study all of the room's strange contents, but Soneste found her eyes drawn immediately to an array of masks hanging from another, less exquisite tapestry on the left-hand wall. There were easily two dozen of them, crafted of wood and bone and painted to resemble grinning white skulls and visages of the animate dead. They stared back like gruesome sentries through empty eyes.

Aerenal death-masks.

It didn't surprise her too much to see these here. Many elves in Khorvaire harbored at least some remnant of their homeland culture—as evidenced by the Aerenal tapestry itself—but unless he'd deceived everyone, Lenrik worshipped Aureon and the Sovereign Host exclusively—*not* the Undying Court of Aerenal.

"Oh, Khyber." There was dread in Tallis's voice.

At his words, Soneste looked beneath the assemblage of masks to what appeared to be a shelf of very old, desiccated skulls. Between a pair of liquid-filled goblets was a human head propped up to face them, the skin ash-gray and plastered tight against the skull beneath. The brown hair was lank, trailing only inches over the lip of the shelf. She stepped closer, *needing* to know . . . and she smelled the astringent stench of embalming fluid.

Unless she was mistaken, she was looking at the severed and preserved head of Ambassador ir'Daresh.

"Sovereigns preserve us," Soneste whispered.

"What is this?" Tallis said, breaking tension with outrage. He stared down at the dead face of Gamnon. "Lenrik can't . . . *can't* know about this."

"Tallis," she breathed. "This is incriminating."

The Karrn gripped his hooked hammer in both hands, knuckles whitening. "What does Gamnon have to do with all this?" He gestured to the rest of the room, where Soneste saw a collection of shelves and other, more innocuous objects reminiscent of Aerenal culture.

Soneste looked back to the head, feeling constricted, helpless. A burning suspicion began to grow within her. The trappings of this room were inconsistent. It was her understanding that the Aereni believed that death was merely a transcendent phase in a much longer spiritual journey. They imitated and revered their own dead ancestors, even called back their spirits to become deathless advisors, but as far as Soneste knew, they only mummified other Aereni. This didn't look like the practice of the Undying Court.

"I don't know. We'll find out." Soneste pulled herself from

her thoughts and set about examining the room, searching every space for further evidence. She drew her crysteel dagger and held it in hand.

"He's blessed water before," she heard Tallis say, his voice hollow. "I've seen him do it. Made it holy. Burned the flesh of the undead. I've *used* it myself. He *can't* have murdered innocents like this."

Soneste shook her head sadly and lifted a hand mirror carved of bronze-vood. Beneath it was a sheaf of folded paper. She separated each piece and examined them. The first appeared to be a letter written in complex shorthand. The second—

A diagram of the Ebonspire, the thirty-fourth level circled in black ink. Skull-shaped symbols were scrawled in the corner.

Just then she heard a muffled cough from the behind the hidden door. She turned, meeting Tallis's eyes. He nodded, his face pale. She set the mirror down and drew her rapier, shifting her dagger to her left hand.

Her heart hammered inside her when she saw that it was Lenrik himself who stepped slowly through the false wall. He looked upon them uncomprehendingly, his angular features wan and vaguely distraught.

"Tallis, what . . ." The elf's voice dissolved into a fit of coughing. He looked ill.

Tallis approached his friend with his weapon lowered but still grasped tightly. "Lenrik, what is this?" He pointed the pick's head to Gamnon's withered head. "What did you do? To him, to his family!"

The priest tried to shake his head, then reached out his hand to steady himself against the wall. "I don't . . ."

"What is this?" Tallis's eyes glistened with tears.

Lenrik's eyes widened as he followed Tallis's gesture. Was it feigned horror or genuine revulsion upon his face? Soneste refrained herself from casting out her empathic net—the anger and shock was too strong here, even within her, to give her an accurate assessment.

Lenrik leaned heavily against the wall, coughing again. His

other hand grasped for Aureon's symbol around his neck. He began to murmur a spiritual incantation, the words slurring slightly. A soft emerald light shone from his fingertips.

Tallis stepped forward and tore the priest's hands away from the symbol, disrupting the spell almost without effort. "Tell me, damn you!" he demanded.

"My friend," Lenrik moaned, then dropped hard to his knees.

Tallis caught him before he collapsed completely to the ground. Soneste steadied him from behind, carefully watching the elf's hands for signs of deception or sleight of hand.

Instead she saw a glimmer of moisture at the base of Lenrick's neck. His hair had fallen away from it, revealing a small but angry red slash. The skin around it was purple and swelling fast.

"Poison," she said, feeling ice riming her guts.

Tallis pulled his friend closer. "Sovereigns," he breathed, unsure what to do. "Try again. Try again!" He grabbed the priest's hand and wrapped it forcibly around the bronzewood symbol. "Aureon, heal him!"

"Give him this," Soneste said, offering the minor healing draught she'd carried with her since leaving Investigative Services. She had no idea if it could help. The Karrn forced the solution down Lenrik's throat, massaging his neck to ease its passage inside. The elf had gone entirely limp

"Upstairs!" Soneste suddenly said. There were priests milling around just above them in the worship hall. "Tallis, carry him. Upstairs. We'll get help."

The Karrn nodded and gathered the stricken elf in his arms. As he rose, they heard muffled voices and the unmistakable clanking of armor beyond the hidden door. Soneste felt resignation sink into her at last. Enough subterfuge, then.

She backed away as a handful of White Lions stormed into the room, evidently well aware of the hidden door or directed by someone who was.

"Drop your weapons!" the lead sergeant demanded with an upraised battle-axe.

Chapter
TWENTY-FOUR

Alinda entered the shrine of Aureon dauntless as any of Karrnath's warlords. Retired Major Jotrem Dalesek, a man she'd known only by name and reputation, had led a squad of Lions into the cathedral only minutes ago, citing the need to apprehend a dangerous criminal within. She'd been hastily summoned to speak with him and decided immediately that she did not like the man. Fifty years in the service of Korth and three major sieges against the city had gifted Alinda with a swift and accurate judgment of character.

"Tallis is a severe threat to the state," he'd said.

"The cathedral maintains its own security, Major." She'd pointed to the Deneith soldiers gathering beside her. "They quarter on church grounds, for Host's sake!"

"It is my understanding that the priest Lenrik Malovyn has harbored this man for a very long time, Prelate," Jotrem said. "With all due respect, we cannot risk treating with others who may have him in confidence."

"Such as myself?" Alinda had smirked. Jotrem was at least a decade younger than she. She wasn't afraid of him in the sleightest.

The very idea of Lenrik, hiding a fugitive of the law. Not likely. She was confident that the elf could dissolve this confusion.

"The men entrusted to me were named by General Thauram himself."

"Very well, Major," she'd said, fully intent upon verifying his claim after the fact, "but I will accompany you."

Aureon's shrine had appeared vacant when they'd entered, but for a single Vassal pulling herself up from prayer in one of the pews. She was a thickset woman almost Alinda's own age, with a kindly face and a startled expression when she saw the prelate and the soldiers arrayed around her.

"Excuse me, my lady," the old woman—Mova, wasn't it?—said and hurried away.

Alinda followed the brazen inquisitive and his squad of soldiers. On the off chance that Major Dalesek's words held some truth, she'd shielded herself and the guards with a prayer. Two of the Deneith soldiers flanked her, magewrought steel ready in hand.

They'd descended to the undercroft of Aureon's shrine, entering one of the storage chambers as Jotrem set about examining the walls as all the guards watched. He'd seemed sure of himself, but she didn't like his pace. Alinda hadn't been down here herself in some time. Most of her meetings with the shrinekeepers took place in the sanctuary or in her own office.

"Here, Prelate," Jotrem had said, pushing away Lenrik's tapestry with the help of a pair of guards. "A door."

The cathedral had many such hidden compartments, but Alinda had not been aware of this one. Why hadn't Lenrik told her? Had there been truth to the inquisitive's claim? Jotrem had ordered his men through the illusionary wall, and Alinda pushed her way through them, unwilling to be left behind the group. The Sovereign Host guarded her, she had nothing to fear.

"Out of the way," she said irritably

"Drop your weapons!" she'd heard the lead soldier shout to someone beyond the illusory wall.

What her eyes took in when she stepped into the hidden room

Alinda was not prepared for. Lenrik, lying limp and sickly in the arms of a bewildered half-elf. A blue-coated, blonde young woman, armed with a rapier and a purple-tinged dagger, both pointed at the White Lions. Behind them, a room draped with adornments, peculiar if not heretical. The Aerenal art was a mere oddity. She'd met many elves in her long life, but only those from warlike Valenar had ever troubled her.

But it was the taint of the necromancy which disturbed her most. The shelf of mummified heads offended her utterly—especially the recently decapitated human head. This place was consecrated ground. How dare *anyone* despoil the shrine of Aureon with such grisly trophies! On impulse, Alinda called to the Host to quell the chamber of its unholy aspect.

● ● ● ◉ ● ● ●

Soneste considered retaining her weapons, considered resisting this. Things needed sorting out. If everyone would just wait, she felt certain she could solve the puzzle of inconsistencies this secret chamber presented.

Then a strong female voice pushed away all other thoughts. "Dol Arrah, purge this corruption from our presence!"

For a moment, blinding white light flooded the chamber. The supplication was followed by a litany of words from an older woman, sounding more like a language of primal power than a wizard's calculated chant. Soneste felt her muscles seize up preternaturally, her limbs overwhelmed with stiffening force.

One of the White Lions smacked her rapier blade with his axe, wrenching the weapon painfully from her frozen grip then plucked the dagger from her hand. Another of the Lions—Sergeant Bratta, whom she had questioned a few days ago—advanced on Tallis and struck him in the head with a mailed fist.

"That's only the beginning, scum!" the man promised.

Soneste's eyes remained on the woman. She found she could not tear them away from that fixed point even if she wanted to,

constrained by magic. She deduced that this must be Prelate
Roerith herself, the high priestess of the Cathedral. Her long silver
hair hung loose, her dark eyes clouded by sudden grief. She moved
beyond Soneste's clear sight over to Lenrik, where the White Lions
had taken hold of Tallis. The Karrn, a dusky shape in her periph-
ery, made no attempt to resist.

"Blessed Boldrei," the prelate intoned with great passion. "Cast
your healing spirit upon this servant of your lord and husband."
More undecipherable, crooning words followed, and tiny points of
bright light shone from the priestess's fingertips as she laid them
upon Lenrik's shoulders and neck.

Anger coursed through her mind as Soneste saw a new figure
moved from the blurred edges of her vision into the sharp center.
Jotrem! Yet there was a measure of anxiety in his still-bruised face.
He met her eyes.

Prelate Roerith's words halted abruptly. She expected to hear
the elf cough again as the healing power of the Sovereign Host
had poured into him through the hands of one its greatest mortal
servants. Instead, cold silence.

"He is dead," she said, her voice lamented. For just that moment,
Soneste was sure she saw relief flicker across Jotrem's features.

Soneste's mind spiraled inward. So much had happened too fast.
Was this meant to frame Lenrik? Who but Lenrik himself could
enter the undercroft of Aureon's shrine and find this place?

She began to follow the path of events backwards more thoroughly—to return along the mystic avenues to that place in
her mind where all images were stored, all words were memorized—when she heard her name spoken aloud. A question had
been asked.

"An inquisitive from Breland," Jotrem answered the priestess,
"who came on her government's behalf to investigate the murder
of Gamnon ir'Daresh. The ambassador, Prelate Roerith, whose
head was—"

"I *know* what happened," the elderly woman said quietly, but
her voice was steady, demanding. "And you?"

Soneste's muscles were slowly easing from the magical grip. She was able to move her eyes again, so she watched as the prelate walked over to Tallis, where he was held by three White Lions. Soneste had never seen him look so defeated, not even after the death of Haedrun.

"You are Tallis? I am told my friend, Lenrik, was safeguarding you from the reach of the White Lions and from the Justice Ministry. My friend is dead now, presumably at your hands. Is this true?"

Whatever the truth of it, Tallis had known nothing of this room, nor the cause of Lenrik's death. Someone had gotten to Lenrik first. Someone close by.

Tallis said nothing, merely stared at the floor like the lost soul he was.

Jotrem walked around the room, peering at its contents. She heard him rifle through the papers on one shelf then clear his throat. "Prelate Roerith, what we have found in this room demands explanation. I understand that, but time is of the essence. We will sort out the details later, and I will certainly call on you when we do. I must escort the criminal to Ministry headquarters. Please leave this chamber as we have found it, so we may—"

"It is blasphemous, Major," she said, looking at the shelf of heads. "I will not tolerate the presence of *these* a moment longer."

"I will send an associate of mine to investigate," he said, "so that it may be quickly removed, but we must document these crimes, prelate, if you would see justice done. As for . . . your friend, I will summon an agent of—"

"Neither the corpse collectors nor any Cultists of Vol will set foot in the cathedral." The prelate stroked the dead elf's hair and closed his eyes for him. Soneste could see that the discoloration had vanished from his skin. The poison had been purged, but the prelate's spell could not bring him back from death. "I will tend to Lenrik myself."

"As you wish." Jotrem nodded. He turned to Soneste. "Miss Otänsin, you may accompany us, if you wish. Out of respect for the King's Citadel, you will not be arrested at this time, but you *will* answer for consorting with a wanted criminal."

He turned to the guards. "Return Miss Otänsin her weapons."

It didn't add up. None of it. Soneste saw evidence to suggest that Lenrik had planned for Tallis to be the dupe but was betrayed in the end by a third, but that wasn't right either. She knew she could solve this but needed some time and the freedom to do it. There was something about the whole scenario that felt . . . intentionally inaccurate?

When Jotrem led them out of the Cathedral, Soneste saw Aegis standing at the base of a statue. Thankfully, the older inquisitive hadn't noticed him. She gestured discreetly for the warforged to stay away, praying he would understand and follow behind from a distance.

Soneste walked behind the squad of seven White Lions, where Tallis was prodded along between them. His wrists were manacled together. His weapons had been seized. Two guards flanked him and a third held a ceramic wand at his back, capped with a piece of amber.

Jotrem strode alongside the group rather than in the lead.

The Lions knew where they were going. Most criminals were brought to one of the barracks situated near the city's major gates, where they were dealt swift release or punishment at the whim of the commanding officer. Men like Tallis, sought by higher powers, were claimed by the Justice Ministry directly. She'd heard that General Thauram himself wanted Tallis's blood. This wouldn't end well.

Her eyes flicked to Jotrem. His jaw was set, his expression exalted. Then she saw his hands at his sides, flexing constantly, the tremor of a nervous man. She'd expected trouble from the older inquisitive, but something had changed within him.

She needed answers. With a thought, Soneste fell into herself and summoned her psychic net. She grasped it firmly in imagined hands and cast it out in a circle, where residue from every emotion within a dagger's throw was snared.

Bravado, Karrnathi pride, and chauvinism in abundance exuded from the White Lions as they paraded their notorious captive between them on the open streets. From Tallis she felt only an emotional hollow, an unknowable ache that dissolved her lingering doubts of his involvement in Lenrik's fate. His head lifted, a torpid curiosity, having heard the fading remnant of her mental song.

Then something else, a gnawing fear, bled in from her catch—Jotrem's strained sensibilities again. But there was more to it now, something she'd felt only a trace of earlier in the day but now roared from his mind as never before. A despondency out of place, a craving . . .

A psionic pulse.

Soneste let her power fade as she fixed knowing eyes upon Jotrem. He still walked with the stride of a confident man, but beneath the veneer of triumph there was a slave. She recalled all that she'd observed of this man since she'd met him in the Justice Ministry. There were contradictions that didn't seem right, a new addiction that revealed him. Unless . . .

This wasn't the same man. The moment she thought of it, she knew she was right.

She spotted an Orien courier further down the street walking in their direction. When the girl started to turn into a side street, Soneste decided her opportunity had come. She took a deep breath to steady her nerves. It was time to cross the line of certainty.

Soneste stared at the back of Sergeant Bratta, who led their procession, and with a thought planted a preternatural interest within his mind. If it worked, he would feel an inexplicable desire to be near the Orien girl. The moment it was done, she pulled out her hand crossbow and primed it.

The other Lions exchanged glances when Sergeant Bratta turned their path into the side street but said nothing. It was something of a detour. The narrow street had fewer pedestrians, sheltered between two tall structures.

"M-miss," Bratta called out, his tone uncertain. "Hold for a moment, please."

The courier turned, startled to see a squad of guards approaching her. Tallis looked up, vaguely aware that something had changed. Jotrem watched suspiciously, tucking Tallis's hooked hammer under one arm as he drew out the Rekkenmark blade at his belt.

Seven armed soldiers, Soneste's instincts warned her, but now wasn't the time for doubt. Only action. Olladra be with me, she prayed. She holstered the hand crossbow, the bolt still loaded. She looked furtively over her shoulder and wished Aegis were there.

Bratta ignored his fellows and approached the girl. The others stopped, unsure. "Sergeant, what are you doing?" Jotrem asked loudly.

Soneste stepped up to the wand-bearing Lion who stood behind Tallis. The Karrn's ear turned in her direction. He was listening, ready.

"Sovereigns save us!" Soneste said, feigning panic in her voice. "What is that thing?" She wrapped her fingers around the wand in the guard's hand and turned him around as if to aim at some invisible foe. She used her body to hide her hands from view of the others.

"What!?" the Lion demanded.

"Oh, gods!" Soneste shouted in his ear then pried the wand upward to point at the man's own face. She didn't know what the magic device would do, but she hoped it wouldn't kill. He locked her fingers around the shaft and shook it.

Orange light flared from the amber tip as the guard flinched. His face slackened visibly, and his eyes lost all focus. The man was physically stunned by the wand's magic and could utter not a word. Elated, Soneste pulled the wand from his feeble grasp even as she drew her rapier.

"White Lions!" she announced as all eyes turned to her. She pointed the wand at Jotrem. "This man is a changeling."

The guards froze, unsure who to attack. Tallis exploited their indecision, erupting into motion even as Soneste released another store of the wand's magic at the false Jotrem. The man threw up one hand defensively, but the spell took hold—he blinked and struggled against the magic that sought to stupefy him.

Even manacled, Tallis was dangerous. He could not move his wrists apart, bound as they were in black iron, but he knew how to turn anything into a weapon. Soneste glanced quickly his way and saw that he'd already struck one of the Lions down with the crossbar of his manacles.

Tallis pushed past the guard nearest him and grasped the pick's head of his hooked hammer, which was still loosely tucked under the pretender's arm. With a two-handed grip, he pulled it away with all his might. The wedge at the hammer's end struck the false Jotrem in the shoulder blade, doubling him over in pain and dropping the sword from his hand.

The White Lions had gathered their wits and attacked now in full. Soneste dodged the axe of the guard who engaged her, knowing her slim blade would not suffice to parry his swings. Out of the corner of her eye, she saw Tallis strike down the stunned Lion with his hammer and turn to face the rest.

Sovereigns, forgive me.

Soneste danced away from her attacker, searching for her opening. She gestured with the wand, but its power had been spent. The guard rushed forward and struck low, aiming to cut her legs. She stepped aside the wild swing and placed the point of her rapier against his collar . . . angled it away from his throat then *pushed*. Her blade sank into his shoulder. He screamed.

"Sovereign bitch!" he swore, clutching at the stream of blood which had opened at his should as he stumbled to his knees. She brought her rapier down against his hand, dropping the axe in one painful strike.

The imposter Jotrem had gathered his senses. He leaned down to pick up his sword and met her eyes. There was fury there, but Soneste still saw that omnipresent fear.

"Who are you?" she demanded, pointing her rapier at him.

With Tallis engaged by the remaining Lions, the man could have attacked her freely now. Why didn't he? Was he no warrior at all? Not half the soldier the retired officer should have been.

"It doesn't matter," he said.

Sergeant Bratta appeared beside the imposter. The sudden battle and the courier girl's flight had erased his psychic attraction. The guard lifted his crossbow, the steel-tipped bolt leveled at Soneste's chest. He stood not ten feet away. There was no way in Khyber she could dodge that.

"Drop it," Bratta prompted her.

She dropped both the wand and her rapier. She let her hands fall to her sides, where she slowly grasped the sleeve of her right hand and searched for the hidden pouch.

"Tallis!" the sergeant called out, spittle flying from his lips. "Throw down your weapon or you'll being pulling this bolt from the wench's heart."

Soneste noted the false Jotrem stepping slowly away. He knew his ruse was up.

"Fine!" Tallis answered, holding his weapon upright for all to see. Only two Lions remained standing around him. The rest lay bleeding and unconscious on the cobbles. The two flanking the Karrn ceased their attack but watched him warily.

The sergeant's eyes flicked to Tallis. "Throw it *down!*"

"I said . . . fine!" Tallis said, bringing his arm down and hurling the hooked hammer straight at Sergeant Bratta. The Lion deflected the spinning weapon with the chain mail of his arm, but the *thwack* of its impact sounded painful. The weapon tumbled from his grip—

—and Soneste pulled her smaller crossbow out, tearing the packet where she'd placed her blue whinnis and applying it swiftly to the bolt's steel tip.

She lifted her weapon and sighted down the retreating imposter. She pulled the trigger.

The dart-sized bolt struck him between the shoulder blades, easily penetrating the wool of his uniform. He cried out and tried to sprint to the main avenue, but already his steps were growing sluggish. Bystanders at the street's edge gaped at the melee.

Soneste looked back to Tallis. Another Lion was down. The Karrn was grappling with Bratta, for he'd attempted to retrieve his hammer and the furious sergeant was fast upon him. With his wrists still locked close together, Tallis couldn't maintain his grip and fend off attacks. He was forced to endure a mace blow to the shoulder from the remaining Lion.

"Just . . . get Jotrem!" Tallis growled through the pain without even looking back at her. He pivoted on his feet, swinging the sergeant's body around to shield him from the next blow. The diamond-headed mace crashed into Bratta's temple.

The Justice Ministry will have my head next, Soneste swore silently.

The imposter Jotrem had almost reached the avenue, but his steps dragged. The sleep poison was taking effect. Soneste paused only long enough to pull out her crysteel dagger.

The imposter reached the end of the street and turned.

And ran headlong into the large metal body of a warforged.

"Aegis!" she exclaimed. "Hold him!"

The construct grabbed the weakening man, who collapsed in his grip and hung there like a puppet. The false Jotrem wasn't unconscious—not yet—but he struggled anyway.

Soneste caught up to them. "Thank you, Aegis. Drop him and help Tallis." The warforged complied, and the imposter crumbled to the cobbled street. "Just don't kill anyone!" she called out after Aegis tramped past.

She crouched down, turned the imposter over, and placed the razor edge of her dagger to his throat. "I know you aren't Jotrem," she said in the man's ear and stroked the blade gently across his skin, "so tell me who you *are.*"

The man's heavy-lidded eyes tried to focus on her.

"Let mmme go, Brel . . . saved you . . . from yyyowler . . ."

Yowler? This was useless. She couldn't question him out here. Already she could see passers-by running off to summon another patrol of White Lions. This had to end now or she was as doomed as Tallis.

At the thought, she looked back. One of the White Lions dented Aegis's shoulder with a sound blow from his battle-axe, for which the warforged pounded the man to the ground. Behind the construct, Tallis brought the hammer's blunted end thudding into the sergeant's stomach. Bratta fell hard. With seven White Lions lying unconscious on the street—Host, let none of them be dead—Soneste watched as Tallis set about searching for the key to his manacles. He looked up and offered her a weak smile.

What was the point? Innocent or not of the murder of ir'Daresh, Tallis was an enemy of the state, and Soneste had just firmly established herself as his accomplice. She thought of the Sharn skyline, her apartment in Ivy Towers, and the proud face of Thuranne d'Velderan. She would never make it home now.

Then Soneste looked to the imposter who lazed stupidly before her. He still shifted, drifting on the edge of consciousness. Therein lay her answers—and she was determined to have them out. If she was going to die for this, she at least wanted to know *why*.

Soneste stood and sprinted after an empty coach that trotted near. "Driver!" she called. "Five dragons to buy my friends passage across the city with no questions asked?"

Interlude

There had been more activity around him than usual, but the man in the chair was ignorant of his only visitor. A promise was made to him—a promise of freedom—but he continued to stare, unhearing.

Sverak stands at the railing, stooped over a panel of scrolls and creation schemas. One of the titans—Rejkar One, the same one to which I have devoted the last week—stands on the ground level below, but the twenty foot tall construct still looms above the railing. It was animated weeks ago, but its ability to take action, to reason at all, is minimal. It should be inoperable, situated at the other end of the hall to await further work.

Yet here it is, one arm raised and frozen in place. A block of granite, bolted between a metal vice, serves as the hand.

A group of workers has gathered near, afraid to approach, with Leonus at the front.

"Stop that!" my nephew shouts.

My eyes return to Sverak. At his feet are several broken slates. He holds a flat, wooden schema in one hand. I recognize it. It contains the recorded instructions for activating one of the creation pods of the forge below. Before our eyes, he takes the schema in both hands and snaps it in half.

Lord Charoth rushes forward, confronting my assistant. "Touch not one more!" he roars, pointing his wand at Sverak. "Back away from there now, or you will die today, warforged!"

These schemas are the lifeblood of the facility, magical possibility in its purest, recorded form. They allow the Cannith machines—especially the creation forges—to function. Sverak has already destroyed the worth of thousands of gold pieces.

"Sverak, please," I say, hoping my assistant will reason with me. "What are you doing this for?" He does not understand the fury of Lord Charoth Arkenen. The director does not give empty threats.

In answer, Sverak holds up another schema before him—one he'd concealed behind his back. In the bright lights of the central hall, I recognize it as I know my superior must: a narrow slate of gold, in which are carved powerful sigils from ancient Xen'drik.

This particular schema is vital to the Orphanage's work, the catalyst from which all of our research springs. It should have been guarded, under lock and ward. Only the director and I have access. How did Sverak get it? Why does he hold it?

"It would be unwise to discharge that wand," my assistant says to Lord Charoth.

Chapter
TWENTY-FIVE

Enthralled
Wir, the 11th of Sypheros, 998 YK

Verdax grunted irritably when he heard Tallis's hammer upon his door again. He set the damaged darkvision lenses down and jumped down from the table, wondering if they had completed their mission. Perhaps the female was ready to talk about Sharn. He cheered himself with the thought of pulling *Kapoacinth* out of port and beginning the long voyage around Khorvaire to the city of Sharn.

He'd had that daydream many times.

Verdax didn't bother checking the spyhole. He knew Tallis would be coming back to restock eventually. That's what he liked about the warmblood. Unlike most of the surface-dwelling races, he didn't lapse into stagnancy at the war's end.

Which meant he kept the gold coming. Yes, Tallis was his best customer.

When the door cracked open, the half-breed elf pushed through with a body in his arms—and it wasn't the female. Another stranger? Moody warmbloods! Verdax revoked his renewed admiration for Tallis.

"Who is you brought now?" he shrieked.

"*Not* now," Tallis said, his face paler than usual. The half-breed's tone was harsh, his words peremptory. Verdax didn't like it.

Tallis and his burden entered the workshop, and the female came aboard behind him. Verdax moved to shut the door, but then the warforged pushed its way in. "Cursed warmbloods and constructs," the kobold muttered in his mother tongue then sealed the door and followed them in.

The stranger showed evidence of a sound beating. Verdax said nothing, hoping he wasn't expected to heal the man. The indignities heaped upon him this day were numerous enough, thanks to his "best customer."

Tallis dropped the man unceremoniously to the ground. Verdax scrambled to clear away his most valuable tools from the area and hastily removed all glass devices. It looked like the Tallis was going to get rough. Apparently he'd forgotten whose boat this was!

"He's still awake," Tallis said. The man who wormed on the ground looked like a military officer. His wrists were locked in by a pair of manacles.

"No more bringing law man here, Tallis," Verdax insisted, baring his teeth. First the half-breed worked *with* them, then he beat them up. Tallis was losing his head.

"Water, Verdax," the half-breed said without looking at him. "Now. Please."

The kobold fetched a wooden cup, the largest one he had, newly filled with water from the Karrn River. Tallis dumped it on the man's face. The military man sputtered and came to. Verdax sympathized—the river water was like ice, especially so late in the year.

"Soneste tells me you are not Major Dalesek," Tallis said to the man, "so tell me who you are."

The battered officer fixed his eyes on his captor. "Forget it. The only good choice for you now is to run from here."

Tallis punched him in the face. "No. What's your name?"

The officer spat at him. The female crouched down low to

the man. "You're a changeling," she said simply. Verdax fumed in silence. He didn't like lawmen *or* tricksters on *Kapoacinth*. Khyber's cauldron, this one was both!

"No changer-mans here!" Verdax exclaimed.

Tallis punched the man in the face again. "What's your name?"

The officer lolled on the floor, one of his eyes too swollen to see. "Just . . . run away, Tallis. You don't . . . want this."

"You *know* me?" Tallis said, his lips twitching. His eyes were wild. Verdax had never seen him so angry. "How?"

The half-breed reached up and took one of Verdax's woodcarving blades from the tabletop. When the officer didn't answer, Tallis pressed the knife point against his ear and with and started to cut. The officer screamed and tried to reach up his ear, where Verdax saw a trickle of blood.

The female reached out her hand and stopped him. "No! Not this way!" she said.

"Gan," the man said feebly. "My name. That's . . .all you get."

"Not enough." Tallis held the blade up, still wet with blood. "*Are* you a changel—?"

Before Tallis finished his question, Verdax watched with disgust as the man's bruised skin quivered as if it were made from wet clay. His already pasty complexion shifted into a faded gray, made sickly by the livid bruises. Verdax didn't know much about changelings, but he felt sure this one was younger than the man he'd been impersonating. The only eye this Gan could see out of was milky white, bereft even of pupils. His thin lips curved into a weak smile.

"Gan, then," the female said. "Where is Jotrem? You haven't been him for very long, have you?"

"He is fine," the changeling said. "He was not to be killed."

"Listen to me, Gan," Tallis said, putting his face only inches from that that blank white eye. "You are going to die if you don't tell me everything you know. Everything, Gan. Two of my friends are dead because of you and whoever you work for. Someone will answer for that, and it will be you alone if you don't tell me more. Do you understand?"

Gan blinked, steadying his breath.

The female stood, a nervous look on her face. "He's not going to speak truth to you, Tallis, because there's someone else he fears more, fears more than anything."

Tallis jammed the butt of the knife into Gan's already swollen eye. He cried out and tried in vain to clutch at the injury. Verdax wasn't sure the changeling would ever see with that eye again. Not at this rate.

"Protect *yourself*, Gan," Tallis said to him, "because your boss isn't here to suffer like you are."

Still the captive said nothing.

"Verdax," the female said, looking to him. "Do you have a device that can cancel magic or other, similar effects?"

Well, at least Verdax would get compensation for this intrusion. A fee would be in order. "The wand of dispelling," Tallis said.

"Thirty platinum," Verdax said, baring his reptilian teeth and taking a stand. The amount was fifty gold coins more than he usually charged Tallis for each use of the wand. They needed reminding that this was *his* ship and their unexpected intrusion was unwelcome.

"Fine," Tallis said, giving in too easily. He'd expected a fierce negotiation of price, in which Verdax wouldn't yield a single coin. But the half-breed elf didn't argue at all. What had *happened* to his favorite warmblood? "We'll settle up later."

Verdax crossed the room, produced the ivory wand from a locked shelf, and returned. He held it out hesitatingly to the female. "Know how to using it?" he asked.

The female merely nodded and took the wand from him even as she placed a strange ceramic one in his hand as if in exchange. Verdax recognized its typical Cannith design. It was an eternal wand! Such wands possessed a limited store of magic each day, but were otherwise everlasting. He accepted it, for now.

The female wrapped her fingers around the dispelling wand in a precise fashion and pointed it at Gan. The changeling struggled under Tallis's grasp. The half-breed elf looked expectantly at her.

The female turned to face the warforged. Verdax had already forgotten about it. "Aegis, I will need your help. Hold down his legs. Tallis, hold his hands."

When they were in place, Gan struggled in vain. Then the female discharged the wand in his face.

* * * * * * *

Gan wanted the dream of his perfect woman to return.

Beneath the throbbing agony of his head and the sharp ache of his swollen eye, he focused his mind solely upon her. Perhaps he could replace this unforgiving reality with his fantasy if he concentrated hard enough, to escape with that sinuous form in silken red. . . .

But no, she wouldn't come. Only that damnable blonde stood over him. The wand she pointed at him buzzed with power as a cyclone of magical *absence* coursed out from his body, leaving only a vacuum of longing within him.

Gan screamed, and in the torrent of pain he couldn't even hear himself. He could hear only that which he craved. It called to him, a liquid panacea that could make sense of his world, give song to his desire, and soften the pain of his unfair, vermiculated life.

The wand's drain upon him had ended, but time seemed to slow. It felt like he'd been locked under its power for hours. The evil device had suffused an ache within his body that he couldn't articulate. Gan felt sick deep within and all throughout. Everything he'd ever dreamed or hoped for seemed unattainable now. Shattered. The beautiful landscapes he'd imagined in his youth, the freedom and peace he'd craved as child—far from Tumbledown, from Sharn itself—all of it dissolved. Life was pain and emptiness, a waiting room to Dolurrh.

"What's wrong with him?" he heard the half-elf ask. Gan wanted to kill him, but could come nowhere near trying. Ever. The man was too dangerous for him.

"The wand strips away magical or other similar effects." The woman—Soneste was her name, he remembered as if from far away—sounded like she was giving a lecture.

"I know that, but—"

"When there are no prominent spells, illusions, or devices left to take from, the spell goes deeper. Now it's removing every trace of magical—or psychic—toxin."

Oh, Khyber! Is that what she—

She hit him again with another infernal blast from the wand. Gan felt like his vital organs were being liquefied, wrenched from his being to evaporate like vinegar in the air. He felt his lungs open, heard pitiful sounds issue from his lips.

"He craves dreamlily," Soneste said calmly, as if every fiber of his being *weren't* rushing out of his spine in a din of torment. "He's an addict, a slave to its power. I'm taking away from him every trace of it that lingers in his body. It's a psionic drug, which makes it susceptible to the wand's effects. He's going into a hastened withdrawal."

How did she know? Even his lord hadn't known until three days ago!

"He hid it well, but when I realized he wasn't Jotrem, the clues made sense. I've seen it before."

Again came the flux from the wand.

"You has enough gold?!" demanded that yapping lizard. Where on Eberron *was* Gan right now? Was he losing his mind?

Gan groaned again. His bones began to throb. His head pounded near to exploding. He just wanted this to end. If he had strength enough, he would kill himself. Gan could feel his body writhing even under the unmoving grip of the warforged's hands. His bowels loosened within.

Traveler, he screamed silently, free me from this! He wished he were a priest that he could call down divine wrath upon his tormentors. The woman's face came close. He knew her face was pretty, but he wanted nothing more than to tear the flesh from her skull, flay her skin and burn it!

"Fortunately for Gan," she said, "I have some 'lily with me to make it all better again." She held a small vial before his eye. His field of vision has blurred, but Gan could see, could *smell* in his very mind, the unmistakable iridescence of that divine nectar. It swished in slow motion inside its hateful glass prison.

Inches from his face, and endlessly out of reach.

❧ ❧ ❧ ❧ ❧ ❧ ❧

What he'd just seen surprised Tallis to no end. Soneste had subjected the changeling to incomprehensible agonies with just the flick of her wrist. Now she held out an illegal drug which she'd pulled from some hidden pocket. At any other time, he might have asked her about it, might have made some witty remark. He'd thought of her as a straight arrow of the law, with only a few colorful fletchings to make her interesting.

But now? He felt only a grim contentment at this turn of events.

Gan fixed his good eye upon the forbidden liquid. His body jerked reflexively toward the dreamlily, but he couldn't break from Tallis's grip and certainly not the warforged's.

"Give it!" Gan pleaded, his voice raw from screaming.

Even Verdax seemed subdued at last. He watched with wide, red-glowing eyes.

"No," Soneste answered. "Not until you've satisfied us. We need answers, and when we have them, this 'lily is yours. I promise."

Gan opened his mouth again. "First the dream—"

"And I promise you will have not a drop until you've talked." Soneste sat cross-legged on the floor as if hunkering down for a long wait. She tucked the vial into her shirt pocket. "So you'd better get your head together. It's going to hurt, but you're going to do it."

267

"My name is . . . Gan," the changeling yielded.

"We're past that." Tallis prodded him with the butt of the knife. "Who do you work for?"

"Lord Charoth."

Soneste met Tallis's eyes. "It *is* him," she said. "All of this! But I don't understand his gain, and I don't think we have sufficient evidence to prove it yet."

Aegis shifted his weight forward, steadily crushing the changeling's ankles in his grip. "Did you kill them?" he demanded in a pitiless voice.

"N-no!"

"The nimblewright," Tallis prompted. "Charoth commands it?"

"No. He doesn't."

"This is too slow, Gan," Soneste said. "You're just going to have to wait longer, I suppose." She folded her hands together on her lap.

The changeling opened and closed his eye as if trying to collect his thoughts amidst a haze of pain. "A woman, a priestess," he rasped. "She commands it. She's a Seeker. She . . . she is working *with* Charoth in this."

Tallis stayed quiet, but he could feel his hatred smoldering. The former Cannith lord had joined with the Blood of Vol.

"What about the contract?" Soneste asked. "The receipt that Lady Erice gave me? It states that the Malovyn family has control of the nimblewright."

"False," Gan said. "Planted. Charoth has eyes in many places, you have no idea. He has contingencies. He is far too smart for you. For all of you. For me."

"Lady Erice works for him, too?"

"No. When we went to the Tower, their divinations revealed my race. When I separated from you I sent word to one of Charoth's servants. He *owns* members of the Twelve. He pulls strings in the Justice Ministry and the White Lions."

"And Jotrem?" Soneste asked. "The Civic Minister? What of them?"

"No. Charoth chooses lesser knowns, those who will not be noticed."

"What's the plan, then?" Tallis asked. "What's he doing? Why have this priestess help him kill a Brelish ambassador?"

"I . . . I don't know why. By the gods, I swear it! He doesn't tell any of us everything. I only do my job, to do what he tells me."

"What *is* your job?" Soneste demanded.

Sweat soaked through the uniform Gan wore. It ran into his eye. He blinked to flush it out. "To follow you. To report what you'd learned. You're just one loose end, Brelish. When the time was right, I was to bring the White Lions in to apprehend Tallis. All the evidence was in place. Planted, as I said. He has eyes and hands everywhere."

"You joined up with me outside the Ministry," Soneste cut in. "Before we went to Charoth's factory, right?" She mused to herself for a moment. "Jotrem had called me Brelander, but *you* knew the correct term. Jotrem didn't mind this cold weather, but you did. You're not from Karrnath."

Gan tried to nod. "Yes. I do spy work for him. I'm from Sharn, like you. Once."

"*You* were his valet!" she said triumphantly. "You knew that bugbear at the factory, didn't you? Because you both work for Charoth."

"Rhazan."

Soneste sat upright, her eyes staring beyond them all. Then she closed her eyes as if searching her own memory. Even with the lids closed, he could see her eyes moving left to right, as if she were perusing a book. The Brelish truly possessed powers he didn't rightly understand.

"Tell me about this priestess," Tallis said. How did they know about Lenrik, and their friendship? How *long* had he known? "Who is she?"

"Lady Mova. She came one day from Atur, from the Crimson Monastery. She knows your work, Tallis. What you do against her faith."

Oh, Aureon. Tallis remembered overhearing Lenrik's conversation with Mova, the worried old woman who claimed to have lost her son in the war and constantly sought spiritual affirmation from Lenrik. She'd been the most troubled of the priest's flock, but she was a bloody Seeker, worming her way in close to him. Now Tallis's oldest friend was dead because of her.

Tallis mastered himself, for Lenrik's sake, knowing this wasn't yet the time for vengeance.

"And Gamnon's head . . . ?"

"I don't know. Her doing, I suppose," Gan answered, "with the nimblewright as her means." Tallis wanted to drive the knife into the changeling's face for his nonchalant tone.

"And Haedrun?" he asked, gripping Gan's head with both hands, forcing him to meet his eyes.

"She was . . . the means to involve you, I think, but I guess she served her purpose." Gan tried to shake his head. "I didn't make these choices. I'm a victim, like you."

Aegis released one of Gan's ankles, made a fist with his thick metal fingers, and slammed it down into the changeling's knee. Tallis heard the crack of the soft, flat bone of his kneecap. Gan screamed and tried in vain to reach it with his hands.

"Do not speak of victims!" the warforged shouted.

"Aegis, no." It satisfied Tallis to see Gan's pain, even so. "We need him awake. Too much like will put him into shock."

Soneste opened her eyes at last. "Tallis, there is more to all this, something bigger in all of this. Remember, before we went to the cathedral? The White Lions were running through the street, responding to something. Something else going on."

Aegis swiveled its helmlike head to look at her. "Yes. There was an incident at the Orien station while you were examining the priest's quarters, an attack on the incoming rail from Rekkenmark. Prince Halix was aboard. Many guards were summoned to see to his safety. I believe he was secured."

"A diversion!" Soneste said. "Just like the ambassador's murder. And you and Lenrik. This whole city is in tumult, but none of it is the real threat. It's *all* just distraction!" Soneste withdrew the dreamlily from her pocket and unstoppered it. "Gan, what is Charoth doing?"

Despite his renewed agony, his eye fixed upon the vial in her hand. "Charoth and Mova. Working together on . . . something. For a long time. I don't know what it is, I swear it!"

"Then what do you know about these diversions?" she asked. "You said Charoth has people within the Justice Ministry and among the White Lions. Where else?"

"I will say . . . but you must give it to me! Promise me!"

Tallis thought about what he knew of Charoth. The nobleman was supposed to be a mercantile lord, a man of industry, a chief player in Korth's exports production. Tallis knew the man's business often called for subterfuge—what noble's didn't? Charoth had once tried to hire *him*, after all. Could all this be the result of the wizard's pride, revenge for declining his offer?

No, Soneste was right. There was more. Tallis hadn't realized the depth of the man's ambition. It couldn't be about wealth. There were plenty of rich men in town, so what did Charoth want?

"I promised you already, Gan," Soneste said. "When we're satisfied that you've told us all you can, this is yours."

"Charoth has people in the Justice Ministry, the Twelve, the White Lions, even the Sivis notaries, but he spent the last year getting his best into Kaius's court, in Korth and in Rekkenmark. I would know, I've . . . I've trained them. They are *my* kind."

"Changelings?" Soneste asked. "What is their mission? What can they possibly hope to do under such heavy guard? They cannot possibly threaten the king."

Tallis looked to Gan. Was he—was Charoth—utterly mad? There was no place more impregnable than Crownhome! Tallis had laughed off every offer ever made to him to infiltrate the king's palace, no matter the gold, and beneath his survivalist veneer, it was simply against his will to do so. It was the home of his king. Tallis wouldn't dare.

Gan coughed, a harsh rasping sound. "When the time was right . . ." He tried to steady his voice. "Their . . . only task was to impersonate the prince and princess of Breland. They are good at what they do."

Chapter
TWENTY-SIX

"Your man is late," the old priestess said.

Charoth looked through the transparent wall of his office to the factory room below, watching his daytime workers leave one by one. Only a select few remained at their stations to maintain the tanks. The magewrights he'd hired to repair the outer wall of the western tank bordered on incompetent, but they'd patched it up well enough. Not that it mattered at the moment. He certainly wouldn't need them tonight.

"Do not bring up the Night Shift until the rest have departed," he told his foreman, who had stood waiting for the order. The work day had ended, but Charoth's true work lay before him. "Once they are here, admit none into the factory. Any who intrude, the fire."

Charoth looked absently to the furnace that adjoined the two heating tanks, necessary to keep the glass in a liquid state. The fire elemental bound there was very powerful; Charoth had hired the best Zil binders gold could buy. Living creatures fed into the mouth of the furnace were inevitably subject to the elemental's ancient wrath and were incinerated within seconds—a convenient method of disposal for when enemies, rivals, or liabilities needed removing.

"Yes, my lord." The foreman exited the office.

"Did you hear what I said, Charoth?" The priestess stepped into his view, demanding his attention. Her ceremonial red and black robes swayed with each step.

"It is inappropriate for my employees to see you here dressed like that." He didn't bother to point. When she did not answer, he forced a shrug. "I must assume that trouble has befallen Gan or that he is otherwise detained. What is done is done, Lady."

"I will send the construct to fetch him."

"No." Charoth leaned his hands against the desk as if weary. "I will not risk giving up any of our defenses now. All resources *must* remain. The nimblewright stays with us." He gestured to the factory doors through the wall. "When all have departed, the doors will be sealed. My sentries will have to suffice."

"So be it," Mova said. "But I am anxious to begin."

Charoth nodded his head, then placed his gloved hands upon the surface of the glass table and looked to the withered shape in the adjoining throne. Without turning to the hulking shadow in the corner of the room, he spoke.

"Master Rhazan, it is time."

❦ ❦ ❦ ❦ ❦ ❦ ❦

Soneste stepped out into the riverside wind, which soothed her mind even as it chilled her skin. The sun had already dropped below the cliffs, tingeing the sky violet in its wake. Thoughts of home returned. She couldn't be farther from it now.

She looked down at the dreamlily in her palm, turning the vial over in her hands to watch the lustrous substance swirl. For her, dreamlily had tasted like the sweet redeye berry wine her father had shared with her on the last day she'd seen him alive.

The drug was an insidious substance, a nepenthe for forgetting. Soneste had used it herself on several occasions in the dream parlors of Sharn and had purchased some to take with her. She'd told her friends that it was for research; if she was going to track down sellers of such contraband, she wanted to *know* their experience. She'd told herself the same thing. She did not tell them of how she'd like to forget the uglier sides of Sharn, to forget how much she missed her father or neglected her mother. It was just one small secret in a city built on them.

The hatch opened behind her. She slipped the dreamlily back into her pocket as Tallis joined her at the railing.

"Do you really intend to give it to him?" he asked.

She thought of little Vestra and her stuffed badger. At least Soneste had only lost her father, not her whole life like Gamnon's children. "No."

The whistling wind filled the empty silence.

"This was my last sanctuary," he said at last, thumping the metal grate beneath them with his foot.

Soneste nodded. "It seems I'm on your side now too."

Tallis touched her hand where it gripped the rail, only for a moment. "For what it's worth, thank you. I'd probably be dead now if you hadn't helped me escape."

"We're even, then."

"I think you're right. The Brelish royals are the mark," Tallis said soberly. "They have been all along. Me and Lenrik, mere scapegoats. Distractions for you and the Ministry to waste its time on. Host! Before I went to the Market, I actually crossed paths with Princess Borina on the street. She was guarded by the Conqueror's Host and a couple of bone knights. Security *has* tightened here, a consequence of Gamnon's death."

Soneste nodded. "If the changeling is telling the truth—and I'm sure he is—we know why Charoth *wants* the city's security shuffled around. When I first arrived, Hyran assured me that General Thauram was assembling more personnel to guard Prince Halix and Princess Borina."

"I have my own fight with the good general," Tallis remarked, "but he's loyal to Kaius. He wouldn't betray his king or his nation.

If he brought in any of Charoth's hirelings, he did so unaware."

"This is why I need to go back to the Ministry." Soneste gripped the metal rail. "The incident at the rail station was probably a ruse. The Halix *there* might well have been one of Charoth's changelings, meant to distract the Lions while the real Halix is captured elsewhere."

"You going back there, not a good idea," Tallis said. "We can find out another way."

Soneste shook her head. "If the Brelish royals really are in trouble, the Civic Minister—Kaius himself—will do *everything* in their power to keep it quiet. You know the consequences if something happens to Boranel's children."

"I do, but you can't just go walking in there." Tallis tapped the pommel of her rapier. "You've assaulted the Lions. There were witnesses. Fraternizing with the enemy. Welcome to my side of town."

Soneste remembered the knave who was killed with his own blade just outside the Ministry headquarters. "I'm here on behalf of the King's Citadel," she reasoned. "I have a certain immunity. It might buy me time."

"On the contrary, Soneste. As a representative of the Brelish crown, your actions may just as easily be construed as an act of war." Tallis let the point sink in a moment. "Even if you can prove you had just cause, by the time they sort all that out . . ." Tallis gestured at the city that rose above them. "Whatever's going on will be over. If your royals are harmed . . . well, I don't think this is going to be a good time for foreign relations anyway. Things will get very ugly very quickly."

"I know." Soneste patted her coat, making sure she had all she needed. "I have to get close enough to be sure. But we can't just go invading Charoth's estate."

"That's exactly what we have to do." Tallis caught her eye and held it. "We'll do it *my* way, and it won't just be you and me. Seems to me we've got a vengeful warforged in our ranks."

Soneste laughed but felt no mirth in it. Her heart was already pounding. She glanced up at the distant, floating lights of the

Tower of the Twelve, wishing they could call down the help of some of Khorvaire's most powerful mages, storm Charoth's estate in force with and lay all secrets bare.

But they didn't know who else Charoth might own. Just how mighty was this one man, self-exiled from his house, disfigured and feared? What in Khyber's lightless depths was he after? She remembered the fear and hatred she'd felt pouring off of him at the sight of the warforged. It seemed his only defining passion, but it wasn't motive enough. Unless his rage extended to the Warforged Decree, warforged had nothing to do with the Brelish royals.

Soneste stepped out onto the dock. "There is a chandler's shop across from Charoth's estate. Wait in the alley beside it, and I'll be there as soon as I can."

Tallis opened his mouth to interject.

"Keep Aegis with you, please," she said. "I'll be there as soon as I can."

❧ ❧ ❧ ❧ ❧ ❧ ❧

Gan whimpered beneath the warforged's grip. "She promised!" he wailed when he saw Tallis return. "I have said what I know!"

Tallis kneeled down to look straight into Gan's good eye. The bruises he'd given the changeling were nothing compared to the sickly lines that now creased his face. Purple bags swelled beneath both eyes, sweat slicked his entire body, and saliva leaked continually from his lips. Tallis had seen Lower District scum starving for their addictions for a variety of substances, but never in such quick order.

"One more question for you," Tallis said. "Why Lenrik? Why was he involved? Why was he silenced?"

Gan forced the words through moist lips. "One of you *had* to be, to complicate the investigation. The priest was more accessible to Lady Mova. She knew she could get close to him at any time. Not you."

Tallis stared at the changeling, wanting nothing more in that moment than the freedom to drive a blade into his throat. "Well, we're out of time, Gan. I'd love to keep talking to you, to find out *more* reasons to kill you, but we'll just have to have that chat later. So for now . . ." In his mind, Tallis could see Lenrik's face in the repose of undeserved death. "You suffer."

"Give it!" the changeling shrieked, flecks of spittle flying from his lips.

Tallis stood. "Verdax, your storage hold. I need to keep him in there for now. I'll return for him later."

The kobold stamped his clawed foot on the ground. "No!"

Gan started to scream again. "Aegis," Tallis said, "Please shut him up." The changeling gave a strangled cry as the warforged held his jaw shut with his metal grip.

Tallis kneeled before Verdax and looked the artificer straight in the eyes. "Verdax, listen to me. I'm going in deep this time, and I need to borrow some things."

"No! This not—"

"You *know* I'm good for it all. Verdax, do you remember Lenrik? My friend, the priest up in the cathedral?"

"Elf man," the kobold said. "He hurt?"

"Dead, Verdax. Killed by vermin like this man, and I need to take them down."

"Charoth," the kobold warned. "Mask Wizard, Tallis. Too many friends. You going with him, not to be back and pay me for what you take."

Tallis nodded. "I understand your concern. I'm good for it, either way." He produced a strip of paper and an ink pen from one of Verdax's piles and scrawled down a series of numbers. He placed it in the kobold's clawed hands. "These are my safe houses in Rekkenmark and Atur. If I don't come back from this job, they're all yours. Collateral, a fair amount of gold and plenty of compensation in goods. It's more than you know. All right?"

"No." The kobold's dragonlike face wasn't as stern anymore. The red glow of his eyes had softened.

"Thank you, old friend. You're the last one I've got. When this is all over, you and I will talk about getting you to Sharn for good."

The artificer's diminutive chest puffed up, then he blew out a long, breathy hiss. "Take Ferine Blade and armor wrist."

Tallis smiled. "Thank you."

Verdax pointed to the spectacles on the table, not yet repaired. "Darkseeing glass not finishing."

"I'll have to do without. How about some sovereign glue?"

He considered his opponents. If they faced a Blood priestess, there was likely a small company of undead under her power. Gods, how he could have used Lenrik's help in this. He maintained a veritable arsenal of weapons perfect for battling the undead—holy water, silver and blessed weapons, and the like—but now Aureon's shrine would be locked up under the prelate's watchful eye. He could go nowhere near it.

Then there was Charoth. Even before today, Tallis knew he commanded a network of informants and street toughs. It made sense that he hired changelings like Gan. A practical mix of mercenaries and spies. None of that surprised him. What did surprise Tallis was that Charoth was resourceful enough to reach the Red Watchers and had somehow learned of his connection to Lenrik. He'd underestimated the infamous Masked Wizard. How long had Charoth been planning this day?

Then there was the question of location. Surely Charoth wasn't sitting around in his house with all his cohorts arrayed neatly around him. What in Khyber was he doing? Why would a man, even an ambitious Cannith lord, risk his entire industrial empire? He was opposing Kaius III himself, arbiter of the Thronehold Treaty, whose military might could not be guessed. Against the king of Karrnath, Charoth could not win—surely?

❀ ❀ ❀ ❀ ❀ ❀ ❀

Soneste stepped into an alley and out of plain sight. She spoke the word that triggered the magic of her shiftweave clothing. The blue coat and stylish Brelish shirt she wore reformed instantaneously into the garments of a noble's servant. Her wide-brimmed hat had become a sensible cap that kept her hair from blowing loose. She unbuckled her rapier and carried it openly in hand.

When she neared the headquarters of the Justice Ministry, she slowed down. White Lions swarmed the street, drawing the murmur of the civilians who wandered through. They'd assembled into ordered formations, awaiting orders, but Soneste detected a note of confusion among their ranks.

"Excuse me, watchmen," she called as she approached the nearest squad. The Karrnathi accent was easy for her. She held up the rapier. "My master, Major Dalesek, instructed me to bring this to him at the Ministry offices when it was repaired. Is there trouble here?"

"Come back later, miss," the closest soldier answered.

"What's going on?" she asked with concern. It wasn't hard to fake it.

"It doesn't matter. Move along."

"I saw the Conqueror's Host mustering," Soneste added. "Should I be concerned?"

The Lion turned to look at her. There was frustration in his expression. "Yes. That is, no. There's been bloodshed on the streets. It's being handled."

"And bloody wizards coming in from House Medani," she heard the man behind the guard whisper to the comrade beside him.

The first Lion spun around. "Private, speak out of turn again and you'll be polishing up the Old Man's privy for the next month."

Medani? The House of Detection. Were they looking for her and Tallis . . . or Halix and Borina?

Soneste slipped away without a word.

Chapter
TWENTY-SEVEN

Infiltration
Wir, the 11th of Sypheros, 998 YK

Night had fully embraced Korth. The dim light of several moons and the cold fire lanterns of the city saw Soneste's way to the Community Ward. She had purchased a few supplies of her own as quickly as possible, altering her shiftweave into the same dark clothing she'd worn at the Midnight Market, and made her way to Charoth's estate.

Aegis's blue crystal eyes glowed faintly in the darkness. She slipped into the alley between the closed shop and the adjacent building. Buckled around the warforged's metal-plated waist was the Rekkenmark blade that Jotrem—then Gan—had carried. In his hands, Aegis carried the long sword Haedrun had wielded. Moonlight seemed to collect along its blade, so the warforged tried to hold it out of plain sight.

Soneste wondered where the *real* Jotrem was. Despite her dislike of the man, she hoped he was all right. At least it was the false Jotrem, Gan, who'd be thrashed by Tallis in Wollvern Park.

The Karrn stood waiting in the shadows behind Aegis, back against the wall. He had discarded his Windwrights garb entirely, wearing the black clothes he favored with their pseudo-military design. A pair of green vambraces girded his wrists. Over his shoulders was a bulging backpack. Most remarkable was the sword strapped in a fine leather scabbard across his back. Its hilt glistened with an emerald light from the jewels encrusted there. A magewrought weapon, for sure.

"Never touch this sword," Tallis said by way of greeting, his eyes fixed on the manor across the way.

With a start, Soneste noticed a man lying against the alley wall with an empty bottle tucked in his arms. She squinted and saw that his head was twisted in a disturbing angle.

"A sentry," Tallis explained. "Our 'forged friend here has the stealth of a herd of gorgons, but it's—*he's*—more observant than I took him for. Know any drunks that carry these around?" The Karrn held up a stiletto, the kind used to slip through the greaves of a warrior's armor.

"Is it common for nobles of Karrnath to place exterior guards?" Aegis asked.

"No," Tallis answered. "Charoth's caution is apparent."

"We were right. Someone *has* gone missing." Soneste kept her voice quiet, though the dark street appeared to be empty. She thought of the nimblewright and Lady Erice's words: *It can wear the illusion of any other person, so it can walk among regular people.*

"But I hope we're wrong," she said.

They turned their eyes upon Charoth's manor, the Murder House. Soneste described her previous visit, the "yowler" outside, and what little she'd seen of the house's interior, while Tallis recounted his reconnaissance around the estate. Five other sentries had been posted in various places outside the gate, but Tallis had dealt with them before her arrival.

"They are no shifts tonight. Our dead friend there said every man had been ordered to guard all night." He turned to Soneste. "This watchdog of his, just how thick was the chain?"

"Strong enough to hold the yowler, it seemed," Soneste answered, "but it *was* uncomfortably long."

The Karrn looked back at the gate. "All right. Just stay behind me. I'll get us in, but your job will be to locate the captives. No lights until we're inside. Understood?"

"Yes," Soneste and Aegis said at once. Weapons in hand, the trio moved across the street, guided only by Tallis, the moons, and the faint light of distant lanterns.

When Soneste had visited the estate the first time, the gates had opened for her. Now the black iron bars formed an impassible stockade. Tallis peered between the tall spikes, searching for any sign of motion beyond. He led them slowly alongside the gate on one side, seemingly counting the individual bars. At last he paused, reaching out with a gloved hand and grasping the black iron. She expected to see a flare of defensive energy, but there was nothing.

"Soul descending," he said with an odd inflection. The bar vanished beneath his fingers, along with several around him. "Inside, now!"

Soneste and Aegis followed, passing through that section of gate before it disappeared again. "How did you . . . ?" she asked.

Tallis stared into the darkness of the estate before them with an appraising eye. With elf blood in his veins, the Karrn could see much better than she in the dark, but the landscaping was obviously not enough cover for his liking.

Finally, he looked back. "I coerced one of the sentries into telling me the watchword," he whispered, offering no details. He withdrew from his pack the ivory dispelling wand and held it out to Soneste. "Take this. Verdax said there are only three charges left, so use it sparingly."

She tucked the wand away, then pointed. "Look, there. The chain."

❂ ❂ ❂ ◎ ❂ ❂ ❂

Squinting in the gloom, Tallis saw a length of heavy chain on the ground, snaking out from a line of bushes. At the end of the chain, an empty collar. "So where is—?"

A ghastly cry, *almost* human, rose up from the night itself, sending a painful chill through his spine. Tallis grit his teeth and forced himself to turn, looking for the source. Soneste stood behind him, eyes searching left and right, her expression panicked. Tallis didn't want to hear that wail again. It made him feel like a child hiding from the dark.

"I see it," Aegis said, and Tallis turned in time to see a lion-sized animal with motley skin and fur crash into the warforged from a low-hanging eave of the house.

The weight of the beast bore the construct to the ground. Tallis lashed out with the mithral pick of his weapon, but it passed harmlessly through the creature. He remembered Soneste had warned him of this, a displacement glamer that made the yowler appear a short distance from its actual location. He swung again, guessing, and felt the mithral bite into the creature's hide.

A yelp of pain that sounded too much like a screaming child turned its glowing, catlike eyes upon him. It raked one hideous paw across Aegis's chest, and the warforged lay perfect still. Tallis wondered if Aegis was dead.

The yowler evidently thought so and padded off the construct to prowl around Tallis. Aegis rolled to his feet and smacked the buckler of his hand against the beast's rump. It turned, snarling, and Tallis buried the pick's head into its hide a second time.

Man and warforged continued this barrage as Soneste backed away, evidently frightened by the preternatural yowl that gave the creature its name. Tallis noted that the creature seemed weakened by their blows only marginally. It was going to take a lot more to bring it down.

Soneste managed to load her hand crossbow and aimed it with shaking fingers at the creature. A dart-sized bolt struck the beast on the head, leaving a welt that Tallis swore vanished only seconds later. It was time for a new tactic. He reached for one of his metal rods. The beast finally gave up trying to fight each of its opponents and focused exclusively on one: him.

Tallis had no time to raise a defense as the thing launched itself in the air. Teeth clamped down on his arm, and its body weight—more than twice his own, easily—threw him to the ground. His sleeve ripped apart under its jaws, and Tallis could feel the sharp edges of its slavering, unwholesome teeth worrying at his flesh. The magic vambraces he'd borrowed from Verdax did their job, preventing the yowler from snapping through to the bone.

Beyond the thing's body, Tallis glimpsed both Aegis and Soneste swiping at it with their blades, but it was still taking too long. The yowler's jaw was strong, and those teeth were bound to get through eventually.

He heard Soneste call out in a quavering voice, *"Audsh! Nerzhaat hak irezh!"*

The yowler paused for only a second, its stubby, hairless ears perking up at the sound of her voice and the peculiar words she'd used.

Tallis used the moment to wriggle his left hand up to its head, where he put all of his strength into maneuvering the magic rod into its mouth. He felt his hand gummed by the creature's saliva as it slid along the length of its tongue, but he pushed again, harder and harder. The yowler made a gagging sound, and Tallis pressed the activating button, locking it in space.

The beast attempted to let out its cry again, but it was impeded by the metal wedged in its throat that *would not move*. The wheeze was painful to hear but not half as frightening. In a panic, it tried to jerk its head this way and that, hoping to break loose, hoping to vomit the offending object. Freed from its attention, Tallis slid himself away. He rose and joined Soneste and Aegis as they pushed their weapons again and again into its body.

Blood spurted from empty space while the perceived body of the creature puckered into wounds too fast for it to mend in full. When the yowler's muscles started to slacken, Aegis stepped over to its head and drove Haedrun's blade into its neck repeatedly until it cut through it completely.

❀ ❀ ❀ ◉ ❀ ❀ ❀

"You speak—what was that, Orc?" Tallis retrieved his magic rod from the yowler's head, which allowed the beast's head drop to the ground.

"No." Soneste smiled and tapped her forehead. "I just have a good memory." In truth, she was embarrassed at the fear that had taken hold of her when the creature had loosed its wail.

The Karrn shrugged. "Disgusting," he said, trying to scrape the beast's vile saliva off his arm even as he returned the magic rod to his belt. He had his share of the yowler's blood caked onto his body as well. "If I live through today, I think I'm going to be very sick later."

The trio approached the porch. Soneste looked up at the statue perched atop the dry fountain in front of it. The vulture-headed demon had not moved—in her imagination, it was a golem, ready to spring to life—but Soneste felt naked under its glass-eyed gaze. They still glowed with a soft, hellish red.

"We need to hurry," she said softly, following Tallis to the front door.

The Karrn examined the entrance for signs of a trap. He didn't bother picking at the lock. He lifted his hammer and brought down the head against the doorknob. Whether the weapon was magical or the metal it was forged from was something uncannily strong, the lock broke apart on the first swing.

Aegis gazed out at the street. "It's snowing," he said.

Soneste looked out into the darkness. She caught the tiny specks glistening in the air. Under other circumstances, she might have appreciated it. It never snowed in Sharn.

❀ ❀ ❀ ◉ ❀ ❀ ❀

Charoth was not bothered by the young woman's screams. He'd worked under more clamorous conditions. Master Rhazan was strong enough to hold her still until the table did its work. Her strength would ebb soon enough. Not for the first time, he wondered if he should have insisted on choosing the other subject—one male's life energy for another's—but Mova had made her choice already and they'd come to an agreement. Today was not a day for changing plans. They'd been too long set into motion. The girl would do.

It didn't really matter. Both had the blood of Galifar flowing through their veins, a lineage that reached farther back in human history than any he'd researched. Mova had explained that the purer the blood, the stronger its memory, the more conducive it was to both arcane and divine magic. His initial experiments supported this claim.

He was counting on it.

Charoth continued his work until a galvanic pulse in his mind halted him again. A moment's concentration revealed the sensory information that awaited him. He saw three figures rendered in the gray shades of darkvision pass below in the courtyard of his estate.

Tallis, blood-stained and flushed from a fight, was the first.

From the start, Charoth had wanted to channel the major's wonderful resourcefulness into something more tangible than foolish nationalism. The half-elf wasted his efforts trying to rid the nation of its own vices—a lost cause. Tallis should *not* have come this far. His presence at Charoth's estate troubled the wizard severely.

A willowy figure followed the half-elf. Soneste, that damnable arriviste. What have you done with Gan? he asked her silently. What did he dare to tell you?

A third, bulkier figure moved at the edge of the statue's vision, but Charoth couldn't refine it. The scrying eyes had its limitations.

At least there were only three of them. They were fugitives of the law, so they would have no help, and who would believe them?

His factory was impregnable tonight. Charoth had layered its entrances with wards of his own, and his magewrights had reinforced the doors. Even if the court wizards turned their magic upon his factory, it would take time to get in.

He wrenched his mind free from the vision and turned to look across the table. Mova worked quietly, smoothing down the young woman's arms with a sanitizing solution.

"Lady," Charoth said, addressing her after long minutes of silence between them. "There are intruders at my estate. And they have killed your pet, Master Rhazan."

The bugbear snarled from his post. "Let me go, my lord," he said with a rattle of his chain.

"You are needed here," Charoth said

"The construct, then," Mova offered nonchalantly.

"No." He would not explain his reasons again.

"I will go there myself," she suggested, "to put your mind at ease. My work, for the time being, is finished."

Charoth considered this. If Tallis found and killed Mova, he should be able to finish tonight's work alone, but the final steps would be more difficult without her. She had already suffused the throne with divine spells. Whether this power originated from Mova, the apocryphal Vol herself, or some ambiguous spiritual "inner spark" Seekers always raved about, Charoth didn't care, so long as it did its job.

Still, he could trust no one else in this. "Thank you, Lady. It is imperative that they do not discover the—"

"I am well aware, Lord Charoth. I will return swiftly."

❦ ❦ ❦ ❦ ❦ ❦ ❦

As they searched the estate, Soneste's thoughts roiled. Had she the time, she could send word by speaking stone back to Thuranne about their suspicion, but what if she was wrong? A clear threat to the peace of the Five Nations would have the King's Citadel dispatching its best agents, including the Dark Lanterns. Would they get here in time, and what would happen to her if it was all a false alarm? After all, their strongest evidence was the testimony of a dreamlily addict.

In less than a quarter hour, they'd searched most of the house.

Adornments and other trappings of a wealthy man aside, the estate was disconcertingly empty. No servants, no traps. And no more monsters. A burglar's dream. It was as though Charoth and his entire staff had vacated the house without selling it or its luxuries first.

The last room to search was the master bedroom. A single crash of Tallis's hammer on the lock and a heavy warforged foot forced the ornate mahogany doors open. The wide chamber was swathed in heavy cloths of green, gold, and black. Expensive furniture and paintings framed in precious metals exhibited the wealth of Charoth's station. Even bereft of House Cannith, he'd obviously done well for himself.

Tallis moved to secure all visible exits, while Soneste set out to find those less obvious. Aegis took up position at the center of the room, watching for intruders. She soon revealed a hidden door in a three-way mirror, which opened up into a spacious walk-in closet. The carpeting from the bedroom stretched into this one as well, while heavy curtains hung from each wall. A single window lay tightly shuttered on the northern wall, with a high-backed, velvet-padded chair facing it.

"For a prisoner?" Tallis asked, stepping into the room behind her.

Soneste dropped to one knee and studied the empty chair. "I don't think so. Why keep a slave or captive in such a comfortable seat?" She ran her fingers along one of the padded arms, then lifted her hand to her nose. "Strange smell. Almost like . . . vinegar. Or brining solution."

Tallis pried open the shutters with the pick end of his hammer. "There's a rumor that Charoth bathes in some sort of pickling liquid to keep his scarred flesh from sloughing off."

Soneste shook her head. "This whole place—the bedroom, the lavatory, this closet—is immaculate."

"He's wealthy, with legions of maids and servants," Tallis said. "Even his secret prisoner had a nice view of King's Bay."

"No, it's more than that. Either his servants are the best paid in the industry or . . . he doesn't actually live here much. If at all."

Tallis turned to face her. "What do you mean?"

"The bed hasn't been used in weeks. Or months. Maybe this house is a front."

"For what?"

"That's why we're here, right?" Soneste looked back to the empty chair. "This chair. . . it *was* occupied. Recently. The carpet shows plenty of movement too. Charoth, or someone, came through here a lot, but he didn't stay here."

"So where next?" Tallis said.

Soneste shut her eyes and visualized the entire house as she'd impressed it within her mind. They'd searched everywhere—the ground floor in its entirety, the two levels above, even the wine cellar. Ahh, but not everywhere! Soneste saw again the sparsely furnished cellar rooms, the blank stone walls—and the wine racks.

She opened her eyes. "We go back down."

❧ ❧ ❧ ❧ ❧ ❧ ❧

She looked like any of the lower wards' residents shuffling across the snow-dusted street in a heavy winter cloak. She might be dismissed as a nursemaid, servant or a baker's wife, someone's wizened mother, but she was so much more, and the importance of her presence in this city would not be understood by the uninitiated.

Mova stepped into the alley and approached the sentry. Her only bodyguard, one of the soldiers assigned to her by the Order, took up a position on the street to ensure none interfered. He needn't have bothered. The authorities were paid well to keep off this street.

Especially tonight.

The sentry lay against the wall like a vagrant, but Mova could sense that all life had been wrenched from his body—confirmed a moment later when she kneeled and saw that his collar bone had been smashed and his neck broken. This one had died differently than the others, not a clean cut delivered quick and painless.

Life was precious, the blood that fueled it sacrosanct, but only Seekers truly deserved to keep theirs. Mova did not mourn this man. He was merely another of Charoth's ignorant marionettes, motivated only by personal desires. Like his master, he saw no glorious plan in the afflictions of the world. Charoth's ambitions were lofty indeed—Mova gave him that much—but ultimately only for his own purposes.

Mova's arrangement with the wizard was a temporal one, as were all between Seekers and those who did not heeded the covenants of Vol.

Seeker or not, the dead man before her still had his uses.

Mova stared into the sentry's dead face, grasping the bone that hung from the beaded bracelet on her left wrist. The icon, which had once been her late husband's ring finger, served as a focus for her magic. She called upon the power of the blood—the spark of divinity that lay within everyone, for those enlightened enough to see it—and spoke the words to make it manifest. She pointed three fingers at the corpse's face, coaxing the settled air within its lungs to surge out through the damaged throat.

"How did you die?" she asked.

The corpse's head tilted slightly to align its neck properly for speaking. She could hear the grinding of splintered bone. "A warforged struck me with a shield," it said, its voice soft and wheezing. Mova had to lean in to hear the words.

"Was the warforged alone?"

"No."

The dead were not very forthcoming, but Mova was feeling patient. "Who accompanied the warforged?"

"A man in black, with a military pick in his hand."

"Lady, there is movement within the house," the soldier called out.

She turned and stood, looking up at Charoth's manor. A white light roved within the upper floors of the otherwise dark house. Tallis, indeed—so close now! And a warforged with him? The nimblewright hadn't mentioned that.

What Mova had gained from her arrangement with Charoth would be inestimable to the abactors of the Crimson Monastery—an opportunity to channel the blood of ancient Galifar and gain leverage over the political powers that be. What *she* would gain would be the abactors' esteem, one great step toward learning the deepest mysteries of her faith. In addition, Arend ir'Montevik had promised a profound donation to her efforts if she returned to Atur with proof of Tallis's demise. There was even talk of animating the half-elf's bones as poetic justice.

Well, she supposed, perhaps we *are* each of us motivated by personal desire, after all. Such was the world the charlatan gods of the Sovereign Host had crafted for their subjects.

Mova kneeled again and produced from her pocket a small black onyx. She inserted it in the corpse's mouth and pronounced the words that would give the husk a semblance of life.

"Follow me," she said. "We have others to tend to."

The dead sentry began to rise, incapable of resisting her power.

❖ ❖ ❖ ❖ ❖ ❖ ❖

Opening the hidden door in Charoth's cellar hadn't been half as simple as finding it. The lack of dust on every bottle in the impressive wine rack suggested an uncanny diligence on the part of Lord Charoth's maids—or a suspicious means of egress for the wizard's secret chambers—and Soneste had discerned a pattern in the lattice of the rack that allowed it to "unfold." Parting down the middle, the rack rolled aside to reveal the stone wall behind it.

Seeing the cracks that formed the hidden door did nothing to actually open it. His and the warforged's combined strength would not budge the obvious portal. Tallis eventually found the stone that loosed the door, but it rewarded him with a tongue of electricity that coursed into his hand. Thank Aureon, it was brief.

The tunnel beyond smelled of the must of centuries and gave way to a mazelike network of passages. "I think we'll find out just why Charoth chose this house," Tallis said. "It looks very old. There are many tunnels beneath Korth, many interconnected, many with limited access. Evidently, he wanted access to *these*."

Tallis produced a sunrod from his pack and struck it against the wall. The iron rod's tip flared up with alchemical light brighter than Soneste's watch lamp.

"This should last us," he said. "Stay behind me, both of you. He may have left his house empty, but that doesn't mean he's not protecting his interests. Be on the lookout for traps. Aegis, stay behind Soneste."

Sure could use one of the Midwife's men right now, Tallis thought, eyeing the walls. Every inch could be trapped, and Charoth was a damned wizard—magical traps were so much the harder.

* * * * * * *

Their exploration ended when they found a closed, iron-bound door at the end of an otherwise empty corridor. Between the imperfect cracks of the door, they could see light. Tallis handed his sunrod to Aegis. "Hold this behind you to keep the light away from the door. Wait here, both of you."

Tallis crept up to the door and listened close, even as he examined the doorknob in what little light he was afforded. An expression of total disgust came over his face, and he looked back at Soneste.

He made his way slowly back. "It stinks of rot by that door," he whispered. "Servitors of the Cult."

Soneste felt a sourness settle into her stomach. "Any voices?" she asked.

"Some. There are some living agents here. Charoth's men."

"We should go through that door—*fast*," Aegis suggested, and both Soneste and Tallis winced at the volume of his "whispering" voice. "Surprise will help. I will force it down."

Tallis nodded. "I agree, but I have a better method. Safer. Are we ready?"

Soneste willed the glowing light of her watch lamp to dissipate. She grasped her rapier in one hand, the Riedran crysteel dagger in the other. Aegis tucked the sunrod under his arm, glowing tip pointed behind him, and he held Haedrun's sword ready.

"Yes," the warforged answered for both of them.

The Karrn grasped his hammer in two hands, angled his right fist so the dragon-headed ring he wore was pointed at the door, and spoke the word *"Telchanak."*

A transparent image took form even as it sped down the hall. Solidifying into the shape of a dragon's head with spiraling ram-horns, it vanished the moment it impacted with the door. Wood splintered and hinges shattered, echoing loudly through the corridor. Large chunks of door struck someone standing on the other side, dropping him with a shout.

"I so rarely get to do that," Tallis said with a humorless smile.

Chapter Twenty-Eight

Striding past the wreckage of the door, Tallis found himself in a moderately-sized dungeon chamber that reeked of moldering bones. Seven hostile figures turned to face him, standing on opposite sides of the circular pit that marked the center of the room. There was a dark shape in one corner of the room and a door in the center of the far wall. A single, wall-mounted wisplight was insufficient to illuminate the whole chamber.

The three leather-clad men on the left—Charoth's toughs, without a doubt—dropped the game of chance they'd been playing at and reached for their weapons. Either they were inured to the smell or had some means of blocking it out. One of their fellows already lay beneath the broken remains of the entry door, unmoving. The four enemies on the right wore plate armor, but where the metal did not cover their bodies Tallis saw only clean white bones. Inscrutable skulls swiveled his way, and the skeletons drew out their own blades.

Good, Tallis thought with an upsurge of anger. Here was something he could understand and deal with on his level.

"Kill them now!" one of the men shouted, leading his fellows in a charge. As all seven enemies made their way around the charnel pit, Tallis noticed a stirring in the shadows in the far corner.

"A little help here?" Tallis asked his companions, raising his hammer to meet one of the living men.

Weapons clashed. The sunrod he'd given Aegis flew end over end through the air—tossing sinister shadows as it went—to land on the far side of the pit. The warforged barreled past him, throwing his weight into the first skeletal warrior and keeping all four—for the time being—away from Tallis. The heavy buckler on Aegis's arm led the way, blasting the undead off its feet. Only the tangled bones of its torso, encased in armor, remained.

Tallis met the eyes of the man before him, stepping near the pit's edge as he did.

"Dolurrh invites, friend," Tallis promised.

Soneste appeared on his left, using her rapier to keep the next man at bay. The third remained behind the other two, turning the winch of a heavy crossbow.

Tallis feinted twice with his hammer, drawing out his foe's attacks as wide as possible. He lunged in at last, connecting the adamantine hammer hard against the man's chest. The thick leather parted like paper, and Tallis heard the crack of a breastbone. The man's eyes widened in disbelief, then he gasped in an attempt to draw breath. Tallis saved him the trouble, burying the mithral pick of his weapon in the man's neck. He shoved hard, launching his victim into the charnel pit.

One of the skeleton warriors broke away from Aegis and circled the long way around the pit. Tallis fixed his eyes on it, feeling the twinge of the rage he reserved for such creatures. He raised his arm, gauged the distance, and threw. The hooked hammer spun end over, and crashing into the skeleton's breastplate, dropped the creature to the floor.

With Soneste still engaged, Tallis turned his attention to the crossbowman. He stepped away from the pit to present himself as an obvious target. The man took the bait, loosing a heavy bolt. Tallis spun away from the missile just in time—feeling the wind of its passage—and let his body drop to all fours, pitching forward in exaggerated overbalance. As he did, the jeweled sword at his back slipped from its sheath, clattering to the stone floor and sliding near the crossbowman's feet.

"Blunted!" Tallis swore loudly.

The man looked at the fallen sword, its blade glowing with a dazzling green light.

Soneste traded swing for swing with her opponent, both of them stepping dangerously close to the lip of the pit. Tallis would have to trust her to defeat the man and Aegis to hold its own against the skeleton warriors for a few moments longer. He looked up to see his own opponent drop the empty crossbow and take the glowing sword in hand. Its baleful light flickered in the man's eyes.

"Khyber!" Tallis said, eyes flashing left and right for some kind of defense.

"I've heard of you," the tough said with an edge of triumph. "Major Tallis, former soldier of Rekkenmark. Who's too clever to die, they say. Where is your cleverness now, Major?"

"Listen," Tallis replied, noting with a glance that Soneste's man was tiring and only two skeletons remained across the room. "Maybe we can work something out. You know, between thieves?"

"I think not." The man stepped almost within reach, smiling as he tested the perfect balance of the Ferine Blade. A savage gleam lit his eyes. "I'm going to be the man who ended you!"

Tallis deliberately backed himself into the wall. He clenched his fists, as if resigned to unarmed combat. The desperate look on his face prompted the man to strike at last. The Ferine Blade trailed green fire as it arched through the air, then leveled out, coming in straight for Tallis's gut.

Soneste saw his predicament, calling out at alarm.

Tallis flinched as he always did—what if it didn't work this time, that ever-gnawing doubt—but he opened his eyes just in time to see the blade vanish from the sword's hilt . . .

Only to emerge from the man's own stomach as though he'd

been stabbed from behind by the same blade. The green fire flared, hissing as it boiled and dissolved the streams of blood that tried to escape the mortal wound. Screaming, the man pitched to the ground, thrashing in his final, agonized moments.

"Still works," Tallis said.

Soneste and her opponent gaped with shock, but the Brelish recovered her wits first and slashed her blade into the man's knee. As he clutched at the wound, her boot came up, catching him on the jaw and setting him off balance. A second kick dropped him, screaming, into the pit.

A loud crash of metal told him that Aegis had dispatched the last of the skeletons, so Tallis took that moment to retrieve his hammer. He caught a look of disbelief on Soneste's face. "Hence, never touch the sword. Ever." He used his hammer to smash the jeweled hilt from the man's preternatural grip, then used the man's own cloak to pick it up by the blade—which had already reappeared on the hilt. "It's called the Ferine Blade. Something went wrong during its creation, I suppose. It's cursed, what we in the business call a 'backbiter.' "

Tallis returned the weapon to its sheath on his back. He kicked the corpse at his feet. "These are Charoth's fodder, muscle recruited from the Low District, but those"— He pointed to the shattered skeletons—"are the Cult's work. It confirms Gan wasn't lying about their involvement. We should expect more."

A muffled voice drew their attention to the corner of the chamber. In the light of the recovered sunrod, Tallis could see that that the shape in the corner was a large, high-backed wooden chair set against an unusually protruded section of the wall. Seated within was a figure lashed with thick rope with its head covered in a black hood.

"Gods, please!" he heard Soneste whisper as she hastened to the captive. Aegis approached beside her, sword and shield ready.

"Be careful," Tallis warned as he made his way over. "It could be a trap."

With her dagger in her left hand, Soneste pulled the hood

away with her right. She gasped, then dropped to one knee and bowed her head.

"Thank the Sovereigns," she said, then looked back up into the disheveled—and gagged—face of a young man who could be no more than nineteen years of age. "Your Highness . . . I am so sorry for this."

Prince Halix—by Aureon's light, it really *was* him!—tried to speak through the muffle. His eyes were wild and he shook his head with alarm.

Tallis held up a hand. "Be care—"

Something fast and hard struck him in the head. He could barely make sense of it, the world spinning too fast for him to guess at his attacker. The room pitched sideways and he felt the hard floor crash into his side. There was some shouting, a woman's grunt and the warforged's bellow. Tallis forced his eyes open again, only to see that he'd fallen to the ground. His brow and cheek stung from the unexpected blow. He looked up to see Soneste and Aegis battling—

The *chair?*

Strange, blunt limbs had reached out from the back of the chair to which the prince was still bound and some even sprouted from the wall behind it. Halix remained in place, though the coils of rope appeared to have loosened as they shook in the attack. Soneste's dagger lay flat against the suddenly mobile chair's back as if held by some magnetic force, and Aegis's sword had been plucked away by one of the sticky limbs and stuck to the wall. As he watched, the chair and wall protrusion undulated weirdly, like an elastic construct, reaching out with ropey strands the texture of the rest of its body to strike at the Brelish and the warforged.

Not a construct. A creature of flesh. That could imitate furniture?

Tallis climbed to his feet even as Aegis attempted to barrel into the moving wall. Instead of smashing it, the thing merely quivered like rubbery flesh. The warforged's whole body remained attached to the creature precisely where it had struck it.

"I am stuck," Aegis announced. He struck at the creature with an empty fist, even as it pummeled him in turn. The flexible limbs rebounded off his plating, but Aegis grunted with each strike.

Halix, held fast by the creature's adhesive body from the start, could only struggle in vain. Even the coil of rope appeared to be part of its body.

Soneste stood back for a moment, unable to get in a clear strike with her rapier without risking the prince harm.

The whole situation was absurd. Tallis rotated his hammer, ready to strike with the sharp mithral pick's head. "At the same time, then," he said to Soneste.

"Watch the prince," she warned him.

At her words, the false ropes tightened around the boy's torso. Even gagged, the prince gasped from the constriction. At the same time, Aegis broke free. He staggered away from the counterfeit wall.

"Prince will die. Move away!" a genderless voice called out. Tallis searched for the source.

It had come from the creature. Something akin to a toothless mouth had formed on the false section of wall and spoke again. "Move away."

Tallis and Soneste both backed up.

"I do not understand this," Aegis said.

"We're away now!" Soneste demanded. "Now let him go. We're not interested in killing you, only freeing your captive."

"Trade," the mouth said. "Your prince for your sword."

"My sword?" Soneste asked, looking down at the rapier in her hand. She was more puzzled than dismayed.

"*Your* sword," the wall said, pointing one of its springy limbs in Tallis's direction. "Green fire sword. Give."

"The Ferine Blade?" he asked, perplexed.

"Prince dies." The coils tightened again, and Halix groaned in its grasp.

"Fine!" Tallis shouted. He pulled the sheathed weapon from

its place at his back and tossed it by the chair's legs.

The foremost legs of the chair stretched and grasped the Ferine Blade and in that same moment expelled Halix. The false ropes melted away into the creature's body. Soneste jumped forward to catch and steady the boy, but Tallis couldn't tear his eyes away from the bizarre creature.

It immediately altered its shape. The stony wall-shaped portion of its body fused with the woodlike chair and together they transformed into a boxlike shape. When it had finished, the creature resembled a massive, iron-bound oak chest. The appendage that still held the Ferine Blade dropped it into the open cavity of the chest's interior, but not all the way. The jeweled hilt protruded from the lip of the chest, gleaming in the light of the sunrod. The creature remained perfectly still.

How inviting, Tallis thought.

Prince Halix ir'Wynarn moved away from Soneste, tearing the gag from his mouth and trying to give himself space. Aegis, in a surprisingly expressive display, unbuckled the Rekkenmark sword from his waist and offered it to him. Halix accepted it without a word, drawing forth the blade. With a weapon in hand, the boy— it was difficult for Tallis not to think of him as such—appeared to regain his composure, as if regaining control of his own fate. Even roughed up as he was, Halix carried himself with an air of dignity. He looked young, dauntless but untried.

Halix gave the chest-shaped creature a final look of disgust then looked around.

"Where *is* this?" he said, gesturing with the blade at the chamber around them. The aristocratic Brelish accent was unmistakable.

Soneste dropped to one knee again. Aegis followed suit. Here in these filthy catacombs, Tallis found the sight almost comedic. "My prince, we are beneath the estate of Lord Charoth Arkenen, whom we have reason to believe is a traitor to Karrnath."

"And you are . . . ?"

Soneste's eyes widened. "My apologies, Highness. I am Soneste Otänsin, inquisitive of Sharn and Thuranne d'Velderan's

Investigative Services, now in Korth by request of the Citadel. This is Aegis, formerly in service to the ir'Daresh family, now sworn to service directly to the crown. This . . ."

Soneste looked over to Tallis, who shrugged. "This is . . . Tallis."

"*Major* Tallis?" the prince asked, eyes widening ever so slightly.

As he heard his name spoken by the young prince, the enormity of Charoth's stratagem sank into his gut like an anchor. Even Lenrik's death, while egregiously painful to Tallis, would go unnoticed to the rest of Khorvaire, but the demise of a Galifar royal like Halix ir'Wynarn? That could unmake the tenuous peace of the remaining nations. Was Charoth aiming to renew war? What did he stand to gain?

No, the prince was still alive. In fact, Halix was still in pretty good shape.

Tallis thought of Crownhome and King Kaius, whose interest in peace had earned him even the disfavor of many of his own warlords. The Conqueror's Host were probably combing the streets above for sign of the Brelish royals, while court wizards employed magic to locate them. Other agents of the king would be working to keep the crisis quiet. If word got out that the royals had vanished under the king's own nose, Karrnathi diplomacy would suffer a crippling setback.

Here in Charoth's dungeon, would Korth's finest have found Halix at all if they hadn't? Tallis looked at the inquisitive, the warforged bodyguard, and their prince. Was Tallis the only Karrn with a modicum of loyalty to Kaius III involved in this situation? The irony defeated him.

"I am," was all he could reply.

"Your Highness," Soneste said, rising to her feet. "We must get you out of here. There is a maze of corridors behind us, but we can see you through it to the streets above."

Halix combed a hand through his unkempt brown hair. "No. Those bastards have my sister. She's alive, so I'm not leaving here without here." His handsome features were resolute.

"What happened?" Tallis asked, needing facts.

The prince's face flushed with shame. "I was grabbed by men at the Lyrandar docking tower when I landed. After that, I don't remember. I suppose I was secreted down here. I can't remember clearly.

"Borina is here, I know it!" Halix said. "They're . . . going to do something to her. I heard some discussion between a man and a woman."

"Charoth and Mova," Tallis said.

"The woman said she'd be coming back to collect me when their business with Borina was concluded." Halix fumed, kicking at the scattered bones of a skeleton warrior. "We have to find her!"

"I *will* do so . . . Highness." Tallis felt a constricting sense of guilt. Would he let Kaius take the blame for this, for allowing Boranel's children to be taken? "I assure you, my king will want you safe . . . every bit as much as your own father. Trust me on that." He looked to the inquisitive. "Soneste, take the prince out of here, back the way we came. Aegis and I will find Borina." He pointed to the door in the far wall—the only way forward.

Halix rounded on him. "I said no, Karrn. I am *not* leaving my sister to mad wizards and walking corpses."

Tallis approached the boy, who stood eye to eye with him. "Will you raise a weapon against an army of foes, people who don't observe national boundaries, who don't respect the honorable strategies taught to you at Rekkenmark? They murdered innocent people just to get to you and your sister, including a Brelish ambassador and two of my dearest friends."

Halix sneered in defiance. "I didn't go to your academy for politics, Major. I went to learn skill at arms from the finest teachers in Khorvaire, to see if you Karrns really *did* know anything about war, after all."

Tallis held the prince's stare, unflinching.

"Prince Halix," Soneste said, her voice exasperated, "Please. I cannot allow you to endanger yourself further. We will find—"

"I appreciate your concern, Soneste," the prince interrupted, his expression dark, "but I am choosing to save my sister. I require your assistance in this."

Soneste merely stared at him for a moment. She'd probably never seen him before today, but he represented the Brelish crown. She had no choice but to obey.

And now we're going to rescue a princess, Tallis thought. If it weren't so bloody serious, he would have laughed.

"Of course, Your Highness," Soneste said firmly.

"Something is coming," Aegis announced, pointing to the doorway where they'd entered. The stench of death rolled out from the dark passage like a living force, stronger than that which already pervaded the charnel pit.

"Get the other door open, now!" Tallis ordered the warforged, readying his own weapon for the coming enemies.

A figure shuffled into the room, stumbling over the wreckage of the door, followed by another.

And another. A total of six men, clad in the tailored leather suits of Charoth's sentries—the very ones Tallis had put down outside the wizard's estate. Each man moved with the preternatural strength of the animate dead, the wounds that had killed them all too prominent, yet their skin was loose and discolored, as if advanced in the grave by weeks of exposure. Where bones jutted through ripped flesh, Tallis noted a metallic sheen. Mova's work. The atrocity in the lead met his gaze with raw malignance—a gift from its creator's magic.

Tallis heard the door open behind him. "Get them out, Aegis. *Now.*"

He'd faced many zombies before, but these were not the intelligent, sinister visages of Karrnath's elite dead—alchemically preserved and fused with the aggressive spirit of their nation. His instincts told him these had been bolstered by various necromantic spells. For one brief moment he thought he saw Valna's face again, grinning in the madness of foul magic.

Tallis fell into a deadly, insensate calm and advanced.

Interlude

He'd been moved. No longer in his private room, the man now sat within a new chair of hard, smooth glass. It was less comfortable, but he didn't notice. Sweat beaded ever so sleightly at his brow, his heart racing within him. The man's mind was terrified.

Lord Charoth's face darkens—he doesn't abide threats—but I notice he lowers his wand. The schema in my assistant's hand is a priceless artifact entrusted to the director by Baron Starrin himself. As patriarch of the house, there can be no greater honor or responsibility.

"If you seek leverage, you have erred," Lord Charoth says coldly.

"I do not," Sverak answers. His sapphire eyes stare back without fear. Have I misjudged him? My own creation?

My superior steps closer, ready with his wand. I fear that if he does strike, the schema will be damaged. He knows the risk.

Sverak tosses the golden rod into the air near the railing. Lord Charoth rushes forward, faster than I would have thought him capable. He reaches for the schema with desperate fingers—

"Now," Sverak says in a loud, instructive voice.

The titan's raised arm comes down.

I watch, horrified, as Lord Charoth catches hold of the schema in both hands, letting his wand drop. A half-moment later, the granite slab of the titan's hand strikes him from above.

I hear the crack of bone as the weight hammers him to the ground.

I hear his cry of agony, the gasp of the workers nearby.

"Again," Sverak says.

The granite hammer lifts and comes down again.

Chapter
TWENTY-NINE

In her mind, Soneste could still see the madness that had overtaken him when the undead had surged into the charnel room. Tallis had insisted they go on without him, had insisted on taking the undead on alone. She'd lingered in the threshold of the door, ready to help yet repulsed by the foul creatures. She'd watched Tallis with a mixture of concern and awe as he battled them alone. Despite their enhanced speed and preternatural resilience, he'd struck them all down in short order. He'd cut them apart and set fire to the corpses that remained, kicking them into the pit. Tallis had rejoined them then, his eyes wet. She'd said nothing then.

Tallis slipped a ring on his finger, discreetly, but Soneste noticed. It was the black opal ring of the Order of Rekkenmark. Evidently he always carried it with him, but she felt he hadn't worn it for a very long time. There was a crisis of identity raging within this man. Soneste wanted to help.

"Tallis," Soneste said at last, the first to break the silence after many long minutes.

After a long silence, he glanced back at her.

"What happened back there?" she asked. When he didn't answer, she spoke again, "Tallis?"

"We're somewhere below the Commerce Ward. Far below." He looked back at her for a moment, shaking his head. "It's nothing. Just another war story. We all have them."

"Tell me."

Soneste could sense Halix paying close attention. The prince remained quiet, his thoughts no doubt consumed by their predicament and concern for his sister. She could hardly digest the fact that King Boranel's youngest son was in her charge.

At the end of the corridor, they found a stone staircase spiraling up into the dark. Tallis stared up. "I led a mission into Thrane, but you know that already, don't you? I was court-martialed for turning on my own men.

"Well, I *didn't*. At least, not living men. My unit was five good soldiers, the finest I'd ever known, but by some cruel joke, Warlord Dehjdan had insisted a rot squad be assigned to us."

Soneste shook her head. "I don't know what that is."

"The animate dead," he said. "Sons and daughters of Karrnath, given the 'glory' to fight for their nation again. The undead legions kept us alive early in the war, and we all owe Kaius the First and his cursed arrangement with the Blood of Vol for saving us. I hate it, but it's true. I've never denied that much.

"Most undead companies consist of the mindless sort, fit only for following basic orders—like those who were guarding Prince Halix—not as adaptable in combat, but much easier for necromancers to raise. Those, in turn, are led by more intelligent commanders, skeletons and zombies augmented with stronger magic and alchemical compounds. I couldn't tell you how they do it.

"We called units of the intelligent dead rot squads. I had one of them assigned to me on this mission, and I had my orders to complete. When I lost every *living* man and woman under my command to a Thrane's fireball, aborting the mission was not an option. It was too important, so I continued on. My days and nights were spent in the company of Marshal Serror, an undead officer, and his rot squad."

Soneste imagined herself traversing a battle-scarred terrain, looking right and left, seeing figures of armor and bone marching tirelessly behind her, and each one lusted for bloodshed, sought it out like rats seek food.

"I kept my distance as much as I was able. I spoke to Serror only when I had no other choice. I did not address his . . . subordinates. I despised them. One night his group captured some Thranes, a soldier and his family, refugees."

Tallis grew quiet again.

"What happened?" she asked.

"Until that night, I'd never seen what the undead were capable of when unchaperoned by the living. I was the mission commander, but I had no authority over the specific actions of Serror and his squad unless it pertained directly to the mission—and I tested those limits. That night, I watched as they tortured the Thranes for 'information.' When they'd learned what they needed, they . . . just didn't stop. They enjoyed it."

"Gods," Soneste muttered.

"I tried to get away, tried to pretend it wasn't happening. I needed them to complete my mission. One man alone couldn't hope to survive where we were going, but I couldn't stand by and just watch. At last I returned, commanded the marshal to relent, to end the Thranes' torment. He refused. I looked, *really* looked, at them . . . the zombies of Serror's squad, standing there in the regalia of my nation, flaying the skin from their living victims. Out of sheer . . . entertainment.

"I lost it. I turned on them, *all* of them. My mission ended there, with the destruction of Marshal Serror, his subordinates, and the Thrane captives. I'd do it again."

Soneste could not find the words to follow this. She wanted to reach out her hand, offer some comfort, but this wasn't the time. She remained silent for a moment, leaving him to his memory, though a question had been gnawing at her for some time.

"Tallis," she asked, her voice low, "when I was searching the Ministry's archives, I found the record of a Captain Tallis, slain in a battle near Scion's Sound." She fished through her pockets and pulled out the faded *Sentinel* article. "This battle. Were you—"

"Recruit number 966-5-1372," the Karrn answered softly without glancing at the clipping. "My sister. Captain Valna Tallis."

Tallis smiled sadly and looked back at Soneste. "I worshipped her. She was the only true flying arrow in my family. Good in a team, dreamed of becoming an oathbound. Said she even would someday join the Conquering Fist or the Iron Band, but she died in 974, five years before I joined the army myself."

Tallis's eyes drifted. There was a darkness there, of deep-rooted fury barely held in check. "I saw her again, Soneste. She was one of those serving under Marshal Serror on my mission, an elite daughter of Karrnath given the . . . 'honor' of reanimation."

Soneste's blood grew cold. She couldn't imagine that, didn't want to try.

"Some Karrns see their slain loved ones again, raised by magic to serve their country, as *I* saw my sister's face again that day—the dead remains of her beautiful face, frozen by some necromancer's alchemy. I saw Valna's . . . joy as she joined the others in their torture of the Thrane captives. *My sister.*"

* * * * * * *

Rhazan never liked waiting, but in his line of work he'd had to get used to it, especially working for Lord Charoth, who'd pulled him out of a very delicate situation back home in Droaam. The man had a frigid patience like no human he'd ever known. Rhazan didn't like the smell of the factory either—the stink of human industry—but he'd grown used to that too. His master spent nearly every waking hour here, and that was a *lot*. The man had stamina beyond his age.

It was Rhazan's job to guard Lord Charoth and had been for years. The bugbear sometimes missed his home in the Great Crag, but he lived better than any tribal chief in the Byeshk Mountains.

To Khyber with all of them. Lord Charoth treated him with respect, recognized his skills, called him "Master Rhazan."

He wrinkled his nose for the thousandth time and pushed his bulk back into the shadows behind one of the heating tanks. It was unusual for his master to order him to do anything but protect him directly, but tonight he'd ordered Rhazan to mingle with the priestess's rancid minions.

So here he was, crouched in the shadows with the Night Shift. Although the largest of these was punier than he, Rhazan was not comfortable around them. He knew neither their battle strategies nor their priorities, and they smelled *wrong*.

"The Night Shift will attack at your command," his master had instructed, "but do not attack until you have surrounded them. None are to escape, not even the prince. Death first, Master Rhazan. I will not be interrupted."

One thought excited him, however: facing Tallis in hand-to-hand combat. When his master had tried to hire Tallis for "mutual protection" some time ago, Rhazan had wanted nothing more than to cave the half-elf's head in and drink from his empty skull. The bodyguard job was *his* alone, and he wasn't going to share it. When Tallis turned down the offer, Rhazan's job was secure again—but the incident had rankled him. Worse, Tallis had killed the feral yowler—Rhazan's only companion from back home.

He'd wanted this opportunity for a long time. Tallis, the undefeated. Tallis, the ghost man who walked on the fringes of the Low District, untouchable. If he died, everyone would learn who'd done it.

Charoth had given him permission to kill Tallis at last.

So Rhazan waited.

⊚ ⊚ ⊚ ⊚ ⊚ ⊚ ⊚

The increasing temperature and muffled drone had been suspicious, but they made sense when Tallis picked the lock and pushed the final door open. An unpleasant and vaguely familiar tang polluted the air. He beckoned the others to follow, pressing a finger to his lips, and stepped out of the stairwell into the chamber beyond.

The room that opened before him now could hardly be called a room at all. Its exits, niches, and devices were myriad—beyond counting. Larger than any cavern he'd seen, the vast space was filled from floor to ceiling with monstrous engines of industry, divided only by aisles and connected by catwalks. Sparse wisplights perched along the balcony that circled the hall, illuminating only enough to light a path from one apparatus to another. A massive furnace bathed the far end with orange light, pulsing like the mechanical heart of the room. There were a thousand hiding places, and every flickering shadow was a threat. It was not a room; it was a trap.

Tallis had been here once before, a year ago when Charoth had given him a private tour. During the night hours, just like this. Of course, back then he'd entered through the front door.

"The factory," Soneste said as she joined him. Halix and Aegis followed, taking in the scene in silence.

Through the rumbling ambience, Tallis detected the murmur of voices—somewhere further in the room. Of course, there *would* be a night staff. The factory could not simply close down when the daylight hours ended, lest the molten glass harden and shut the entire operation down.

Tallis eyed the two cylindrical tanks at the far end, where chutes from the wall fed in raw materials. Within each, glass was heated and maintained in a liquid state until ready for shaping. Such maintenance required manpower at all hours.

The factory room had too many variables. Charoth's men could be many, and in a space this big they were sure to use ranged weaponry. Tallis pulled two potion vials from his pack, pressing them into Soneste's and Halix's hands. "Drink these *now*. They'll keep you alive while you get in close. Once we're discovered, it's going to get tricky in here." He looked to Aegis. "Sorry, I only have two."

"It is well, Tallis," Aegis said, lifting the shield on his arm.

"Good man," he said with a smile of camaraderie. Tallis wished he'd known more warforged like Aegis.

"And you?" Soneste asked.

"I'll be fine. Stay here until I call for you."

She nodded, seeming uncertain, and Tallis set out across the room. He kept to the shadows as much as possible.

※ ※ ※ ◎ ※ ※ ※

After five minutes had passed without any sign from Tallis, Prince Halix bristled.

"I'm not waiting for him," he said, drawing his sword.

Soneste nodded. "We go together then, Your Highness. Aegis, please take the lead."

"Of course."

The warforged strode forward with loud, echoing steps, eliciting a wince from Halix. Soneste didn't want to make the prince a target, so she kept him in front of her where she could keep an eye on him, and followed cautiously.

When they neared the far end of the great room, she spied Tallis and a handful of men, most of whom lay unmoving on the ground. Only three remained. Dressed like the glassworkers she'd seen earlier in the day—Host, had that been today? she thought—they surrounded Tallis with brandished weapons. She glanced at the stairs that led up nearly fifteen feet from the factory floor to the glass door of Charoth's office.

One of the glassworkers spotted her. He turned to face her and pointed a wand at her. Soneste hadn't seen the bolt coming, had no time at all to decide which direction to try and dodge. She gasped as the missile struck her in the chest. She felt an unpleasant stab of pressure and winced at the splintering *smack*, but she felt no pain. When she realized she was still alive and unhurt, she smiled.

I need to get myself more of those potions, she thought.

Soneste looked up in time to see the same man loose another bolt—this one aimed for Halix—and felt her inhibitions drain away. She drew her crysteel blade, ran close enough for a throw, and sent it through the air. The glassworker threw up his arm and watched in horror as the blade sank to the hilt in the flesh of his forearm. He screamed—

And the hooked end of Tallis's hammer caught him at the back of the neck, dropping him to the ground.

Halix engaged another glassworker, a man who wielded both a Karrnathi scimitar and a mace. Sword clashed against mace repeatedly as the prince's face lit with delight. He was utterly unafraid, using speed and precision against the man's wilder attacks. Soneste moved to flank the man, but the glassworker pivoted hard and slapped the rapier from her hand with his scimitar.

"Unholy Six!" she swore.

Aegis could not hit his new opponent, who labored for breath. Face flushed as he worked to dodge every one of the warforged's heavy swings, the man did not see Tallis place one of his magic rods in the air at knee level behind the man. When he stepped away, the Karrn pointed with his hammer at the glass door at the top of the metal stairs.

"Something's going on up there," he told her. Soneste nodded, turning to retrieve her dagger.

When Aegis's man stumbled over the floating rod, the warforged sank Haedrun's blade to the hilt in his exposed stomach. He withdrew the sword and ended the man's suffering with a second, careful stroke. Tallis retrieved his rod.

Soneste and Tallis both turned to help Halix, only to see him slip the Rekkenmark blade beneath his opponent's arm. With a scream of fury, the prince ran him through. The glassworker dropped to the ground as his blood welled beneath him.

Seven bodies lay around them, unmoving.

Mounting the metal stair, Tallis crouched when he neared the top. Soneste joined him, aware that a glass wall would allow those within the room to look out just as easily as looking in. Tallis's expression was one of revulsion.

Soneste heard the sounds of Halix and Aegis climbing the stairs behind her, but as she looked through the perfect glass herself, she tried to make sense of the scene within.

Chapter
THIRTY

Three figures oversaw what Tallis could only assume was some sort of blasphemous ritual: Lord Charoth, swathed in his customary midnight robes and mask. A woman in the ceremonial black and red vestments of a Seeker priest—presumably the Lady Mova. Standing behind both, as rigid as a statue, the nimblewright. Undisguised, it resembled a helmed, elven knight whose armor covered every inch of its body—except for one hand. That one was still missing. The rest of its metal body showed no sign of their battle from the previous night.

Before them, a young woman lay bound to a thick table of smooth glass obviously sculpted for this very purpose. Tallis recognized Borina from the night before. She lay awake, cognizant of her surroundings but too weak to struggle. Her bare feet were shackled. Her arms were splayed beside her, strapped to the table at the elbow, the sleeves of her soiled shirt torn away. The exposed skin was pierced in three places along each arm by sharp glass tubes like the proboscises of giant insects.

Dark with her blood, these siphoning tubes attached to the tabletop itself, where they threaded through the glass like arteries and attached themselves to the next component of the ritual—an outlandish throne, its back affixed to the table, also composed entirely of transparent glass. Where the tubes fed into the back of the throne, red blossomed and hung frozen as if the blood were soaking slowly into ice. It faded to a cloud of pink that pervaded the whole.

Sitting limp in the throne was a cadaverous figure in a smart, but utilitarian blue uniform, a living man of indeterminate age and sickly, mottled skin. Tallis could see black, wormlike veins through the man's own translucent flesh. He looked like he was dying or had been for a long time. Eyelids only half open, his head lolled to the side. A livid glow suffused the throne around him, evidence that magic was at work. There was some sort of emblem on the man's shirt and a ring on one skeletal finger.

Tallis had spied upon ceremonies of the Blood of Vol before, had witnessed variations of the Sacrament of the Blood that was vital to the faith. He'd personally sabotaged many of them. But *this* was different. This was something more . . . clinical. It repulsed him in a primal way.

"Gods," Soneste breathed as she stared in horror at the gruesome scene. "What is this?"

Halix came up beside them, but Soneste tried to hush him before he could call out. Tallis could feel the tension boiling out of the boy at the sight.

● ● ● ◉ ● ● ●

Through the lenses of his mask, Charoth saw the nimblewright's head swivel ever so sleightly to face the door of his workshop. The ancient construct had finer senses than he.

Charoth had spent too many months planning this moment—too many *years* researching the spells necessary to dissolve the matrix of polluted Positive Energy—to suffer this interruption. His factory had been compromised, and a very dangerous opponent had arrived to terminate his work.

Tallis and his allies stood at the door, peering within.

Charoth quelled the panic that threatened him. His opponent was too judicious to storm in without taking precautions, but Charoth's own resources were stretched thin. Most of his spells had been expended to protect the factory, hide the royals, and execute the procedure itself. But he would not take any chances with Tallis.

He produced a pinch of gem dust, spoke the catalyst, and directed his hand to the door, giving the spell kinetic force. At the edge of his vision, there was motion at the throne, ever so sleight.

It was working! His hope had not been in vain. With the spell-barrier in place, Charoth regained control of the situation once again.

"Welcome, Major," he said, returning his attention to the procedure—he was very nearly done—trying his utmost to keep his voice calm, to temper his rage. "Your intrusion is unwelcome."

Magic carried his voice through the slit of his mask, through the glass walls of his workshop, and into the factory room beyond. Lady Mova looked up, jarred from her cabalistic trance.

❖ ❖ ❖ ◉ ❖ ❖ ❖

Tallis heard the wizard's voice reverberate across the vast room behind him like the words of a god. He didn't bother to respond or even open the door. Leading with the adamantine head of his hammer, he crashed into the door with all of his strength.

When the shards fell away, an invisible, unyielding force barred his entry. "Blunted!"

"Tallis," Soneste said, urgently.

His instincts flared a warning of their own as he turned around. He looked to the factory floor below and immediately set to counting the number of new enemies emerging from the shadows.

There were at least a dozen already and more coming. Leading them forward was Rhazan, an eight foot wall of coarse hair and bristling goblin features, his massive chain grasped in both hands.

At each end of the spiked chain was a large, bladed weight.

The creatures that slunk out from around Rhazan had hairless, haggard frames sheathed in desiccated, gray skin which stretched tight across angular bones. They wore the same clothing as the glassworkers, though soiled and in disrepair, and some even carried weapons. Filthy, jagged nails sprouted from fingers half again as long as they ought to be. The ghouls looked up in malignant glee and an unearthly howl of laughter rose up from them.

Servitors of the Blood of Vol.

Rhazan snarled when the ghouls surged before him, cutting off his path.

Tallis heard curses from his companions—neither was likely accustomed to fighting the ravenous dead. They were cornered, backed to a wall, but they did have the higher ground. He tried to formulate a plan—when an arrow loosed from somewhere within the horde, smashing against Charoth's invisible wall. A second ricocheted off Tallis's vambrace.

"Aegis!" he shouted, pointing to the base of the stairs. "Stand at the base. Keep them down there, if you can—they can't poison *you*." The necrotic toxins in a ghoul's body could paralyze living victims with even the slightest scratch, but the warforged's physiology was quite different—the construct could not be afflicted. "Halix, Soneste, stay up here and by Aureon do *not* let them touch you! Soneste, if you—"

"Tallis, I have an idea!" she said. She took hold of his shoulder and pointed to the brick-walled glass tank not fifteen feet behind Rhazan. "The wall is damaged. Together we might break it open!" Following her lead, he fixed his eyes on the tank and spotted the sleight break in the otherwise even brickwork.

Even as the first of the ghouls reached Aegis—who swept them back with a mighty swing—Tallis turned to meet the Brelish's eyes. "Perfect," he breathed, forcing a smile.

"If you can cover me, I can—"

"No," he said. "I'm going. I know what to do. Cover me. Use

that fancy blue poison of yours on Rhazan if you've still got it, but only if you can get a clear shot!"

"Tallis, alone you can't—"

He ignored her, eyeing Rhazan as he climbed atop the metal railing.

The ghouls hissed and clamored to reach them all. Aegis stood with his legs spaced apart for maximum stability. The ghouls' weapons and clawed fingers scrabbled against the warforged's metal plating. Most rebounded without effect, but slowly they were wearing the construct down. With flashing blades, Halix and Soneste cut back those who tried to climb up along the rail or reach through the gaps of the stairs.

Sidestepping a few pale-skinned claws, Tallis stepped once then jumped out into the air, buoyed by the magic of his enchanted boots. He sailed over the ghoulish crowd, clearing them completely.

Rhazan had guessed his move and lashed out with his chain. Even from ten feet away, the spiked weight clipped him in mid-air. Tallis hit the ground in a roll, gritting his teeth as pain coursed through his arm from the bone-numbing blow. His bracers had kept the blade from tearing through.

Tallis leapt to his feet and turned to face Rhazan. "That's all you've got, Rhaz-bag? You're more bug than bear!"

Staying in one place would ensure a quick death with Rhazan so close, so Tallis started moving. He held his hammer ready in one hand, even as he fished in the pocket of his backpack with his other. He produced a metal flask—and just in time! The next swing of Rhazan's chain tore the haversack from his shoulders, spilling its contents to the ground.

Speeding out from the corner of his vision, a dart-sized crossbow bolt sank into the thick fur at the bugbear's collar. Rhazan growled in pain. Sleep well, Tallis thought, remembering how quickly Soneste's poison could take effect.

Rhazan opened his mouth and bellowed a challenge in the Goblin tongue, spinning both ends of his chain and looking for an opportunity to strike his foe. The bugbear advanced on him just as two of the ghouls peeled away from their fellows and rounded on Tallis, their hunched bodies loping toward him like animals. He'd been ready for this. He stopped moving only long enough to skewer the first with the mithral pick, then rushed on again when Rhazan's chain swept a little too close. One head blow from that thing would finish him.

The second ghoul swiped at him, its claws coming away with ribbons off the back of his shirt but failing to draw blood. Tallis stopped again, turned, and threw his weight into a one-handed hammer swing. The blow balked the creature's advance but didn't knock it down. He dodged aside just as Rhazan's chain soared in, the heavy weight catching the ghoul instead. The thick spike opened the creature's hideous head, spilling its contents to the floor as the body dropped.

Khyber! Was Soneste's poison doing nothing against the brute?

As Rhazan drew his chain back in, Tallis sprinted directly *at* him. He'd get only one chance at this.

Mere feet away, Tallis dived at the bugbear's feet and upended the metal flask across his foe's hairy, sharp-nailed toes. A pale amber substance slipped from the flask in one large gob and landed squarely across a bearlike foot and the stone beneath it. Good enough!

"Stick it out, Rhaz-bag!" he quipped.

Rhazan roared, released one hand from his chain, and punched Tallis between the shoulder blades before he could move away. Grimacing under the wave of pain that coursed through his spine, Tallis pulled out one of his immovable rods and locked it in place along Rhazan's shin only one foot off the ground. I'm not getting this one back, he thought darkly.

Tallis kept on rolling, and the bugbear moved to follow with his chain spinning through the air. His lower shin pressed against the floating rod, keeping him in place for just a few seconds.

That was all Tallis had needed. He gained his feet when he heard the bugbear's roar of frustration, then he looked to back to see his handiwork.

The amber substance connecting Rhazan's foot to the ground had solidified into a mass harder than the bugbear's own bones—sovereign glue, a magical adhesive far stronger than any tanglefoot bag. Expensive, but worth it. Rhazan wasn't going anywhere.

Sovereign glue? Tallis thought. Lenrik would have made a pun from that.

The bladed weight at the end of Rhazan's chain whistled past his head. Damn, the bugbear was good with that thing! Soneste's poison hadn't even slowed him.

"Coward!" Rhazan shouted.

Moving in a half circle around the bugbear and dodging a second swing, Tallis reached the brick-walled tank. Just as Soneste had said, there was erosion in the brickwork, an imperfection yet to be fully repaired.

Tallis gripped his hammer in two hands and struck. He felt the brick crumble under the impact. Adamantine was the hardest metal on Eberron. A few more blows like that and he could break through!

He raised the hooked hammer again. Metal slapped against metal as Rhazan's chain encircled the shaft and wrenched the hammer from Tallis's grip. The barbs on the chain cut into his hand and the weapon spun away, the sheer strength of the bugbear's pull sending the weapon clanging to the ground fifty feet away.

Blunted!

Tallis knew staying a moving target was his only way to survive Rhazan. The sheer force of those spiked weights could break bone—yet Tallis couldn't breach the wall without a weapon.

Then the idea hit him fast, and he had no time to reconsider it. Staying right where he was, Tallis called out. "Rhaz-bag!"

Rhazan, trying in vain to pull his foot free from the ground, looked up. He set his chain spinning again. The spiked weight lashed out—perfect aim, as always.

Tallis danced aside only a step aside, ducking as fast as he was able. The heavy weight whistled just above him and sank its spike into the brick wall of the tank. When the bugbear yanked it free, Tallis stepped back again.

"By the Six, Rhaz-bag!" he laughed. "That was terrible aim."

The spiked weight came in at him again, and Tallis dodged. He felt the weight clip his arm then heard it smash against the wall again, scattering chunks of brick. Intense heat washed over Tallis from where he crouched on the ground. He looked up to see a leak of bright yellow fluid from the wall's sleight breach.

That will have to do, he thought. He leapt to his feet, glancing at Rhazan only long enough to note the next attack.

Tallis threw up both arms as he tried to dodge and felt the concussive force of the spiked chain glance away. Were it not for the magic of his vambraces, he knew he'd be dead by now.

As the chain was pulled back for another rotation, Tallis looked to the tank again, aimed with his right fist, and looked at the dragon-headed ring he wore.

"*Telchanak*," he said, willing as much power as the ring could expend at one time. The ghostly manifestation of the ramlike dragon's head surged out from the ring and struck the wall of the massive bricked cylinder.

The wall broke under the impact. The magical force dispersed, and Tallis felt a wave of caustic heat roll over him, along with the yellow-white glow of molten glass as it spilled out in a torrent of burning death. With a stab of fear, Tallis *knew* that he was too close to escape the deadly flood. He started to turn, but the liquid glass moved like water. Rhazan's scream came first and Tallis understood that he was only a second or two behind.

All shadows receded as light and heat surged around him.

In a desperate move, Tallis reached for the only thing that could save him and jumped without direction as high as he could.

Chapter
THIRTY-ONE

Wir, the 11th of Sypheros, 998 YK

The air rippled above the yellow liquid as it spilled out onto the floor in a frightening deluge. Soneste's idea had worked, but in effecting it Tallis might have doomed himself. She lost all sight of him through the rippling air and the chaos of the ghoulish horde. Her stomach lurched as she imagined the Karrn swallowed by the burning tide.

"Aegis, get back up the stairs!" she shouted.

The warforged had kept the undead from gaining the higher ground, but he'd paid a heavy price for it. The polished metal plating was scored all across his body. Half of the slavering creatures had been hewn down by his blade or knocked aside by his thick shield, but to keep them down he'd had to remain at the bottom of the stairs.

"What in Khyber?" she heard Halix shout. She looked up.

The liquid glass flowed across the ground, destroying everything in its path as easily as volcanic lava. The bugbear Rhazan, stuck fast to the ground by Tallis's trick, had been unable to move in the sleightest. He let out an agonized wail as the glass burned away the lower half of his body. The rest of him caught fire.

Soneste prayed that Tallis was not suffering the same fate. All she could hear was the monstrous scream.

The burning yellow liquid spread out across the factory floor, engulfing the legs of the ghoulish crowd. The creatures shrieked and cavorted in a parody of pain, but Soneste couldn't tell if it was from real agony or some unnatural semblance of self-preservation. They were already dead—but the molten glass was destroying them.

All of them.

Aegis wasn't fast enough. Still under assault from the ghouls, he'd stepped back up to the lowest stair, but the hateful creatures pulled back at him. The heated liquid washed over his feet. His head swiveled back and forth in astonishment as he watched the wooden components of his legs burn away. The stone liquefied, the metal became white-hot.

"Mistress!" The warforged panicked, dropping the gore-spattered sword and reaching wildly with his hands to find the railing behind him. "Soneste! Please . . . help . . . "

"Aegis, no!" she cried.

Soneste and Halix both stepped down and tried to pull him up, but the metal plating of his arms became unbearably hot in mere seconds. They fell away, skin blistered from the contact. Halix cursed and pulled Soneste up, lifting her bodily away from the dying warforged.

The molten pool rose no higher. It had spread itself out as far as it could, a wide radius forty feet or more around the ruptured vat. The undead creatures had become blackened, human-shaped lumps. They were still burning, their bodies glistening with slowly-cooling glass.

At the base of the stairs, Aegis lay still, the lower half of his body ruined.

Soneste was weary, spent. As much as she wanted to weep for Aegis, she couldn't. Yet enduring anger coursed through her limbs as she thought about the cost of Lord Charoth's deeds. The bastard was just behind them in his office. She'd make certain he paid.

The air thinned somewhat as the molten glass began to cool. It had become viscous but was far from being solid again.

There, hanging mere feet above the yellow pool, was Tallis. With two hands he clung to one of his floating metal rods. The Karrn looked exhausted, his skin slicked with sweat and blood and his clothes scorched by the heat.

"Tallis!" she shouted to him.

He coughed, gasping for air, and looked over his shoulder at Soneste. He looked down at the cooling but still deadly mass of heated glass.

"It was . . . a great plan!" he said hoarsely and offered a weary smile.

Then he deactivated his magic rod and dropped. A shock of fear stabbed through her at the sight, but when he hit the ground he started moving immediately. The glass had become thick, almost gummy, but she could see it was eating away at his boots.

Tallis reached the edge of the pool and jumped to the unmarred floor of the factory room. He looked down with something like regret at his boots—the remaining strips of leather barely clung to his legs. The Karrn shook his head, scooped up his hooked hammer from where it lay safely outside of the glass pool, and worked his way around the glass pool.

Climbing atop portions of machinery, he finally reached the metal stairs and vaulted the railing. Tallis's face was reddened from the heat, his black hair gray from the fumes.

"Aegis," she said.

Tallis looked sadly to the the valiant warforged and nodded grimly then touched her briefly on the shoulder. "I'm sorry."

He looked to Prince Halix. The young man's eyes brightened with anger. They were all of same mind. "Let's finish this."

Tallis smashed away portions of the glass door that his first strike against it hadn't cleared, only to discover that Charoth's invisible barrier was gone entirely. Thank the Host, she cheered. The magic had run out.

❂ ❂ ❂ ❂ ❂ ❂ ❂

Appropriately, the office resembled a wizard's laboratory. It was spacious and well-furnished with an arcanist's equipment, but Soneste's attention was fixed firmly upon Charoth and his allies. The nimblewright, standing still behind the wizard, sprang into motion.

"Borina!" Halix shouted, moving forward as he looked to the glass table and the young woman bound to it.

"Enemies *first*," Tallis said, grabbing the prince's shoulder, then pointed to the woman in black robes. "Now spread out!" The Karrn dashed to the right, intent on the wizard himself.

The nimblewright produced its remaining rapier-blade and advanced on Soneste. Her heart hammered in her chest. She feared this elemental construct more than anything. By rights, it had already killed her once.

She raised her rapier fast enough to parry its first attack, but two strikes sent her sword spinning out of her hand and across the room.

Aureon, not again. . . .

"Kill *Tallis*," the black-robed priestess commanded.

Without a sound, the nimblewright sprinted away from Soneste. Relief for herself and fear for the Karrn gave way as she and Prince Halix faced the priestess together.

Soneste's first thought was that Lady Mova looked like a wise woman, a grandmother with eccentric taste in clothing, but her eyes were cold, entirely bereft of humor or compassion.

"Death for you, dear," the old woman spat, holding up a curving dagger that glowed with a poisonous light.

She rattled a bracelet of bones and swept her arms outward as if she were conjuring a shield. A thick layer of frost appeared on Mova's skin and clothing, then fell away to form a cloud of tiny ice crystals in the air around her. As Soneste and Halix closed in, the inquisitive could see their breaths puffing in the air.

Soneste drew out her own dagger. Halix himself was distracted—his eyes returning again and again to his vulnerable sister and her prison of glass—but he kept pace with Soneste.

Lady Mova raised a hand in the air and spoke a twisted, undecipherable phrase. Soneste knew very little about true scriptural prayers to any god, but the old woman's words felt offensive to her very soul. A ray of crackling black energy coursed from her fingertips and struck Halix in the chest.

The prince gasped for breath as if all air had been expelled from his lungs in an instant. He clutched at his chest and fell hard to his knees, his sword clanging to the ground. His body slackened. Mova wasn't going to kill Halix, Soneste realized. From what the prince had said earlier, he was probably supposed to be Mova's prize just as Borina was Charoth's. She needed the prince intact for her own purposes, and young Halix was no match for her magic.

You won't harm another soul, Soneste promised the woman silently.

Soneste rushed willingly into the aureole of freezing crystals that encircled the priestess, hoping Mova would be no match for her physically. She focused her mind as she closed in, as fast as she could, drawing on the last reserves of her psychic power. Quick as a thought, she recalled the last few seconds in her mind: Mova uttering a prayer of her bloody faith and smiting Halix with its power. Grasping the memory fragment with mental fingers, Soneste flung the vision into Mova's own mind.

Soneste prayed to Aureon that the priestess could not use the same spell again—a severe risk.

The memory took hold. Lady Mova readied her blade for Soneste then stopped. Her eyes were wild, alarmed, as she raised her hand in the air against her will and spoke the same foul prayer she had only seconds before. This time there was no spell unleashed as she pointed her fingers at Halix.

With her defenses lowered, she was not prepared for Soneste. The cloud of freezing air hit Soneste like a storm of ice, chilling her to the core, but she pushed through and plunged the sharp Riedran crysteel into Mova's body. The old woman's breastbone resisted then split as the last vestiges of Soneste's psionic power surged through the blade.

❀ ❀ ❀ ❀ ❀ ❀ ❀

Tallis wanted to bring Charoth down, wanted to hurt the wizard again and again for Lenrik's death, but the nimblewright had appeared before him to meet his challenge instead.

He steeled his rage and struck first, denting the nimblewright's armored forearm.

Charoth's incanting voice rolled across the room as he issued another spell from his defensible position behind the table. At once, the nimblewright's body appeared to flicker. Tallis reversed his weapon then struck again. The pick's head slashed harmlessly through the metal body as if it were mere illusion.

"No!" Tallis screamed, exasperated.

His world divided into a series of long, desperate moments, and he was forced fully on the defensive. His efforts were in vain. To have come so far, to find the very man behind all this pain, and to fail. Tallis was once again at the Ebonspire, helpless to stop the killer. Only *he* was the victim.

Well, why not? he despaired. Lenrik, I tried.

The nimblewright's blade broke through his slowing defenses once, then twice. The rapier would have cut through his stomach, were it not for the bracer's invisible armor. How long could he last?

❀ ❀ ❀ ❀ ❀ ❀ ❀

Shivering from the hideous cold, Soneste stepped away from the old woman's body. Lady Mova—priestess, murderess, Seeker of the Blood—writhed on the stone floor, her lips mouthing a meaningless litany.

Soneste turned away, hoping she could do something for Halix.

327

He slumped on the ground looking as helpless as his sister. Soneste's teeth chattered uncontrollably as she tried to say his name, to offer him some comfort as her mind inventoried her resources.

Her eyes were drawn to the desperate battle between Tallis and the nimblewright. Crippled by its missing hand, the construct was effectively outmatched, but the Karrn's every strike passed through its body without effect. This was obviously the same magic that had allowed it to enter the Ebonspire and exit again without a trace.

Her hand trembled as she reached to her haversack and she pulled out the ivory wand. "Take this," Tallis had said. "Verdax said there are only three charges left, so use it sparingly."

According to Tallis, this very wand—empowered to strip away magic effects—had been used to dispel the alarm wards at the Ebonspire, allowing him to enter undetected. Soneste herself had used it to extract the truth from the changeling Gan. It was only fitting that she use it here, at the end.

She pointed the wand at the nimblewright, her hands still shaking from the numbing cold. Invisible energy streamed from its tip, but she saw no change in the construct's form. She tried again, to no avail. One charge left.

Aureon, she prayed. Justice, Sovereign Lord, *please!*

She flicked the wand again and was rewarded by a flash of light from the nimblewright's armored frame. She heard the impact of Tallis's hammer against its body, and smiled.

"Thank you," she said aloud.

Then her body shook from the impact of several pulses of energy which slammed into her from out of nowhere. She was thrown from her feet, and the world chose that moment to spin in every direction at once.

Then darken.

❖ ❖ ❖ ◉ ❖ ❖ ❖

Charoth felt a constricting sense of loss as Lady Mova fell. The Seeker herself was unimportant now, but his servants were far too few. The nimblewright would carry out the final command of its mistress, so he'd had to trust in its skill to occupy or defeat Tallis.

The spell of incorporeality had been a difficult one to master, but he'd researched it solely for use with the nimblewright. Once he'd imbued the construct's blades to exist in both the corporeal and incorporeal realms, the perfection of his spell in conjunction with its peerless swordplay could not be denied.

The nimblewright had been sold to Mova's family by the Twelve more than a century ago. Entombed beneath the Crimson Monastery for many years, the moment the priestess had introduced it to him, Charoth knew it needed to be in his power. He was not comfortable in its presence—its eyeless gaze judged him, he was sure—but from the moment he'd seen its skill put to work, its role had been vital in his plans. The nimblewright could go where he could not and leave behind no evidence.

Until now, it had been invulnerable, but the Brelish girl had just taken that away from him with some second-rate tinkerer's wand.

Charoth had paused in his work to strike her down with a spell—a minor force attack he could afford to expend—which should have been sufficient to kill her. It was about time. He'd considered having the nimblewright kill Soneste shortly after her interview with him, but the death of Breland's sole investigator might have brought in Boranel's Dark Lanterns—a more troublesome possibility.

Still, this was entirely too distracting. She shouldn't even have *been* here.

Charoth looked down at Princess Borina. Her eyes were open, timorous, her gaze fixed upon his mask, pleading for cessation. In mere minutes, the arcane lineage of her blood would be siphoned away completely. She was just another privileged human undeserving of her noble inheritance. Such power, such purity of youth and mortal divinity, should belong to those whose brilliance deserved recognition. The world should be shaped by those with the will to shape it.

He had not labored in the Orphanage those many years ago to see things go wrong again.

The way it weaved its body from side to side, Tallis could well imagine the watery spirit that occupied the nimblewright's body. His own body was drenched with sweat, his fingers slick with blood. The bracers Verdax lent him had staved off many blows, but his body ached from every hit.

Even with only one hand, the construct was a fierce opponent, but at least he could hurt it.

"You've killed innocents," he said, needing to understand the creature's motive.

They traded blows, the clash of steel and adamantine the only thing he could hear.

"I do not care," the nimblewright said between strikes, surprising Tallis so much he nearly failed to parry its next one. The construct's voice was like a wet hiss of steam issued from a human throat.

According to what Soneste had learned, the nimblewright would simply obey its master. It had no moral base, no opinions of its own. Like a golem, it knew obedience and nothing more. It was not evil. It simply was.

"Well I *do*," Tallis answered.

He knew he was winning now, could feel the construct's movements slowing not out of exhaustion but from the sheer damage it had sustained. The armor plating of its body was dented and gouged in ways that would have killed any man.

He struck again, pounding the adamantine hammer soundly against one shoulder.

There was no cry of pain. Tallis expected none. One moment it was a fluid creature of death and metal. The next, it was an inanimate suit of armor crashing to the floor. A cloud of vapor rose from his enemy and dissipated around him.

There was no elation, no satisfaction, from its demise. Tallis merely stepped past it, taking his remaining rod into his left hand and hefting his hammer in his right.

He glanced to his left and saw Soneste lying on the ground. She might well be dead. Halix struggled to stand. The young prince looked half-dead. There was no time to tend to either of them.

To Khyber with you, Charoth.

The wizard stepped away from the table, fully aware that he was all that remained of his cabal. Princess Borina cried out when his gloved hand moved away from her body, drawing wisps of power from the pulsing table. In the adjoined glass throne, the cadaverous man stirred. Whatever Charoth had been doing— whatever *all of this* was for!—it was nearing its end.

Tallis knew something about magic weaponry, armor, and various enchanted devices. Like his immovable rods, they had well-defined rules, limitations, and numerous applications, yet he could make no sense of this bizarre experiment, ritual, or whatever it was. The spells and variations of a wizard's work were beyond him.

He *did* know that Borina was dying from it.

At the sound of his sister's voice, Halix pulled himself to his feet. Tallis wanted to shout at the boy to get down—another spell from Charoth would end him. Damn it!

Tallis needed to make *himself* a target.

He held his arms out. "I'm sorry," he said to Charoth, gesturing to the shattered door and the laboratory itself. "Is this the wrong room? I was just looking for the latrine."

Charoth struck the ground with the tip of his blue-glass cane. "We are at a stalemate, Major," the wizard said, his voice reverberating across the room clearly. He twisted the silver vulture's head at its top and withdrew a jeweled wand from the concealing shaft. "It needn't end in violence. We are rational men, you and I."

Tallis wasn't intending to trade words with Charoth any longer. He made sure his grip was good on both rod and hammer then took a step forward.

"Sss . . . sver . . ."

Tallis looked to the figure in the glass throne. The voice had been barely audible, but it had certainly come from the withered man. More importantly, it had drawn Charoth's full attention.

He would not waste the opportunity.

Tallis placed all his strength and focus into the throw, sending his hooked hammer into the air. The weapon spun end over end, spanning fifteen feet and rebounding off whatever magic shielded the wizard's body, but the force of the blow sent Charoth stumbling back. He recovered quickly and swiped the wand in Tallis's direction.

Accuracy didn't matter. Electricity sprayed from the jeweled device, twisting in the air and skewering Tallis. Overwhelming vibrations, the inability to control his own muscles, and the smell of his own burning flesh assailed Tallis's senses for several agonizing seconds. He regained control with time enough to catch himself from falling, but he had to steady himself with one hand to the ground. He labored for breath, his body quivering.

One more hit like that . . .

Tallis looked up, ready to spring away.

"Can you *hear* me?" the wizard asked the figure in the throne, his voice sounding almost subdued. Was that a House Cannith emblem upon the man's uniform? Pain blurred Tallis's vision.

The bright colors of Charoth's mask turned to face Tallis again. The sleightest flick of his gloved hand loosed another bolt of blue-white lightning. Tallis jerked his body sideways and forward, whiplash sending a blossom of pain through his neck. He felt the charge in the air as the splintering bolt streamed past him.

Tallis dived to the ground and grasped his hammer. Even as he rose, he brought the mithral pick arcing through the air—

Where it cut into the back of Charoth's hand. The jeweled wand whirled free. There was no blood, just a gash in the glove and a glimpse of gray flesh as the wizard recoiled without a sound.

Tallis stood face-to-face with his adversary, expecting a paralyzing or fiery blast of magic, but Charoth wasn't fast enough, not by far. Tallis struck again with his hammer, feeling it pass through invisible armor and rebound off the wizard's own chest. The resistance of the man's breastbone was stronger than he'd expected, but he felt it crack. The blow should be beyond painful.

Charoth made not a sound. He merely stumbled back, doing his best to get away from Tallis. Was this all the feared wizard could do?

The words of Karrn the Conqueror flashed through Tallis's mind, from *The Analects of War:* "Only utter destruction prevents a foe from rising again."

Tallis spun the weapon in his grip and aimed for Charoth's damnable face. Come, he thought, let's see how hideous you *really* are.

The mithral tip of the pick clove the darkwood mask in two even pieces.

"Stop," the withered man whispered.

Interlude

Shouts and angry voices surrounded him, but the man in the glass chair couldn't quite hear them. The world around him struggled to merge with his thoughts, but he could think of only one thing.

"Stop!" I shout. In this moment, it is the only word I know.

Sverak echoes me. The titan's arm stops.

Lord Charoth Arkenen lies in a sickening heap before us. Blood pools beneath him, his back arched in a dreadful angle. I cannot give voice to my horror. I cannot speak at all.

"You are free, master," Sverak says. "Free from him." I know my assistant is speaking to me, but I cannot bear to look at him. I made him. I made this monstrosity.

My superior stirs. He may yet be saved! I reach for the wand of healing that I'd never had to use before. As one, the magewrights rush to save him. More workers appear at the edge of my vision, warforged guards with them.

Sverak now holds Lord Charoth's wand. He waves his thin arm in the direction of the incoming guards, unleashing a bolt of lightning. The electricity arrests the first man's movement even as it kills him, but the bolt arcs through his body to the next, then the next, then the next. I hear a woman's scream, but it dies as quickly as she. In a single gesture, Sverak has slain five Cannith workers.

One of the warforged nears my assistant, but Sverak shrinks away and turns the wand against it. Lightning sprays from the deadly instrument. Charoth himself had fashioned that jeweled wand for his own personal protection.

Leonus, my dear nephew, lies on the floor now too. His face is twisted in pain, frozen in death.

I look at the wand in my own hand, an instrument coiled with Positive Energy, empowered to knit blood vessels together again, to repair scorched skin, to restore fading life, but destruction is easier to deliver and so much faster.

I push the screams away, not wishing to see or hear what Sverak has planned. I am aware only that the titan is moving away from the balcony, acting on Sverak's orders. From somewhere along the central pillar of the great creation forge, there is an explosion, quieter in my mind than it really must be. Without looking up, I can sense that the titan is destroying it.

Sverak grasps my hand. His delicate, five-fingered grip is not strong, but I do not resist. I follow, stricken by guilt. I have not the courage to end this. Wherever opposition arises, Sverak strikes it down with wand or spell. In three short months, he has already learned the rudimentary spells of a wizard.

Flashes of light play across my vision. Destruction like I have never seen. The creation forge is collapsing. Errant rays stream from the birthing pods, white tongues of energy clawing the air. Positive Energy, very deadly. Used in trace amounts, it restores damaged life, like the wand in my hand. It even gives life to the inanimate, life to created materials. Like the warforged.

But in such a deluge, unguided . . .

What has Sverak done? What have I done?

Time means nothing. There is only muted sound. More distant screams.

The world brightens unimaginably. Like a white burning sun manifesting before me. I feel . . . invigorated, invulnerable. Why does immortality feel like agony?

"Master!" I hear Sverak shout. He is screaming. I have never heard him shout or sound so human. "Master Erevyn! I am sorry! I did not mean this! I will save you. I will save you!"

Sverak is concerned for my well being, but I am all right. I am impervious to all harm.

But not pain?

Sverak is carrying me now. I cannot see him, but I can sense him. He is carrying me from ruin, delivering me from death. Can I not carry myself?

"Sverak?" I say, but my voice is louder than I remember it. "Where am I?"

Chapter
Thirty-Two

The Blood of Galifar
Wir, the 11th of Sypheros, 998 YK

The crack of electricity brought Soneste back to consciousness. She felt like she'd been stabbed in four different places, but there was no warmth or wetness of blood. In one painful instant, she remembered where she was.

She pulled herself to her feet and looked around.

Halix leaned heavily upon the glass table, struggling to free Princess Borina from her prison. Tallis leapt to avoid a bolt of lightning, which snaked out beyond the laboratory and vanished into the factory beyond.

The Karrn rose from the floor and met Charoth face-to-face. With dagger in hand—its blade still slick with Mova's blood— Soneste circled around the table. Her body protested every step, her head throbbing.

It didn't matter. She saw Tallis's weapon come away on a back-swing, and pieces of Charoth's mask fell away. The wizard fell hard to the ground without a sound.

Soneste felt her blood freeze as she advanced and looked down upon the prone man. Tallis struck again, sweeping the pick across Charoth's midsection. The wizard's body jerked from the impact, the sharp tip of Tallis's weapon catching on something more than flesh and bone. With effort, the Karrn pulled it free, tearing away ribbons of fine cloth.

A skull-sized head of wood and metal looked up at both of them from beneath the hood, a ghulra carved into the forehead. Two faceted eyes of dark blue stone pulsed with a weak light. The wizard's jaw was metal, hinged at the side of his head. Where Tallis's pick had torn away robes, Charoth's torso lay exposed. It was wood—*darkwood*—banded with strips of silvery metal and engraved with eldritch symbols.

Tallis looked at Soneste, seeking an answer.

She opened her mouth, not sure what to say. If Charoth was some kind of warforged, he was the strangest she'd ever seen. His frame was skeletal enough to pass for a human body beneath thick robes.

"Sverak . . . where . . . am I?"

Soneste turned to look at the gaunt man in the glass throne. He leaned heavily upon the arm, his sunken eyes watery as he tried to blink, tried to focus.

"Master. . ." Charoth—*Sverak*, or whoever he was—struggled to sit upright. The voice sounded like Charoth's as she'd known it, but its timbre was sharper, more metallic, lacking the resonance and volume afforded by the magical mask he'd worn.

Tallis raised his hammer, but Soneste held up her hand. *Wait.*

She briefly met the old man's eyes. The uniform he wore was familiar, the traditional gray-blue of a Cannith-employed artificer. Then she saw the gorgon emblem upon his breast and a faded, lyre-shaped tattoo at his collarbone. No, not a tattoo. A dragonmark.

The Mark of Making. This man was of House Cannith!

"Sver—" he rasped. "Sverak, it hurts . . ."

The skeletal warforged at their feet reached out a gloved hand. "Master Erevyn! I am here!"

Erevyn. Soneste recalled the *Chronicle*: *Among the thirty-two presumed dead at the Orphanage was Erevyn Korell d'Cannith, chief artificer and minister of the facility.*

The warforged yanked off one glove then the other. Sickly, translucent skin—not unlike the mottled flesh of Erevyn himself—sent a putrid stench into the air. More delicately, the construct Sverak also began to peel the skin from his arms as though they, too, were mere gloves. The end of each was cut off at the elbow with ragged cuts and dry, exposed veins. Even as he discarded these, the dead skin twitched with a semblance of life—or necromancy.

Whose skin was that? Soneste felt sick.

"What are you?" Tallis asked, disgusted.

"It is me, Master," the warforged continued, holding up its arms. The metal fingers—five on each hand—were thin, delicate, nothing like the strong digits of a normal warforged.

She thought of Aegis and Soneste's anger flared again.

"Sverak," Erevyn said, his voice slightly stronger. "Where . . . are we?"

"You are safe, Master." The lean warforged sounded weak, but there was a desperate elation in his voice. He crawled on his hinged, metal-capped knees, reaching a hand out to his master. Tallis watched Sverak carefully, primed to strike him down. Without his mask and robes, the construct seemed so much smaller.

"I have *saved* you, at last. Look! Master, I have used what you taught me. I have learned how to undo the damage to your body. The energies that hurt you—they kept you alive, impervious to harm, but they were too much for your body to sustain. You have been . . . asleep, but I learned at last to reverse the effects!"

"I don't . . ." Erevyn d'Cannith turned his head—an effort which seemed to pain him—to look upon the room, the shattered glass door, and the factory beyond. "Where is the director, Sverak? What have you done to Lord Charoth? He is badly hurt." The artificer was still feeble, unable to do more than writhe slowly in his seat.

Soneste saw despondency in the man's watery eyes, the weight of some terrible knowledge. Erevyn—and not Charoth, the *real* Charoth d'Cannith—was the sole survivor of the Orphanage disaster.

"He is gone, Master," Sverak said. "He sought to destroy all that we worked for."

"We? Sverak . . . no."

"Master, I have done *all of this* for you. Your body is infused now with the power of Galifar's own pure blood—the oldest human lineage on Khorvaire! Its power is your power, its vitality *yours*. You will live strong again! We can do whatever you like, go wherever you want to go. I have wealth, influence, prestige. We will be untouchable, you and I. House Cannith will offer us so much for your return!"

Minister Erevyn turned his head to look again upon the warforged—*his* own creation—and then to Tallis. "Who are . . . ?" he asked weakly.

Tallis opened his mouth but nothing came out. He probably didn't know what to make of this exchange, but Soneste was piecing it together. She remembered the empty chair in Charoth's estate. She remembered the articles' words:

"It was not mere fire that has scarred me," was all he told the Korranberg Chronicle *regarding his condition . . .*

. . . While most creation forges in the late 980s produced the rank and file units that House Cannith sold to the Five Nations, the Orphanage facility worked to augment the warforged mind . . .

. . . "I cannot speak to the destructive properties of such devices. That is not our province. I can, however, confirm that Positive Energy, such as that channeled by the Mark of Healing, can be deadly if not used correctly."

It was Erevyn who had been stricken in this way. He had languished for six years while his assistant, an unorthodox product of the Orphanage, claimed the identity of the wealthy and influential Lord Charoth. All for this *one* moment, to capture scions of Galifar blood for an attempted reversal of the damage.

The royals! Soneste's desire to unravel the mystery disintegrated instantly. She looked back at the glass table. Halix had freed his sister and was laying her gently on the ground. Soneste could see the young woman's chest rise and fall. Still alive, thank the Sovereigns.

"Who are—?" Erevyn started.

"No!" Sverak screamed, his voice shrill with anger, with arrogance. Soneste looked at the warforged's narrow head, his faceplate bereft of expression. "Do not speak to them, Master! They would destroy us, just as Charoth would."

Tallis's lips twitched. She could see the darkness in his eyes returning.

"*Us?*" Erevyn's face became a grimace of agony. Soneste had seen dying men in less pain. Tears soiled by his affliction traced a watery black path down his lined face. "He would have destroyed you, not me, destroyed you as he should have. As *I* should have. You are *my* mistake. Onatar, forgive me for what I've done. You . . ."

"Master, no, listen," Sverak leaned forward, reaching his hand out again as if physical contact with his master would bring him absolution.

The artificer shrunk away the best he was able. "You are . . . animate material, Sverak . . . nothing more. A tool of industry . . . and my failure."

Soneste looked back at Sverak. The warforged froze, speechless.

"By the . . . Host." Erevyn's head slumped, his mouth working to speak. "Kill me, please."

"Master, no," the warforged said, struggling to stand. "You will be strong again, and I will *make* you understand."

"No, you won't," Tallis said, his voice cold.

The hooked hammer came down in a two-handed grip, splintering the wood of the construct's back. Sverak collapsed to the ground and lay still.

Chapter
THIRTY-THREE

The windows of her room had frosted over. When Soneste leaned in close against the glass, she saw that a fine layer of snow had dusted the streets of Korth.

She hadn't yet decided whether she loved or hated this city.

It was dusk. She'd spent the last two days in Crownhome, which despite its elegance had felt like a prison. Confined as she was to a series of well-guarded chambers, she'd had a great deal of time to reflect. The view was marvelous and the food, when she forced herself to eat, was extravagant. She wanted for nothing.

Except answers.

She'd been allowed to leave only once—under escort—to the House Sivis enclave. There she'd sent a brief and cryptic message to Thuranne to let her know that the ir'Daresh case had been closed, that she was all right, and that she'd be returning soon. She'd dare to presume.

When Kaius's court wizards had at last breached the doors of the glass factory, even the White Lions had been denied entry. Soneste had been allowed only a brief exchange with Prince Halix and Princess Borina before they were escorted away by

341

the Conqueror's Host. Strangely, even Aegis's remains had been taken.

Tallis had been claimed by the king's royal guard, who operated above the Justice Ministry's jurisdiction. The bone knight, Laedro, personally oversaw Tallis's apprehension. There was finality in the Karrn's quicksilver eyes when they'd taken him. He'd given her a nod, a sad smile, and then he was gone. She knew nothing of his fate. It had occupied her mind for the last two days. Was he even—

"Still alive," a woman's deep voice spoke behind her.

Soneste whirled, heart hammering. She hadn't heard anyone open the door, much less move so close to her.

The woman wore royal garments of white and gray, embroidered with black designs. The effect was subtle, exhibiting wealth in reserve. Long silver hair was bound in a tight bun at the nape of her neck. Her dark eyes were unsettling, and the deathly pallor of her age-lined face was traced with the faint scars of a blade. Soneste knew this woman by her reputation. She was the king's aunt, and prior to Kaius III's coronation, ruler of Karrnath for seventeen years.

"Regent Moranna," she said, offering a respectful bow.

Soneste couldn't help but stare at the older woman's bloodless lips as she spoke again, her Karrnathi accent thicker than most. "The deeds of Major Tallis are known to us. Your efforts, Miss Otänsin, have erased *certain* recent events from his record, but he will still answer for crimes against the crown."

He may have *saved* the crown, Soneste thought bitterly, but she forced herself to nod. "May I request, Regent, the opportunity to speak with him?"

"Spare yourself, Brelish, and move on." Moranna's severe face turned away as she approached the window, looking out into the deepening twilight. Soneste found herself looking out at the city as well.

"You are free to leave now, Miss Otänsin. On behalf of King Kaius III, I thank you for your actions and ask for your discretion in these events. Articles addressing the brief disappearance of the prince and princess of Breland, the fate of Charoth d'Cannith, and the events at the glass factory will be circulating among various chronicles very soon."

Soneste looked back to Moranna. "What will they—?"

The woman turned, fixing Soneste with fierce dark eyes. "It is our *strong* recommendation that any accounts of your experience in Korth, should you be asked to describe them, not deviate from these articles."

"I . . . understand," Soneste said, unable to meet Moranna's gaze. Her presence was formidable.

"Do you? King Kaius has worked very hard for the peace we all enjoy. Prince Halix and Princess Borina are our honored guests in this land, yet even they appreciate the need for discretion. The troubling events of the last week have reminded us how quickly such peace can be taken away by insurgents and outlaws."

How true, Soneste thought. She dared to look back at the Regent. "Princess Borina. How is she?"

"Both children are well, in excellent health, and are grateful for your part in these events. Be assured that they will never again face such peril on Karrnathi soil." Moranna withdrew an envelope from her pocket and held it out. "They leave you with this parting letter and a recommendation to their father that you be commended for your work on the case of Ambassador ir'Daresh. Ask for nothing more, Miss Otänsin."

Then Soneste remembered Mova. "Regent, what of the Seeker priestess—?"

"The king is no friend to the Blood of Vol," Moranna interjected. "Trust that the Cult's involvement in these events will be thoroughly explored."

Soneste knew she should be content with this. She held the envelope in her hand and stared back out at the city, her eyes drawn to the distant lights of the docks.

"You have King Kaius's personal gratitude, Miss Otänsin, *and* his trust that you will keep certain secrets to yourself. We wish to keep you as an ally." Moranna smiled, with no warmth in her eyes, and turned to go.

"Is he to be executed?" Soneste blurted without turning to face the woman.

The Regent pause at the door. "No."

"Will he be released?" she pressed. She turned, but Moranna had gone.

The door remained opened, so Soneste was free to go, given both recognition and a sinister warning. Five days ago, she had thought the world had looked different, that her part in it had changed. How did it look *now?* She had no answer.

Perhaps it was just wishful thinking. Perhaps she'd grown fond of a Karrn and wanted to believe she'd developed some kind of understanding with him. What sentence or service did Major Tallis of Rekkenmark await?

Perhaps her investigation in Korth *wasn't* finished.

As Soneste walked out into the snow-dusted streets, she decided upon her first course of action. There was a certain diminutive artificer who deserved to know a little bit more about Sharn.

THOMAS M. REID

The author of *Insurrection* and The Scions of Arrabar Trilogy
rescues Aliisza and Kaanyr Vhok from the tattered remnants
of their assault on Menzoberranzan, and sends them off on
a quest across the multiverse that will leave
FORGOTTEN REALMS® fans reeling!

THE EMPYREAN ODYSSEY

BOOK I
THE GOSSAMER PLAIN

Kaanyr Vhok, fresh from his defeat against the drow, turns to hated Sundabar for the
victory his demonic forces demand, but there's more to his ambitions than just one
human city. In his quest for arcane power, he sends the alu-fiend Aliisza on a mission
that will challenge her in ways she never dreamed of.

BOOK II
THE FRACTURED SKY

A demon surrounded by angels in a universe of righteousness? How did that
become Aliisza's life?

November 2008

BOOK III
THE CRYSTAL MOUNTAIN

What Aliisza has witnessed has changed her forever, but that's nothing compared
to what has happened to the multiverse itself. The startling climax will change the
nature of the cosmos forever.

Mid-2009

*"Reid is proving himself to be one of the best up and coming authors
in the FORGOTTEN REALMS universe."*
—fantasy-fan.org

RICHARD A. KNAAK

THE OGRE TITANS

The Grand Lord Golgren has been savagely crushing
all opposition to his control of the harsh ogre lands of
Kern and Blöde, first sweeping away rival chieftains, then
rebuilding the capital in his image. For this he has had to
deal with the ogre titans, dark, sorcerous giants who have
contempt for his leadership.

VOLUME ONE
THE BLACK TALON

Among the ogres, where every ritual demands blood and every ally can
become a deadly foe, Golgren seeks whatever advantage he can obtain,
even if it means a possible alliance with the Knights of Solamnia, a
questionable pact with a mysterious wizard, and trusting an elven slave
who might wish him dead.

December 2007

VOLUME TWO
THE FIRE ROSE

With his other enemies beginning to converge on him from all sides,
Golgren, now Grand Khan of all his kind, must battle with the
Ogre Titans for mastery of a mysterious artifact capable of ultimate
transformation and power.

December 2008

VOLUME THREE
THE GARGOYLE KING

Forced from the throne he has so long coveted, Golgren makes a final
stand for control of the ogre lands against the Titans . . . against an
enemy as ancient and powerful as a god.

December 2009